POINT OF NO RETURN

Adventures in ODYSSEY

Paul McCusker

TYNDALE
Tyndale House Publishers, Inc.
Carol Stream, Illinois

Point of No Return
Copyright © 2006 by Focus on the Family
All rights reserved. International copyright secured.

ISBN-10: 1-58997-332-1
ISBN-13: 978-1-58997-332-9

A Focus on the Family book published by
Tyndale House Publishers, Carol Stream, Illinois 60188

TYNDALE and Tyndale's quill logo are registered trademarks of Tyndale House
Publishers, Inc.

All Scripture quotations, unless otherwise indicated, are taken from the *Holy Bible, New International Version*®. NIV®. Copyright © 1973, 1978, 1984 by International Bible Society. Used by permission of Zondervan Publishing House. All rights reserved.

The books in this collection were originally published as:
Point of No Return, © 1995 by Focus on the Family
Dark Passage, © 1996 by Focus on the Family
Freedom Run, © 1996 by Focus on the Family
The Stranger's Message, © 1997 by Paul McCusker

A note to readers: The Adventures in Odyssey novels take place in a time period prior to the beginning of the audio or video series. That is why some of the characters from those episodes don't appear in these stories; they don't exist yet.

Editor: Liz Duckworth
Cover design: Greg Sills
Cover illustration: Gary Locke
Cover copy: Larilee Frazier

Library of Congress Cataloging-in-Publication Data
McCusker, Paul, 1958-
  [Selections]
  Point of no return : four original stories of suspense, time travel, and faith / Paul
McCusker ; [cover illustration, Gary Locke].
    v. cm. — (Adventures in Odyssey ; 3)
    Summary: Four stories set in the fictional town of Odyssey follow the adventures of the Whit's End gang as they learn valuable lessons in helping their fellow man, forgiving, and living their faith.
    Contents: Point of no return—Dark passage—Freedom run—The stranger's message.
    ISBN-13: 978-1-58997-332-9
    ISBN-10: 1-58997-332-1
    [1. Conduct of life—Fiction. 2. Christian live—Fiction. 3. Friendship—Fiction.]
I. Title. II. Series: McCusker, Paul, 1958-
  Adventures in Odyssey ; 3.
  PZ7.M47841Po 2006
  [Fic]—dc22

Printed in the United States of America
1 2 3 4 5 6 7 8 9 /10 09 08 07 06

To Matt and Sam Butcher

With special acknowledgment to Marshal Younger and his Underground Railroad episodes for the "Adventures in Odyssey" radio series.

CONTENTS

BOOK ONE

POINT OF NO RETURN

CHAPTER ONE

Friday Night

JIMMY BARCLAY looked into the deep blue water. It was still. Faintly, he could see his reflection looking back. It didn't look much like him, though. In fact, it could have been a complete stranger . . . but it wasn't. That had to be his young face looking up out of the water. The blue, still water.

There was also the scent of pine.

He got on his knees and looked closer at the deep blue water—pondering it. He waited.

This was really stupid, he knew. At his age—a mature and wise 10 years old—he shouldn't be in this situation. He never should've let Tony talk him into it. How many kids of 10 try to smoke their best friend's father's cigar? What made it worse was that Jimmy thought people who smoked cigarettes were Neanderthals. So why did he try the cigar?

He rested his head against the porcelain, sending a tiny shiver through the toilet bowl. The deep blue water rippled. The scent of pine was overwhelming. *Mom must have cleaned in here today,* he thought. He couldn't imagine when, though. His mother worked part-time as a dental receptionist and was on every committee the church could think up.

A new wave of nausea worked its way through Jimmy's stomach, and he prepared himself for it. Again, he stared into the deep blue water. Again, it was so still.

At that moment, he tried to remember how many puffs he had taken on the cigar before Tony said he was turning green. He couldn't remember. Too many. Way too many.

The wave subsided, and he sat down. He rested his head against the cabinet that housed the sink and prayed for deliverance. He begged his stomach to make up its mind: *Either do it or don't do it. Let's stop playing around.*

Of course, I wish you wouldn't *do it,* Jimmy told his stomach.

From his room down the hall, he could hear music. Tony, his best friend, was listening to—singing along with—some CD he had brought over. Jimmy winced. It sounded as if Tony had the volume turned up full blast.

Jimmy wondered how long it would be before Donna, his older sister, would hang up the phone downstairs and yell at him to turn off the music. He thought about hollering for Tony to turn it down but was afraid to. He didn't know what it would do to his stomach or his mother's freshly cleaned bathroom. He leaned over the deep blue water again in case.

Tony screamed along with a song.

How could he be so energetic when Jimmy was sitting on the bathroom floor ready to die? Easy. Tony was good at talking Jimmy into doing stupid things and never doing them himself.

Jimmy grabbed the sides of the bowl, sure that something was about to happen. He held on and waited.

This is so very very very dumb. When will you learn? When will you stop acting like such an idiot? You're a jerk, Jimmy Barclay, and you'd better never let this happen again.

As if to say it agreed, his stomach settled down. It seemed suddenly at peace.

After a moment, Jimmy stood up slowly. His head swayed a little. He dropped the cover over the deep blue water and turned to the door. Everything would be just fine.

He paused at the mirror and looked hard at himself. *A little green around the gills maybe—but nothing too terrible. Just Jimmy Barclay looking a little sick. Boy, it's a good thing Mom and Dad are out.*

He opened the door, turned out the light, and headed for his room. He didn't notice that the music had stopped. It didn't click in his mind that all was deathly silent. When he entered his room to find Tony sitting quietly on the edge of his bed, he still didn't think much of it. . . .

Until he saw his mom at his CD player and his dad looking over the remains of the cigar.

There are no words to describe the look on their faces, but most kids know it when they see it. Jimmy knew it well. His stomach turned upside down, and he considered running back to the bathroom.

"Get ready for bed, Jimmy," his dad said as he walked out of the room with the cigar. His mom looked at him with an expression of complete disappointment and followed.

And that was it.

Jimmy looked at Tony.

Tony shrugged and said, "I didn't hear them coming. I would have done something if I knew they were coming."

"How could you hear them with the music going full blast?" Jimmy asked. "They probably heard it at the restaurant and came home to investigate."

His dad yelled from the kitchen, "Do you need a lift home, Tony?"

Tony looked at Jimmy. Jimmy shrugged.

Tony shouted back, "Oh, no thanks. I'd better walk."

"Good night, then," Mrs. Barclay called out.

"I guess that means I'm leaving now," Tony said to Jimmy, grabbing his jacket from the foot of the bed.

"I guess so."

"See ya," Tony said as he drifted out of the room. "Call me when you get paroled."

"Thanks, *pal*."

Tony opened the front door and called out a final farewell to Mr. and Mrs. Barclay before retreating into the crisp Friday night.

Jimmy sighed.

From somewhere on the front lawn, Jimmy could hear an outburst of Tony's laughter.

George Barclay, Jimmy's dad, was sitting at the kitchen table drinking coffee. Mary, Jimmy's mom, was at the counter pouring herself a cup. Donna also sat at the table with a stricken look on her face. Obviously, his mom and dad had already read her the riot act. Jimmy guessed that they held her partly to blame for what had happened. She had been on the phone when she should have been keeping a closer eye on him.

"You're home early," Jimmy said brightly.

After a moment of silence, his dad spoke. "We're home early because I decided to go see your grandmother tomorrow. I may leave first thing in the morning."

Grandma Barclay was Jimmy's dad's mom. She had been sick over the past couple of weeks, and they were worried it might be a relapse of her cancer. She lived a couple of hundred miles away.

"Oh—you're going by yourself?"

His dad looked darkly at him and said, "Your mother was going to come with me, but it's clear that we can't leave the two of you alone."

Guilt poked at Jimmy's stomach. "I can go with you," he offered.

"No, you can't." His dad looked Jimmy full in the face now. *That* look was still there. "You're on restriction. For the rest of your life. Maybe longer. And when we get a minute, your mother and I are going to talk about what to do with you. I can't figure which is worse: the fact that you lit matches in your room or the fact that you tried smoking a *cigar*. Maybe they're equal. And there's Tony coming tonight when we told you before you left that you weren't to have friends in. And that music you were playing at a speaker-blowing volume. Not forgetting to mention the water balloon battle you had in my study *last* weekend, the fire you started in the garage with the blowtorch the week before, the call we got from the librarian about you and Tony knocking books off the shelves, the fight you had with Kelly next door over that bike, and, and . . . Jimmy—"

He stopped as if his anger had tied up his tongue. "Just go to bed," he finally said.

In his room, Jimmy began unloading his pants pockets. It was something he always did before undressing and going to bed because, if he didn't, his mom might accidentally wash something like coins, a crumpled dollar, some gum he had bought at Town Center Drugs, lint . . . .

So much for the left pocket. He emptied the right. More lint.

He tossed everything onto his dresser, where his eye caught the framed photo of Grandma Barclay. She'd lost a lot of weight since that picture was taken. The cancer did it. It had been eating her alive a few years ago, but everyone prayed for her, and it went into remission. Jimmy wasn't so sure prayer had made her better, but he didn't dare say so out loud.

You wouldn't know how ill Grandma was if you saw only the picture with its soft-focus close-up that made her wrinkles less noticeable, gave a nice shine to her white hair, and accented her bright blue eyes. They were stunning eyes, the kind that made Jimmy feel funny because he suspected they could somehow see much deeper than eyes should be allowed to see.

Grandma Barclay was a very devout woman. As far as anyone knew, she had never missed a day of church in her life. Hers was a deep-rooted, practical faith. It was as real and natural to her as breathing. Jimmy's father felt the influence of that faith and tried to instill it in both Jimmy and Donna. Donna liked church. Jimmy thought it was boring. He would've stopped going if his parents didn't make him attend. He once talked to them about letting him stay home, but they wouldn't hear of it. He had to go, and that was that.

Jimmy's parents fussed with him for a while about his lack of faith. They did everything they could to get him interested. But lately it was as if they had given up on him. His mom said that they had decided to stop worrying and let God do the rest.

That was fine with Jimmy, because God seemed to want to leave him alone, too.

Grandma didn't fuss about it at all. When she found out Jimmy didn't like church, she just smiled and said he would enjoy it eventually. *He would have to. The call in his life was too strong.*

Jimmy didn't know what she meant by that. He wondered but didn't want to risk a lecture by asking. He got off easy, and that's all that mattered.

But sometimes he thought about *the call* and tried to figure out what a call would sound like. Not that it would make any difference. When Jimmy grew up, he wanted to be a singer in a rock band.

All these thoughts swirled around in his churning mind as he fell asleep. The last thing he would remember was the sound of thousands of fans cheering him as he performed in a huge auditorium.

Saturday Morning

THE OCTOBER SUN played peekaboo with Jimmy's left eyelid through the crack between the half-drawn curtains on his bedroom window. Swimming to the surface of wakefulness, he was aware of the irritation the sunlight caused him. He moved his head. The sunlight hit his right eyelid. He moved his head again. Relief.

But not for long.

Right on cue, his head throbbed. He rolled over with a groan and tried to open his mouth to lick the cobwebs off his lips. His tongue felt like a fuzz ball. His eyes twitched but wouldn't open. He was numb all over.

He rolled over onto his back again and rubbed at his eyes until they could open.

His room looked as if someone had hung a giant piece of gauze over it. He blinked. The gauze separated like a curtain, and he made out the specifics—so familiar and so cluttered. Posters covered almost every inch of wall space. The small desk was piled high with magazines, school papers, comic books, and only heaven knew what else. The closet was an outpouring of clean and dirty clothes, games, games, and more games. A chair was covered with more clothes. A small table held his CD player and surrounding stacks of CDs. And there was the ancient oak dresser with the Old West wagon-train lamp and 96-ounce beer mug half filled with pennies. Also on top, as a testimony to the night before, was the junk he had taken out of his pockets last night.

He moaned as he remembered what had happened.

He remembered Tony, the cigar, deep blue water, and . . . his parents coming home.

He scanned the room, trying to remember where he threw his alarm clock. He had no idea what time it might be. He sat up, and his head protested.

As he struggled to get out of bed, the door slowly opened, and Donna peeked in. She looked annoyed until she saw Jimmy swing his legs off the side of the bed.

"Mom wants to know if you want some breakfast," she asked.

He shook his head. "Maybe later" was all he could manage. His tongue wouldn't let go of the roof of his mouth. After a moment he asked, "What time is it?"

"Almost lunchtime." She retreated.

"Donna?"

She returned and said, "What?"

He hesitated, then: "Are Mom and Dad . . . still mad?"

"What do you think?" she asked and left again.

He gingerly stepped out of bed and grabbed at the nearest stack of clothes.

In the bathroom, Jimmy tried to use water to flatten some of his hair. It stuck out in 12 directions. He looked at his face. His eyes looked tiny. He leaned closer to the mirror and checked his chin and top lip for anything that might look like a beard. He couldn't wait until he was old enough to shave.

Grabbing the skeletal remains of a bar of soap, he scrubbed his hands. And he began to think—not the way the world's great thinkers do, but with all the concentration he could manage. He replayed the night before in his mind and wondered what made him act the way he did.

He searched his mind for something or someone to blame.

Blank.

Nothing.

He did what he did because it was what he *wanted* to do. That was all. There really wasn't any other reason, was there?

Something was just out of reach in his mind. A thought, a feeling . . . he wasn't sure. But it made him feel that something was wrong. Maybe something was wrong with *him*. Maybe he should try harder to behave himself. Maybe he should change somehow.

But he was only 10 years old. What could be wrong with him at the age of 10? How much can a 10-year-old be expected to change? He shrugged and walked out of the bathroom.

Mary Barclay sat silently at the table drinking a cup of tea. Jimmy half-heartedly ate some sugar-coated cereal that promised to be part of a nutritious breakfast. His head still sent dull thuds to his eyes. Did cigars make everybody feel so bad?

His dad had gone to Jimmy's grandma's house. It didn't really sink into Jimmy's mind what was happening, but someone called that morning to say his grandmother was in great pain and had to be put back in the hospital, and the doctors were playing guessing games about radiation and maybe chemo, but there were no promises, no guarantees, because she was almost 80 years old and not as strong as she used to be.

His mother looked Jimmy directly in the eyes and asked, "Why, Jimmy? Why do you get into so much trouble? The past few months have been one incident after another. Last night was the last straw. Why do you do it?"

His mouth was full of sugar-coated cereal, so he couldn't answer her.

"I wanted to see your grandma, too, but—" She looked down at her cup of tea. "I can't trust you anymore."

Jimmy swallowed hard. He could tell by her tone that she wasn't just trying to make him feel guilty. She wasn't even trying to make him feel bad. She was speaking in a neutral voice as if she were telling him about the weather. That made it even worse. Jimmy searched frantically for the right words to say—something to convince her he could be trustworthy.

He couldn't think of anything. So finally he offered, "I'm sorry, Mom. I just got carried away. It won't happen again."

The words sounded hollow even as he said them.

"That's what you keep saying over and over."

"This time I mean it," he said, on the edge of pleading. All his life there had been a bond of trust between him and his parents. Even when he misbehaved, the bond somehow stood firm. To lose it, to feel he had truly failed them, was more than he could handle. "I'll behave."

"Don't tell me you'll behave. I know better. You feel bad this morning, but that won't last. You'll get with Tony and forget."

He stood up to take his dishes to the sink. "It's not Tony's fault," he said. He stood there, looking out the window into the backyard. The swings on the swing set moved gently in a breeze.

"I'm not blaming Tony. He's been like another son in this family. But he *does* influence you. You can't deny that."

He turned back to face her and said, "Maybe I'm influencing *him*."

She took a drink of her tea. "I hope not," she replied. "I hope I raised you better than that. But since you got bored with church—" Her voice faded, the sentence left unfinished.

Jimmy knew where the conversation was going. He closed his eyes. He didn't want to talk about that. He wanted to go out.

"You say you'll behave, and then you don't. I don't think you *can* behave by yourself. I think you need help." She watched him as she spoke. "So, until further notice, Tony can't come over, and you can't sleep over at his house. You're on restriction. And that means you have to come straight home from school—no Tony, no Whit's End, nothing."

Jimmy's jaw tightened, and he looked away. He hadn't expected his punishment to be *that* bad.

Just then, somebody knocked at the front door.

Mary stood up, saying as she walked out of the kitchen, "I want you to think about how you behave and what it does to us . . . *all* of us. Another night like last night and I . . . I don't know what we'll do."

Jimmy brooded as he listened to his mom walk to the front door and open it. Probably the mailman with a personal delivery, he figured.

"Ever since you got bored with church—" she had said to him. *Church, church, church*, he moaned inwardly. Church was the last thing he needed. He knew plenty of people who went to church, and they weren't any better than him. In fact, he could think of a whole list of people who seemed worse off because of church.

"Jimmy," his mom called from the living room, "there's someone here to see you."

Huh? he thought. *Who in the world would come to see me in the middle of a Saturday except Tony?* He pushed off from the sink and rounded the corner into the living room. It might have been his imagination, but he thought he could still smell the cigar somewhere.

That's when Dave Wright and his son, Jacob, entered Jimmy's life. Dave was the ever-smiling, ever-friendly kids' pastor from Calvary

Church—his family's church. Jimmy had heard of him and seen him in the pulpit to make announcements, but he stayed clear of him whenever he could. But there he stood, right in Jimmy's own living room, grinning from ear to ear. His 10-year-old son, Jacob, stood next to him with the same smile. Jimmy's mom stood next to them both.

It was a setup. A trap.

"I'll go to the kitchen to make some tea," she said and quickly departed.

Dave stepped forward, hand outstretched. "I'm Dave Wright from Calvary."

Jimmy hesitated and then shook his hand. His grip was firm. *Obviously a weightlifter,* Jimmy thought. *That's a surprise. Most of the church leaders I've ever met turned out to be meek, mousy, turn-the-other-cheek types.* "Hi," Jimmy said.

"This is my son, Jacob," Dave said.

Jimmy nodded to Jacob. Kids their age didn't shake hands unless they were making a deal.

"I've heard a lot about you, Jimmy," Dave said. He moved to the couch to sit down.

"Oh," Jimmy said, bugged that Dave sat down. That meant he planned to stay for a little while. Jacob leaned against the side of the couch.

"You're wondering why we're here, right?" Dave asked, then gestured to the end table. "I had to drop off some Sunday school material for your mom."

Jimmy glanced down skeptically at a couple of Sunday school books sitting there.

Dave chuckled and said, "Actually, that's a lie. I really came by to talk to you."

"Isn't it a sin to lie?" Jimmy asked.

"Yeah, it is," Dave said with mock shame. "I guess that's why I'm still just a kids' pastor. I'll graduate to pastor when I can stop sinning."

Jimmy looked at him blankly.

Dave's smile faded. "I'm kidding," he explained.

This guy is really weird, Jimmy thought. He was wearing a normal-looking sport coat and tie and had longish brown hair, a plain face, and an athlete's build. He wasn't at all what Jimmy thought a kids' pastor should be. Kids' pastors were supposed to be wimps. Even Jacob looked like his father, except he was too young to lift weights.

"I have to go now, okay?" Jimmy said as he moved toward the stairs. "My mom's in the kitchen if you want to talk to her some more."

"Wait a sec," Dave said, waving him back. "What's the problem? We're here to talk to you."

Jimmy stopped. "Yeah, and I know what you wanna talk about, and I don't wanna talk about it, okay? I don't like church."

Dave laughed. "I know," he said. "Sometimes I don't like it either."

"I guess that makes us even." Jimmy faked a smile and turned away to head for his own room.

"How does that make us even? I still want to talk to you." Dave stood up and followed Jimmy up the stairs. He obviously wasn't going to let Jimmy go without a fight.

"About what?" Jimmy asked.

"I want to know why you don't like church."

"I don't know. It's boring, that's all. No offense."

"No offense? Are you kidding? What have I said, what have I done?" Dave pretended he was hurt. "It's my breath, isn't it? Go on. You can be straight with me."

At the top of the stairs, Jimmy stopped. "It doesn't have anything to do with you." This guy really was a wacko.

"Then you have something against the church?"

"I just don't care, okay?" He went into his room, hoping Dave and Jacob would go away.

But they didn't. Dave and Jacob stepped into the room. Jimmy felt invaded—it was *his* room, for crying out loud. Why wouldn't these guys go away? Jimmy looked for something he could busy himself with.

Dave smiled and continued, "You're evading the question, Jimmy. I want to know what *your problem is.*"

"I don't know!" Jimmy said.

"Not an acceptable answer. Try again."

Jimmy felt uneasy. "What is this—a quiz?"

Dave smiled. "Sort of," he said. "Why don't you come to the church youth group?"

"'Cause I don't feel like it." It was all he could think of.

"Not acceptable. You're oh for two." Dave frowned and shook a finger at him. "You're flunking, Jimmy."

Jimmy was tongue-tied. He didn't know how to get out of this. But he had to say *something* . . . so, he grunted.

"I'm sorry," Dave said, "was that a grunt?"

"Yes, it was. Do you want me to do it again?" And he did.

Dave laughed. "That's the most intelligent thing you've said so far."

Jimmy sighed and said, "What do you want from me? What's it gonna take? Do you wanna hear my life story? I could tell you a lot. I could make up even more."

"I'll bet you could."

"What do you want to know? Just ask."

"I did, and you grunted. I'm afraid of what you might do if I ask anything harder." Dave sat down on Jimmy's unmade bed and leaned forward, his elbows on his knees. "I want you to come to one of our youth meetings. Just one." His voice was low and very serious.

Jimmy grimaced. "And do what? Drink punch? Sing some boring folk songs? Pray?"

"Maybe."

"Forget it," Jimmy said firmly and glanced at Jacob, who seemed to be admiring some of his posters. It bothered Jimmy that Jacob didn't speak.

For a second, Dave seemed at a loss for words. But only a second. "That's it? There's nothing I can do to get you to come?"

"You can tie me up and drag me, I guess," Jimmy said.

Jimmy knew right away that it was the wrong thing to suggest. Dave looked as if he might consider the idea. Instead, however, he stood up and offered, "How about a deal?"

Jimmy cocked an eyebrow. "What kind of deal?"

"What sports do you play?"

"I don't know. Most of them." Jimmy looked at him suspiciously. "What kind of deal?"

"Pick a sport."

Jimmy eyed him, trying to figure out what he was up to. "A sport?"

"I saw a basketball hoop over the garage. You use it?" Even as Dave asked, he began taking off his sport coat.

"Me and my dad play sometimes. Why? What are you going to do?"

Dave knelt down and tightened his shoelaces. "We'll play one-on-one. First to reach 10 wins." He untied his tie and pulled it off. "You lose and you'll have to come to the youth meeting."

"Play *you*?" Jimmy laughed. "No way."

"Don't be silly," Dave said. "I'll just referee. You'll play against Jacob."

Jacob looked at Jimmy without smiling. Jimmy realized Jacob stood about an inch shorter than himself. "And if I win?"

"We won't nag you ever again," Dave said with a smile.

"That doesn't sound like much of a deal."

Dave laughed and said, "You've never seen us really nag."

Jimmy sized up Jacob and thought about his chances of winning.

"Well?" Dave asked.

"I don't know." Jimmy ran his fingers through his short, curly hair, his habit when thinking hard.

"They call me the Hound of Heaven," Dave said. "I'll stay on your tracks for the rest of your life. For eternity."

Jimmy looked at him closely. This situation had all the elements of a *Twilight Zone* episode. But this was a dare, a challenge. It intrigued him too much not to see it through to the end. "I'm gonna regret this," Jimmy finally said. "Deal."

Jacob and Jimmy silently shook hands.

Dave smiled again and moved to the door. "I have a ball in the car," he said. "Let's go."

Jimmy dug under his bed to get his basketball shoes. He tried to figure his chances of winning. Jacob was shorter and looked a little wimpy. Jimmy, on the other hand, considered himself a pretty good basketball player—not because he loved the game, but because he played against his dad. It would be a good match. And as Jimmy put on his shoes, he psyched himself up. He told himself all the reasons why he would win. Why he *had to* win.

Jimmy's mom caught him at the bottom of the stairs. She asked what was going on. Outside, Jimmy heard Jacob dribbling the basketball on the driveway. "I just moved the car so you could play . . . basketball?"

Jimmy explained the deal.

She shook her head. "I don't like it," she said. "I don't like it at all."

"You're right," Jimmy agreed. "It's risky. Jacob could win."

"That's not what I'm afraid of." She turned and walked away.

Thanks, Mom, he thought. *Glad to have you in the cheering section.*

CHAPTER THREE

Early Saturday Afternoon

BEFORE LONG, JIMMY WAS leading off with three baskets. Then he made four and five before Jacob got his first. *Piece of cake,* Jimmy thought even as the midday sun bore down and his pace slackened. His lead slackened, too. Jacob got two more baskets. Then—after a long stretch where neither scored—Jacob got another one.

"Jimmy: five; Jacob: four!" Dave announced from the side. What bugged Jimmy the most was Jacob's silence. He never said a word: no jokes, commentary, or exclamations that were usually part of the game. It was killing Jimmy's concentration.

Donna stood off to the side, watching with delight. She screamed and cheered . . . for Jacob.

"Get lost, Donna!" Jimmy shouted at her.

Then it was Jimmy: five; Jacob: five.

Good going, Jimmy, he thought. *Give the poor kid a false sense of security.*

Jimmy pushed his inner power button and got two more baskets in rapid-fire succession.

"Whoa," Dave cried out, "maybe we should've challenged you to darts."

Mrs. Barclay brought a round of drinks, giving both Dave and Jimmy a disapproving glance as she served them. She didn't like this one bit. She said so again.

Back to the game.

Jimmy stole the ball from Jacob and shot from halfway down the driveway. Jimmy: eight; Jacob: five.

They traded baskets after they both alternately knocked the ball out of bounds. Then it was Jimmy: nine; Jacob: six.

One more basket and it would be all over. Jacob, still silent, breathed hard, and looked tired. Jimmy figured he couldn't lose. The thought gave him a shot of adrenaline, and he plowed through for an almost-perfect layup. *Almost* perfect. He missed.

Jacob rebounded, recovered, and scored. To Jimmy's irritation, he then snatched the ball from Jimmy and scored again.

Jimmy: nine; Jacob: eight.

Jimmy went up again, with style and grace, and fired a shot. It hit the basket and rolled round and round. And around. And out.

"I've been robbed!" Jimmy cried.

Jacob got a swisher to tie things up.

The excitement and tension were at their peak. Donna could barely contain herself.

"Why don't you go find a friend or something?" Jimmy growled at her. This wasn't right. It wasn't fair. He'd had the lead most of the game, and he should have made those last two baskets with no problem. He looked at Jacob and said, "No fair if you're praying."

For the first time, Jacob made a sound. He laughed. Dave laughed with him. And while they laughed, Jimmy realized he liked them both.

That was a good thing, because Jimmy went up for another shot knowing full well that this time it would be perfect, and he would get the basket and win and not be at the mercy of this lunatic father-and-son team that he liked in spite of his better senses. And there it was— the ball at the very tips of his fingers, reaching up and up and up toward the basket, and all he had to do was let go and it would be in, and . . . .

Then Jacob was up with him, jumping higher than Jimmy would have ever imagined someone of his size jumping. In that instant, Jimmy remembered reading about a guy from a nearby college who was known as the "Thieving Kangaroo" because he could jump high and steal the ball from anybody, and his name was Dave Wright, and he had given up his future in basketball to go into the ministry.

That's when Jimmy lost—no, he *quit*—because he realized he'd never had a chance to begin with and that Jacob had inherited his dad's jumping ability and natural talent and probably could have slaughtered him at any time.

Sure enough, Jacob knocked the ball away and, in less than a minute, scored and won.

"You didn't tell me who you were," Jimmy panted as they all walked back into the house.

"You didn't ask," was Dave's reply.

CHAPTER FOUR

Late Saturday Afternoon

JIMMY SAT ON THE EDGE of his bed and fingered the small booklet Dave and Jacob had left with him. He didn't read it. He simply turned it over and over absentmindedly while he tried to come up with a good excuse to go back on his word and skip the youth group meeting that night. At the moment, his only ploy was that it was unfair for Dave and Jacob to lure him into a basketball game when Jacob was the son of a great player. *No, that won't work*, he decided.

Maybe he could come down with something contagious.

Jimmy's plotting was interrupted by a tap at his window. Tony sat on a tree branch outside looking like the serpent in the Garden of Eden. Jimmy opened his window.

"Hey, Jimmy," Tony said as casually as if he were sitting on the living room sofa instead of an unsteady branch.

"Get out of here or I'll get in worse trouble than I already am," Jimmy said.

Tony smiled as he asked, "Did your mom and dad give it to you good?"

"You know they did," Jimmy said. "They were really ticked off, and you're not supposed to be here."

"That's too bad. You're gonna miss a great time tonight."

Jimmy frowned. "Tonight? What's going on tonight?"

"A couple of us are going out to Allen's Pond. I heard that a bunch of Nathan's friends are gonna get drunk and stuff." Nathan was Tony's older brother and did things like sneak out and get drunk. He hated Tony and Jimmy for hanging around, but they did it anyway.

Jimmy thought of how fun it'd be to follow Nathan and his pals like a couple of secret agents on a mission. But he knew he couldn't—not tonight of all nights. "I can't anyway," he said. "I have to go to church."

"Church!" Tony nearly fell out of the tree.

"Yeah. I got tricked into going."

"But it's not Sunday! Why're you going to church on a Saturday night?"

Jimmy toyed with the booklet he still held in his hand. "Because that's when the kids get together. I guess it's kinda like a Saturday night Sunday school."

"Oh boy! I wish I could go with you!" Tony said in the singsong voice he used to tease Jimmy.

"Why don't you?" Jimmy asked seriously. "Then maybe I won't get so bored."

Tony scowled at Jimmy. "You're kidding."

"No."

"Forget it," Tony said.

"Thanks, *friend*," Jimmy said and closed the window.

Tony laughed as he slithered down the tree branch and out of Jimmy's sight.

Jimmy sat down on his bed again and looked at the booklet. "If you were to die tonight . . ." the black letters on the front said. Jimmy had seen the booklet before in a rack in the lobby of his church. He had never paid attention to it. Why should he? At his age, why would he think about death? Kids his age didn't die unless they were in car accidents or got some kind of weird disease. And Jimmy didn't plan on getting in any car accidents or coming down with a weird disease—unless it would get him out of going to that meeting at church. What did death have to do with him? Death happened to other people that Jimmy didn't know. Death happened in the make-believe world of movies. Death happened to old people.

The last thought gave him an uneasy feeling as his grandmother came to mind. She was old and sick. She might even die. What would happen to her after that? She always told Jimmy she wasn't afraid of death. Because of Jesus, she knew she would go to heaven. Jimmy believed her. She *would* go to heaven because she was the best grandmother anybody could ever have.

"If you were to die tonight . . ." the booklet said.

It wasn't talking about Jimmy's grandmother. It was talking to Jimmy.

He threw the booklet onto his nightstand. *What a stupid idea,* he thought as he fell back onto his bed and looked at the ceiling. Then he remembered when he was smaller and his parents prayed with him at bedtime. They used a little poem, and part of it said: "And if I die before I wake, I pray the Lord my soul to take."

If I died tonight . . .

Jimmy didn't like it. And suddenly he didn't like Dave or Jacob or the way they had tricked him into going to church that night. *What kind of maniac would give a kid my age a booklet that talks about dying? They must be warped,* Jimmy concluded.

Once again, he set his mind to coming up with a scheme to get out of going to church.

CHAPTER FIVE

Saturday Night

JIMMY FAILED TO DEVISE an escape. Dave and Jacob picked him up right on time. *They want to be absolutely sure I make it*, he figured.

The club meeting started 10 minutes late in what everyone at the church called the "fellowship hall." It was a large, auditorium-like room just off the main sanctuary. Jimmy knew it from the Sunday school assembly his parents made him attend every week. It had multiple purposes, with a marked floor for sports games and enough blackboards and wall space to work for teaching. With the addition of a few long tables, it also served as a banquet hall for events like Valentine's Day or back-to-school or end-of-school get-togethers, depending on the time of year.

Because he'd never paid much attention on Sunday mornings to know who attended, Jimmy was surprised by some of the faces he recognized. Many of the most popular kids from school were there. Kids of all ages showed up. Jimmy dropped himself onto a folding chair along the wall and figured that those kids were there because somebody *made them* go—just like him.

Jack Davis, who was in the same grade as Jimmy, sat down next to him. "Hey, Jimmy, what're you doing here?" he asked.

"I don't know," Jimmy said with a shrug. "I got tricked into coming. What are *you* doing here?"

"I come every week."

"Really? Your parents make you?"

"At first they did, but now I come because I want to. It's a lot of fun," Jack said. "There's Lucy and Oscar! I'll see you later." And Jack took off to greet his friends.

Jimmy was surprised. Jack's answer wasn't what he would have expected. As he looked more closely at the expressions on the faces of the kids mingling around, saying hi to one another or talking about how they had spent their Saturdays, he realized they didn't seem dejected like him. They didn't look as if they minded being there at all.

Jacob walked in, saw Jimmy, and waved. Jimmy nodded. Jacob looked as if he might come over but was distracted by his dad whistling through his fingers to get everyone's attention.

As they quieted down and took their seats, Dave took hold of a microphone attached to a portable podium. He welcomed one and all in a voice made thin by the cheap speaker. He asked any visitors to stand up and say their names, and a couple of kids scattered through the crowd complied. Jimmy didn't. Dave realized it and, not to be undone, announced that Jimmy was there. Jimmy blushed and leaned forward, resting his arms on his knees, wishing he'd never agreed to that stupid basketball game. He didn't belong here. He didn't belong with any of these people. He belonged with Tony somewhere at Allen's Pond, spying on Tony's older brother. But it was too late now. All he could do was hope the evening would slip by as quickly as possible.

Dave introduced a guest speaker, Mr. Lucas, one of the church's deacons. Jimmy recognized him from the times he got up to pray in the services.

Mr. Lucas talked for almost 15 minutes, and about halfway through, Jimmy realized he was having a hard time understanding a word the man was saying. A couple of times he mentioned having an abundant life and calling on some sort of power and being born again by being washed in the blood of the Lamb for remission of something or other and inheriting some kind of eternal thingy in a kingdom of a lot of big words in a fullness of time affixed before Adam fell in his garden and . . . .

Jimmy felt as if he were drowning in a sea of weird words. He had a vague idea of what Mr. Lucas was trying to say, and Mr. Lucas was obviously sincere, but Jimmy got so lost that he could only stare at the pattern of marking tape on the floor.

Mr. Lucas finished his talk on a loud and excited note and stepped away. Dave took the podium again and announced that it was time to split up into various grades for games. Jimmy was relieved to find himself in a game of dodgeball with Jacob, Jack, Lucy, Oscar, and a few other kids he knew from school. He was especially proud when he held out the longest and was the last one in the circle to get hit.

Then they played a beanbag toss, ran a relay race, and played a game

Jimmy had never seen before where they lay down on their backs and kicked an enormous ball from one side of the room to another. The idea was to score by hitting the other team's wall. Jimmy alternately screamed and laughed through all the games. Time slipped away. He was shocked when they stopped for snacks and drinks and he realized it was after nine o'clock.

All the kids gathered again for a few final words from Dave. Jimmy braced himself for another sermon with a lot of words and expressions he didn't understand.

Dave spoke simply, however. "I can't let any of you out of here tonight without making a few things absolutely clear," he said. "We try to have a lot of fun when we meet like this, but we're not here just for fun. We're here to get to know each other. We're here to have fellowship with other Christians. And we're here to see that there are ways to enjoy ourselves without doing what a lot of our friends think is fun—the kinds of things that get us in trouble, that lead nowhere, and don't give you anything except a few seconds of pleasure."

Dave held up a booklet just like the one he gave Jimmy earlier that day. "I've handed out this booklet to a lot of you over the last few days. I'll bet most of you haven't read it. You looked at the front and said, 'Hey, I'm just a kid. What do I care about dying?' "

Jimmy squirmed in his chair and wondered how Dave knew that.

"I understand how you feel," Dave continued. "You don't care about the past or the future. All you care about is *right now*—what games you play, what's on television, what kind of music is really hot, what all the other kids are doing. Today is all there is for you. Living for the great big *right now*. You're too young to feel you have a past. You're too young to feel there's really a future. And if there *is* a future out there for you, dying isn't part of it. So why did I give you these booklets?"

Good question, Jimmy thought.

Dave laughed and said, "I gave you these booklets because we have two boxes of them in the church office and we didn't know what else to do with them."

Some of the kids snickered.

Dave's laugh tapered off. "Actually," he said, "I gave them to you because of what they say inside. Did any of you read what was on the inside?"

Jimmy glanced around, but no one raised a hand.

Dave went on. "See, these booklets are supposed to make you *think*, if only for a minute. Any of us could die at any time. Any of us could die *right now*. The same *right now* that you live in day after day. I'm not trying to scare you. I'm just saying there's something *more* to this world than we realize. There's a lot more to it than games, television, music, what the other kids are doing, finishing your homework, or eating all the right vegetables. In fact, there's a whole *other* world. An eternal one. One that goes on forever. And it's not some kind of comic-book place. It's *God's* place. It's *real*. And it's even more real than *this* world."

Dave knocked on the podium as if to say that the "this world" he was talking about was the one that could be rapped with your knuckles. It was the world Jimmy could see with his two eyes and touch with his two hands.

It made Jimmy sit up. He stared at Dave and wished he *could* see the other world or touch it somehow. Maybe that would make a difference. Maybe then Jimmy could . . . .

Could what? he wondered. *Could what?*

"But y'know," Dave said with a smile, "when I was your age, I figured there was no point in thinking about any other worlds, because I have to live in this one. None of us can be Alice slipping through the looking glass or Peter stepping through the closet into Narnia or a captain on the Enterprise warping to another galaxy. We're stuck *here* for now. And that's why God had to do something radical. God had to make a move. Do you know what He did?"

Jimmy waited for the answer.

"God stepped into *our* world. He put on skin and hair and muscles and clothes and became just like *us*. He took on a name—Jesus. He did it so we could have some of that other world in *our* world. He did it so we could go to that other world and be with Him when the time is right. But it wasn't easy for Him. It cost Him *a lot* to do it. I know some of you guys know what I'm talking about."

Jimmy knew, but he wanted to hear Dave say it anyway.

Dave said, "That other world is a perfect place, just as God is perfect. But we're not. Not matter what we do, we can't be good enough to go there. So God had to do something even *more* radical than just walk around in our world. He had to come up with a way to get us imperfect people into His perfect world. And the only way to do that was to die for you and me and all our imperfections—our *sins*—and He did it in the most painful way possible: on a cross. He did it because we couldn't do it for ourselves. I can't do enough or be good enough. You can't, either. No matter what you try to do to make yourself better, it won't be good enough. Do you understand? He *had to do it*—and He did it *for you*."

Those words hung in the air, and for a moment Jimmy felt as though it were just him and Dave in the room. *He had to do it, and He did it for me,* Jimmy thought.

"But dying wasn't enough," Dave continued. "Anybody can die and be put in a grave to rot. Nothing special about that. But Jesus died and then came out of the grave. Death couldn't hold Him down. He rose up so that we could rise up, too. And when we rise up, we rise to that other place, the place where God lives. And we'll live with Him. But until then . . . ."

Dave shoved his hands into his pockets and moved away from the podium. He walked into the crowd of kids sitting on chairs and on the floor and spoke as if to each one. "What's the catch? you're wondering. He did all that for me, but what's He want in return? Well, I'll tell you . . . ."

Jimmy held on to his chair. Dave was now in the middle of the crowd.

"He wants your *life*," Dave said in a harsh whisper. "He wants every bit of you: your heart, your mind, your body, your *soul*. And He doesn't want it so He can lock it away somewhere and make you a miserable, boring religious person from now on. He wants it so He can work on it, turn it into something new . . . and then give it back to you in better shape than it was before."

Dave turned and scanned the crowd before he spoke again.

"Maybe you think you're too young; this is stuff for grown-ups. It isn't. Even if dying is years and years away for you, the decision to believe in Jesus, to accept Him into your hearts and give Him your lives, begins *right now*." Dave looked Jimmy square in the eyes. "Jesus wants you *right now*."

Late Saturday Night

JIMMY WAS SURPRISED by how he felt as the meeting ended. Somehow it had never struck him that Jesus might actually *want* him or that Jesus died *for him*. Yeah, he'd heard those things in Sunday school and church. But for some reason it hadn't hit him until now that Jesus' death and resurrection demanded that he do something in return. Until now, Jesus was always something he could pick or not pick—like an answer on a multiple-choice test. But there He was . . . wanting Jimmy *right now*.

Jimmy thought about it as Dave and Jacob gave him a lift home. Jimmy hoped Dave wouldn't say anything to him or ask him any questions. He was afraid an additional word or question might spoil the whole thing. Maybe they sensed it, too, because neither of them spoke. They drove in silence except for an exchange of "Good night" when Jimmy got out of the car and walked to his front door.

He died for me . . . . He wants me . . . . He wants every bit of me. My heart, my mind, my body, my soul. And He doesn't want it so He can lock it away somewhere and make me a miserable, boring religious person from now on. He wants it so He can work on it, turn it into something new . . . and then give it back to me in better shape than it was before.

Jimmy drifted past the living room. His mom called out from her reading chair. Jimmy peeked in.

"How was it?" she asked.

Jimmy shrugged and said, "Okay, I guess."

"Not as bad as you thought?"

"I guess not," he answered. "A bunch of kids I know were there. We played some games and stuff. It was okay."

Mary smiled. "Good," she said. "Now do me a favor and go have a bath."

"A bath!"

"Uh-huh. We have church tomorrow, and after tonight's exercise, I'm sure you need one. Go on," she insisted.

"Okay," Jimmy said and went up the stairs.

Donna came out of the bathroom just as he reached the door. "What happened to you?" she asked.

"What do you mean?" Jimmy said.

"You look like something's wrong."

"I'm gonna have a bath," he answered.

"Oh. That must be it." She giggled and strode to her room.

Jimmy went into the bathroom, turned on the water, and stripped down. He thought about God putting on skin, hair, and muscles so He could be like us . . . so He could die like us . . . for us. *For me.*

The words wouldn't leave Jimmy alone. The were like rubber bands, so that no matter what his mind wandered to in the warm cocoon of the bathwater, it snapped back to those words. *For me. And He wants me right now.*

Jimmy absentmindedly scrubbed himself, then pulled the plug at the bottom of the tub. The water gurgled and gulped. He stepped out of the tub. *What if I said yes?* he wondered as he dried himself off. *What would happen if I said He could have me right now?*

His heart beat a little faster at the thought. Would angels sing? Would he hear God whisper in his ear? Would lightning strike the house? What would happen?

Jimmy wrapped the towel around himself, strolled toward his room—got halfway there when he remembered he had left his clothes on the bathroom floor and went back to get them—then resumed his journey. *Jesus wants me right now. What if I say yes?*

Say yes.

In his room, Jimmy looked around for the small, black Bible his grandmother had given him for his birthday a couple of years before. It had his name in gold letters at the bottom of the front cover. What had he done with it? He got down on his hands and knees to look under the bed. Was that it in the far corner? He got up and rounded the bed, kneeling once again to get the Bible. But it wasn't there. Nothing was there. *It must've been a shadow,* Jimmy thought.

He stayed on his knees. Quietly, without fanfare or announcement, the yes slipped from his head to his heart. It happened in the fraction of a second while Donna's muffled radio played on the other side of the wall, his mother coughed once downstairs in the living room, and the night was otherwise silent enough for him to hear the pounding in his chest and the blood rushing past his ears. *Yes.* He pressed his head against the side of the bed. *You died for me, and I'm sorry, and now You want me—all of me—and I'm saying yes.*

Jimmy opened his eyes and stood up. That was that. It was done. He looked around, but there was no flash of lightning, no supernatural appearance, no voices. He didn't even feel any different. It didn't matter. He wasn't disappointed. He had said yes.

He went downstairs and didn't say a word about it to his mom. Instead, he talked her into letting him have a small glass of chocolate milk before he went to bed.

It seemed so simple. And as he went to sleep, he thought about how everything would get better. Jesus would take his life, fix it up, and hand it back. All Jimmy had to do was watch it happen.

Jimmy had no idea what he'd gotten himself into.

Sunday Morning

With bleary eyes, fluffy bathrobe, and worn slippers, Mary Barclay walked into the kitchen to make coffee. She yawned as she passed the kitchen table where Jimmy sat. She nodded at him and turned to plug in the coffeemaker. Her hand, holding the plug, stopped in midair as the vision of what she had just seen registered on her sleepy brain. She swung on her heel to face the table again.

Jimmy sat at the table in his church outfit—washed and ready to go. Mary's mouth fell open.

Donna walked into the kitchen in the same state of early morning disrepair as her mother and also gasped when she saw Jimmy. "You . . . you're up," Donna said.

"Uh-huh," Jimmy said.

"You're dressed and ready to go to church," Jimmy's mom said.

"Uh-huh," Jimmy said.

"He doesn't have a fever," Mary told Donna.

"Then what's wrong with him?" Donna asked.

"I don't know," Mary said, then looked at Jimmy. "What's wrong with you?"

Jimmy smiled and said, "What makes you think something's wrong?"

"Because we usually have to drag you out of bed kicking and screaming to go to church, that's what," Donna said.

"Really? That's terrible. I'll have to work on that," Jimmy said. "Mom? Are you gonna plug in the coffeemaker or stand there with it in your hand for the rest of the morning?"

Mary looked at the plug in her hand, then turned to plug it in.

"Okay, what's going on?" Donna demanded with her hands on her hips.

"If you hang around asking me questions, we're all gonna be late for church," Jimmy said.

"But—"

"He's right, Donna," Mary interrupted. "I don't want to spoil whatever's gotten into him by asking a lot of questions. Let's just . . . make the most of it."

The routine to get ready for church continued as usual—except that this time Jimmy was the one waiting for everyone else. He didn't tell them what had happened the night before. Not yet. He wanted to relish their surprise and curiosity at his mysterious behavior.

Jimmy walked to his Sunday school class as if it were his first time there. Rather than drag himself down the hall with a scowl on his face as he normally did, he walked quickly, taking in all the sights with a nervous anticipation. *What* he anticipated, he didn't know. But it was the first Sunday he was in church after he had said yes, and everything seemed new to him. He felt as if it were the first day of school. He felt like a stranger, even though he'd been there week after week since he was seven years old. He felt that way not because no one knew him, but because he didn't really know them. All the kids moving to and from their Sunday school classes from various assemblies, clutching their Bibles and lesson books, looked as if he'd never seen them before. No longer were they Sunday school zombies as he had always thought of them. Now—*now* they were alive because Jimmy was alive. And he was alive because he had said yes.

Jimmy's wide-eyed reverie was suddenly interrupted by someone grabbing his arm. "Whoa! Where're you going in such a hurry?" Dave Wright asked.

Jimmy was too startled to answer right away.

Dave took a step back and looked him over. "Something's happened," he said. "You look different. This isn't the frowning, I-don't-want-to-be-here Jimmy Barclay I'm used to seeing on Sundays. What's going on?"

Jimmy smiled awkwardly. His heart picked up a few beats as he tried to say the words. If anybody should hear first, it was Dave. But how could he say it?

"Well?"

Jimmy nodded. "You said Jesus wanted me, and I said yes—He can have me."

Dave's face instantly lit up. "Jimmy! Are you serious? You really accepted Jesus?"

Jimmy smiled and said, "Yeah!"

"Yahoo!" Dave shouted, scooping Jimmy up in his arms. It wasn't what Jimmy expected, and he was a little embarrassed when everyone in the hall stopped to look. "Praise God!"

"Hey! Cut it out!" Jimmy said.

Dave put Jimmy down. "Jimmy, that's *wonderful*! Wonderful!" And he grabbed Jimmy again for a bone-crushing hug.

"Lay off!" Jimmy said.

"Sorry." Dave let him go. "I'm a tactile person."

"I hope it isn't catching."

"It means I'm a huggy kind of person," Dave said with a laugh.

"I hope that isn't catching either," Jimmy said.

A bell rang.

"We're late for Sunday school," Dave said, moving away. "You go on and I'll . . . invite myself over to your house for Sunday dinner or something so we can talk about it. See you in church!" He gave Jimmy a thumbs-up and smiled before he disappeared down the hall.

Just like Sunday school, the church service took on a whole new meaning for Jimmy. The hymns, the Bible readings, and the prayers all seemed created just for him. The pastor's sermon still made him fidget and want to doodle on the offering envelopes, but besides that, he *liked* it. For the first time, he *really liked it.*

During the final hymn, Jimmy leaned over to his mother. "Mom?"

She continued to sing while she leaned her ear toward Jimmy.

"Mom," Jimmy began. He wanted to say it just right, so he used the phrase Dave used earlier. "I accepted Jesus last night."

Mary sang another few words, then the hymnbook in her hand slumped a little. She closed her eyes for a moment. When she opened them again to look at Jimmy, they were tear-filled. She pulled him close with her free hand. It wasn't enough. She laid the hymnbook on the pew and embraced him long and hard with both arms. Jimmy wasn't as embarrassed as he was with Dave. This hug was all right.

From the corner of his eye, he saw Donna stare at them as if they'd lost their minds.

Sunday Afternoon

DAVE, HIS WIFE, JAN, and Jacob invited themselves to a Sunday meal at the Barclays'. Mary said there was plenty of food to go around and she'd love to have them. She wished George would get home from his mother's in time, she added, but she didn't know when he'd make it. Besides that, it seemed like a perfect way to celebrate Jimmy's decision.

Jimmy wasn't sure if the dinner felt more as if it were his birthday or Thanksgiving. Either way, it felt like a special occasion. Jacob was as quiet as always, while Dave entertained them all with stories of other churches where he had been a kids' minister. Jimmy thought Jan was rather quiet but really pretty. Now that he saw her up close, he realized Jacob looked more like her than Dave.

After dinner, Jacob gently smiled and gave Jimmy a small box. Jimmy opened it to find a new Bible.

"We didn't know if you already had one," Dave said, "but I figured some of the study helps in there might be good for you."

"Thanks," Jimmy said and flipped open the cover. On the inside was written: "To Jimmy Barclay, for saying yes to life's greatest adventure . . . with Jesus! Love, Dave, Jan, and Jacob."

After they all helped to clear away the dishes, Dave took Jimmy into the living room and sat him down. "How do you feel?" Dave asked.

Jimmy shrugged. "I don't know," he said. "How am I supposed to feel?"

"It's hard to say. Some people feel like crying, some feel like laughing, and some don't feel anything at all."

"I guess I feel funny about all this fuss," Jimmy said.

"I would, too," Dave said, "but I brought you in here to talk about some things you should know."

"Like what?"

"Well . . ." Dave paused as if trying to choose his words carefully. "Being a Christian isn't like anything you've experienced before. You and Jesus are directly connected now because His Spirit is living inside you. That means things are going to change for you."

"Change? Like how?"

"For one thing, you're going to grow as a Christian. That means you'll develop and mature in the faith. And that growth is just like any other growth. Sometimes it happens in spurts, and other times it happens so slowly you hardly notice."

"Okay," Jimmy said, wondering when his growth would start to happen.

Dave said, "It takes work, Jimmy. The Spirit doesn't just take over and automatically do things. You have to read your Bible every day and obey what it says. You'll want to pray as much as you can. You'll need to spend time with other Christians at church. And you'll want to tell others about your faith. It's a great adventure, Jimmy. It really is."

Jimmy smiled. He liked adventures—especially adventures that changed things for the better.

Dave leaned forward and said quietly, "But make no mistake, Jimmy. It's an adventure that can be difficult and painful sometimes. You'll see."

Jimmy looked at Dave uneasily. That didn't seem like a very nice thing to say.

The front storm door banged, and the inside door opened. George Barclay stepped through, clumsily lugging his overnight bag. "Oh, hi," he said with a weary smile. "I didn't know we were having a party. Hi, Dave."

"We figured we'd take over while you were gone," Dave said.

"Hey, Dad!" Jimmy called out. "You'll never guess what happened!"

"Yeah, you wouldn't believe it in a million years," Donna said as she emerged from the other room with Mary, Jan, and Jacob.

"Why? What happened?" George asked. He dropped his bag, and Mary kissed him hello. Then he waved hello to Jan and Jacob.

"Go on, tell him," Mary instructed Jimmy.

"I accepted Jesus last night," Jimmy said.

George looked from Jimmy to Mary and back again. "You did?"

"Uh-huh," Jimmy said.

"Jimmy . . . Jimmy . . ." George simply said his name over and over as he moved across the room toward him. He pulled Jimmy close for a hug. "Son . . . I don't know what to say."

"Just say you're glad," Jimmy answered.

George whispered, "I'm glad, son. I'm so glad." Suddenly he held Jimmy at arm's length. "Wait a minute. This isn't a trick to get out of being punished for that stunt you pulled the other night?"

"No, Dad," Jimmy said and rolled his eyes.

George laughed and pulled Jimmy back for another hug. "Good."

Everyone gathered in the living room for coffee and soft drinks while George reluctantly reported that his mother's health was going downhill. Even with treatment, the cancer was ravaging her body. The doctors couldn't guess how long she had to live.

Jimmy sat silently while his dad spoke. He was a Christian now, and his grandmother was going to die. It didn't seem right somehow.

Dave suggested they take a minute to pray for her, so they did. Jimmy was horrified when Dave asked him to start.

"Me?"

Dave nodded.

"Out loud?"

"Yes, please."

"But I don't know how," Jimmy said.

Just do it like you've heard it in church," his dad suggested. "You can do it."

Jimmy looked on helplessly as everyone bowed his or her head and waited. Finally he started: "Um . . . heavenly Father . . . uh, we thank Thee for the things which Thou has, uh, spoken to our faces, and, uh, we pray that as we disregard the things we know today that, uh, You will be ever-pressured, uh, while we, uh, remain mindless of You . . . ."

Donna snickered.

Jimmy told her to shut up.

George put his hand on Jimmy's arm. "Son, just pray what's on your heart, okay? Just pray for Grandma."

Jimmy nodded and bowed his head again. "Dear God, please make Grandma better. Amen."

"Amen," everyone echoed.

Then Dave prayed long and hard for Jimmy's grandma, saying all the things Jimmy's heart had wanted him to say without knowing how.

CHAPTER NINE

Late Sunday Afternoon and Evening

THE WRIGHT FAMILY went home late in the afternoon, but not before confirming that Jimmy would go to the evening church service. They wanted him to go to forward at the closing altar call to present himself as a candidate for baptism. Jimmy wasn't keen about going forward in front of all those people. Dave assured him it was nothing to be embarrassed about. It was the next step of obedience in his yes to Jesus. Jimmy reluctantly agreed.

In the silence of his room, he decided to read his new Bible. He figured the best thing was to start at Genesis 1:1 and read through the whole Bible.

He was asleep before he got to Genesis 2:3.

Amid dreams of firmaments, ocean waves, and blinding light, a gentle knocking woke him up. It was Tony at the window again. Jimmy threw it open.

"Hey, Jimmy," Tony said. "What're you doing?"

"Do you have a death wish or something? Why do you keep coming to my window?" Jimmy responded.

"Because your parents won't let me come to the front door," he said. "Don't you wanna hear about last night?"

"Last night?"

"Allen's Pond! Me and Brad Woodward followed my brother and his friends up to the barbecue area on top of the hill. They took beer and everything! You should've seen them!"

"Did they catch you this time?"

Tony shook his head. "Nope. This time we hid around by the utility shack. Dale Miller walked right up to us to throw a bottle away and didn't even see us!"

Jimmy wished he could've been there.

"You really missed it," Tony said. "That's what you get for going to that stupid church meeting."

"It wasn't stupid," Jimmy said defensively.

"Oh, really?"

"Yeah, it was . . . good." Jimmy felt a hot rush of embarrassment. He didn't know what to say to Tony, how to tell him what had happened.

"What was so good about it?"

"I . . . well, we played a lot of games and stuff," Jimmy said. "And then . . . then . . . I came home."

"Sounds like a blast," Tony said sarcastically.

"Something happened . . . ."

"Like what?"

Jimmy's eyes darted around the room nervously. He didn't dare look Tony in the face or he'd lose his nerve. How could he tell Tony he'd become a Christian when he and Tony used to laugh at them?

"This branch is hurting my arm. I gotta go," Tony said when it didn't look as though Jimmy would answer his question.

"Wait," Jimmy said, then blurted out, "I became a Christian last night."

Tony laughed. "You did what?" he said.

"I became a Christian," Jimmy repeated.

"Cool!" Tony said. "What a great idea!"

For the first time, Jimmy looked him in the eyes. "What?" he asked, surprised.

"It's a great way to get your parents off your back! Hey, maybe they'll take you off restriction!" Tony said.

Jimmy frowned. "That's not why I did it!"

Tony smiled as if to say, "I don't believe a word you're saying."

"I'm serious, Tony," Jimmy said. "See, Dave talked about how Jesus died for us and . . . how He wants me and . . . and I said yes. I'm even going back tonight to tell the church I want to be baptized."

It sounded so ridiculous to Jimmy's ears, he could imagine what Tony must've been thinking.

"You're lying to me," Tony said.

"Huh-uh," Jimmy answered.

Tony renewed his grip on the tree branch. "I don't get it, Jimmy. Did they brainwash you or what? You're tellin' me you're turning into a Chip Bender or something?"

Chip Bender was a former friend of theirs who became a Christian and talked about Jesus all the time after that. It drove everybody at school nuts.

"No!" Jimmy said, then added, "I mean, I don't know. It just happened!"

"Oh, man," Tony said, shaking his head. "This isn't good."

"What's wrong?"

"You're gonna become a monk and preach to the raccoons in the woods. I just know it," he said.

"I am not!" Jimmy protested.

From downstairs, Jimmy's mom called that it was time to go to church.

"You'd better go to *church* now, Jimmy," Tony said and began to back away on the branch. "You don't wanna miss your chance to preach."

"Cut it out!" Jimmy said.

"See ya, Mr. Sunday School," Tony said before he disappeared at the bottom of the tree.

"I don't care what you say," Jimmy shouted after him.

Some friend Tony turned out to be, he thought as he closed the window. But, of course, Jimmy *did* care what Tony thought. He cared a lot.

Jimmy brooded on Tony all during the church service. At first, he worried that he'd lost his best friend. Then he got angry about Tony's teasing. Then he wondered if he had made a big mistake in saying yes to Jesus. Would he become Mr. Sunday School? Then he got mad again because Tony spoiled the night he was going forward for baptism.

The pastor finished preaching, and everyone stood to sing the closing hymn—the *invitation*, it was called. George Barclay put his hand on Jimmy's shoulder and leaned close to his ear. "I know it's a little embarrassing," he said. "Will you let me go up with you?"

Jimmy smiled as thoughts of Tony disappeared instantly. "Yeah," he said.

George kept his arm across Jimmy's shoulders as they stepped into the aisle and walked to the front of the church. Jimmy was vaguely aware of the rows of people on both sides, but they were merely trees in a human forest.

The pastor greeted them with a big smile. "Hi, George. Hello, Jimmy," he said.

George cleared his throat and said, "Jimmy accepted Jesus last night and would like to be baptized."

"Congratulations!" the pastor said warmly. He then looked at George expectantly, as if there were something else to be said.

Jimmy looked up at his dad's face and suddenly realized tears were rolling down his cheeks.

"Because my son accepted Jesus, I want to rededicate my life to Christ," George said and squeezed Jimmy's shoulder.

"Me, too," came a tear-filled voice from behind Jimmy. He turned. It was his mother.

"So do I," came a younger choked-up voice. It was Donna.

As the organ played softly, the Barclay family collected themselves into a tender embrace. And Jimmy found himself crying, too.

Monday at School

JIMMY SET HIS RADIO alarm clock for Q96—Odyssey's only Christian station. He thought he would wake up to music. Instead, he awakened to a fiery preacher who was making a case about lazy Christians who never talked about Jesus to their families, friends, and neighbors. He made his point by citing Acts chapter two. "Look what happened here," the preacher said. "After the Holy Spirit descended upon the disciples, Peter went out into the street to preach the story of Jesus. At first, the people thought the disciples were drunk because they were so filled with the power of the Spirit. Peter set them straight. He said, 'Hey, you heathens, we're not drunk! We're just fulfilling what the prophet Joel said would happen! He said that in the last days, young men and women would prophesy and see visions and dream dreams! And that's exactly what's happening right here, right now!'"

Jimmy rolled over in his bed and listened.

"Then Peter went on and laid the gospel down for everyone who was listening. He told them about how God sent Jesus of Nazareth to them, and they crucified Him because their hearts were hard, but it didn't matter because Jesus rose from the dead to prove He's their Lord and Messiah! And look at what the people did.

"The people said, 'What're we supposed to do?' and Peter told them to repent and be baptized in the name of Jesus the Messiah, and then their sins would be forgiven.

"You see what he did? He told them the gospel, plain and simple, and they responded. He *witnessed* to them.

"Do you know what witnessing is? Witnessing is telling what you know. Like if you saw a car accident, you'd act as a *witness*—you'd tell the police and the court what you saw, what you know. That's what Peter did. He told them what he knew. And they responded by asking how they could know Jesus the way Peter did. And look at verse 41. Do you see that verse? *Three thousand* people were added to the church that day! *Three thousand*—all because Peter took the time to share the gospel. He could've made all the excuses we make—about how we're tired or embarrassed or don't want to be pushy. Did Peter care? No! He obeyed Scripture, called on the power of the Holy Spirit, and explained his faith, and *three thousand* became believers."

Someone knocked on Jimmy's bedroom door.

"Yeah?" Jimmy called out.

"Just making sure you're up," his mother said. "We don't want you to be late for school."

"Okay," Jimmy said and sat up. The preacher had finished speaking, and an announcer was telling about booklets listeners could order. Jimmy turned off the radio and got ready for school.

It would be his first day there as a new Christian, and he wanted to make it count. If Peter could bring three thousand people to their knees, Jimmy could at least do the same with a couple of kids. One way or another, he was going to make an impact.

And he did.

how they could know Jesus the way Peter did. And look at verse 41. Do you see that verse? *Three thousand* people were added to the church that day! *Three thousand*—all because Peter took the time to share the gospel. He could've made all the excuses we make—about how we're tired or embarrassed or don't want to be pushy. Did Peter care? No! He obeyed Scripture, called on the power of the Holy Spirit, and explained his faith, and *three thousand* became believers."

The morning at school slipped past in a blur of history, English, and math. Jimmy and Tony were in different classes, so he didn't get to see him until lunch. Tony was sitting with Brad Woodward when Jimmy walked up to their table.

"Hey, Tony," Jimmy said as he sat down.

Tony and Brad stopped their conversation to look at Jimmy. "What's up, Jimmy?" Tony said.

"Not much," Jimmy said. That was one of their normal exchanges, like when adults say "Hi, how are you?" and the other says "Fine" even if he isn't fine.

"Brad and I were just talking about Saturday night at Allen's Pond," Tony explained. Then he said to Brad, "Jimmy couldn't go with us 'cause he was in trouble and had to go to church. Right, Jimmy?"

Jimmy answered, "Yeah, well, I—"

Tony continued saying to Brad, "Did I tell you that Jimmy's all religious now? He's gonna grow up and be one of those TV evangelist guys." Tony and Brad laughed.

"Cut it out, Tony! I am not," Jimmy said.

"He'll have to paint his hair white and get sweaty and talk in a REAL LOUD VOICE," Brad added.

"He'll have to buy a white suit," Tony said with a laugh.

Jimmy wondered if Peter had to put up with this kind of junk. "Don't be stupid," Jimmy said.

"I still think you're just pulling something to get out of trouble with your parents," Tony said.

"No, I'm not," Jimmy said.

"Then come on, tell us what happened," Tony said.

Jimmy thought back to what the preacher had said that morning: Witnessing is just telling what happened, and then *three thousand* could be saved. So Jimmy sent up a quick prayer for the Holy Spirit to help him make Tony and Brad fall to their knees and become Christians right there. He began, "See, I went to church the other night, and I thought it'd be really boring, but it wasn't. We played games, and then Dave, one of our pastors, talked and said that—"

"What kind of games?" Brad asked.

"I don't know," Jimmy answered impatiently, "dodgeball and stuff. Shut up and listen, will you? Anyway, Dave told us how we all live in this world, but there's another world that God lives in, and so God sent Jesus to *this* world to—"

"So Jesus was some kind of astronaut," Tony teased. "A UFO."

"No," Jimmy said. "But, see, He came over and dressed in skin and stuff so He could be like us."

Brad raised his hand as if he were asking a question in class. "How did He put on the skin?" he asked. "Did it have a zipper up the back, like the monster in *Creature from the Black Lagoon*?" He and Tony laughed again.

Annoyed, Jimmy folded his arms. "He was *born*, you idiots! Don't you know what Christmas is all about?"

Tony smiled and said, "It's about a big tree and presents and Santa Claus."

"Maybe Santa Claus was Jesus in disguise," Brad said with a chuckle.

"Will you quit fooling around?" Jimmy pleaded. "Do you wanna know what happened or not?"

"Yeah, but skip the history lesson," Tony said.

"It's not a history lesson, it's part of the story," Jimmy said. "You have to understand why He came! See, we're no good, and God is perfect, so Jesus had to come and die so that we could be with God. We can't go to the other place unless we're made perfect, kinda like Jesus is and . . . and . . ."

Tony's and Brad's blank expressions told Jimmy he wasn't making any sense at all. Why couldn't he say it the way Dave did? Why couldn't he sound like Peter? Why were Tony and Brad giggling? *I'll bet Peter's audience didn't giggle*, he thought.

Tony burst out laughing. "I wish you could see your face," he said. "You don't even know what you're talking about!"

Tony and Brad laughed harder, then harder still.

"I do, too! You just don't understand!" Jimmy protested.

They kept laughing and making more jokes about Santa Claus, aliens, other worlds, and everything else Jimmy had tried to say.

It wasn't supposed to happen this way, he thought as his emotions twisted up and nearly squeezed tears out of him. *They're supposed to understand and say yes to Jesus just like me. Why don't they?*

Finally, he grabbed his tray of food and stormed off to another table.

Jack, Oscar, and Lucy were sitting together as Jimmy passed their table. Jack called out, but Jimmy ignored him. He wanted to ignore everyone. He couldn't stand the thought of being laughed at anymore.

Monday After School

AFTER SCHOOL, JIMMY avoided Tony and went straight home. He was still moping about what had happened at lunch, but in case he was asked, he had worked out an excuse about rushing home to finish building a model of a ship. His dad had given him the model two Christmases ago, and it was still unassembled in a box at the top of his closet, but Jimmy ran home anyway.

It nagged at Jimmy that he had prayed for the Holy Spirit to help him—just like Peter—and they had laughed at him anyway. He couldn't understand why they didn't want to say yes to Jesus the same way he had after hearing Dave.

In his room, he paced and tried to figure it out. He wished—no, it was really a prayer, though Jimmy didn't realize it—that he could talk to somebody who understood how he felt. At that moment, he thought he was the only person in the world who had ever become a new Christian and was teased about it.

His mind went back to the ship model, so he climbed up on a chair to pull it down. As he pushed and lifted various games and boxes of long-forgotten toys, something caught his eye in the corner of the shelf. It was the Bible his grandmother had given him—the one with his name embossed on the front cover. He grabbed it, climbed off the chair, and threw himself onto his bed. Dust flew from the book's jacket. The binding cracked as he opened it. On the inside, his grandmother had written:

For Jimmy,
Do not let people look down on you because you are young, but
be to them an example in your speech and behavior, in your love
and faith and sincerity. (1 Tim. 4:12)
    Love, Grandma B.

Was this the answer to his wish-that-was-really-a-prayer? "Don't let people look down on you," it said. "Be an example in your speech and behavior." Is that what God wanted him to know? He couldn't be sure.

Then Jimmy thought about his grandmother. He suddenly felt a longing to talk to her, to see her. She had always acted as though Jimmy would become a Christian one day, and now that he had, he wanted to make sure she knew about it. Had his dad told her? Would they let him call her? Maybe he could go and visit. He wanted to do *something*.

He remembered once again how his family used to pray together. He wondered how it would feel now to pray—and really mean it. He closed the Bible and crawled off his bed. Getting on his knees next to it, he carefully folded his hands and began, "Dear God—"

Just then, Donna walked into the room. "Jimmy," she said.

Jimmy instantly fell to the floor and pretended he was searching for something under his bed. "What?" he shouted. "Don't you ever knock?"

"Sorry!" she said. "What are you doing?"

"I'm looking for something!" he said, still talking loudly from his embarrassment.

Donna looked puzzled. "Oh," she responded. "Well, Jacob's here to see you."

"Jacob Wright?" Jimmy asked as he stood up.

"How many other Jacobs do you know?" Donna said as she walked out. Jimmy heard her call down the stairs for Jacob to come up.

Jimmy was surprised. He couldn't imagine that Jacob would show up without his father. He wondered what he was doing there. He also wondered what he would have to talk about with a kid who never seemed to talk.

Jacob peeked into the room. "Hi," he said softly.

"Hi," Jimmy said.

"I heard you had a hard time today," Jacob said.

Jimmy knew that Jacob was taught at home by his mom, so he didn't go to their school. "How did you hear about it?"

"My dad saw Jack Davis at Whit's End, and he said your friends were teasing you at lunch. You tried to witness to them, huh? They didn't act the way you thought they would."

Jimmy stared at Jacob for a moment. "They're idiots," he finally said, and all the feelings from lunch came rushing back to him. He felt angry and wanted to cry.

"They don't get it," Jacob said quietly as he sat on the edge of the bed. "Maybe they'll *never* get it. That's the way it happens sometimes. They all make up their own minds. All you can do is what God says to do and *try* to tell them."

"But Tony's my best friend! He was supposed to . . . to understand." Jimmy hung his head. "I said it all wrong."

Jacob smiled. "Just because you became a Christian doesn't mean you'll turn into Peter or Paul and be a great preacher right away," he said. "I know. The same thing happened to me the first time I tried to tell someone about Jesus."

"Really?" Jimmy asked, brightening a little.

"Yeah," Jacob confirmed. "I felt embarrassed and mad, and . . . I thought I might cry in front of everybody. It was terrible."

Jimmy sat down on his bed next to Jacob. He looked intently at the brown-haired kid who didn't talk much but came by at just the right time as if he had been sent by someone.

Jimmy realized he wasn't alone after all. His wish-that-was-really-a-prayer had been answered.

They talked until dinnertime.

CHAPTER TWELVE

Tuesday at School

JIMMY KNEW HE WAS OFF to a bad start at school when, that morning, he found a handwritten note in his desk that said, "Hi, Saint James—Super Christian." It was Tony's handwriting.

At lunch, Jimmy decided to eat by himself. Tony and Brad had other plans and sat down with him.

"So, how's the preaching, Super Christian?" Tony asked.

Brad chuckled.

"Leave me alone," Jimmy said.

"Oh, come on, Jimmy. Quit being so serious," Tony said.

"Then quit teasing me," Jimmy said.

"Okay, Saint James, I won't tease you anymore."

Jimmy scowled at Tony.

"We really wanna know more about all this church stuff," Tony said, barely keeping the smirk off his face.

Brad leaned close and added, "Are you gonna start wearing one of those white collars like the priests do?"

"He'll wear a blue shirt with a big S in the middle of it," Tony said. "For *Super Christian*!" Then Tony sang the *Superman* theme and stretched out his arms as if he were flying around the table.

Jimmy tried to remember the verse his grandmother had written in the front of his Bible. "Don't let people look down on you. . . . Be an example and behave," or something like that. He stuffed the last of his sandwich into his mouth and got up to leave.

Tony grabbed his arm. "Don't you wanna pray before you go?" he asked with a laugh.

Brad said, "Isn't he supposed to dismiss us with a hymn or something?"

Jimmy jerked his arm away and said through his mouthful of sandwich, "Just leave me alone!"

As he marched away, he heard Brad ask, "What did he say?"

Tony laughed again and said, "I think he said to *weave him a home.*"

Jimmy tried to figure out why Tony was being so obnoxious. Okay, so Jimmy had become a Christian. Why did that make Tony so mean? Just a few days ago, they were best friends. Now Tony acted as if they were enemies. What was going on?

Since there was still some lunchtime left, Jimmy walked out to the playground. On the dodgeball court, he saw Jack and Oscar, with Lucy standing nearby, talking to a group of girls. Jimmy didn't know any of them very well, except that Jack and Lucy went to his church. He wasn't sure about Oscar. Maybe he should try to be friends with them now that he was a Christian.

He was thinking about going over to talk to them when he heard an approaching hissing noise, like air coming out of a balloon. He turned around just as Tony and Brad, arms outstretched, raced around him like two Superboys. They hissed through their teeth to make it sound as if they were flying through the air.

"It's Super Christian!" Tony announced. "Faster than a speeding Bible!"

"Able to leap tall churches in a single bound!" Brad said.

"It's a bird . . . . "

"It's a plane . . . . "

"Go away!" Jimmy shouted.

"It's Super Christian!" they yelled together as they circled around and around him.

Jimmy tried to move past them, but they stayed with him no matter where he tried to go. "Cut it out!" Jimmy shouted at Tony.

"Super Christian! Super Christian!" Tony said over and over.

Finally, Jimmy had had enough and stuck out a leg to trip one of them. He caught Brad's foot. Brad spun to the ground, landing in a way that knocked the wind out of him.

Tony nearly tripped over the ashen Brad, but he caught himself in time. He angrily pushed Jimmy. "What're you doing, Super Christian?" Tony demanded. "Super Christians aren't supposed to make people trip."

"Leave me alone," Jimmy said through clenched teeth.

"Make me," Tony said and pushed Jimmy again.

"Go away."

"What're you gonna do, cry like you almost did yesterday? Huh, Super Christian?" Tony teased as he pushed Jimmy once more.

Tony's remark wouldn't have been so stinging if Jimmy hadn't felt like crying—but he did. Tony was supposed to be his best friend, and it made no sense that he would act like this.

Jimmy then did the one thing he never thought he'd do. He looked straight into Tony's face, with its twisted smirk and defiant eyes . . . *and punched him in the nose.*

Tony's expression of surprise burned itself into Jimmy's memory, but no more so than the way Tony staggered backward, tripped over Brad, who was trying to stand up, and fell flat on his backside.

The image stayed on Jimmy's mind even as Mr. Parks grabbed his arm and led him to the principal's office.

"What did you think you were doing?" George Barclay asked Jimmy as they drove home from the school half an hour later. "Is that your way of bringing people to Jesus—by punching them in the nose?"

"He was teasing me, Dad. He's been teasing me ever since I told him I was a Christian," Jimmy complained.

"So let him tease you. Who cares what he thinks?" George said.

"I do. He's supposed to be my best friend. Why's he being such a creep?"

George shrugged. "Maybe he doesn't like Christians."

Jimmy thought about it, then shook his head. "I never saw him act like this with the other Christian kids at school."

George was thoughtful for a moment. They drove on. Finally he said, "But the other Christian kids at school weren't his best friend, were they?"

"Huh?"

"Think about it, Jimmy. You were best friends, and suddenly you go through a change that Tony's not part of. Since then, he's been teasing you and picking on you, right?"

"Right," Jimmy said.

"And now you're thinking that he's rejected you, right?"

"Well, yeah."

"And what's *he* thinking?" George asked.

"That's what I can't figure out!" Jimmy said.

George rubbed his chin. "I'm just guessing—and I'm not trying to excuse what you two have been doing to each other—but . . . isn't it possible that Tony thinks *you* rejected *him*?"

"What!"

"Sure," George said. "You're a Christian now, and you think Tony should come along with you into your new adventure. But what if Tony's afraid you're going to leave him behind? Maybe he resents what's happened to you because it'll take you away from him."

"But we can still be friends if he'd stop acting like such a jerk!"

"Can you?"

"Yeah!" Jimmy said. Then he thought about it for a moment and added, "I mean, can't we?"

"I don't know," George said with a shrug of his shoulders. "Sometimes Christianity can tear friends—even families—apart."

They pulled into their driveway, and George turned to Jimmy. "You know you'll have to be punished. I can't have you going around punching kids in the nose—even if it seemed like self-defense."

"At this rate, I'm gonna be grounded for life."

"It's going to seem like it. I'm adding *two weeks* to your restriction," George said.

"But Dad!"

"Don't argue. You might get time off for good behavior, but you're going to have to be *really good.*"

George opened his door to get out.

Jimmy sat and stewed. Tony had gotten him in trouble *again.*

CHAPTER THIRTEEN

Tuesday Evening at Home

JIMMY WENT STRAIGHT to his room and paced around like a lion in a cage. Two more weeks' restriction, and all because of Tony. It wasn't fair!

His mom peeked in on him. "Hi, Jimmy," she said.

"Hi," he said unhappily.

"Sorry you had a bad day."

Jimmy frowned at her.

"Dave left some material on your study desk, if you want to look at it," she continued. "Considering what happened today, you should probably read it." And she retreated from the room.

Jimmy went to his desk. He wished he'd been there when Dave came. He needed to talk to Dave or Jacob. He frowned again and thought how stupid it was that Jacob was taught at home. If he'd been at school with Jimmy, he could have helped Jimmy deal with Tony and Brad.

"To Jimmy B," said the writing on the large, yellow envelope. He flipped up the clasp on the back and dumped out the contents. A small paperback book fell on top of his normal junk. "Tips for New Christians," the cover said.

In his frame of mind, Jimmy didn't have the patience to read the book. He simply flipped through the various sections about the importance of Bible study, prayer, sharing the faith—and one particular section about the life of a new Christian.

"Purity is a vital part of the new Christian's life," the book said. "You need to be pure in what you see and hear and do. As a new believer, you don't want to expose yourself to anything that will stunt your growth in Jesus. With a prayerful heart, look closely at the books you read, the television shows you watch, the music you listen to. Maybe it's time to clean your house and—and your soul—of risky, un-Christian material."

Jimmy had the sense to know that as long as he was mad at Tony, he wouldn't have a very "prayerful heart." But he glanced over at his CD player and saw some CDs Tony had played the night Jimmy smoked the cigar.

He picked one up and thought about purity. *This'll stunt my growth in Jesus,* he said to himself. Clenching the thin disc between his fingers, he angrily broke it in half. Then he grabbed a second CD and broke it.

It made Jimmy feel good. *Pure,* he thought.

He broke one CD after another—until he exhausted his own collection and wondered how pure his parents' and sister's collections were.

"I'll kill him!" Donna Barclay said.

"All right, let's not get carried away," George said.

Jimmy sat on the living room sofa and watched his judges and jury. He was no longer mad at Tony. That emotion had been moved to a position of lesser importance now that his family was ready to hand him over to a juvenile detention agency.

"When did you do it?" Mary asked in a bewildered tone. "How did you do it so *fast?*"

"We were in the family room watching the movie," Donna offered. "That's when he did it. We thought he was upstairs doing his homework or . . . or reading his Bible."

George leaned against the doorway into the dining room. "I can't keep up with you anymore, Jimmy," he said. "Today you punched your best friend in the nose, and tonight— What possessed you?"

"We don't want anything in the house that'll stunt our growth in Jesus, right?"

George and Mary looked at each other as if to decide who would answer. George shrugged helplessly.

"Right," Mary said. "But you should leave the decision of what will stunt *our* growth to *us.*"

"Did you see what he did to my room?" Donna growled. "He took down my posters! He went through my books! He broke my CDs!"

"Not the *Christian* ones," Jimmy said in his own defense.

"That's not the point! You're supposed to keep your hands off my stuff!" Donna insisted.

"Okay, calm down," George said to Donna. Then he turned his attention to Jimmy. "Son, I appreciate your enthusia—"

"Enthusiasm!" Donna cried out as if she might tear at her hair in exasperation.

"Yes," George said. "If I remember right, enthusiasm is normal for a new Christian. Don't you remember, Donna? When you became a new Christian, you tried to plaster Christian bumper stickers all over the car. And I don't think you asked us first, either."

"That was different."

"No, it wasn't. You were enthusiastic about your newfound belief— just like Jimmy. But what we need is *balance* and *consideration*. So, Jimmy, next time you get the . . . uh, inspiration to purge the house of things you consider less than Christian, talk to us first, okay?"

"Yes, sir."

"Where did you put Donna's things?" Mary asked.

"In the garage. I put everybody's stuff in a box next to the garbage can," Jimmy answered.

George shook his head as if he hadn't heard correctly. "*Everybody's* stuff? Which everybody's stuff?"

"Yours and Mom's," Jimmy said.

Mary was on the edge of her seat. "*Our stuff?*" she asked. "You went through our stuff, too?"

"Yeah! You guys really oughtta be ashamed of yourselves," Jimmy said.

But his words were lost in the commotion as George, Mary, and Donna raced to the garage.

CHAPTER FOURTEEN

Wednesday Afternoon

JIMMY DIDN'T SEE Tony again until the next day at recess. He had just finished a round of dodgeball when he noticed that Tony was sitting on the sidelines, watching him. Mr. Parks blew the whistle for everyone to go back into the building.

"Hey, Jimmy," Tony said as he ran up to him.

Jimmy prepared himself another clash, maybe even a fight. "What?" he asked.

Tony walked at Jimmy's side. "Slow down, I wanna talk to you."

"What about?"

"You know," Tony said.

At a glance, Jimmy noticed that the punch in the nose hadn't done any damage. He felt a twinge of disappointment that he didn't have more power in his punch. "No, I don't."

"What happened yesterday. Do I have to spell it out?" Tony asked.

At that moment, Jimmy realized that in all the years of their friend-ship, they had never had to say they were sorry to each other. Even when they got on each other's nerves or had an argument, apologies were simply understood, not spoken.

"Look," Tony said, "I shouldn't have teased you so much. It's just that . . . well . . . I don't get this Christian thing. That's all."

Dad was right, Jimmy thought. Tony acted like a jerk because he felt Jimmy was rejecting him—leaving him behind by heading into a new experience. So that was it. That was Tony's apology. "Forget about it," Jimmy said.

They walked silently to the door. "A bunch of us are going to the gazebo in McAlister Park after school," Tony finally said. "Tim Ryan has something he wants to show us. He says it's real cool. You wanna come?"

Tim Ryan was well known for finding all kinds of neat things for

Jimmy and his friends to look at. A few weeks ago, he had brought bullets from his dad's gun. But Jimmy said, "My parents said I have to go straight home after school. I'm still on restriction, remember?"

"Just tell 'em you stayed after school to do homework or something. You can figure it out," Tony suggested.

Jimmy knew this was like offering him a peace pipe. It was a way to be friends the way they were before. If he said no, it would be the same as hitting Tony in the nose all over again. He had to say yes. "Well . . . okay. I'll try."

"Good," Tony said, and he spun on his heel to go to class.

The gazebo in McAlister Park was a popular place in the summer, even though it was out of the way. It was shaped like a large, round, wooden porch with open sides and a white roof. Bands often played there, politicians made speeches from it, and couples sat in it with their arms around each other while dreaming the warm days away. As the cloudy afternoons of September rolled into October, that part of the park saw fewer people come through. It was a perfect meeting place for a group of kids.

By the time Jimmy got there, Tony, Brad, and a few of their other friends were gathered in the center of the gazebo. "Tim's not here yet," Tony explained when Jimmy joined them.

"What's he got?" Jimmy asked as he dropped his schoolbooks onto one of the benches that lined the gazebo.

"You'll see," Tony said.

"There he is!" Gary Holman said, pointing.

They turned to look. Tim ran toward them, all smiles as he carried a brown bag. He took the stairs to the gazebo two at a time and was breathless when he reached the other boys. "Hi, guys," he gasped.

"Did you get them?" Tony asked.

"Yeah!" Tim said. "My dad almost caught me, though."

"What is it?" Jimmy asked.

"Here." Tim opened the bag for everyone to look. Inside were strings of firecrackers, a small rocket, matches, and a small can of lighter fluid.

"Great!" Tony said.

"What's the lighter fluid for?" Cory Sleazak asked.

"Oh, just in case it's too windy to light the fuses," Tim answered. "I figured it'll help keep everything burning."

Tony took charge. "Gary, keep an eye out. We don't wanna set these things off when somebody's coming."

"We're setting them *all* off?" Jimmy asked.

Tony smiled and said, "Yeah! Fourth of July at the beginning of October!"

"The noise'll make people come running. We'll get in trouble," Jimmy said.

Tony frowned at him. "Not if we light the fuse and run, you idiot. We'll soak the long fuse in lighter fluid so it'll burn while we run. Then we can watch the fireworks from the woods." He turned to Tim and instructed, "Let's get it going."

"I don't think it's a good idea," Jimmy said, knowing full well that he would look like a party pooper.

"Quit being a spoilsport!" Cory said. "Or should we call you *Saint James?*"

"Shut up," Tony snapped at Cory. "He's not like that. Now come on, let's put everything on the floor and get it ready."

Jimmy watched silently as Tony and Tim stretched the string of firecrackers along the wooden floor, paying careful attention to the fuse.

"What should we do with the rocket?" Tim asked.

"Put it at the end of the firecrackers so its fuse'll catch when they go off," Tony said.

"Let's point it toward the field," Cory suggested.

Tony grabbed the rocket. "Good idea!" he said. He positioned it so it would shoot through the opening between the banister and the roof. He tied the rocket fuse to the firecracker fuse so it would catch.

"Get back. I'm gonna pour the lighter fluid on it now," Tim said.

Everyone took a few steps back. Tim poured the fluid onto the firecracker fuse.

He laughed as he said, "I'm spilling it."

"Put some on the rocket fuse," Tony told him. "Hurry or it'll evaporate."

Tim laughed harder as he spilled more of the fluid. Finally he just turned the can upside down and poured it all over the firecrackers and rocket. "That'll help it go up faster," he said.

Jimmy didn't know a lot about lighter fluid, but something told him this was a bad idea. Even if it evaporated quickly in the cool breeze, it might make the fireworks explode faster than they wanted and hit them before they could run. Jimmy was about to protest when Tony lit a match.

"Run!" he shouted and threw the match at the fuse. It caught immediately. The kids ran out of the gazebo and toward the woods about 25 yards away. Jimmy ducked behind a large tree with Tony and watched.

From where they stood, Jimmy could see the smoke—more than there should've been for just a fuse. "What if the gazebo catches on fire?" Jimmy whispered to Tony.

Tony looked as if the idea hadn't occurred to him. He shrugged.

Suddenly—*Pop!*—then another *Pop!*—then *Pop! Pop! Pop! Pop!* as the string of firecrackers sparked and exploded like a gangster's machine gun. From behind various trees, the kids pointed and laughed.

"That's *better* than the Fourth of July!" Tony shouted.

The firecrackers were still banging away when the rocket hissed loudly and took off. But the trajectory was all wrong. Instead of shooting toward the field, it spun and spiraled upward into the roof of the gazebo. Jimmy watched in wonder.

Kaboom! The blast echoed throughout the park. Smoke poured out the top of the gazebo.

"It's on fire!" Jimmy gasped. "It's on fire!"

"Get out of here!" Tony yelled and raced into the woods. The rest of the kids followed. Jimmy stood mesmerized where he was, not sure of what to do as smoke blew from the gazebo. "Jimmy! Run!" Tony screamed from a distance.

It was enough. Jimmy panicked and ran home.

"Oh, God, I'm sorry I'm sorry I'm sorry I'm sorry," Jimmy puffed as he ran. He didn't know which direction Tony and the other kids went, nor did he care. He shouldn't have gone to the gazebo, he knew. He shouldn't have let them light firecrackers. *The gazebo's going to burn down, and it's all my fault.*

What should he do? Tell his parents? Call the fire department? He didn't know. What was the *Christian* thing to do? "God, help me. I'm sorry I'm sorry I'm sorry . . . ."

By the time he reached his front door, he knew he had to tell his parents. *They* could call the fire department. But Jimmy figured the gazebo would be burned down by that time. And then he'd be an arsonist and go to jail.

He burst through the front door on the verge of tears. In the living room, several heads turned in his direction. He stopped dead in his tracks. His mom and dad, Donna, Dave, and Jacob were sitting with very serious expressions on their faces.

They already know! Jimmy thought.

"Jimmy!" his dad said. "Where've you been? We've been looking for you."

As an automatic response, Jimmy nearly said he'd stayed late at school to do his homework. Then he realized he didn't have his books with him—he had left them at the gazebo, where they were either ashes or evidence for the fire chief. That was the end. His life was over. He began to sob.

Mary rushed to Jimmy and wrapped her arms around him. "Aw, that's all right, Jimmy. It'll be okay." His ear pressed against her, he heard her say to the others, "I guess he got the message at school."

Jimmy looked up at her through misty eyes. "Message?" He was confused.

"About your grandmother," she said and stroked his hair. "She's taken a turn for the worse. We have to leave right away."

CHAPTER FIFTEEN

Wednesday Evening

THINGS WERE HAPPENING too fast for Jimmy's mind to cope. Suddenly he had to jump from the gazebo to his grandmother.

"I need you to pack," his mom told him. Then she glanced around and asked, "Where are your schoolbooks?"

"I left them—"

"You're going to need them," she interrupted. "Your teacher told me what homework you can do while we're gone."

"I'll drive you back to school," his dad said.

Jimmy opened his mouth to tell them his books weren't at school. They were at the burned-down gazebo. But Dave spoke first.

"I know you have a lot of things to do," Dave said. He and Jacob stood up. "How about if we take him to get his books? That'll be one less thing for you to worry about. Besides, I'd like to talk to him before you go."

"If you don't mind," George said.

"I don't," Dave said with a smile. "Let's go, Jimmy."

Jimmy felt as if he were caught in a strong current that carried him down a river. But whether he was headed for a peaceful lake or a rocky waterfall, he couldn't be sure.

Dave hugged Mary, then George, then Donna. "God be with you," he said. "We'll pray for you."

"Thanks," everyone muttered.

With a hand on each of their shoulders, Dave guided Jimmy and Jacob to the door. "I'll have him back in a few minutes," he said.

In the car, Jimmy confessed to Dave that his books weren't at school but at the gazebo.

"Gazebo! In McAlister Park?" Dave asked.

Jimmy nodded.

"What were you doing at the gazebo? I thought you were on restriction. Weren't you supposed to come straight home after school?"

"Yeah," Jimmy answered. "But I didn't."

From his place behind the steering wheel, Dave glanced across the seat at Jimmy. "Then you didn't get the message about your grandmother."

"No," Jimmy said.

"So you weren't crying about her. You were crying about something else."

Jimmy's chest tightened. "Yeah."

"Why were you so upset?"

"You'll see," Jimmy said.

They parked the car at the edge of the park and got out. Jimmy looked around for some sign of the fire department or police, but everything seemed quiet as usual. They walked down the path through the woods to the gazebo.

It was still there.

Dave and Jacob both noticed Jimmy's wide-eyed expression as he approached it. "Jimmy?" Dave inquired.

"It's still here," he whispered.

They mounted the steps. "Of course it's still here. What did you think?" Dave asked.

"There're your books," Jacob said. They were still sitting on one of the benches that lined the gazebo's banister. Jimmy picked them up. There was no sign that they had been touched by the fire.

"That's a shame," Dave said. He pointed to the floor of the gazebo.

Jimmy looked down. There were bits of paper, black powder, and scorch marks where the firecrackers had been. The marks led to a large black mark—a black circle that looked as if someone had dropped a bottle of ink on the floor and it had exploded. *The rocket*, Jimmy knew. He glanced up at the roof. It was also scarred with black marks like those on the floor. Other than that, the gazebo looked the same as it always did. Obviously their prank caused a lot of smoke but no fire. Jimmy slumped onto the bench with relief.

"What do you know about this?" Dave asked.

Jimmy gazed up at Dave and confessed everything.

"You have to tell your parents," Dave said as they drove home.

"I know," Jimmy said.

"Don't make excuses. Just tell them what happened."

"Okay."

"I'm sure they'll understand," Dave said.

Jimmy wasn't so sure of that.

"They'll probably make you pay for the damage," Dave said. "Maybe your friends'll help."

Fat chance, Jimmy thought.

Dave stopped at a traffic light and studied Jimmy. "This isn't unusual, you know. You're going to have battles with your old friends. They're going to want you to act like you always did, and you won't be able to. It'll cause a lot of conflict—more than you've had already. Jacob knows."

Jimmy turned in the seat to look at Jacob, who sat in the back.

"My best friend wasn't a Christian," Jacob said. "And he didn't care when I became a Christian. But he thought I'd keep doing all the stuff we used to do, and I couldn't. I mean, we weren't *bad* kids, but everything changed. I wanted to do more things at church, and he wouldn't come with me."

"What happened?" Jimmy asked.

"He stopped being my friend," Jacob said sadly.

"But Tony and I have been best friends since the first grade!" Jimmy said. "I don't have to stop being his friend just because I'm a Christian, do I?"

"If he expects you to do the kind of mischief you did today, how *can* you stay friends with him?" Dave asked.

Jimmy settled back in his seat and thought about it. He didn't have an answer. *There has to be a way for us to stay friends*, he thought.

"You need courage," Dave said. "We'll pray that God will give you the courage to do the right thing. Go on, Jacob."

Jacob prayed for Jimmy, for him to have courage, for Tony, and for Jimmy's family as they went to visit his sick grandmother. It was a simple, heartfelt prayer that sounded strange to Jimmy's ears, particularly since it came from someone Jimmy's age.

How come it seems so easy for Jacob to talk to God? Jimmy wondered. "I wish I could pray like that," he said after Jacob finished.

"You will eventually," Dave said. They pulled into Jimmy's driveway.

"When?" Jimmy asked.

Dave chuckled. "Be patient," he said. "You've only been a Christian for a few days. Give yourself a chance to grow."

"Does that mean I'll be like Jacob—or you?"

"Wait a minute," Dave said. "I don't think you'd want to be like either one of us."

"But I do! You guys are so smart. You always know the right thing to do."

Dave tapped the steering wheel with his fingers. "No, Jimmy. That's not true. We make a lot of mistakes. You only get to see us when we're on our best behavior. Right, Jacob?"

Jacob nodded.

"I don't believe you," Jimmy said.

"Don't do this to us, Jimmy," Dave said with a sudden seriousness. "Keep your eyes on Jesus. If you look at us, you'll only be disappointed. We have problems; we make mistakes. Keep your eyes on the One who saved you, okay?"

Jimmy said okay, but his heart wasn't in it.

Dave playfully pushed at Jimmy. "Now go on. And don't forget to tell your parents about the gazebo."

"I promise," Jimmy said and climbed out of the car.

He watched Dave and Jacob drive away. He had no idea it would be the last time he'd see them.

Wednesday Night and Thursday

WITH A FOUR-HOUR DRIVE ahead of them, Jimmy decided it would be better to tell his parents about the gazebo after they were well on their way.

When he broke the news, his mom was instantly upset and couldn't believe he'd do such a thing. His dad said he appreciated Jimmy's honesty, but that Jimmy would have to pay for any damage *and* plan for an extra punishment when they got home.

Donna rolled her eyes and said, "It seems you're getting in more trouble now than you did before you became a Christian."

Jimmy hadn't really thought about it, but now that Donna brought up the idea, he had to agree. It seemed *everything* started going wrong after he went to Dave's youth group meeting. He said yes to Jesus and had since made Tony, his other friends, and his family mad at him, and now his grandma was sicker, too. It was as if he couldn't win no matter what he did. What was the point of being a Christian if things weren't going to get better?

These thoughts swirled in his head as the lights from passing streetlamps and buildings mixed the shadows in the darkness of the backseat. They lulled him to sleep.

"Jimmy," his dad said, bringing Jimmy back to consciousness.

"Yeah?" Jimmy looked up to see his dad's eyes in the rearview mirror.

"You have no idea how thankful to God I am for your newfound faith. Hang in there."

They arrived at Grandma Barclay's house in a town called Newberry just before midnight. It wasn't the house George or his brother and sister grew up in. Grandma had sold that house after Grandpa Barclay died. This was a smaller, cottage-sized house in the middle of a village for retired people. George identified himself to the security guard at the gate and was allowed to pass. He used his key to get in the house itself. There was a note from Mildred, one of Jimmy's grandmother's friends, saying that she'd made them sandwiches and would call in the morning. Grandma Barclay was in the intensive care section of the hospital, the note finished.

The Barclays sleepily ate the sandwiches and organized who was sleeping where. Mom and Dad slept in the guest room. Donna got the couch in the small living room. Jimmy used his sleeping bag on the floor. No one wanted to sleep in Grandma's bed.

The next morning, Mildred arrived as they were having breakfast in the tiny kitchen. She was a lively old woman with wild, silver hair and dancing, blue eyes. She told them Grandma Barclay had collapsed the morning before, with a sharp pain in her abdomen. Her doctor at the hospital said there was no doubt about it now—the cancer had returned. This time there would be no therapy. There was nothing any-one could do but pray.

Jimmy remembered that he had prayed for his grandmother a few days before. *A lot of good it did*, he thought.

They drove to Rock Creek Hospital. Jimmy didn't like hospitals much. They had a peculiar smell, the nurses seemed unfriendly as they rushed around, and patients sometimes moaned from their rooms. Hos-pitals gave Jimmy the creeps.

Intensive care was a quiet area with a lot of softly beeping equip-ment and gadgets Jimmy couldn't identify. The nurses and doctors looked tired. After George assured the nurse that they were all family who'd traveled a long way to see his mother, she said she'd bend the rules a little and let them all in to see Victoria. Jimmy wondered who Victo-ria was, then remembered that was his grandmother's name. He'd for-gotten that grandparents once had first names like that.

As they walked toward Grandma Barclay, Jimmy caught sight of other patients in the ward. They were young and old. Most of them lay very still. One man with white skin looked as if he had died. Jimmy hoped the nurses knew.

They came to Jimmy's grandmother. He hardly recognized her. Her normally clean and styled hair was matted and greasy. Her skin was a pasty color, and without her makeup, she looked a hundred years older than she was. She had tubes and wire hanging from her face and dangling from odd angles under her sheets.

Mary's eyes filled with tears. Donna put her hand over her mouth. George touched his mother's arm tenderly. Jimmy watched with a mixture of wonder and fear. He was far, far away from any of the things that gave him comfort: his room, his school, his Odyssey, his youth, his future. There his world didn't include the old and the dying.

"If you were to die tonight . . ." the booklet said.

Grandma Barclay slowly opened her eyes. A shadow of a smile moved across her lips when she saw George. "You came," she whispered in a distant voice.

"Hi, Mom," George said. "We're all here."

Grandma tried to adjust her head so she could see them. "Mary . . . Donna . . . ." She lifted her hand weakly. "Where's Jimmy?"

Jimmy moved toward the bed so she could see him.

"Ah," she coughed. "I knew it would happen. I always knew it." She wiggled her fingers for Jimmy to come closer. He did. She touched his hand. "I've been praying for you since before you were born. I knew you would meet the Lord. I prayed every day."

Jimmy felt tears burning at the back of his eyes. "Thanks, Grandma."

"I want to talk to you," she said. "There are . . . things . . . I want to say to you."

"When you're stronger, Mom," George said.

She smiled and closed her eyes. "No strength until . . . later."

George quietly ushered the family out of the room.

George insisted on staying at the hospital—at his mother's side—if they would let him. But he gave Mary, Donna, and Jimmy the okay to leave for a while. Mary and Donna decided to go to the mall. Faced with the prospect of shopping for clothes with his mother and sister or watching TV in the waiting room, Jimmy opted for the TV. Besides, he was curious about what his grandmother wanted to say to him and didn't want to miss the chance to talk if she woke up.

An hour or so later—after Jimmy had sampled one of the dried chocolate cupcakes in the vending machine and watched all he could stand of the TV soap operas—his dad came back. "She's awake," he said. "She wants to talk to you."

Jimmy leapt to his feet.

"Now, son, don't do anything to excite her, all right? Take it easy."

"Okay," Jimmy said. He followed his dad back through the corridors to his grandmother's room. When they reached the door, George gestured for Jimmy to go in and walked away toward the nurses' station.

She looked better this time. Someone had brushed her hair, and she was propped up in a way that made it appear as if she were at home in bed with a book. Jimmy smiled at her as he rounded the bed. She smiled wearily back to him. "Hi, Jimmy," she said in the same distant voice he'd heard before. It was her voice, but it seemed to come from another place.

"Hi, Grandma," Jimmy said. "How're you feeling?"

"Awful, but I'll get over it," she said, chuckling. "How are you doing?"

"Okay," he said.

She patted the mattress as a signal for him to come closer. "I mean, how are you doing now that you've met Jesus?"

Jimmy was puzzled. "I asked Him into my heart, Grandma," he said. "But it doesn't feel like I really met Him."

"Those feelings will come," she said. "Keep your faith and the feelings usually follow."

"Is that what you wanted to tell me?" Jimmy asked.

Grandma closed her eyes as if she felt a deep pain somewhere. Then she opened them again. "I have so much to tell you. I wish we had years. I would love to . . . to see you grow up in your faith."

"You will, Grandma. We're praying for you!" Jimmy said.

"Good," she said, her voice raspy and broken. "Pray hard. Not because I'll get better, but because you should pray. Learn to talk to God, Jimmy. Talk to Him all the time. He's listening. He's always listening. Things won't always work out the way you want, but He's always there. He knows what's best."

Jimmy leaned forward, his elbows pressing into the mattress. "You have to get better, Grandma. It wouldn't be fair for you to leave me right after I became a Christian." He paused as the full reality of the situation came to him. She was going to die and leave him. "I need you."

Grandma turned her head so she could look Jimmy in the eyes. For a moment, her eyes seemed as bright and clear as when she was healthy—the way Jimmy always remembered her. "You don't need me," she said firmly. "You need Jesus."

"But Jesus isn't here," he said. "And I don't have anybody else."

"You have your family. You have your church. You have friends—some you haven't even met yet. Jesus is in them." She raised a finger and pointed at Jimmy's chest. "You have Him in there."

"But it isn't fair. I didn't know it was going to be this hard."

She coughed and grabbed Jimmy's hand. "Fair has nothing to do it with it. Look at me, Jimmy. Nobody said the Christian life was fair—or easy. Nothing in this world is fair or easy. Growing old and dying of cancer isn't fair or easy. But God is good."

She gasped and lay back with her eyes closed. She still had hold of Jimmy's hand. He waited, worried she might die right then and there.

A minute passed, and she opened her eyes again. She whispered, "You want to meet Jesus? Well, sometimes the Lord has to strip everything away from us before we can truly meet Him. And sometimes it really hurts. I felt it when your grandfather died, then my brothers and sisters, then my friends . . . and then my own body stopped working a little at a time. It's the Lord's way of getting me to pay attention. He's taking it all away from me so He can give it back in a newer, more wonderful way. It's like He gives us a good, hard scrubbing—and it hurts a little—so we'll be cleaned up to see Him face-to-face." She squeezed Jimmy's hand. "You see, He strips it away *here* so He can give it back to me nice and new *there*."

A chill ran up and down Jimmy's spine. Those were the same words Dave had used the night Jimmy said yes to Jesus. It led to a new life for Jimmy. In a strange way, Jimmy now understood how it would lead to a new life for his grandmother—a new life in that other place where God lives. But it still meant she would leave him, and he didn't want that. Not now, not yet.

"Oh, Jimmy," his grandmother said, and he saw a small tear slip from her eye and slide down her temple. "I'm so happy for you . . . all the adventures you have ahead of you. I'll be watching . . . ."

She closed her eyes again. Her grip on Jimmy's hand relaxed completely—and let go.

❖   ❖   ❖

That evening, Jimmy, Donna, and Mary had dinner at a restaurant with Uncle Donald and Aunt Gwen, George's younger brother and sister. They had arrived that afternoon. Jimmy's dad insisted they should go while he stayed at the hospital, as long as they promised to bring him back something to eat. Since Uncle Donald, Aunt Gwen, and their families rarely came to Odyssey, they had the usual conversation about how big the kids had gotten and how they were doing in school and what the adults liked or didn't like about their jobs. Jimmy zoned out. He thought about his grandmother and once again prayed that God would let her live.

Toward the end of the meal, Mary realized she hadn't asked George what he wanted her to bring back for him. She excused herself and went to the pay phone. Jimmy and Uncle Donald exchanged knowing looks as Aunt Gwen and Donna started talking about hairstyles. The minutes ticked away. Jimmy glanced over at the pay phone just in time to see his mother hang up the receiver and wipe tears from her eyes.

Jimmy knew.

Mary reached the table and put on the brave face that Jimmy had seen at other times when there was bad news. "I'm so sorry," she said, choking back the tears. "Grandma died 10 minutes ago."

Friday and Saturday

OVER THE NEXT TWO DAYS, Jimmy battled more against boredom than
against grief. George, Donald, and Gwen made arrangements at the
funeral home. Distant family members came to the house, cried, and
left again. Errands were run. Members of Grandma's church brought
food. Friends dropped in to pay their respects.

Amid all the activity, Jimmy didn't have anything to do. He tried to
watch television on Grandma's portable black-and-white, but she didn't
have cable, and the aerial only picked up three snowy channels. He
made an effort to finish his homework, but the buzz of activity distracted him. And there was nowhere to go in the middle of a retirement
village.

Friday evening arrived, and Mary handed Jimmy his Easter suit
from last year. He didn't even know she had packed it—and only then
realized that she had because she had known Grandma would die.

"Where are we going?" he asked.

"The viewing," she replied.

"Viewing?"

Mary explained that it was a time for everyone to see Grandma in
the coffin at the funeral home—a time to offer comfort to the family
and to say good-bye to Grandma. "Don't you remember when your
grandfather died?" she asked.

Jimmy didn't. He was just five years old when that happened and
had only the vaguest memory of black suits and a long, black hearse at
a graveyard.

The funeral home smelled like flowers. So did the funeral director.
He took Jimmy's hand in a cold grip and shook it while he said in a soft,
deep voice how sorry he was about "Victoria's passing."

Dad guided Jimmy, Donna, and Mary into a cozy room with dim
lighting and chairs, lamps, and tables that looked as if they belonged in

somebody's house. Near the wall on the far end of the room sat a long, brown coffin. Grandma's head was barely visible above the shiny box and lacy linen it rested on. Donna froze in her steps. "I can't go," she cried.

Mary hugged her and took her aside. "Whenever you're ready, Donna," she said. "It's okay."

George looked at Jimmy. "Do you want to wait?" he asked.

"No," Jimmy said. "Let's go."

George and Jimmy approached the coffin. At first, Jimmy thought someone had made a mistake. It wasn't his grandmother. But he looked closer and realized it was. She looked as though somebody had done a bad job of making a wax mannequin of her. Her hair was all wrong. Her eyes looked painted closed. Her lips were stretched too tight.

"It doesn't look like her," Jimmy whispered to his dad.

George put his hand on Jimmy's shoulder. "In a way, it's not really her," he said. "This is just an empty shell where she used to be."

Jimmy carefully studied the face in the coffin. *An empty shell where she used to be.* Her hands were folded across her waist. Jimmy reached up and touched them. Waxy and cold. All life had gone to another place— that place where God lives. And for a moment, Jimmy imagined her rushing into the arms of his grandfather, shaking hands with all those friends who'd left her, and turning to see the One she longed to see face-to-face.

Jimmy patted her hand and asked Jesus to say hello to her for him.

The funeral service on Saturday was a strange mixture of joy and tears. It was as if they couldn't make up their minds how they felt, Jimmy thought later. One minute a pastor was talking about the joy of going home. The next minute, family and friends wept as they said how much they'd miss Grandma and her wonderful sense of humor, her faith, her love, or her homemade cookies.

George got up and captured what Jimmy felt most when he said, "Our loss is heaven's gain. For those of us who know Jesus, we can be assured that this isn't good-bye, but simply 'Until we meet again.'"

Jimmy cried when he heard that and felt a flood of grief rise up within and pour out of his eyes. Grandma was gone. Gone for good. He couldn't stop crying until they drove to the grave site and threw flowers onto the coffin as it was lowered into the ground.

After that, Jimmy brooded that it still wasn't fair. Now that he was a Christian, it would've made a lot more sense for God to let his grandmother live so she could help him. He still didn't know what to do about Tony. He didn't know about a lot of things. His mood sank into self-pity. He'd only been a Christian for a week, and he had probably lost his best friend and definitely his grandmother. What else could go wrong?

He fought with Donna in the car on the way home. She was listening to music with her old headphones. Jimmy thought the tinny guitars and drums that leaked from her ears would drive him nuts. He jerked at the headphones and told Donna to turn down the volume. She told him to lay off and pushed him away. He pushed her back. They yelled at each other.

Dad pulled the car over to the side of the road. "Stop it!" he shouted at them. "This is tough enough without you two acting like babies!"

The harshness of his voice brought wide-eyed silence from Jimmy, Donna, and even Mary.

Dad turned away from them, lowered his head onto the steering wheel, and let the tears flow. Mary moved close to him, put her arm around his back, leaned her head against his shoulder, and cried with him. It struck Jimmy that he hadn't seen his dad cry at the hospital, the funeral home, or even Grandma's house.

"I'm sorry," George said. And he kept crying.

Donna glared at Jimmy and whispered, "See what you've done!"

Jimmy felt awful for being so selfish. *What else could go wrong?* he asked himself again. *Nothing*, he answered. *This is as bad as it gets.*

CHAPTER EIGHTEEN

Sunday

JIMMY'S MOM TIGHTENED the belt of her dress. "I don't know if I can handle everybody saying how sorry they are," she said. "I'll cry. I just know it."

The family was back in Odyssey. They were getting ready for church.

"Just take some extra tissues," George advised and kissed his wife on the cheek.

"My purse is stuffed to the top," she replied.

Jimmy drained the last of the milk from his cereal bowl. He was eager to get to church so he could talk to Dave or Jacob. He felt confused about a lot of things—his grandma's death, how to decide about his friendship with Tony, why so many things went wrong after he became a Christian—and he knew they'd tell him what to do.

"Donna, let's go!" George called out.

The Barclay family got into the car and drove to church for what should have been a normal service. It wasn't.

Jimmy looked for some sign of Dave or Jacob in the Sunday school assembly. He couldn't find either of them. He sat down in the auditorium and waited for Dave to take the podium as he usually did. Instead, Mr. Lucas led the morning devotional and prayer.

Jimmy went to class distracted and annoyed. He bumped into Lucy and asked if she had seen Dave or Jacob. She hadn't but said that rumors were flying all over the place about where they were.

"Where are they?" Jimmy asked.

"Kidnapped by aliens if you want to believe Jack Davis," she said and walked off.

Jimmy's mood worsened. Maybe they took the day off. But that didn't make sense. Dave was an assistant pastor; he couldn't be allowed to take Sundays off!

In between Sunday school and church, Jimmy saw his dad. "I can't find Dave or Jacob!" Jimmy said.

"Really?" George said. "Maybe they're gone for the weekend."

"But they *can't* be gone! I wanna talk to them!"

George laughed. "I'm sure they would've canceled their plans if they'd known."

"Find out, will you, Dad? Please?"

"Okay, there's Tom Riley. He should know; he's a deacon. I'll see you in church in a minute." George strode off.

How could they leave me like this? Jimmy fumed. *They knew my grandmother was sick. How could they take a vacation when my grandmother died?*

Jimmy walked into the sanctuary and dropped himself onto the pew next to his mom.

"Well, hello, Mr. Happy," she said.

Jimmy grunted.

George arrived just as the organist started the first hymn. Jimmy looked at him expectantly. George's brow was furrowed into several worried lines.

"Dad?" Jimmy whispered.

"I'll tell you after church," George said.

"*Now*, Dad. *Please*. Are they on vacation?"

"No," George said. "They're gone."

"What!" Jimmy said so loudly that people around them turned to look.

George gently took Jimmy's arm and led him into the hall. "Look, son," he said when they were away from the sanctuary, "I need you to be calm, okay? Pray that God will help you be calm."

Jimmy was worried. "Be calm? But what did you mean—"

"They're gone, Jimmy. Dave and Jacob left the church."

Jimmy's mouth fell open.

George continued, "Do you remember Jan? Dave's wife?"

"Yeah."

"She wasn't happy. Do you understand? She didn't like being a minister's wife. So she left them right after we went to see Grandma. Rather than put the church through a difficult time, Dave and Jacob went back to Dave's family in California." George kept his grip on Jimmy's arm, as if he thought Jimmy might pass out.

"All the way to California?" Jimmy asked weakly.

"Yes."

"But . . . they didn't say good-bye. I didn't get to say anything to them."

"I know." George knelt down next to his son. "They wanted it to happen fast and quietly to stop any gossip. Now do you see why I wanted you to pray?"

Jimmy understood. And he *did* pray. He asked God, "Why are You doing this to me?"

CHAPTER NINETEEN

Sunday Afternoon

"I KNOW HOW TOUGH this week has been for you," Jimmy's dad said to him after their Sunday dinner, as Jimmy lay on his bed. "You've been through a lot."

Jimmy didn't say anything. He had hardly said a word since he found out about Dave and Jacob. All he wanted to do was mope.

George rested his hand on Jimmy's arm. "We've had our share of losses. But . . . that's part of life. We gain family and friends, and we lose them."

Not all in one week, Jimmy thought.

"Your mom and I talked about it, and we're going to give you a break this afternoon," Dad said. "Consider it a short reprieve from your restriction—an escape. Go take a walk or something. Try to . . . I don't know . . . use the time to pray. Maybe that'll help." He stood up and headed for the door.

"Thanks, Dad," Jimmy said and rolled off his bed. *A walk might be good*, he thought. *A chance to get out of the house.* He tugged on his shoes and grabbed his jacket. But where would he walk? Would he go to Tony's house?

No. He wasn't ready for Tony.

So he was allowed to leave the house, but he didn't have anywhere to go. He felt even more depressed as he walked out the front door into the cloudy October afternoon.

He thought about the past week as he walked: all the trouble he'd been in with his family and his best friend. Then he lost his grandmother and two people he had *hoped* would be his friends.

He felt completely alone.

Is this what saying yes to Jesus means—walking alone on a Sunday afternoon, with no one to talk to and nowhere to go? he wondered.

He thought about Tony again. He hadn't lost Tony. Not yet. But could he stay friends with Tony and still be a Christian? Or maybe the real question was this: Did he really want to be a Christian if he *couldn't* stay friends with Tony?

It'd be easy enough to forget it, right? Just tell everybody it was a dumb idea—being a Christian caused too many problems—and give it up. Yeah, his family would be disappointed, but they'd get over it. Things could go back to the way they were.

Jimmy looked around and realized he was walking in McAlister Park. He felt a twinge of guilt as he remembered the incident at the gazebo. He hadn't talked to Tony since it happened. He wondered what Tony was thinking. Did word get around the school about Jimmy's grandmother? Did Tony know?

Again, Jimmy felt alone. And restless. He wanted to do something. He wanted to be normal again and run around with his friends and quit having so many things go wrong. Could he quit being a Christian now? Would God let him change his mind?

"Hey, Jimmy."

Jimmy nearly jumped out of his skin. Tony stood directly in front of him.

"What're you doing here?" Jimmy asked.

"I was gonna ask you the same question," Tony said. "I stopped by your house, and your dad said you took a walk. I thought you were on restriction."

"They let me off today."

"Why didn't you come over?"

"I was going to, but . . ." Jimmy sighed and started to walk again. "I'm confused."

Tony stayed at his side and took the lead in setting their direction. "Really?" he asked. "About what?"

"Everything," Jimmy said. "You don't know what it's like. It's a big mess. My grandma died, and Dave and Jacob left, and I keep getting in trouble, and . . . I didn't know it would be like this."

"Be like *what*? What're you talking about?"

"You know," Jimmy said, "being a Christian."

"I could've told you that was a dumb idea," Tony said.

"I don't know if it's a mistake. I mean . . ." Jimmy faltered. "Oh, I don't know what I mean."

"You're saying it's not all it's cracked up to be, right?"

Jimmy thought about it for a moment, then said, "Right."

"So why don't you give it up?" Tony asked. "You joined the club, and now you wanna unjoin it. It's not against the law."

"I know, but—"

"Looks to me like it's nothing but trouble. You never punched me in the nose before," Tony said with a laugh.

Jimmy smiled and answered, "Huh-uh. And . . . you know, I'm . . . you know."

"Forget about it."

Jimmy looked at Tony and couldn't imagine why he thought he could give him up as a friend. "Tony, I—" He stopped himself when he noticed where they had walked to: the gazebo.

"What're we doing here?" Jimmy asked.

"Just walking," Tony said. "So, what are you going to do? Are you gonna keep doing this Sunday school stuff, or are you gonna get things back to the way they used to be?"

"I don't know, Tony," Jimmy said.

"I think you have to make up your mind. A lot of the kids at school are talking about you. They think you're weird. Some of the guys are saying you're a tattletale."

"Huh?"

"I don't believe it, but they're saying you told what happened with the firecrackers. Did you tell anybody?"

"No!" Jimmy said, then remembered he had confessed everything to Dave and Jacob and then his parents.

"Oh . . ."

"You *did*, didn't you?"

"Only Dave—and then my parents," Jimmy said.

"You got us in trouble," Tony said, his voice stiffening.

"How? We've been gone! My dad didn't say anything to anybody."

Tony poked Jimmy in the chest with his finger. "Yeah," he accused, "but it turns out your friend Dave played racquetball with one of the guys from my dad's office, and he told him all about the firecrackers. My dad found out, and he was furious. So we all got in trouble—and there'll be more trouble later."

Out of the corner of his eye, Jimmy saw Gary walk around from behind the gazebo. Then Tim came around the other side. Cory stepped out from behind a tree and headed toward them. Jimmy didn't know for certain what they planned to do, but he figured it wouldn't be very nice.

"Look, Jimmy," Tony said, "as long as you wanna keep playing the religious nut and getting us in trouble, we don't wanna be your friends anymore. Okay?"

At that moment, Jimmy knew that if he promised Tony and the guys that he would quit being a Christian, they might leave him alone. Maybe they could be friends again and do things the way they did before. At that moment, it was possible. At that moment, it was a serious consideration. But at that moment, Jimmy couldn't make such a promise and decided on another course of action. . . .

Run!

He pushed Tony and took off as fast as he could. He made it as far as the path into the woods before one of the kids tackled him. Then they were all on him with wild, flying fists that didn't hit hard but connected with enough places on his face and body to hurt. Jimmy swung back just as wildly, but it didn't help.

Someone slugged him in the stomach. It knocked the wind out of him. He gasped as the fists kept coming.

He barely heard the deep and powerful voice that commanded the kids to stop. The fists—and the boys connected to them—withdrew, scattered, and ran off in several directions through the woods.

Strong hands lifted Jimmy to a sitting position. "Take it easy, Jimmy. Breathe slowly. Slowly."

Jimmy tried to take in some air. A handkerchief was pressed against his nose and his lip. "You're bleeding a little. Can you stand up?" the deep voice asked.

"I think so," Jimmy croaked.

"Good. My shop is right over here. Come on."

Jimmy looked up into the face of his rescuer. It was John Avery Whittaker.

CHAPTER TWENTY

Sunday Evening

JOHN AVERY WHITTAKER—or Whit, as a lot of people called him—owned a soda shop and discovery emporium on the edge of McAlister Park. He called it Whit's End. It was a popular gathering place for kids and adults, with room after room of exhibits, interactive displays, a library, and a theater. Whit was dedicated to anything that would help bring the Bible to life for kids. Jimmy went there on occasion with his parents. He didn't go more often because Tony didn't like it.

"I don't open on Sundays," Whit explained as he unlocked the front door. "But we should get some ice on that nose of yours."

He led Jimmy past the soda counter, into the kitchen, and over to a chair next to a small table. He disappeared into a walk-in freezer and returned a few seconds later with a clump of ice. He methodically broke it up with an ice pick, wrapped it in a cloth, and gently placed it so that it covered the side of Jimmy's nose and upper lip.

"Ow!" Jimmy said. His nose and lip throbbed.

"Just tilt your head back and hold it there while I call your parents," Whit said. "What's your number?"

Jimmy told him. Whit went to the phone and had a brief conversation with George. He hung up, then turned back to Jimmy. "Your dad's on his way," he said. He grabbed a chair and pulled it up close. "Do you want to tell me what that was all about? I assume you weren't being robbed."

"No," Jimmy replied. "Do I have to say who did it?"

"Not if you don't want to," Whit said.

Jimmy thought for a moment, then said, "I don't know where to start."

"Why did they beat you up?"

"Because I became a Christian."

Whit cocked an eyebrow quizzically. "I heard about that. But I didn't think kids got beat up for it around Odyssey."

"They do." Jimmy sighed. "Mr. Whittaker, I became a Christian, and it's ruined everything. I'm driving my family crazy, I lost my best friend, my grandmother died, and Dave and Jacob left."

Whit nodded slowly as if he understood completely. "I knew about Dave and Jacob. But I didn't know you were so close to them."

"Dave was the one who talked me into becoming a Christian, and Jacob helped me this week," Jimmy explained, then sighed again. "It's all gone wrong."

"So being a Christian isn't what you thought it would be?" Whit asked, echoing the question Jimmy was asked earlier.

"I guess not. I thought things would get better, and they didn't."

Whit took the ice pack, adjusted it a little, and put it back against Jimmy's face. "How did you think things would get better?"

"I thought that Jesus was going to change me—take everything, make it better, then give it back nice and new."

"I see," Whit said thoughtfully. "And you thought it would happen right away."

Jimmy shrugged. "Maybe not right away. Dave kept saying I had to be patient. But I didn't think everything would go wrong while I was being patient."

"So why don't you give it up?"

Surprised, Jimmy looked at Whit. It was the last thing he thought Whit would ask.

Whit chuckled and said, "Well, why don't you?"

"Because—" Jimmy began, but he didn't know how to go further. Finally he blurted, "Because I *can't*."

"Why not?"

"Because my mom and dad would be upset," Jimmy stammered.

"I thought they were upset with you already. What's the difference?"

"It's a different *kind* of upset," Jimmy explained. "*That's* the difference. See, now they're upset because I keep making dumb mistakes. Before they were upset because I kept doing things to get in trouble."

Whit's eyes lit up with laughter. His white mustache spread across his round face. "That's wonderful!" he said. "I've never heard it explained so well. So you're telling me you became a Christian to please your parents?"

"No."

"Then what were you thinking when you did it? I mean, I'm sorry you had a bad week. And I'm *deeply* sorry you lost your grandmother. Because of her poor health, though, I think you would have lost her whether you became a Christian or not. So I don't understand why you think it all connects to your becoming a believer."

Jimmy thought about it for a moment. "It connects because it happened after I said yes to Jesus."

"Because you thought He'd make everything all right when you said yes. Is that it?"

Jimmy nodded. That was it in a nutshell. He thought Jesus would make everything all right, and instead everything went wrong.

"Do you know what I think?" Whit asked. "I think everything *is* connected. It makes perfect sense—*if* you think about how God works sometimes."

"What do you mean?"

"Jimmy, God loves you more than anyone in this world ever could. He loves you so much that He sent Jesus to die for you. But Jesus didn't die so you could walk around with a smile on your face or so you'd never have a problem. The fact is, He died so you could be friends with God; so you could learn to love God the best you can; so you could be *changed* into the person He wants you to be. Do you understand that much?"

Jimmy said he did. It was another way of saying what Dave had said the night Jimmy became a Christian.

"Here's the next part," Whit continued. "Jesus' death didn't come easily, and neither does our change. It's a struggle, a battle, against all the things inside us that want everything to stay the way it was. That's why we make a lot of mistakes. We do things we know better than to do. Our family might get annoyed at us. And I'm not surprised that your friends have turned against you, though I'm a little surprised they went as far as knocking you around. They want to keep you the way you were. But Jesus is inside you now and wants you to fight to be more and more like Him. Are you still with me?"

Jimmy nodded again.

Whit went on, choosing his words carefully. "Sometimes God strips away the things in our lives that keep us from relying on Him."

A light went on in Jimmy's head, and he sat up straight.

Whit noticed Jimmy's change in expression but slowly went on. "Sometimes God strips away the things we think are important to make room for us to see Him more clearly. Only then can He make the changes He needs to make. That's what growth is all about. And, yes, sometimes it hurts as we lose friends or suffer the loss of those we love. Sometimes we feel completely alone and figure that no one else in the whole wide world knows how we feel.

"But that's wrong. God knows. And that's why you're never alone. God is there, first and foremost. Then there's your family—who love you even when you get on their nerves. And then there are friends you have who are Christians—or the friends you haven't made yet. Like me, Jimmy. I'm always here if you need to talk."

"Thanks," Jimmy said softly and hung his head.

"Oh, now, Jimmy," Whit said with a smile. "Don't be too hard on yourself. You're only at the *start* of this new adventure. It's bound to be overwhelming for you."

"You never met my grandmother, did you?" Jimmy asked.

"I don't think so. Why?"

"Because she said the same things you just said," Jimmy answered.

"She must've been a very wise woman," Whit said, chuckling.

"Yeah," Jimmy said. "I'm going to miss her a lot."

Whit took the ice pack from Jimmy and looked closely at his wounds. "Just remember, Jimmy," he said, "that God never takes anything out of our lives unless He's going to replace it with something else—something that will help us the same way or more. You just have to keep your eyes open for it."

Whit pressed the ice pack against Jimmy's face again. Jimmy looked into his eyes and saw heartfelt kindness looking back. *I need to hang around Whit's End a lot more,* he decided.

CHAPTER
TWENTY-ONE

Monday

JIMMY SAT DOWN at a lunch table with his tray of food. At another table across the room, he saw Tony and his old friends laughing at a joke Jimmy would never be a part of again. He wished he could be friends with them. But at this point in his life, he didn't know how. He closed his eyes, said a quick prayer of thanks for the food, and hoped no one saw him.

He opened his mouth to take the first bite of his pot roast, and his lip stung. It was a cruel reminder of the day before. There wasn't a lot of swelling on his face, but it still hurt a little. "Okay, God," he prayed, "it's just me alone at this table with a face that hurts. But it'll be all right if You'll help me." He sighed. It had been another bad day so far.

Jack Davis came up to Jimmy's table with a brown lunch bag in hand. "Hi, Jimmy," he said. "Okay if I sit down?"

Jimmy shrugged. He was afraid Jack had come over to tease him.

"What happened to your face?" Jack asked.

Jimmy self-consciously glanced over at Tony.

Jack must have noticed, because he said, "Never mind. You don't have to tell me." He shook his head and continued, "Boy, you've really been through it."

"What do you mean?" Jimmy asked.

"I dunno. It seems like a lot's happened to you lately. I've never seen a kid go through the wringer like that." Jack bit into his sandwich. He kept talking, even with a mouth full of food. "I guess you and Tony are on the outs, huh?"

"Yeah," Jimmy said, wondering what Jack might be up to.

Jack silently chewed his food, swallowed, then said softly, "That happened to me—y'know, being friends one minute, then not being friends the next. You remember Colin."

Jimmy did. He was a kid Jack had befriended who turned out to be an uncontrollable liar.

"Anyway, I was thinking that I know how you feel," Jack said. Then he stayed silent for a while.

Jimmy gazed at Jack while Jack looked down at his potato chips. Could they be friends? Jimmy wondered. Did God send him over to be a replacement for Tony, as Whit said? But there was no way to replace Tony or the years they had as friends, any more than his grandmother could be replaced.

That didn't mean, however, that God couldn't bring someone *new* into his life.

"Jimmy," Jack said, and Jimmy was suddenly embarrassed for staring him.

"Yeah?"

"I saw you at the youth group meeting that night, and then I heard a rumor that you became a Christian."

"So?"

Jack scrunched his face up as if he didn't know how to ask what he wanted to ask.

"Well, I was wondering . . . I mean, what's going on? I think about Jesus sometimes because, you know, my parents are Christians, but . . . I can't make up my mind about what it means."

Jimmy looked at Jack intently. "You want to know Jesus? I can tell you how to get to know Him. But it isn't easy, and it isn't always fun. In fact, right now it hurts more than anything I've ever done in my life. But you know what? It's all there is . . . and I wouldn't trade it for anything. Jesus'll get me through this. I don't know how, but He will."

"I figured you'd say something like that." Jack smiled and paused. "Y'know, me and Oscar and Lucy are going to Whit's End after school today. You wanna come with us?"

"I'll ask my parents," Jimmy said.

The day didn't seem so bad after that.

BOOK TWO

DARK PASSAGE

Author's Note: Most of the details in this story were taken from firsthand, factual accounts of slaves who worked in the South and escaped with the help of the Underground Railroad. Other details were provided by a variety of historical reference works, writings from the time period, and eyewitness sources. To convey historical accuracy and portray the true horror of the slaves' treatment, many words, phrases, and colloquialisms have been maintained.

BANG! THE DOOR TO the hatchway slammed shut. The noise echoed down the dark tunnel and left nothing but a ringing in the ears of Jack Davis and Matt Booker.

"Oh no," Jack said. The tunnel was so dark he couldn't see his friend at all.

Matt scrambled up the ladder-like steps, turned the thick, metal handle, and pushed as hard as he could. The door wouldn't lift. "Well don't just stand there," Matt snapped. "Climb up here and help me."

Jack felt his way up the splintered wooden steps and stopped when he was side by side with Matt at the top. "Quit breathing on me," Jack said.

"You're the one with the bad breath," Matt replied. "Now *push!*"

With grunts and groans the two boys pressed on the door with every ounce of strength they had. It refused to lift.

"It must've locked when it slammed down," Matt gasped.

"What do we do now?" Jack panted.

If they had been in the afternoon light outside, Jack would've seen Matt scrunch up his nose as he often did when he was thinking. "Scream for help?" Matt finally suggested. He pounded on the door and yelled at the top of his lungs.

"Hold it! Wait! Stop it!" Jack called out to Matt. "Who's going to hear us?"

Matt groaned. Jack was right.

The two 11-year-old boys had been playing catch with a football behind Whit's End, a large soda shop and "discovery emporium" where most of the kids in Odyssey liked to hang out. Jack had gone long for a pass from Matt, but the ball flew over Jack's head and into a patch of woods nearby. While searching for the ball among the fallen leaves and dry branches, Jack stumbled onto a large, metal covering on the ground. It was half covered with leaves. A small sign bolted to the top said to "Keep Out." For the naturally curious Jack and Matt, that meant "Get in if you can." It was an invitation to a new adventure.

Jack had flagged Matt over and turned the latch while both of them yanked at the door. It creaked and opened. A large, black, square hole beckoned them.

"What do you think it is?" Matt had asked.

Jack had shrugged and told Matt to go down and look.

Matt had refused and said *Jack* should be the first to have a peek since he discovered it.

They had argued back and forth for a few minutes until accusations of "chicken" and "coward" were thrown around. Finally they agreed to go in at the same time, using a rock to prop the door open for light. But no sooner had they reached the bottom of the stairs and faced the yawning, dark tunnel than the rock slipped and the door closed.

"Maybe we should follow the tunnel to see where it leads," Jack suggested.

Matt snorted. "And get lost in some kind of ancient maze under Odyssey? No way."

"Then let's just follow it a little ways in," Jack said irritably. "If it doesn't go anywhere, we'll come back here."

"And then what?" Matt wondered.

"I don't know. I guess we'll just sit on these stairs until we starve to death."

"That's not funny," Matt said as he crept down the stiff, wooden steps to the tunnel floor.

Jack slowly followed him. "Hello?" he called out, not really believing that anyone would call back. He coughed. The air smelled of earth and mildew, like an old basement.

They pressed against the cold, stone wall of the tunnel and inched forward into the blackness. They couldn't even see their hands in front of their faces.

"I heard that a man'll go crazy in a couple of hours in this kind of darkness," Matt said.

"Thanks for the encouragement," Jack growled. "What kind of place is this? An old mine shaft maybe?"

Matt suddenly stopped. Jack walked right into the back of him.

"Hey," Jack complained.

"Watch where you're going," Matt said.

Jack wanted to ask him *how* he was supposed to watch where he was going, but he decided against it. "Why'd you stop?"

"If this is a mine shaft, there might be big holes," Matt said in a voice full of worry. "I think we'd better go back to the steps."

Jack sighed. "And do what? Eat wooden-step sandwiches until somebody finds us? I think we oughtta—" Jack stopped mid-sentence with a sharp intake of air.

"If it's a snake or a rat, I don't want to know," Matt whispered.

"No," Jack replied. "Look up ahead. It's a little red light."

Matt squinted deep into the wall of black but didn't see anything. The darkness was simply *dark.* Then the small dot of red light appeared to him as if out of nowhere. "What do you think it is? I mean, you don't think it's anything *alive,* do you?"

"Huh-uh," Jack answered. But his tone wasn't confident. "Let's check it out."

Matt didn't budge. "*You* check it out."

"Why do *I* have to do everything around here? You're in front; *you* check it out."

"Nope," Matt said. "You saw it first, so you can do the honors."

Jack grumbled his disapproval as he carefully navigated around Matt, keeping his hands on the wall and tapping the ground with the tip of his sneakers to make sure it didn't suddenly open up to a bottomless pit. He listened hard to make sure it *wasn't* some kind of red-eyed monster waiting to devour lost kids. He moved closer and closer until—

Suddenly the red dot turned green.

"Hey," Jack called out to Matt. "The light turned gr—"

Jack heard a soft click, and the tunnel exploded with white light.

"Ow," JACK SAID AS he winced, covering his eyes with his hands. "Is somebody there?"

"What's going on here?" Matt asked. He squinted against the light and could barely make out Jack's silhouette ahead in the tunnel.

No one answered.

After a minute, their eyes adjusted and they realized there were floodlights attached to the length of the tunnel wall—from the steps to a door about 20 yards ahead.

"The lights must be motion sensitive," Matt observed.

"Motion *what*?" Jack asked.

"They turn on if something moves," Matt explained. "We have them above our garage. That red light was probably the sensor."

Jack breathed a sigh of relief. "At least we know we're not trapped in some abandoned mine shaft. Let's go see where that door leads."

With renewed confidence, the two boys walked quickly to the end of the tunnel. The door was large and heavy-looking with square, decorative panels and a round, bronze doorknob. Jack reached out, grabbed the knob, and turned it. The latch clicked freely, and the door opened a crack. "Unlocked," Jack whispered happily.

"You know, there might be somebody on the other side of that door who won't like us barging in," Matt said.

"Do you want to go back to the steps and wait until someone finds your skeleton?" Jack asked.

Matt frowned. "The least you can do is knock first."

Jack thought that was a reasonable idea. He ran his fingers through his dark hair nervously, then rapped his knuckles against the hard wood.

"Nobody's going to hear that," Matt said and quickly pounded on the door with his clenched fist. They waited. No one answered.

Jack looked at Matt with a smug expression and grabbed the doorknob again. "Ready to go in?"

Matt lifted his shoulders and raised his eyebrows as if to say, "If you insist."

The door swung open silently on greased hinges. They peeked in uncertainly. Beyond them was a workroom, obviously situated in someone's basement from the look of the rectangular windows high on the walls. A dusty sunshine broke through to give the room a warm, orangy glow. Jack and Matt stepped inside.

The muffled sound of kids talking and laughing made its way down the stairs leading up from the room. "We're back at Whit's End," Matt said.

Jack nodded. "This has to be where Mr. Whittaker comes up with all his inventions."

Mr. Whittaker—or Whit, as most people in town knew him—owned Whit's End and ran it as a place where children of all ages could enjoy themselves and even learn something in the process. Whit's End was originally Odyssey's old recreation center; a building that was part house, part church tower, and part gymnasium. Whit completely renovated it to include a soda shop, library, theater, the county's largest train set, and room after room of interactive displays, exhibits, and constantly changing activities.

Standing in the workroom, Jack and Matt suddenly realized just how much time and effort Whit put into his shop. Workbenches littered with tools, electronic parts, and gadgets sat beneath Peg-Boards adorned with schematics, diagrams, cords, wires, safety glasses, and even more tools. Boxes, sawhorses, large drills, a tool chest, and what looked to Matt and Jack like pieces of computer hardware were scattered around the floor. The room was an explosion of half-finished devices, bizarre contraptions, and peculiar equipment—all there for the purpose of making Whit's End a fun and interesting place to visit.

But the thing that caught Matt's and Jack's attention was a large machine sitting in the very center of the room.

"What is it?" Matt gasped as he circled the odd-looking invention. It looked as if someone had combined an old telephone booth with a helicopter cockpit. Through the smoke-colored glass, he could see multicolored lights blinking inside. A low, constant hum seemed to vibrate through his chest.

"Maybe it's one of those booths that takes your picture," Jack suggested. "You know, like they have at the mall."

Matt shook his head. "No way. Why would Whit invent something that he could just *buy*? It's some kind of ride."

Jack, who circled the machine from the other direction, nearly tripped over a large cable. It ran from the invention over to a large box that looked like a washing machine. On second glance, Jack realized that the "washing machine" was some kind of computer. "Check this out," he called to Matt.

Matt was at Jack's side in an instant. "This is great! The computer must be feeding information into the ride." Matt gazed at several books, encyclopedias, magazines, and newspaper clippings scattered on a nearby workbench. They referred to the Underground Railroad, slavery in America, and the Civil War. Jack picked up one particular headline that reported Odyssey's "November Riots." The year 1858 was handwritten in the upper right-hand corner.

"This is *great*! It must be some kind of Civil War ride." Matt dashed around to the door of the machine. "I love that time in history."

"Really? I didn't know that," Jack said offhandedly. History wasn't one of his strong subjects.

The door didn't have a handle, so Matt had to look for a way in. "My great-great-great-great-great-grandfather was a slave," he said simply.

Jack did a double take as if realizing for the first time that Matt was black. "You're kidding. You mean he was a slave, like on one of those plantations in the South?" he asked.

"Uh-huh."

Jack rubbed his chin thoughtfully. He had never thought much about skin color—his own pale, pink flesh or the honey-brown tone of Matt's. They were friends, and that seemed to be enough. Their parents never drew attention to the difference in their races, either. Why should they? But the thought of Matt having someone in his family who was once a slave made Jack uneasy. What if *his* great-great-great-great-great-grandfather was a slave owner?

"Aha!" Matt exclaimed and pushed a button. *Whoosh!* Just like an elevator, the door on the "booth" slid back and disappeared into the side of the machine. Jack suddenly realized what was happening.

"What are you doing?" he asked as Matt climbed in.

"I want to see what it does," he replied.

Jack glanced around nervously. "What if Mr. Whittaker comes down?"

"Then we'll get in trouble," Matt said with a shrug. "But we'll still be the first ones to try his new ride."

Jack couldn't argue with his point, so he smiled and squeezed into the chair next to Matt. It was large and comfortable. They faced a board of buttons, small lights, and digital displays. "This is an dash-" Jack said. He picked up a large sheet of blue paper with crude s of the machine, numbers, lines, and, on the bottom, the words *Imagination Station (Revisions & Improvements)*.

"The Imagination Station?" Matt mused. A flashing red button larger than the rest—beckoned them. "Let's push this one and what happens."

"Are you sure it's worth it if we get in trouble?" Jack asked.

Matt smiled. "We won't know until we try it, will we?"

For an instant, Jack understood why their parents complained that the two boys weren't good for each other. He dismissed the thought and said, "Push it."

Matt poked at the red button with his finger. It clicked down. Nothing happened.

Disappointed, Jack slumped a little in the seat. "Maybe Mr. Whittaker hasn't finished it yet."

Matt was about to answer when the door quickly slid shut with another *whoosh*. The machine made a low, rattling sound that soon got louder and louder.

"It sounds like it's going to fall apart," Jack said, worried.

Matt reached for the red button. "Maybe I should stop it."

It was too late. The Imagination Station shifted into a higher gear with a shrill, whirring sound.

Jack opened his mouth to speak, but his breath was taken away as the machine lurched forward. *Or did it?* Neither of them could be sure. All they knew right then was that it felt as if they had just been blasted out of a rocket silo into warp-speed hyperspace. Butterflies danced in their stomachs. Their eyes grew wide.

The colors of the lighted dashboard, the smoky glass, and the workroom beyond spun out of control. Jack and Matt cried out.

Then everything went dark.

CHAPTER THREE

S IS WEIRD," Jack said in the darkness. He was on his knees, but he
't know how he got that way.

"*Too* weird," Matt replied from Jack's left. "We're back in the tunnel
gain."

"Are you sure?" Jack asked, but all his senses told him it was true.
The cool earth beneath him, the smell of damp, and the endless night
ahead and behind him confirmed it. Matt patted the tunnel wall with
the flat of his hand. "It's the tunnel all right. But I can't figure out how
we got back here."

"Maybe we've been stuck here for hours and only dreamed about
Mr. Whittaker's workroom and the Imagination Station and . . ." Jack
stopped himself. Two people couldn't have the same dream, could they?
"You remember the workroom and the machine, right?"

"Uh-huh," Matt answered. "That's what makes it so weird. How
could we be sitting in the machine and the next second be in the tunnel again?"

Jack suddenly gasped and reached out. His hand collided with
Matt's chest.

"Ouch. What's wrong?" Matt asked.

Jack shushed him. "Don't you hear those voices?"

Matt listened for a moment. Muted, almost unhearable voices
drifted down the tunnel. They were quiet, as if someone had left a radio
on somewhere.

"This way," Jack said as he felt his way forward into the tunnel. He
looked for the red light that had signaled the motion-sensitive lights. It
wasn't there. Instead, he saw a thin, yellow line stretching across the
ground and up the tunnel wall. As his eyes adjusted, he realized it was
light coming out from under the bottom and side of a door. By the time
they were only a few feet away, they could see its outline completely.
The door was slightly ajar. The voices were more distinct. Two men
were arguing.

"This is *really* weird," Matt whispered as they got closer. Together the boys huddled at the crack in the door and peered through. The workroom was completely different from the one they'd seen before. The workbenches were gone. In their place sat a couple of sleeping cots covered with ragged wool blankets. The walls were bare wood and stone. In the center of the room, a scarred wooden table and wooden chairs crouched on fragile legs. Two men stood on opposite sides of the table. Jack and Matt didn't recognize either one of them. One was a tall, slender white man with salt-and-pepper-colored hair that stuck out in wavy tufts. He wore a clerical collar atop a blue shirt and trousers. The other man was taller and stockier. His coat, shirt, and pants were an ill-fitting patchwork that made him look even larger than he was. His face was dark brown and glistened with sweat. He shifted nervously from one foot to the other while clinging with both hands to a frayed hat.

"Is this the basement to Whit's End?" Matt whispered.

Jack shrugged. "I think so . . . I don't know. Listen." They turned their attention to the argument inside.

"No, sir, Reverend Andrew," the black man was saying. "I'm tired of running. We're free now, and I won't hide in someone's cellar. No, sir, I won't."

The clergyman spread his hands in appeal and said with a soft English accent, "Listen to reason, Clarence. They'll catch you and take you back to your old master. That's what they're paid to do, and that's what the Fugitive Slave Law allows them to do. Even here."

The man called Clarence tightened his grip on the hat. "With all due respect, Reverend Andrew, I'm tired of laws that take away a man's freedom."

"So am I," Andrew said sadly. "But what you or I want makes no difference for the moment. Odyssey is in the midst of an all-fired argument about slavery. Douglas and Lincoln have everyone riled up from their debates. The town is split in two. My advice to all the runaway slaves is to keep moving north. None of the American territories are safe. You won't be truly free until you get to Canada. So, tomorrow morning we have to get you back on the Railroad and—"

Clarence interrupted, shaking his head slowly. "We can't take another step. Not so soon. We've come a long way and we're tired all to pieces. I have to think of my daughter here."

"It's your daughter I'm thinking about as well," Andrew said as he gestured behind him. Jack and Matt took a couple of steps to the right to get a clearer view of who they were talking about. A black girl—about the same age as Jack and Matt—sat quietly on the edge of a cot. She was wrapped in rags that barely passed for a dress and coat and looked as if she might fall over from lack of sleep. Their movement caught her eye. She squinted at them.

"Somebody's at the door," the girl said softly.

Wanting to hide in the darkness of the tunnel, Jack pushed back against Matt, who stumbled and fell backward to the ground with a grunt. Jack then tripped over Matt and found himself flat on his back in the dirt.

Hands seemed to come from everywhere and hauled Jack and Matt to their feet. Instantly they were both dragged into the room and dropped onto the rickety chairs. Andrew and Clarence leaned into their faces with expressions full of accusation.

"Who are you?" Andrew demanded. "Why were you spying on us?"

"We weren't spying," Matt stammered.

Jack tried to explain. "We got lost in the tunnel and couldn't figure out where we were—er, *are*. We were just playing football and—"

"We thought we were in a machine in Mr. Whittaker's workroom," Matt chimed in, "but then we were in the tunnel again and—"

"Do you know what he's talking about?" Clarence asked Andrew.

Andrew shook his head no. "Beats the thunder out of me."

Clarence turned to Matt. "Where's your papers, young 'un?"

"My papers?" Matt asked.

"Are you free or running away?" Andrew asked.

"I don't understand what you mean," Matt said.

"Come now, son. Where are you from?" Andrew asked.

"Odyssey."

"I've never seen you around Odyssey," Andrew challenged him.

"He *is* from Odyssey!" Jack shouted. "And so am I! And if you don't let us go right away, our parents are going to send the police here, and you'll be arrested for kidnapping."

"Kidnapping!" Clarence exclaimed.

"Yeah *kidnapping*!" Matt added.

Andrew waved his hands as if trying to bring calm to the confusion.

"Wait just a minute. Nobody is being kidnapped. Look, lads, I know everyone in Odyssey. So just tell me who your parents are and I'll make sure you get home safely. But first I want you to tell me how you found the entrance to the tunnel. It's important that—"

"Somebody else is here," the little girl said.

All eyes went to the door. Another black man stood in the half-shadows. "I'm sorry to bother you," the man said as he shyly stepped into the room.

"This has turned into a major thoroughfare," Andrew said with a hint of distress.

Clarence couldn't mask his alarm. "Just what's going on here? Who are you? Are you all together?"

Jack and Matt vigorously shook their heads. "We've never seen him before," said Jack.

"No, sir. Those boys aren't with me," the stranger replied. His out-fit was worn and dirty like Clarence's, and the sweat-stained hat on his head drooped down like it was terribly sad about something. "I'm a run-away slave who's come to you for help because I heard you were part of the Underground Railroad. Have I come to the right place?"

Andrew was about to answer when suddenly Clarence interrupted. "Where are you from? How did you hear about the Railroad?"

"I'm from Hattiesburg, where any slave with a good pair of ears has heard about the Railroad," the stranger explained. "I've been on the run for weeks."

Clarence eyed him skeptically. "You look awfully healthy for a man who's been running for weeks."

A sliver of a smile crossed the man's face. His eyes narrowed humor-lessly under the brim of the hat. "I can't help how I look. Why're you asking me so many questions? Did I understand wrong? I thought run-aways were taken care of here. Aren't I welcome?"

"Of course you're welcome," Andrew said.

"Don't trust him," Clarence said boldly.

"What?" Andrew asked, startled. "Why not?"

Clarence kept his eyes on the stranger. "There's something wrong here."

"Don't know what you're talking about, sir," the stranger said.

"Clarence, please explain yourself," Andrew insisted.

"I've learned never to trust a so-called slave who'd approach a white man without taking his hat off first," Clarence said.

"You doubt this man because of his *hat?*" Andrew asked incredulously.

"I'm telling you, sir, that it's one of the first things any slave learns. You always take your hat off around white folks. It's a habit. It stays a habit your whole life. The only ones who don't know it aren't really slaves." Clarence stood up to his full height as if he expected the stranger to jump at him.

The stranger chuckled and took his hat off. "Maybe we do things differently in our part of the country."

"Maybe you do," Clarence said. "And maybe you're a free black man who's working for the slave hunters. Maybe you're one of those treacherous snakes who pretends to be a slave to help the slave hunters find the stops on the Railroad. Maybe this is how you find the fugitives!"

"You've no call to speak to me that way. I think you must be sick with a fever," the stranger said.

"I can settle this," Andrew announced, then gazed at the stranger. "Tell me who sent you here. If you've been traveling on the Railroad, I'll know who told you to come."

The stranger frowned and said, "I don't ask for names, sir. It was an old woman—in a cabin about a mile on this side of the Mississippi."

"That would be Mrs. Cunningham," Andrew said with a smile. "Keeps bees to make her own honey, I believe."

"Mrs. Cunningham. That's right. Kept bees. I remember now. Gave me some of the honey," the stranger said, obviously relieved.

Clarence folded his arms and grunted his unspoken doubt.

Andrew seemed satisfied and held out his hand. "Come on in. Forgive us for being so suspicious."

The stranger took a step forward and shook the Reverend Andrew's hand. "Thank you, Reverend," he said.

Suddenly, Andrew's eyes turned cold as he tightened his grip on the stranger's hand. "Peculiar that your hand doesn't have calluses. I've never met a slave who didn't have calloused hands."

The stranger's eyes widened. "I was a house slave," he explained.

"Really now?" Andrew questioned as he pulled the stranger closer. He continued in a low, threatening voice. "That may be true. But unfortunately for you, there's no Mrs. Cunningham who keeps bees. I made it up."

The stranger jerked his hand away from Andrew and, with his other hand, put two fingers in his mouth and let out a loud, shrill whistle. Immediately, somewhere deep in the tunnel, men shouted. Oil lamps danced like fireflies in the darkness.

"It's a trap!" Clarence cried out.

"Run!" Andrew shouted. "Run for your lives!"

EVERYTHING HAPPENED at the same time. The stranger leaped at Clarence in a flying tackle and the two crashed onto the table. It collapsed under their weight with a wrenching, splintering sound. The girl screamed. With surprising power, Clarence grabbed the stranger, rolled him over, and delivered a hard blow to his jaw.

The Reverend Andrew grabbed Jack, Matt, and the girl and pushed them to the stairs. "Run!" he shouted.

"Daddy!" the girl cried out.

Clarence jerked his head around and yelled, "Go, child! You know where to meet me!"

Andrew spun around to face the crowd of men as they appeared in the tunnel doorway. The girl and Matt raced up the stairs. Jack followed, but not without first seeing the men from the tunnel pour into the room, their lamps and guns lifted. They descended like a pack of wolves onto Andrew and Clarence.

"What in the world's going on here?" Matt called over his shoulder.

"I don't know," Jack shouted back, "but I sure hope Whit's End is at the top of these stairs."

Matt and the girl reached the top landing and disappeared around the corner. As he reached the doorway himself, Jack wished that he would find himself in the soda shop, with Whit serving ice cream behind the counter and kids crowded into every booth, table, and corner. Whatever he and Matt had done by getting in the Imagination Station and pushing that red button—whether it was a weird dream or some kind of ride—Jack was sorry and wanted to put an end to it now. He didn't like being chased by strange men in a strange place. He didn't like the feeling that he and Matt had gotten themselves into something that they wouldn't get out of easily. *Please, please, please*, he thought, *let it be Whit's End.*

Jack stopped dead in his tracks. It *wasn't* Whit's End. To his surprise, it was a modest-sized church with stained-glass windows, wooden pews, and, on the far end, an altar, podium, and choir loft.

Matt stood a few feet away from Jack and they shared the same open-mouthed expression. "Where are we?" Matt asked.

"Don't you know?" the girl asked, bewildered.

They weren't given time to answer, as another group of men burst through the double-doored entrance to the church. "Get them!" one of the men shouted.

Instinctively, Matt, Jack, and the girl ran in the opposite direction toward the altar. There they found a door that led to a small room filled with books, chairs, and choir robes. It looked to Jack like a small Sunday school room. Slamming the door behind them, the three fugitives looked around wildly. There weren't any other doors out.

"We're trapped," Jack gasped.

Matt fumbled with the door handle, hoping to find a lock. It didn't have one. "Oh, great."

More shouts and the sound of pounding feet on the hard church floor approached.

"What are we going to do?" Jack asked in a shrill voice.

"We didn't do anything wrong, did we? Let's talk to them!" Matt suggested.

"I don't think they're the listening types," Jack replied.

"This way," the girl suddenly said and climbed on a chair. A small window peeked out at them from above a tall wardrobe. By the time Jack and Matt reached her, the girl already had the window open and was squirming out like a rabbit from a hole. Matt was next. Jack took up the rear, just getting his head and shoulders through when their pursuers exploded into the room.

"Stop!" one of them shouted. Another man knocked over a chair and scrambled after Jack. His hands reached out and caught the edge of Jack's jeans. Jack kicked out at him. The rubber sole of his sneaker grazed the man's chin. With a curse, the man fell backward into his friends. It gave Jack the time he needed. Like a rocket, he shot out of the window, falling to the ground with a heavy thud. Matt helped him to his feet and half dragged him away from the church.

A meadow stretched out before them to a thick patch of woods about 20 yards away. Near it sat a burned-out shell of a house. All was quiet. Jack was surprised that, in spite of the commotion inside the church, no one seemed to be waiting to catch them outside. The girl was halfway across the meadow and beckoned them to follow.

"Well, Matt—where to?" Jack asked, blinking against the afternoon sun.

"Wherever *she's* going, I guess," was Matt's reply.

The two boys ran after her.

Jack felt like a frightened deer as they ran through the forest, scattering fallen leaves, tripping on branches, and leaping over giant logs. A breeze caught the tops of the trees in steady crashes that reminded Jack of waves on a beach. They slowed down only when they were sure they weren't being followed. Jack collapsed against a log and clutched his aching side as Matt fell into a pile a leaves.

"No," the girl said, "not yet. We have to go on. It's not far."

"What's not far?" Jack groaned. The girl hardly seemed winded. Where did she get the energy?

"Come on," she said and jogged onward.

Matt rolled his eyes and struggled to his feet. "Guess we'd better go," he said as he stumbled after her.

Jack pushed off the tree and dutifully followed.

They crossed a large field that was autumn brown and baking in the sun. It felt soothingly warm after the coolness of the woods. Jack wanted nothing more than to lie down right there and bask in it. But the girl continued on relentlessly. They soon came upon another thicket that was abruptly scarred by a dirt road. Crossing it with careful looks in both directions, they entered a small grove, and finally the girl stopped in a clearing within sight of the road.

"Here?" Matt puffed.

"You're kidding," Jack panted, his dark hair matted against his skull.

"My daddy and me said we'd meet here if we got split up. We passed it on the way to the reverend," she said simply.

Jack and Matt looked warily at each other. They were standing in the middle of a small assembly of wooden crosses, small grave markers, and gray tombstones.

"A *graveyard*?" they asked together.

"A GRAVEYARD," THE GIRL said with a nod as she sat under a tree. "Daddy said I'd remember it—and I did," she added proudly.

Jack looked around for a church, a house, or anything else that might explain why there was a cemetery in the middle of nowhere. "This is weird. Why are these people buried way out here?"

"I asked my daddy, and he said these folks were probably buried out here because they died of some kind of disease."

"Oh, *great*," Matt said as he moved away from the solemn gathering of the dead.

"Forget about that," Jack said as he stooped next to the girl. "I want to know what's going on here. What happened back at the church? Why were those men chasing you?"

"*Us*. They were chasing us, too," Matt amended.

"Yeah."

The girl looked from Matt to Jack and back again. Her expression made them feel as if they'd just stepped off a spaceship from another galaxy. She suddenly frowned. "How do I know I can trust you?"

"You mean, besides the fact that we've been running together for the last three miles?" Jack asked sarcastically.

The girl pondered the idea and seemed to agree with it. "My daddy and me ran away from Alabama. Those men wanted to take us back, I guess."

"Why did you have to run away from Alabama?" Matt asked. "Did you escape from jail or something?"

She smiled for the first time, her teeth yellow and crooked. "Heavens no. We ran away from our master."

"Your master?" Jack asked.

"Yes, sir," the girl replied. "He was really mad because my Mama ran off to Canada, and he swore he'd make me and Daddy pay for it. He was going to sell me down the river. So we ran away first chance we got.

Been using the Underground Railroad the whole way here. We're going to Canada to meet Mama."

Jack scrubbed a hand over his face. "This doesn't make any sense."

The girl looked earnestly at Matt. "You don't act or talk like any slave boy I ever met before. Are you a runaway or are you free?"

"I'm free," Matt said as though the girl was crazy.

Jack stood with his hands on his hips, his brow furrowed. "What happened to us?" he asked Matt. "One minute we're in a tunnel, then we're in Whit's workroom, then we're in the Imagination Station, then we're in the tunnel again, then we're running for our lives. *What happened to us?*" His voice bounced from the trees to the cemetery and sounded unusually loud.

Matt's eyes suddenly grew wide. "I have an idea," he said. He spun on his heel and raced over to the grave markers. He seemed to be looking for something in particular as he went from one to another. He finally stopped and gazed down at a tombstone.

"What are you doing?" Jack asked impatiently.

Matt waved him over. "Here. This one looks new."

Jack joined him. "What?"

He pointed to the tombstone. *Safe in the arms of Jesus,* it said in carved letters that curled at the ends. Underneath was the name Josiah Slade, followed by the birthday: June 4, 1824. Under that, it said: *Parted this life the 10th of October, 1858.*

"New?" Jack said. "It's over a hundred years old."

Matt slowly shook his head.

The truth hit Jack so suddenly that he whipped around to the girl. "What's the date?" he called out.

The girl had been sitting with her eyes closed. She opened them wearily. "Date?"

"You know, like, on a calendar? The *date?*"

The girl looked perplexed. "I don't know the date. The leaves fell, we had a full moon the other night . . ."

"What year is this?" Matt asked more gently.

"Oh, that." She frowned for a moment, then said, "It's 1858, my Daddy said in the summer. I guess it still is."

Jack paced nervously. "I don't believe it. You're saying you think that somehow we went back in time to 1858? No way. Not a chance."

"Do you have a better explanation for everything that's happened?" Matt countered. "The Imagination Station, Jack. It's some kind of time machine. We're back in 1858, probably Odyssey."

The girl agreed. "This is Odyssey. I saw the signs when we walked in. I can read, you know."

"No way, no way, no way," Jack said as he paced nervously between the graves.

Matt wandered back to the girl. "That's what happened. The reverend is part of the Underground Railroad—"

"Everybody keeps talking about a railroad, and I don't know what they're talking about," Jack said.

"You never paid attention in history class," Matt rebuked him. "Don't you remember the stories about Harriet Tubman and Frederick Douglass? The Underground Railroad was the secret way that runaway slaves got out of the South. There was a whole network of people and houses where the slaves could stop to get food or a place to sleep. It stretched from the South all the way to Canada." He nodded to the girl. "That's how you got away, right?"

"Uh-huh," she replied.

Matt went on, "So the reverend is part of the Underground Railroad and those guys that suddenly showed up were like slave hunters who catch slaves and take them back south."

"How can they do that? I thought once the slaves got to the North, they were safe," Jack said urgently. He seemed to hope that by proving Matt wrong on that one point, it would prove his whole crazy theory wrong.

Matt opened his mouth to answer, but he closed it again. He was clearly stumped.

"The law," the girl interjected. "I don't know the name of it but, when I was a little girl, they made a law so the slave hunters could go north and take the slaves back to their masters."

"See?" Matt spread his hands. Case closed.

The girl frowned and stood up to look around. "Where's my daddy?"

"I'm sure he's okay," Matt said. "I'll bet he got away and is running here right now." His voice betrayed him, though. He didn't believe it.

Jack shoved his hands into his jeans pockets and turned away. It was still too much for him to believe. How could Whit create a machine that sent them back in time? But the evidence—and his own senses—told him it must be true.

Matt was at his side before he realized it. "Let's go into Odyssey to see if we can find her father. And maybe we can figure out how to get back to Whit's End."

It sure beats waiting around a graveyard, Jack thought. "Yeah, sure," he answered.

"You can't," the girl said to Matt.

"Why not?"

"You're a Negro," she said, as if that answered the question in full.

"So?"

"Do you have any papers that say you're free?" she asked.

Matt was indignant. "No! Why should I carry around papers to say that?"

"Because the slave hunters will think you're somebody's slave and if you can't tell them whose slave you are or show them papers that prove you're free, then they might take you."

"They'd better not!" Matt snapped. "I don't have to prove anything to anybody!"

"Yes, you do," the girl said softly. And it was in the soft resignation of her voice that Matt knew she was absolutely right.

"Better not take the chance," Jack affirmed. "I'll go into town. Maybe I'll find the reverend and he can tell me what's going on."

"Okay," Matt said unhappily.

There was a silent moment as an expression passed between them like a shadow. It wasn't as if Jack were running to the store to buy them a couple of sodas. There was unknown danger ahead and they both knew it.

"It's only Odyssey," Jack offered.

"Yeah. Only Odyssey," Matt agreed.

Jack strode away, lifting his shoulders and picking up his pace just to show them he wasn't afraid. When he reached the edge of the trees that led to the road, he paused and turned back to them.

He shrugged with embarrassment and called out, "Which way is Odyssey?"

CHAPTER SIX

SOMETHING NAGGED AT Jack during the three-mile walk to Odyssey.

Apart from getting lost because he couldn't find anything he recognized to guide him, he kept thinking something was different about the world he was now in. Eventually, the ringing in his ears solved the mystery.

It was the silence.

In a world without cars, trucks, buses, or passing jets, the silence was deep and seemed to go on forever. The forest whispered its life through birds singing, leaves rustling, and branches rubbing dryly against each other. The air carried the soft sound of wind, waving grass in the meadows, the yawning moo of a cow, and the occasional snort of a roaming horse. The crunch and scrape of Jack's sneakers against the dirt road seemed out of place, and it felt as if all living creatures for miles around must be wondering what the awful racket was.

Jack was eventually relieved to hear the teapot whistle of a distant train. Then he came upon houses scattered distantly on both sides of the road, some no more than large single-storied cabins with plank-floored porches. Most had wooden sheds and outhouses in the back, bordering modest fields and farmland. One woman, wearing a long dress and apron, her hair up in a bun, smiled and waved at Jack as she pinned flapping sheets to a clothesline.

Soon the number of houses increased, along with their sizes and sophistication of design. Simple square boxes evolved into more elaborate styles with rounded turrets, arrowlike eaves, circular porches, ornamental windows, and chimneys that jutted up from the rooftops. Brick, stone, and nicely painted siding replaced plain wood. Fences sectioned off each property. *The houses are bigger, but the land is smaller*, Jack thought. Crudely painted signs offered rooms for rent, cheap rates at boardinghouses, piano lessons, and an attorney-at-law.

"Welcome To Odyssey," a large, wooden sign said. Jack couldn't believe his eyes as he got closer and closer. He followed the road—sign-posted as Main Street—which broadened out from a ruddy dirt path to a thoroughfare smoothed over with paving stones. The clip-clop of horses' hooves and the rattle of wagons and carriages came and went. Residential houses yielded to tall, square buildings and businesses. Jack strolled down a wooden walkway, passing the displays for barbers, dentists, blacksmiths, shoe and boot repairs, tin shops, saloons, a general store, and dozens of other shops and offices long-since removed from Jack's Odyssey.

From Jack's point of view, Odyssey—even the *world*—of 1858 was like visiting another planet. There were no fast-food restaurants or convenience stores on this street; the store windows contained no microwaves, appliances, CD players, televisions, movies, computers, or even calculators; he saw no telephones or booths to put them in; no electric lights hung above the doors or on the lampposts. He suddenly realized that almost all the things he would take for granted hadn't been invented yet.

A group of boys suddenly rounded a corner and nearly ran straight into Jack. "Watch it," he said.

"Sorry, mister," a freckle-faced boy said, then stopped to look at Jack long and hard. Adults might not notice a strange boy walking in town, but kids noticed when someone their age was around whom they didn't know. "You're a stranger here," the boy said.

Jack sized him up, just in case the boy wanted to fight. He was a couple of years younger than Jack. "I'm just visiting," he answered.

The boy eyed Jack up and down. His gaze rested on Jack's jeans and white sneakers. The other boys also noticed them, and whispered among themselves. Jack thought he heard them say something about "strange shoes."

The freckle-faced kid looked at Jack curiously. "Where'd you get those clothes? I don't know anybody who has clothes like that. Are you from out West?"

"San Francisco?" a sandy-haired boy asked. "I heard they dress funny in San Francisco."

"No, I'm from . . ." Jack's voice trailed off. Where *was* he from, if not from Odyssey? "Near here," he finally said. He glanced away self-consciously and decided to change the subject. "Maybe you can help me.

I'm looking for anyone who knows the pastor of the church that's—"
Again, he had to stop himself. He didn't know the name of the church
or where it was.

"Must be Reverend Andrew you're talking about," the sandy-haired
boy said helpfully. "He's rector of that church yonder." The boy pointed
through a gap between the buildings to a church sitting about a hundred yards away in the middle of a parklike area. It looked peaceful in
the afternoon sunlight.

Jack was astounded. It was the church all right. "We must've
climbed out of the back and run *away* from town," he muttered.

"Pardon?" the freckle-faced boy asked.

Jack shook his head. "Nothing. I just need to talk to someone about
the church."

The sandy-haired boy asked, "Why don't you go over and talk to the
reverend himself at the church?"

Obviously whatever had happened in the church wasn't common
knowledge around the town. "I'm not sure anyone's there," Jack said
honestly.

"Then you better check the hotel," the freckle-faced boy said. "The
reverend stays there when he isn't at the church."

"At a hotel?"

"Yep. He's been living there ever since his house got burned down,"
the boy said.

"That's what he gets for fighting with the slave hunters," another
boy interjected.

"Quiet, Jeb," the freckle-faced boy snapped, then pointed down the
street. "Now, just go across the street there and the hotel is on the end—
at the corner."

"Thanks, guys."

"Guys?"

"Er, *friends*." With a quick nod to them, Jack dodged the horses and
wagons that seemed to come from every direction on the street and
made it to the other side. He looked back at the group of boys who
talked animatedly between themselves while they watched him. He
waved and headed down the sidewalk.

The Odyssey Hotel sat at the corner of Main Street and McAlister.
It looked familiar to Jack with its large, frosted windows embedded in

richly carved doors. Then he remembered that he'd only seen pictures of it while he was on a school field trip to Odyssey's historical museum. Jack's feeling of being out of place was intensified when he also remembered that the hotel burned down in 1904 during Odyssey's great fire. It was like seeing the *Titanic* before it sailed.

Parallel to the hotel but on the other side of McAlister Street sat City Hall, with its large, ornate clock tower. The huge face of the clock peered at him like an old friend. It was the only thing so far that Jack was certain he recognized, though the tower still had scaffolding along one side for workers to add some finishing touches. Jack searched his memory from that field trip. The clock tower was finished in the fall of 1858. *That's now*, he thought and smiled. Mrs. Sexton, the museum guide, said that it was completed around the same time that Big Ben was put into the tower at Westminster Palace in London. Folks in Odyssey were proud to share the experience with their foreign cousins.

Jack walked into the hotel and was immediately impressed by the marble and by the plush, red decoration of the lobby, tastefully matched by patterned wallpaper, shelves with Chinese-looking vases, flowers, and dark brown woodwork along the edges of the ceilings and floors. The entire reception desk was also dark brown wood. Camel-backed sofas, loveseats, and wing-backed chairs with frilly skirts were scattered around the room. An elegant staircase led away from the lobby and up to parts unknown. On the other side of a wide, curtained entryway just to the right of the stairs, Jack could see what looked like a restaurant or saloon. Somewhere inside, a piano player announced that he would play a new song and fumbled his way through "The Yellow Rose of Texas."

Men and women, in varying styles of formal and casual clothes, wandered around the lobby. Businessmen in smart suits chatted seriously in a corner. A man wearing a large, round hat and carrying a long, silver-headed cane plucked a gold watch from his waistcoat and checked the time. The women wore bell-shaped dresses that rustled as they walked past. Overburdened porters moved quickly about with their patron's luggage in hand.

Jack stepped up to the reception desk, but a man with a thick mustache stepped in front of him and slapped a coin down on the counter. "This should take care of my room and any extras," he said quickly. He was obviously in a hurry.

The spectacled clerk eyed the small, gold coin warily. "Ah, I see. One of those new three-dollar pieces. It's the first one I've seen."

"Not sure they'll last," the man said simply. "Apply the difference to my account. I don't want to miss the train."

"Yes, Mr. Prentice," the clerk said, but the man was already on his way out the door.

Jack approached the counter and stood on the tips of his toes to get the clerk's attention. "Excuse me—"

"I'll be right with you, son," the clerk said as he turned his attention to shoving pieces of paper into a collection of cubbyholes on the wall behind him.

Jack waited patiently as bits of conversations around him drifted by. One man complained to a woman, "It just doesn't make sense that Minnesota can get the statehood and Kansas can't. I swear, you give those Washington politicians a new capital to meet in and they lose their marbles."

"I'm telling you, Beck and Russell say Cherry Creek is teeming with gold. I'm thinking of making the trip out myself," one traveler said to his companion on the way through the lobby.

His friend replied, "All the way to Colorado? That's clear on the other side of the Kansas Territory! It'll take a mighty long time to get there."

"Not so long these days," he countered. "The Overland Stage Coach made it from St. Louis to Los Angeles in *20* days!"

A lady sat in a corner chair reading a book. A younger girl eased down next to her and asked what she was reading. "*The Courtship of Miles Standish* by Henry Wadsworth Longfellow," she said, holding it up proudly. "I just received it by post from New England!"

A man reading a newspaper suddenly laughed and said to his friend, "It's been over a month since the transatlantic cable stopped working and now they aren't sure they'll ever get it fixed. I reckon President Buchanan and Queen Victoria won't be able to send messages across the Atlantic anymore."

His friend chuckled. "Not sure why anyone would *want to* send cables back and forth across the Atlantic."

A cheery, roly-poly fellow—obviously a salesman—entreated another bored-looking man about the "revolution" that the new "Mason

Jar" would have on the country. He was giving the man the chance to invest a small sum that he assured him would yield 10 times the amount later.

But the conversation that caught Jack's full attention was between two wealthy-looking gentlemen nearby who spoke in hushed but agitated tones about a debate on slavery between Abraham Lincoln and someone named Stephen Douglas.

"I'm tired to death of hearing about it," the first man said. "Let the politicians decide and be done with it."

The second man shook his head. "I don't think this is a matter to be legislated. People like John Brown and those abolitionists won't let it lie. The way it's going, I figure there's going to be fighting."

"A war?"

"God forbid," the man said. "But you see how it's tearing Odyssey apart. If that's any indication of the mood of the rest of the country . . . well, I can't predict what'll happen."

Someone loudly cleared his throat. Jack realized it was the hotel clerk. "You wanted something, young man?"

"I'm looking for Reverend Andrew. He lives here, right?" Jack said.

"He does, but he isn't here at the moment. Did you look for him at the church? That's where he generally is at this time of day," the clerk said.

Suddenly a man rushed in through the door. He called out breathlessly, "Has anyone seen the sheriff?"

"Not here. Why? What's wrong, Albert?" the clerk asked.

"We've got another *incident* behind the church!" he replied.

There was a flurry of activity as some of the men reacted and ran to Albert, then all squeezed out the door.

The clerk groaned, "Not another one."

"Incident?" Jack asked.

"Yep." The clerk frowned at Jack. "That'll probably be Reverend Andrew's doing. Reckon you'll find him wherever that crowd's going."

Jack sped out of the door after the men.

CHAPTER SEVEN

MATT AND THE GIRL sat under an elm tree near the cemetery. Normally, Matt might've thought what a beautiful day it was to sit under an elm tree, with the birds chirping happily and the yellow and brown leaves gently falling. It was another gorgeous fall day in Odyssey, only it wasn't his Odyssey, and the edge of danger cut through the pretty picture like a razor blade.

"What's your name?" Matt suddenly asked the girl.

She had been staring wearily at the tombstones and answered so softly that Matt barely heard her. "Eveline."

"Eveline who?"

"Not Eveline *who.* Just Eveline."

"Don't you have a last name?"

"I think we did once, but I don't remember what it was."

They sat in silence again while Matt tried to grasp the notion of a girl who didn't know her own last name. It made him uncomfortable. He knew a little about slavery from his classes at school and some of the books he read. But this was the real thing. He didn't like it. He squirmed impatiently. What was taking Jack so long? he wondered. Where was Eveline's father? Did he get away from the men in the tunnel? *I sure hope so,* he thought. *Otherwise I don't know what we're going to do.*

"Can you read?" Eveline asked.

"Sure I can read," he replied, surprised by the question.

"So can I," Eveline said with a big smile.

"That's what you said before." Matt shrugged and couldn't figure out why it was so important to her. "Everybody I know can read."

She looked at him carefully, as if trying to decide whether or not he was teasing her. "Everybody? Even folks of color?"

"Yeah. What's the big deal? You go to school and they teach you to read."

"You went to *school*?" she asked, awed.

"Of course I did, er—*do*," Matt said. He was getting a little irritated with this game. "Don't you go to school?"

Eveline shook her head. "Huh-uh. Slaves aren't allowed to go to school. Our masters don't want us to learn nothing but the work we do. That's why I had to learn to read in secret. Aunt Tabby taught me how, but she said I wasn't ever supposed to let white folks know or they might put me in jail or hurt me."

"Put you in jail for knowing how to read?" Matt nearly shouted. "That's crazy! Why would anybody do that?"

"Aunt Tabby said that they don't want us to read because it gives us ideas," she said.

Matt didn't know how to react. He remembered from history class that most slaves couldn't read, but it never occurred to him that they weren't *allowed* to read.

The distinct sound of horses' hooves beating the road worked its way through the air. Then came the sound of churning wagon wheels. Matt stood up to look. "Somebody's coming," he said and turned to Eveline, but she was gone. He was amazed by how quickly she had disappeared. "Eveline?" He looked around for her. She was a few yards away, waving at him from behind a large tombstone. "What are you doing?"

She waved frantically at him.

Torn between running to the road for help or going to her, he hesitated for a moment. She waved with greater agitation, and he decided to find out what her problem was first. "What's wrong? Maybe it's your father."

"And maybe it's the slave hunters!" she whispered. "We have to hide until we can be sure."

Matt knew instantly that she was right. He didn't have much to fear in his world, but in *her* world there was plenty to be afraid of. He ducked behind the tombstone with her and watched the road.

First came a man on horseback. Matt thought it might've been one of the men in the tunnel, but he couldn't be sure. Following behind him, another horse pulled a wooden wagon with two men sitting up front. Matt still couldn't be sure whether they were slave hunters or not—how could he?—until Eveline gasped and pointed. Tied up in the back of the wagon, beaten and bloody, was Eveline's father. She made as if she might rush out to him, but Matt grabbed her arm. They didn't breathe as the wagon drifted past. Curls of dust were kicked up by the horses and the wheels.

"They got my daddy," she moaned. "They're gonna take him back."

Matt didn't know what to say or do. "Maybe when Jack comes back with the reverend, we can—"

"No. I have to follow them. I don't wanna lose my daddy!" With that she took off before Matt could stop her.

"Wait! You'll get caught!" he whispered as loudly as he dared.

"Freedom's no good without my daddy," Eveline snapped back, then weaved her way quickly through the graveyard as the wagon disappeared around the bend.

Matt leaned against the cold, damp tombstone and groaned. What was he supposed to do? He glanced hopefully up the road—praying that Jack, the reverend, and a posse of good guys might be following the slave hunters to rescue Clarence and keep Matt from having to make a decision. A rabbit scurried out to the center of the road, then dashed on to the other side. That was all.

Matt couldn't see Eveline anymore. What was he supposed to do? But he knew that there was only one answer.

He couldn't let Eveline follow the slave hunters alone.

A CROWD OF MEN had gathered in a grove of trees not far from the church. Jack rushed up anxiously and maneuvered so he could see what had happened. A man knelt next to a tree—to cut the ropes that held Reverend Andrew. A small ribbon of blood slid down the side of Andrew's face. Jack's heart pounded furiously as he looked all around for Clarence. He wasn't there.

Reverend Andrew climbed to his feet and, in a voice filled with anger, told the crowd what had happened. "They burst into the church, grabbed us, and dragged us here. They tied me up and proceeded to beat the poor slave mercilessly. They wanted to know where his daughter was, but he wouldn't tell them. That made them even angrier, so they beat him more. I protested until they gagged me. They tied me here and hauled the slave off."

"What was a runaway doing in your church, Reverend?" one man asked with undisguised annoyance. "You're not part of that there Underground Railroad, are you?"

"What do you mean by the question, sir?" another man answered. "If the church can't be a haven to *all* men in *all* conditions, then what's it for?"

"I better run home and check my fences then," the first man sneered. "What'll become of my business when my cows and pigs know they need only run away to the church for protection!"

A few men snickered at this remark.

"You go too far, Thomas," a man snapped back. "We're talking about *men*, not animals!"

"Are we?" the sneering man replied.

"Yes, we are!"

The reverend held up his hands in appeal to the men. "This isn't the time or place for a debate. I ask only that the men here who abhor the practice of these slave hunters come with me. We must rescue the poor unfortunate who is even now being unwillingly taken back to the South!"

Half the men murmured their consent, while the sneering man and his group grunted and turned away. One muttered something about the reverend getting what he deserved for helping runaways.

After the men had gone, Reverend Andrew gathered the remainder around him. "My guess is they took the Connellsville Road. But there's a girl—the runaway's daughter—who is hiding somewhere in the region. We must scour the area and find her lest she fall into their hands as well!"

With this, Jack stepped forward. "Excuse me, Reverend, but—"

At the sight of Jack the reverend's eyes grew wide. "You! You were in the church!"

"Yes, sir. I know where the girl is. She's with my friend just a couple of miles from here. I came back to find you to—"

"You know where she is? Excellent!" Andrew exclaimed, then turned to the crowd. "Get your horses and wagons and meet me at the church. God help us to stop this horrendous deed!"

With roars of approval, the crowd scattered. Reverend Andrew put his hand on Jack's shoulder. "Well done, son. What's your name?"

"Jack," he replied.

"It's providential that you came when you did," he said. "Where is the girl and your friend?"

"At a cemetery a couple of miles from here. The girl said it's where her dad would meet her."

"Clarence was a smart man to prearrange a meeting place if anything went wrong. Which cemetery? Odyssey has several."

Jack frowned. He had no idea *which* cemetery it was. Then he remembered: "The girl said that diseased people are buried there."

"I know the graveyard," the reverend said with a nod. "Now I need to impose on you further. Run as hard as you can to the girl and your friend, and keep them hidden until I arrive with help. Trust no one. Clarence didn't tell the slave hunters where his daughter was, but they might be searching for her! Now, *go*, lad!"

The sun was going down by the time Jack reached the graveyard. His side hurt from all the running and he couldn't remember a time when he felt more tired. "Matt?" he called out. "It's me—Jack!"

Silence.

"Don't mess around, Matt," Jack called out again. A cool breeze blew past, and his skin went goose-pimply. Something was wrong. He crept around the tombstones and wooden grave markers, hoping that they really were just teasing him. He then widened his search to include the surrounding woods up to the road. No sign of them.

"Where *are* you?" he eventually shouted with exasperation.

His voice echoed and came back to him empty.

With no better ideas, Jack slumped down next to a tree by the road. All he could do was wait for Reverend Andrew.

WITH THE SOUND OF THUNDER, the reverend and about 20 men from Odyssey arrived at the cemetery just as the sun ducked below the horizon. They carried rifles and blazing torches. Jack, with obvious relief, ran out to the road to meet them.

"Well?" Andrew called as he leaped off of his horse.

"They're not here," Jack said.

"Are you sure?" a man with thick whiskers asked. Then he signaled for some of the men to fan out to search.

"Believe me! I already checked," Jack said. "They aren't here."

"That's enough for me," another man shouted. "Let's go after those blasted slave hunters and show 'em we don't tolerate this kind of thing in Odyssey."

The men shouted their approval and were yanking at the reins of their horses when another posse raced up and surrounded them. Curses and insults were exchanged between the two groups, and Jack was afraid a fight might break out.

"Hold on, boys," a lean man shouted from the front of the group as he reined his horse to a stop. He had a star pinned to his gray flannel shirt. "Just what in tarnation do you think you're doing?"

"Slave hunters again, Sheriff. Nabbed a runaway slave and probably his daughter."

"Sorry, boys, but the law says the slave hunters can take runaways back to their masters. Nothing you or me can do about that."

"We'll show you what we can do about it!" a large man shouted.

"Whoa now! I won't have it! Not in my territory. You go after those slave hunters and sure as I'm sitting here, there'll be a fight. Somebody'll get hurt or killed. So just put your guns away and go home. No point getting worked up over somebody else's problem. These slaves aren't our business."

"But my friend might be with them—and he wasn't a slave!" Jack called out.

The sheriff jerked his head around to look at Jack. His eyes narrowed. "What are you talking about? Are you saying they kidnapped somebody?"

Jack shuffled uneasily. "We *think* they took him."

"Well, I'll be doggoned. Not like them to be kidnapping white boys," the sheriff said.

"Matt isn't white—" Jack said.

"But he's free," Reverend Andrew interjected.

"Matt? I don't remember a free black Negro named Matt registering at my office."

Jack was surprised. "Register at your office? Why would he have to do that?"

"For his own sake. Free blacks are supposed to register so that the slave hunters won't have a right to capture them. Everybody knows that." The sheriff leaned forward on the front of the saddle. "Did he do that?"

"No," Jack said. "We didn't know he was supposed to. I mean, where we come from, you don't—"

"That's all that can be done, then," the sheriff announced. He turned his attention to the crowd of men. "Now I'm going to ask you all *nicely* to go home and forget about this thing. I won't have a pack of vigilantes riding across the countryside shooting or getting shot by the slave hunters. Now, you can go home or spend the night in jail. It's up to you."

In a tense moment, the sheriff stared down the reverend's posse until, one by one, they yanked their reins and spun their horses toward Odyssey. Reverend Andrew stood alone with Jack.

"Well, Reverend?" the sheriff asked.

"Have it your way, Sheriff," Andrew said in a cold tone.

The sheriff sighed heavily. "I don't like this business, you know. I don't like it at all." He loudly clicked his tongue and spurred his horse away. With various grunts and "yahs!" his men followed, leaving a cloud of dust to coat Jack and the reverend.

"That's it?" Jack asked with disbelief. "We're just supposed to sit back and let the slave hunters take Matt?"

Reverend Andrew put his hand on Jack's shoulder. "This thing isn't over yet," he said with determination.

MATT AND EVELINE CRAWLED beneath a thick bush and watched the clearing where the slave hunters had set up their camp for the night. The hunters had tied their horses to the buckboard wagon's wheels, gathered wood for a fire, and pulled out a tin pot to make what smelled to Matt like meat broth. It made his stomach ache for the food. That's what he wanted more than anything, he thought: to be home for a hot meal and to sleep in his own bed.

The thick brown forest dirt under the tangled branches of the bush was moist and cold. Matt cradled his head in his arms and closed his eyes.

They'd followed the slave hunters for miles. How many miles, Matt didn't know. It was all he could do just to keep up with Eveline, whose speed and energy seemed without limit. *How did I get into this,* he kept asking himself, *and how do I get out of it?* He clung to the hope that Jack was not far behind them with Reverend Andrew or, better yet, Mr. Whittaker. Matt was sorry he'd ever laid eyes on the Imagination Station.

"There's my daddy." Eveline whispered so softly that, again, Matt almost didn't hear her. He lifted his head and looked. She pointed to an enormous oak tree in the shadows on the edge of the clearing. Clarence was tied tightly to it. He hung his head. Matt couldn't tell if he was sleeping or just too exhausted to sit up straight.

The three slave hunters fixed their meal silently and seemed to be listening for anything in the woods that sounded unusual. Matt guessed that they were worried that someone from Odyssey might follow them. Little could they know they were right. But they were expecting men and horses, not two kids hiding under a bush.

"I don't think anyone's coming," one of the slave hunters said.

For the first time Matt was able to take a hard look at the men. The one who just spoke was tall and wiry, with a bushy mustache perched under a hooked nose. Even in the firelight, Matt could see he had a dangerous-looking face, with deep lines going every which way like a road map. He had long, thinning, gray hair that sprayed out from under an old, weather-beaten cowboy hat. Eventually Matt picked up that he was named Hank.

"I didn't believe they would. The sheriff would see to that," said a man named Sonny. He was a round-faced, clean-shaven man in a bowler hat. He pulled a pipe from his waistcoat pocket—its buttons stretched to their limit by his bulk—and settled back against a rock.

The third man was the one Matt was sure he had seen in the basement at Whit's End. He had squinty eyes as if someone had drawn two quarter moons above his cheeks. Thick eyebrows crowned them and splayed out like bird's wings. His face was lean and looked even longer by the way his mouth pushed downward in a permanent frown. He was the boss, which was obvious only because it was what the other two men called him. He grabbed the coffeepot from the fire and poured himself a cup. "We need to take shifts to make sure nobody sneaks up on us tonight," he said in a hoarse, scratchy voice.

Matt took in the scene and couldn't imagine how to help Clarence. He thought he might be able to sneak around and untie his ropes. But then what? The three slave hunters would quickly catch them again. *What are we going to do?* he wondered.

"You wanna give the chattel some of this soup?" Hank asked.

Boss glanced over at Clarence, then shook his head. "Not sure I'm interested in wasting any good food on him after the trouble he's caused us."

"You call this good?" Sonny grimaced and threw his tin down playfully.

Hank sniffed indignantly. "You're welcome to eat something else if you have a better offer."

"Let's just get to Huntsville and we'll have all the offers we want," Boss said with a chuckle.

"So long as our buck here gets us the reward money we want," Sonny said.

"How 'bout that, Boss?" Hank asked.

Boss scrubbed his prickly chin and stood up. "Not gonna fetch as much as we expected without the daughter." He walked over and kicked Clarence's leg.

Clarence stirred and slowly lifted his head with a groan.

Boss kicked him again. "You've robbed us, boy. We were supposed to get you and your daughter and you helped her get away. You're gonna have to pay us the difference—or I reckon you'll have to be punished somehow."

"You wanna punish him? Give him some of the soup," Sonny said.

"You want some soup?" Boss asked Clarence. As if on cue, Hank walked over with a tin of the soup and knelt down next to the bound man. "You must be hungry after such a long trip."

Hank held the tin of soup up to Clarence's mouth. Clarence looked as if he didn't want it.

"Go on. Take some," Hank said.

Clarence turned his head away.

"Can't you hear, boy? He said to *take some soup*." Boss kicked Clarence harder.

Clarence shook his head. "No, thank you, sir. I'm not hungry."

"What? That's not the point. We want you to eat. We want you to be a big, strong buck for your master when we march you in. Now *eat!*"

Hank kicked at Clarence.

"Daddy!" Eveline gasped.

Every muscle in Matt's body tensed as the two men taunted and kicked at Clarence. Sonny sat nearby and laughed at the scene. Matt knew they had to do something, but he couldn't think what. Then he wondered, *What if we could create a diversion?* If he could get the slave hunters away from Clarence, Eveline could untie her father. He turned to Eveline to tell her the plan but didn't get the chance. She scrambled out from under the bushes and raced into the clearing.

"Not again!" Matt groaned.

"Stop it! Stop doing that to my Daddy!" Eveline cried.

The two men, startled by the girl's sudden appearance, swung around. Sonny dropped his pipe.

"No, child!" Clarence shouted as he strained at the ropes.

Hank let out a bark of a laugh. "Well, as I live and breathe! Look, Boss, it's the girl."

"I see her," Boss replied. "What are you doing here, my little pickaninny? Come to help your daddy?"

Eveline stood frozen where she was, but her eyes moved quickly from man to man in case one made a move for her.

"Eveline—" Clarence croaked.

"You want me to grab her?" Hank asked.

"Shut up," Boss snapped. Then he smiled at Eveline. "You wanna help your daddy, *Eveline*? Then give me your hand. Come with us. It'll help him more than anything else you can do."

Matt realized that this was as much of a diversion as he could have planned himself. He crawled backward, keeping out of sight behind the bush, and then rushed around the edge of the clearing toward the tree to which Clarence was tied. He knew he had little time and ran as fast and as quietly as he could.

"Come on, Eveline," he heard Boss say.

Through the limbs of the trees, he saw Eveline standing perfectly still by the firelight. Her eyes still darted like a rabbit's who'd been surrounded by wolves. But they also betrayed that she had acted on impulse and didn't know what to do next.

"Run, child," Clarence shouted. "Don't let 'em take you. *Run!*"

Matt was now behind the tree and at the ropes holding Clarence. He peered around and saw Eveline shuffle anxiously. She was stricken by her indecision. Boss took a step toward her. "Come on, girl."

In the darkness of the woods, Matt had a hard time seeing the ropes. He felt around for the knots and, with a sinking heart, realized they weren't there. They must be on the other side, with Clarence.

"Don't listen to him, Eveline," Clarence commanded his daughter. "You run now, you hear? Don't let him get any closer! Run!"

The words somehow got through, and with a last, despairing look, she tore away just as Boss dove for her. Gazellelike, she bounded into the dark woods.

"Get her!" Boss yelled. The three men disappeared into the darkness after her.

Matt's mind reeled as he tried to think. How could he get Clarence untied? Peeking around to make sure everyone had gone, he circled the tree to Clarence.

"What are you doing here?" Clarence asked him, amazed. "Are you crazy?"

"We're here to rescue you!" Matt announced.

"Rescue me! Oh, son, you *are* crazy."

"How can I get you free?" Matt asked as he tugged at the ropes.

Clarence looked around frantically. "You'll never get these knots undone. A knife. Look around the wagon for a knife."

Matt ran to the wagon and searched through the bedrolls, saddle-bags, and a crate filled with ropes, tools, and tarp. No knife. In a harsh whisper he called back to Clarence, "I can't find it. Are you sure there's a knife here?"

"Watch out!" Clarence shouted, looking beyond Matt.

Matt heard a low chuckle behind him and turned.

"MAN ALIVE, THIS BEATS the dutch!" Hank wheezed happily as he secured the ropes on Matt's and Eveline's wrists. "Good thing you came along, Wylie."

"I guess it was," Wylie replied. Matt stared at him with all the hatred he could muster. He recognized Wylie as the black man who had arrived in the tunnel right after Matt and Jack. Clarence had accused him of pretending to be a slave in order to catch runaways. Clarence was right.

"You're gonna get it for tying me up like this," Matt fumed.

"Shut up," Hank hissed in Matt's ear.

"I figure you can add this boy to what you owe me. You have *three* to take back with you now," Wylie said with a smile.

"That wasn't part of the deal," Boss said.

"Neither was you going so far out. We were supposed to meet in Gower's Field, you'll recall. All this riding hurts my hind parts," Wylie complained. "So just add a few dollars to what you owe me."

Boss looked as if he might argue, then changed his mind. "I swear, I've never known a darky to haggle the way you do. But you do good work and I won't begrudge you that." Boss marched over to his saddle-bag and pulled out a small pouch. Coins clinked as he poured them into his palm, counting carefully as he did. When he was satisfied with the amount, he held out his hand to Wylie. "What we agreed and then some."

Wylie took the money. "Pleasure doing business with you."

"You oughtta be ashamed of yourself," Clarence growled at Wylie. "Betraying your own people for 30 pieces of silver. You're a *Judas*! You sold yourself to the devil."

Wylie chuckled in response. "I'll be thinking about you when I have a hot bath and good meal in Connellsville tonight." He tipped his hat to the three slave hunters. "Good hunting, my friends. You know where to find me if you need me again!" He bowed, then made his way into the woods.

"I never liked him and never liked doing business with him," Sonny said. "I hope you didn't give him much. Do you think this boy'll fetch a good price?"

Boss grunted. "We'll get what we expected for the buck and his girl, but this one's scrawny." He nudged Matt with the edge of his boot.

"You do anything to me and you'll be in *big* trouble," Matt challenged.

Hank and Sonny laughed at the boy's spirit. Boss didn't. He squinted at Matt thoughtfully. "Strange. He doesn't act like a slave."

"I'm *not* a slave!" Matt shouted.

"Then I reckon you better explain yourself," Boss said. "Where're you from and what're you doing here?"

Matt sat up proudly. "I'm from Odyssey."

"Are you?" Boss said skeptically. "You sure don't dress like anybody I've ever seen in Odyssey. Where'd you get those funny-looking clothes?" He tugged at Matt's jacket and sweatshirt.

"Well, I'm not from the Odyssey you know but from a different Odyssey . . . one in the future."

The slave hunters looked at each other, bewildered. "What in blazes are you talking about?" Boss asked.

"See, Jack and I went through the tunnel to the workroom in Whit's End, and that's where we found the Imagination Station."

"Whit's End?" Boss shook his head.

"Crazy as a loon," Sonny mumbled.

Matt protested, "I'm serious! We got into the Imagination Station and the next thing we knew, we were in the tunnel again, but it wasn't the tunnel leading to Whit's End, but to the church where we saw Reverend Andrew—"

"What a yarn," Hank said with a chuckle.

"I'm telling the truth!" Matt shouted.

Boss nudged him harder with the toe of his boot. "Listen, boy. I wasn't born in the woods to be scared by an owl—or to have a little urchin cut shines with me."

"Huh?"

"Do you have papers? I need to see some proof that you're free," Boss demanded.

"We don't need papers where I come from!" Matt said.

"I reckon that's too bad for you," Boss said. He turned to his companions. "Looks like he goes with us."

Matt squirmed. "I don't know who you guys think you are, but you're going to be arrested for kidnapping if you don't let us go *right now!* I mean it. Mr. Whittaker is going to show up any minute, and the police are going to lock you up and throw away the key!"

"Shut up, boy," Boss said.

"No, I *won't* shut up! You have no right to tie us up and—"

Matt didn't get to finish his sentence. Boss suddenly backhanded him across the face. "I said to *shut up* and that's what I meant!"

Matt was so startled that he didn't notice the pain in the side of his face like a bee sting, or the tear that slid down his cheek without permission.

"All right, boys, let's get some shut-eye. Tomorrow we take to the river," Boss said. "You're on the first watch, Sonny."

"Me!" Sonny complained.

"Yeah, you. Then me. Then Hank."

After the slave hunters were settled down for the night, Eveline leaned over to Matt. "Are you all right?" she whispered.

Matt swallowed back his tears and nodded.

"Don't you fret," Eveline said soothingly. "You'll get used to it. That's how they treat us."

Matt thought, *No, I won't. I'll never get used to it.*

REVEREND ANDREW LIVED in a modest two-bedroom apartment in the Odyssey Hotel. To Jack, it looked the way rooms did in Western movies. Andrew had assembled a makeshift study on one side of the room, with a rolltop desk, shelves overburdened with books, a small sofa and reading chair, and an end table with a kerosene lamp. All of it sat atop a large, patterned throw rug that covered most of the wooden flooring. Small, painted pictures of country hills hung at odd angles on the walls.

At the moment, Jack and Andrew were sitting on the opposite side of the room at the dining table. Since he didn't have a stove on which to cook, Andrew had brought up a meal of beef and potatoes from the hotel restaurant.

"No doubt you're wondering why I'm living in the hotel," Andrew said as he chomped on a particularly chewy piece of beef. "The apartment was given to me by some of our parishioners after slave hunters burned down my house several years ago."

"They burned down your *house*?" Jack asked, vaguely remembering that the boys on the street had mentioned the fact. That conversation seemed like a long time ago.

"It was the rectory not far from the church. Perhaps you saw what's left of it today," Andrew said.

Jack nodded as he remembered the shell of the house near the woods. "But why did they burn down your house?"

Reverend Andrew shook his head. "It's a long story. They didn't appreciate the way I helped a family of runaways. The house caught fire when the fools decided to smoke the family out of the tunnel. That incident secured my place in the abolitionist movement. If I doubted the importance of the Underground before, I didn't afterward. I've dedicated all I have to helping where I can to stop this abomination before God."

Jack frowned. "I don't understand how people can treat other people that way . . . just because of the color of their skin."

"Obviously I agree," Reverend Andrew said. "The Scriptures are clear about the dignity of all those for whom the Son of God died—regardless of their color. Slavery makes a sham of our humanity, a lie of our place as a Christian nation. The love of Christ cannot be spoken of with our mouths while our hands whip the backs of our brothers and shackle their arms and legs. God must weep in heaven. He must!"

Jack sat up, captivated by the power of Andrew's words.

But Andrew didn't continue. He simply sighed. "In many ways it's worse now than it ever was. The debates have certainly stirred things up."

"Debates?"

"You don't know? Where have you been, lad? I thought everyone knew about the Douglas-Lincoln debates."

Jack thought of the snippet of conversation he'd heard in the hotel lobby that afternoon. "Oh, yeah. But why is everyone so upset about a debate between Abraham Lincoln and that other guy? Or is it because Lincoln is president and—"

"*President* Lincoln!" Reverend Andrew bellowed. "I hardly think he's likely to ever become president. Not now. Not after taking such a hard stand on slavery. I'm all for him, of course, but I can't imagine the majority of other people are. Douglas will probably win because of his confounded stand on states' rights."

Jack shook his head. None of it made sense to him, and he said so.

Reverend Andrew leaned back and spoke patiently. "Senator Stephen Douglas and Abraham Lincoln recently conducted a series of debates about the issue of slavery. It is Lincoln's intention to be the next Republican senator from Illinois. You see, he caused quite a stir earlier in the year when he made a speech at the Republican convention. He said that a 'house divided against itself cannot stand. . . . I believe this government cannot endure permanently half slave and half free.' I'll never forget those words—an echo of the very sentiments of Christ." He paused for a moment in reverent silence.

Jack took another bite of his beef. It was tough and stringy.

Reverend Andrew continued. "Douglas, a Democrat, argued that democracy itself was at stake if states—and the new territories in the West—aren't allowed to decide the issue of slavery for themselves. He was quite eloquent. So was Lincoln. And by the end of the debates, Lincoln laid his cards on the table. He turned the subject of slavery from a political issue to a *moral* one. He has appealed to the whole nation to reject slavery as an institution."

"And he's right!" Jack said.

"He is indeed," Andrew said soberly. "And though the nation may not accept his message, *I* certainly do. Which is why I won't let those slave hunters get away with taking Clarence, Eveline, and your friend. I've never lost a runaway. I'm not about to lose any now."

Jack bit into a potato. He was surprised by how plain it tasted but didn't want to offend Andrew by saying so. "But how will we get them back?"

"Ah! I have a very clever plan, if I may say so myself," the reverend said with a smile.

"What are we going to do?"

Andrew frowned. "We? I'm sorry, lad, but it's a bit too risky for you to help out."

"But Matt is *my* friend. I *have to* be allowed to help!" Jack exclaimed, nearly spilling his glass of water.

Reverend Andrew rubbed his chin thoughtfully for a moment. "An assistant would be helpful. But I need you to tell me who your parents are so I can speak to them about it."

Jack grimaced. "I can tell you who my parents are, but you won't be able to find them."

"Won't I?"

"No, sir." Jack poked at the last of the potato with his fork as he tried to decide how to tell Reverend Andrew the truth. He realized that he couldn't. The truth sounded ridiculous, even to his own mind. Who would believe that he had been transported from the future by a machine called the Imagination Station that some inventor named Whit had created? Jack sure wouldn't.

"Are you an orphan?" the reverend asked gently.

Jack mused on the question. In a way, he and Matt *were* orphans since, technically speaking, their parents hadn't even been born yet. "Something like that," Jack replied noncommittally.

"Then I'll assume you have nowhere to stay tonight."

"No, sir. I don't."

"You do now. I have a guest room for just such occasions. It has a feather bed—not straw. I believe you'll find it comfortable. I'll put some fresh water in your washbasin so you can clean up before you go to sleep." The reverend stood up as a signal that it was time to call it a night.

"But . . . what about the plan?" Jack asked as he also stood up.

"In due course, lad," Andrew said. "We'll have plenty of time on the train journey to Huntsville to talk it through."

"Huntsville?"

"It's in Alabama. I'm sure that's where the slave hunters are taking Clarence and Eveline."

"How do you know that?"

"Because it's where Clarence's master lives." Reverend Andrew began clearing up the dishes. "Now, if you need anything at all, simply let me know."

Jack hesitated for a moment. The reverend looked at him quizzically. Jack cleared his throat. "Well . . . I was wondering where the bathroom is."

"There's one on the second floor. But it's terribly late to order a bath," Andrew said.

"Actually, I don't need to order a *bath*. I need to *use* the bathroom."

Reverend Andrew look at him perplexed.

"You know, the bathroom? The *toilet*?"

Suddenly the reverend's face lit up. "Oh, I see! The *necessary!* You want to use the chamber pot!"

Jack shrugged. "Whatever you call it."

"Certainly! Why did you have to ask? It's where you would expect it to be."

Jack shuffled uneasily. "And . . . uh . . . where would I expect it to be?"

"Under your bed, of course," Andrew said, giving Jack an odd look. "Now, go on, first door on the left. Make yourself at home."

"Right," Jack muttered as he walked down the small hallway. "Make myself at home."

CHAPTER THIRTEEN

AT DAWN THE NEXT MORNING, Matt, Clarence, and Eveline were thrown into the back of the wagon by Hank and Sonny. Still tied up, they bounced along the dirt roads that led them four hours later to an old cabin somewhere along the Mississippi River. A toothless old woman leered at them as Boss paid her to hire a flatboat. They haggled over the price, but there was a playfulness to it that made Matt think the two were old friends. Matt suspected that Boss and the old woman had done business to transport slaves many times before.

Sonny slapped the reins, and the horse drew the wagon down a pot-holed path to a small dock on the river. The sound of the rippling water normally would have brought Matt pleasure. Today, it filled him with fear. He knew that once they were away from shore, Jack would never be able to find him.

Hank gruffly pushed the three of them off of the wagon and guided them to a large, raftlike boat at the end of the dock. It was the flatboat, or "ark." Matt didn't have to guess about how it got its name. The flatboat had a shelter in the center for passengers or cargo. Matt considered jumping over the side, but he realized he wouldn't get very far (except to the bottom of the river) with his hands tied.

Hank shoved them into the cabin of the boat. "Get down there next to those crates," he barked. The three prisoners obliged, sitting down in what looked like a mixture of straw, dirt, and seeping river water.

Another man appeared—scowling and shriveled beneath a sailor's cap. He spat a wad of tobacco into the corner. "I'm captain of this vessel," he announced, "and I don't want to hear a word out of any of you. No shouting, no talking, no singing. Not a peep. Can't stand the sound of you." He spat again.

"But I have to go to the bathroom," Matt said.

The captain looked at him a moment as if he needed to translate the words. Then he frowned. "I don't care!" He stomped out and slammed the small door behind him.

The cabin had windows, but they were closed off by hinged boards. The air was sickly cold with a smell that reminded Matt of a backed-up sewer. He looked helplessly at Clarence and Eveline, wondering if they were as scared as he was. If they were, they didn't show it. Clarence leaned back against the crate and closed his eyes. Eveline simply drew her knees up under her chin and rocked back and forth.

Matt felt something nudge against his foot. He looked down in time to see a large, gray rat scamper by. He screamed.

They spent three days on the boat. Or was it four? Matt couldn't be certain. The boarded-up portholes of the cabin kept daylight to a minimum, and Matt couldn't tell anymore. A storm that turned the day into night threw his internal clock completely off.

They were a tiny vessel on a large river of mud and monstrous logs with tangled roots that stuck out like matted hair. Sometimes the flatboat would bump into the floating trees with a hard thump. Matt was certain that sooner or later, they'd hit something that would send them to the bottom.

Except when they were allowed out of the cabin for exercise and a meal of water, bread, or a suspicious-looking fish concoction, Matt's routine was to lie on the floor, kick at the rats, scratch at the fleas, and pray that somehow, some way, Jack or Mr. Whittaker would rescue him. A couple of times he tried to talk to Clarence and Eveline, but they shook their heads. "Those slave hunters'll whip you something awful," Clarence dared to whisper. "Just keep your mouth shut."

Once in a while he heard the splash and patter of a steamboat's paddlewheel. The captain almost always hailed somebody on the riverboat—maybe the captain or a crewman—who'd respond with a quick toot of a whistle. It gave Matt hope. *There are people out there*, he remembered. *Somebody will rescue me*.

One afternoon when they'd all gathered on deck to eat, a steamboat passed by. Matt stared at it openmouthed. It was like a long, trim palace on the water with two fanciful chimneys, a large, glass-encased pilothouse, and vast decks with people milling around happily behind white, ornate railings. The paddlewheels were enclosed in painted coverings that depicted a scene taken from the river itself: a wide expanse of water with a shoreline of thick forests and, in the center, a lonely, green island. Matt watched the people on deck and wished that one might look at him. He prayed that somehow he could let them know he wasn't a slave and didn't belong on this awful boat. It took every ounce of strength and willpower to keep from shouting at the top of his lungs for help. But he knew if he did that, Boss would do more than just backhand him.

Late that night, Matt was awakened by the frantic clamoring of a distant bell followed by a loud explosion. His heart pounded furiously as he heard people screaming. Something terrible had happened, he knew. The slave hunters stomped around the deck of the flatboat, shouting to each other. The captain commanded them to help him get the boat away. They must have succeeded, since the night drifted back to the river's normal sounds of water and frogs singing on the shore.

The next morning, Hank told them that a riverboat had collided with a massive collection of river debris—trees, roots, and mud—and blown up. When Matt reacted with shock, Hank laughed at him. "Guess you don't know much about riverboats, do you, boy? They blow up all the time."

The hours and minutes drifted by endlessly, like the river they rode upon. *Forever*, Matt thought as he slipped into despair again. *I'll be trapped here forever.* He thought of his parents and brother and sister who must be worried about him. Maybe they had even called the police by now. Would they think to look in Whit's workroom? Did the machine have some way of letting Whit know that two boys had gone inside and turned it on? Matt turned these questions over and over in his mind. But he didn't know the answers.

Early one morning, Clarence sat up and muttered, "Must be Columbus."

Matt also sat up, wondering why Clarence mentioned the explorer's name until he heard the noise. Actually, it was a mixture of noises: horses' hooves on stone, rolling wagon wheels, shouts of hellos, barks of commands, a clanging bell, splashing water, wood banging upon wood —it was the noise of activity. Matt crawled expectantly onto his knees as the captain brought the boat to a halt by thumping it against a landing dock. Sonny threw open the cabin door and told the three prisoners to come out on deck.

"Columbus, Kentucky," the captain called out, as if it were his duty to announce to the people on board where they were.

"We know, you old fool," Boss replied. "Now drop us off and be on your way." He sounded harsh, but then he clasped the captain's hand affectionately in his and thanked him for the service.

Matt glanced around. The town sat on a flat and marshy stretch of land circled by sickly-looking trees. Half-houses were built along the dock area next to square buildings with shops. The streets bustled with merchants, customers, and travelers. Clerks sat in wooden chairs, tilted back against the wall, snoozing under their hats until a customer brought them awake. Pigs made feasts of watermelon rinds near the porches. Freight piles and skids littered the crumbling, stone wharf.

Again, Boss had made arrangements for another wagon and two horses to be brought to the boat. The three prisoners were put straight onto the wagon and, with a loud "Yah!" from Hank, taken away. No one around the busy dock seemed to notice that a man and two kids were tied up like animals. Sadly, Matt noticed that other blacks were doing the majority of work, lugging freight on and off the boats in chains, wearing rags.

Don't fret. You'll get used to it. That's what Eveline had said. Matt clenched his teeth and fought the resignation that wanted to lay claim to his heart. This nightmare would end, he knew. Somehow it would end.

THE OLD WAGON RATTLED along the rutted roads across the south-western tip of Kentucky, with its low plains and thick forests of oak and hickory. Their travel in the wagon was painfully slow compared to the speed of the cars Matt was used to. He began to wish that they'd just hurry up and get to where they were going—*anything* had to be better than the tediousness of the journey itself.

As they drove deeper into slave territory, Boss, Hank, and Sonny seemed to relax. They joked more often with each other and even made an effort to make Matt, Clarence, and Eveline more comfortable by throwing fresh hay in the back of the wagon. The food didn't improve—Hank was a lousy cook—and Matt was never really sure of what they were eating. Mostly stew, he figured, with contents he couldn't identify.

No matter how friendly things seemed, however, the ropes stayed securely bound on their wrists and ankles, and one of the slave hunters was always nearby to make sure they didn't escape. Matt couldn't forget the casual way Boss had backhanded him. He was black and, for that reason alone, was a slave. He was a piece of cargo that they were taking somewhere to sell like an animal. If they had to beat him to keep him in line, so be it. Fortunately, Matt was careful not to give them any reason to hit him again. But that didn't erase the painful memory—the burning shame—of being struck at all.

They cut across the black-bottomed land of western Tennessee, over gentle slopes, along river swamps, and through endless woods of trees shorn of their red and yellow leaves. They glided past the fertile fields that, in their time, yielded lilies, orchids, wild rice, tobacco, corn, and the all-powerful cotton. They reached a town called Paris—"Named after Paris, France," Hank offered—where they got caught in a traffic jam of cows and pigs being brought in to market. Matt hoped that this was the end of their trip. It wasn't. After giving the horses a rest and picking up supplies, they continued southeast to Danville, where they crossed the Tennessee River.

From the river, the land gave way to rolling bluegrass country and rich plateaus. Oaks and cedars rose high, their barely clothed limbs stretching up to the blue sky. Somewhere along the road, they stopped for the night and Sonny announced that it was his intention one day to marry a girl from this part of Tennessee. "If I ever settle down, I'm settling right here," he said. "I'm gonna get me some Tennessee land and raise some Tennessee horses and cure some Tennessee ham with Tennessee hickory and—"

"What in tarnation are you talking about?" Boss growled. "You're from Baltimore!"

Sonny shook his head mournfully. "I know it. But I should've been born in Tennessee."

The next day they reached the Natchez Trace, where Hank felt duty-bound to inform his "ignorant passengers" about its importance. "It's one of the first roads ever done by the government. Goes all the way from Natchez, Mississippi, to Nashville, Tennessee. I saw a gunfight in Natchez once."

"Nobody cares," Boss said sleepily from under his hat.

Hank glanced around at their expressions and realized it was probably true. He settled back into a sulky silence.

One Sunday morning, nearly 12 days after they had left Odyssey, the hills of northern Alabama yielded to a valley where Huntsville sat waiting under the early sun. Matt noticed that Clarence began to get edgy, his eyes growing wide and dangerously wild as they got nearer to their destination. Eveline nestled closer to her father.

"What's wrong?" Matt whispered.

Clarence simply stared straight ahead and ignored the question.

"Eveline," Matt whispered again.

She slipped from her father's arms and leaned over to Matt. "No telling what Master Ramsay will do to us for running away."

Matt felt like a fool for not realizing it sooner.

Hank laughed from the buckboard seat at the front of the wagon. "Well, now, I guess this is your Judgment Day—eh, Clarence?"

Boss, who had been on a horse ahead, whistled for Sonny to pick up their speed and follow him. Still north of town, they suddenly turned left onto a smaller road. A canopy of tree branches formed a natural tunnel that led to a large, white, two-storied mansion with pillars along the front, tall windows, and large balconies. Matt was reminded of a famous old film called *Gone with the Wind*.

They drove around to the right of the house and followed a smaller path that took them into a compound of stables, workhouses, shacks, and, farther beyond toward the fields, a cluster of log houses.

"That's where we live," Eveline said, with a catch in her throat.

Boss dismounted and walked up to the back door of the mansion. He shuffled from foot to foot as he rang the bell and waited. After a minute, the door opened, and a black servant appeared. Matt couldn't hear what Boss said to him, but the servant suddenly looked at the wagon, put his hand to his mouth with surprise, then disappeared into the house. Boss strolled back to the wagon.

"Well?" Sonny asked, crawling down from the buckboard seat and rubbing his rear. Hank did likewise.

"He's coming," Boss replied.

The door slammed, and Matt looked up in time to see a short man with a chiseled, white face and billowing housecoat race down the walkway.

"Boss! What're you doing here at this ungodly hour on a Sunday morning? Don't you know that—" He stopped himself when he saw Clarence and Eveline in the back of the wagon. "Good heavens, look at that!"

"I thought you'd be wanting your property back, Mr. Ramsay," Boss said.

Ramsay glared at Clarence and Eveline. "As a matter of interest, no. I *don't* want my property back. And it's taking every ounce of strength to keep from grabbing a horsewhip and driving these two troublemakers into the next county!"

Clarence refused to look at Ramsay in the eyes. Eveline kept her gaze locked on her hands, which were neatly folded in her lap. Matt felt like throwing up.

"Wait, now, Mr. Ramsay," Sonny gulped. "You say you don't want them back? But you put out a reward! You said you—"

"Oh, don't start sniveling. That doesn't mean you won't get money for them. Come into the kitchen, Boss. I have a proposition for you."

Boss followed Ramsay back up to the door, and the two of them went inside.

"This better not be some kind of trick," Hank snarled. He pointed a finger at Clarence. "If we don't get what's coming to us, I swear I'll skin you alive."

Fifteen minutes later Boss returned to the wagon. Sonny and Hank watched him expectantly as he ran his fingers through his greasy hair, then put his hat on. "He doesn't want them. He said they're too much trouble, trying to run away every chance they get. It's bad for the other slaves. Doesn't even want the boy."

Matt wasn't sure whether to feel relieved or insulted.

"So what's he want to do with them?" Hank asked.

"He's selling them to us."

"Us!" Sonny complained. "We don't have that kind of money."

"No—but we might in Huntsville. He wants us to sell them, and in return we'll give him part of what we make. I think it's a fair deal. We stand to make more from that than we would've just with the reward money."

"I'm not sure I like it," Hank said. "But I reckon we don't have much of a choice."

Sonny scratched his nose thoughtfully and said, "It suits me."

Boss came alongside the wagon and peered in at his three packages. "Did you get all that?"

Clarence and Eveline nodded. Matt looked perplexed. "I don't understand. What're you going to do with us?"

"I'm selling you, boy," Boss said earnestly. "Tomorrow you're gonna be on the auction block."

CHAPTER
FIFTEEN

SUNDAY WAS A SLAVE'S day off for rest or to go to church or to visit nearby relatives. Since Clarence and Eveline were runaways, the over-seer—a man named Watson who was in charge of the slaves—locked them up in an empty storeroom. Matt wasn't considered a threat and Watson waved his hand at him in dismissal.

"But I have to talk to you," Matt said.

"You can go on," Watson scowled as he locked the door on Clarence and Eveline. "Go play or something."

"But I don't want to go play. I need to talk to somebody in charge. There's been a big mistake!"

Watson pushed him away. "You wanna talk to Mr. Ramsay? Forget it. Consider yourself fortunate that we're letting you stay here until the auction. It's not as if you belong to us."

"That's what I mean!" Matt persisted. "I don't belong to *anybody*. I don't belong here. I'm free."

"Leave me alone," Watson snapped and walked away.

Matt followed him. "Boss picked me up without having a right to. Don't you have laws against that? Somebody's going to be in big trouble. Understand? I'm *free!*"

"Shut up, boy," Watson said. "I don't want to know."

"But you *do* know."

They rounded the corner of a stable and nearly ran straight into Boss. He was brushing down his horse.

"What's wrong, Watson?" he asked casually.

"This boy says he's free, but you're selling him anyway," Watson replied.

"I am and you know it!" Matt said.

"Shut up," Boss said to Matt.

Watson looked at Boss uneasily. "We don't want anything illegal going on here, Boss. Mr. Ramsay won't like it."

"There's nothing illegal about you putting up *my* slave for the night—as a favor."

"I'm not your slave!" Matt said.

Boss grabbed Matt by the shirt and yanked him so close to his face that he could smell yesterday's potatoes on his breath. He spoke softly, "You won't be *anybody's* slave if you don't close your mouth. That back-hand I once gave you is nothing compared to what I'm willing to do." He thrust Matt away so hard that Matt fell and hit his head on a post.

"Do you have papers for him?" Watson asked.

Boss smiled. "I might have them around here somewhere. But you don't have to see them."

"Mr. Ramsay might ask."

"Only if someone gives him a reason to ask. I won't and this boy won't—how about you?"

"Depends on what it's worth," Watson said.

Boss nodded, went to his saddle, and pulled out a bag of coins. He fished around until he found an appropriate number and tossed them to Watson. "That should help to keep things quiet."

Watson considered the money. "I reckon it will."

Boss threw him another coin. "This is to help make sure the boy keeps quiet, too."

"Easily done," Watson said. He walked over to Matt, who was standing up. He put his hand on the leather hand of the whip attached to his belt. "Come on, boy."

Matt looked at Boss's face, then Watson's, and realized what was going to happen. "No!" he said and tried to run in the opposite direction.

Watson was too quick for him and had him by the collar instantly. Matt shouted. Watson gave him a hard thump on the back of the head with the end of his leather whip handle. Stunned, Matt began to cry. "No, no, no," he said over and over.

Watson dragged Matt back to the empty storehouse where Clarence and Eveline were held prisoners. He opened the door and shoved Matt inside. "Keep this boy quiet or the three of you won't live to regret it," he said to Clarence. He closed the door again and locked it.

Splinters of light came through the uneven boards on top of the shack. Matt lay on the ground and continued to cry. All his pent-up emotion had been unleashed and wouldn't be stopped. Eveline leaned down and held him close. "It's all right," she said gently.

Clarence also knelt down next to him and stroked his back. "Go ahead, Matthew. You go ahead and cry. Cry for all of us."

CHAPTER SIXTEEN

JACK SAT IN THE STEAM train's passenger car at the Corinth railway station and stared at the Western Union Telegraph office across the platform. He fidgeted anxiously in the brown cloth seat. What was taking Reverend Andrew so long? he wondered.

It was yet another delay in what seemed like a trip of endless delays. First, they couldn't leave Odyssey until Reverend Andrew found someone to take his pulpit and pastoral responsibilities for a couple of weeks. That raised questions about *why* he was leaving and though Andrew answered discreetly, word got back to the sheriff who warned him not to try any of his "abolitionist" stunts. Jack remembered well how the sheriff had squinted an eye and said, "I promise you, Reverend, that if you intentionally bring any runaways back to this town, there'll be more trouble than either one of us'll know how to handle."

The reverend politely thanked him for the warning.

Later that day Jack and the reverend rode down to a wharf on the Mississippi and caught a riverboat headed south. Andrew insisted that he and Jack stay in their stateroom for the journey, since Jack's "obvious unfamiliarity with the ways of the riverboat" (he said) would make him stand out in a crowd. Jack suspected that there were things on the riverboat that Andrew didn't approve of. The heavily made-up, perfumed women and the card games were probably two of those things, Jack guessed.

They made good time on the river until, just south of Cairo, Illinois, they came upon a boat that had hit some river debris and blown up. For that, they were delayed a day getting to Columbus, Kentucky.

At Columbus they took a train deeper into the South. Jack was surprised by the overall sootiness and dinginess of the steam train. The passenger cars were plain and boxlike with seats barely covered in thin fabric for marginal comfort. Jack had complained to Reverend Andrew about it. The reverend then informed him that some of the cars—particularly the ones the blacks were allowed to ride in—had hard wooden seats. "Be grateful for what you have," he said.

Travel on the train was anything but smooth. There was a great deal of jolting and rocking, noise, and grating screeches. At night, the sparks from the engine flew past the dirty window like wild fireflies. Jack worried that the sparks might land on the wooden cars and turn to flames.

"You don't have to worry about that," Andrew said as he hooked a thumb toward the stove in the middle of the car. "That'll start a fire long before the sparks will."

Jack wasn't comforted and didn't sleep much.

According to his plan, Andrew reminded Jack not to call him "Reverend" anymore. Now he was simply Andrew Jamison or, to Jack, *Uncle* Andrew. He had given up his role as a minister and was now an ornithologist—a man who studied birds.

"Isn't that lying?" Jack had asked.

Andrew had smiled and said, "Not at all. Studying birds has been a hobby of mine for years. That I choose to omit the fact that I'm a Northern minister who abhors slavery is no one's business but mine. We'll get onto the plantations to spread the word among the Alabama slaves about the Underground Railroad. Meanwhile, we'll look for your friend in Huntsville."

The plan seemed terribly simple to Jack. What if Matt wasn't in Huntsville? What if they took him somewhere else? What if they hurt him along the way?

They stopped at the station in Corinth, Mississippi, where they would then catch another train heading east to Huntsville. That's the train Jack was now sitting in. He squirmed in his seat and tugged at the collar of the shirt Andrew had bought for him. It was stiff and uncomfortable. The new, wool trousers also made his legs itch. And the shoes pinched his toes.

Andrew emerged from the telegraph office and leaped onto the train. He sat down across from Jack. "Well, that's done."

"What did you do, Rev—er, *Uncle* Andrew?" Jack asked.

"I telegraphed ahead to a friend of mine in Huntsville. He'll help us when we arrive." He smiled and rubbed his hands together. "I'm quite pleased, Jack. If my estimations are correct, those slave hunters will only just be arriving with Clarence, Eveline, and your friend. I believe this excursion will yield much fruit for their freedom—and the freedom of others."

"Just so we find Matt," Jack said.

"Don't worry, lad. God is with us. What could go wrong?"

A man in a blue uniform and matching cap opened the door and poked his head into the train. "Sorry, gentlemen, but this train'll be delayed a few hours."

"What!" Jack responded.

Andrew put a restraining hand on his knee. "What is the problem?" he asked the man.

The man scratched impatiently at his ear. "Train went off the track just outside of Decatur. Awfully messy. Since it's the Sabbath, they can't rally the men they need to get it cleared until morning. Corinth's a nice little place. I'm sure you'll find lodgings."

"But what about Matt?" Jack asked.

CHAPTER
SEVENTEEN

On Monday morning, Boss took Matt, Clarence, and Eveline to Huntsville. They had been given fresh clothes to wear, for reasons Matt learned later. After a half hour's drive they made their way past the homes and businesses on the outskirts of town to a cluster of rough, wooden buildings. Several saddle horses were either tied or held by servants as their owners assembled around a building in the rear.

"This is the slave market," Clarence told Matt. While Boss spoke to a bearded man off to the side, Sonny pulled them off the back of the wagon and led them to a dozen other slaves standing along a wide gate. As they walked, Clarence took Matt's hand in one of his own. He held Eveline's in the other. Matt's heart beat so fast that he thought it might explode.

"Listen to me, son," Clarence whispered. "You've got to learn to keep your mouth shut or you'll get sold to the worst possible master. You hear? Because none of the nicer masters will want a black who is too big for his britches. Keep your eyes down—never look 'em full in the face—and just say yes, sir and no, sir."

"I'm afraid," Matt said.

"We all are," Clarence said.

Matt glanced around at the other slaves. They were men, women, and children of all sizes. Some clung to each other with tight fists and eyes wide and unblinking. They weren't dressed in the raggy work clothes that Matt expected, but had on clothes given to them for the auction. The men had on black fur hats and coarse corduroy trousers with nice vests and white cotton shirts. The women wore peasant dresses with scarves on their necks or over their heads. Clarence called them "market clothes"—which the slaves would be stripped of as soon as they were sold. That's why the three of them had been "dressed up": to make a good impression and bring a higher price.

On a signal, the slaves entered through the gate into a narrow courtyard, where they were ranged in a semicircle for the white buyers to get a good look at them.

A woman fell to her knees and wept loudly, only to get a swift kick from the bearded man who was obviously in charge of the day's business. He turned to the white buyers as if nothing had happened. "Good morning, gentlemen! Would you like to examine this fine lot? It's as fine as ever came into a market!"

"This can't be happening," Matt said to himself.

The buyers moved down the line of blacks, looking them over from head to foot and checking their teeth and muscles as if they were horses or cattle. The slaves stood perfectly still.

A man with a goatee stepped up to Clarence, looked him over, and passed his gaze down to Eveline and then Matt. "Is this a family?" he asked.

The bearded man nodded. "They are. For what service in particular did you want to buy?"

"I need a coachman," he replied.

"I have an excellent coachman right here," the bearded man said, stepping past Clarence to another slave. "He's strong and good-looking. A nice adornment to sit atop your coach."

The goateed man leaned forward to look at the slave. "What's your name?"

"George, sir."

"Step forward, George," the goateed man said. George obliged him. "How old are you?"

"I don't recollect," George replied. "I'm somewhere around 23."

"Where were you raised?"

"On Master Warner's farm in Virginny."

The man stroked his goatee. "Then you're a Virginia Negro."

"Yes, Master, I'm a full-blooded Virginny."

"Did you drive your master's carriage?" he asked.

The slave nodded enthusiastically. "Yes, sir. I drove my master's and my missus' carriage for more than four years."

"Have you got a wife?"

"I had one in Richmond and wish you would buy her, Master, if you're going to buy me."

The goateed man grunted indifferently then issued a series of orders like "Let me see your teeth and tongue. Open your hands. Roll up your sleeves. Have you got a good appetite? Are you good tempered? Do you get sick very much?" He seemed satisfied by George's answers and finally said to the slave trader, "What are you asking for him?"

"He's worth a thousand dollars, but I will take $975."

The goateed man talked him down to $950.

Just as the deal was concluded, another man named Mason stepped forward and thumped Clarence in the chest. "He's a sound one," Mason said. "I'll take him."

The slave trader smiled and said, "Oh, he's a good one, all right. A hard worker and—"

Mason turned on the slave trader with a cold look. "Don't butter me up. I know this slave belonged to Mr. Ramsay and is notorious for running away. But I'll get that notion out of his head. I'll give you $850."

The bearded slave trader looked over at Boss, who'd been standing quietly by the courtyard fence. Boss nodded. "Sold!" the slave trader announced happily.

"Come along, boy," Mason said.

Clarence hesitated.

The slavetrader grabbed Clarence by the collar and pushed him along. "You heard him. Go."

But Clarence couldn't go very far, because Eveline and Matt held firmly to his hands.

"What's this?" Mason asked angrily.

The slave trader punched out at Eveline and Matt to let go. He caught Matt in the side and knocked the wind out of him. Matt slumped to the ground.

"No, no!" Eveline cried out.

"Don't lose your head," Clarence told her. "You know how to behave."

Eveline stubbornly held on to her father's hand. "Please!" she cried.

The slave trader struck out at her with both fists, sending her to the ground. Clarence spun around with wild eyes. A whip cracked the morning sky like a gunshot, and all Matt could see was the expression of agonizing pain on Clarence's face.

"You're coming with me, boy," Mason shouted as he prepared his whip for another strike. Clarence leaned down to his daughter and said only "Behave" before he stumbled after Mason.

"Lord Jesus, help me!" Eveline cried. Matt, still winded, crawled over to her and put his arms around her.

The slave trader stepped forward, his teeth grinding with anger. "You young ones need a lesson, I think." He started to kick at them with his pointy-toed boot. Matt threw himself between the trader and Eveline to take most of the blows.

"Stop it! Stop it right now!" someone shouted.

The kicking suddenly stopped as the slave trader backed away. "Yes, Colonel," he said obediently.

Colonel Alexander Ross knelt down next to Matt and Eveline. "Can you sit up?" he asked gently.

Matt nodded and, with aching ribs, sat up. Eveline wiped away her tears and did the same.

"What a brave boy you must be," Colonel Ross said to Matt. Then he gestured to the slave trader and said, "I want them."

Matt looked away to keep him from seeing the tears gathering in his eyes.

"For what service, Colonel?" the slave trader asked.

"House servants," he answered. "What's their price?"

"Normally, I would ask—"

"I'll give you $500 for the two of them."

Once again the slave trader looked at Boss. Boss slowly nodded. "Five hundred it is, Colonel."

The colonel helped them both to their feet. "Come on, children. You're coming home with me," he said with a smile.

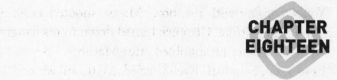

JACK AND ANDREW ARRIVED in Huntsville close to noon. At the Liberty Hotel, a telegram was waiting for Andrew. He opened the envelope, read the message, and then leaned against the counter with a grimace.

"What's wrong?" Jack asked.

"My friend investigated Mr. Ramsay's stock of slaves and learned through the overseer that Clarence, Eveline, and Matthew were taken to the slave market." He folded the telegram and shoved it into his coat pocket. "That's a setback. I wouldn't have expected Ramsay to dispose of them so quickly."

"What do we do? We have to find them!" Jack said, his worst fear becoming a reality.

Andrew nodded and turned to inquire casually if the clerk knew of any slave markets taking place that day.

"I'm not entirely certain," the clerk replied. He then held up his hand and turned to a black porter nearby. "How about it, Sam? Do you know of any markets going on today?"

Sam took off his glove. "Well, sir, Monday is usually a good day for buying. But I heard of only one market and that was this morning."

"Are you sure?" Andrew asked.

"Yes, sir," Sam answered. "My cousin Ishom was to be sold there."

"Take us," Andrew said.

Sam looked to the clerk for permission. The clerk shrugged and said, "At the usual rate."

On the street, Sam flagged them a carriage, climbing up next to the driver while Jack and Andrew got into the back. They made their way through the city streets at a speed that Jack thought might drive him crazy. He kept looking out the window just in case he could spot Matt in the business-day crowds. At one junction he did see something that caught his eye.

"Look!" he shouted to Andrew.

Andrew leaned over. "What?"

"That wagon. Aren't those the slave hunters from Odyssey?"

As Andrew got into a better position to look, the wagon turned out of sight. "Missed it," he said.

Jack wiped the sweat from his brow. "It was them. I swear it was."

"Then perhaps we're closer than we could've hoped."

The carriage weaved through the traffic to a less-crowded area of town. The driver pulled up to a cluster of brown buildings that Jack would've called shacks.

"This is the place," Sam said, leaning down from the driver's seat. "That courtyard yonder."

Jack and Andrew climbed down from the carriage. Jack nearly ran to the wide gate, but Andrew put a firm hand on his shoulder. "Not so fast. You can't look too interested," he whispered.

They walked to the gate, opened it on creaky hinges, and stepped into the empty yard. On the opposite end, a bearded man spied them and waved. "Hello!" he called and crossed over to them.

"Greetings," Andrew said. "Is this the slave market?"

"One of them," the man said. "The only one today."

Andrew smiled. "I see. What time may we have the pleasure of seeing your . . . your slaves?"

"Nine o'clock this morning," the man replied.

"We missed it?" Jack asked anxiously.

The man looked at Jack as if surprised that he would speak. "Yes, you did."

"Did you have a man with a boy and girl about my age?" Jack asked quickly.

The question raised the man's eyebrows. "We have a lot of men, boys, and girls. Women, too. What's your interest?" The man's tone was suspicious.

Andrew cleared his throat. "We had heard of three particularly valuable slaves from Mr. Ramsay's plantation. We're sorry we missed the opportunity to buy them, that's all."

The man eyed them carefully. "Well, they were here—and they've been sold."

"Sold!" Jack shouted.

"Oh, dear. And we've come all this way," Andrew said with mock unhappiness. "May we ask to whom they were sold?"

"I don't remember," the man said, but he gestured so subtly that Jack almost missed it. He rubbed his fingers together.

Andrew sniffed casually, reached into his waistcoat pocket, and retrieved a couple of coins. He handed them to the bearded man.

Back at the hotel, Jack and Andrew entered their room. No sooner was the door closed than Andrew grabbed Jack by the arm.

"Hey!" Jack reacted, alarmed.

"Listen to me, young man," Andrew said sharply. "Our lives—and the lives of many others—are dependent on being as unassuming as possible. We cannot draw attention to ourselves. No one must ever suspect that we're up to anything unusual or everything we hope to accomplish will be completely destroyed. For that reason, you must *keep your mouth shut* and *do only what I tell you to do*. Do you understand?"

Jack nodded his head. "Yes, Uncle Andrew."

"Good," Andrew said and let him go. "We'll have to pray that the slave trader doesn't run back to his customers and tell them about our questions."

"But you paid him!"

Andrew unbuttoned his shirt and toyed with a necklace just beneath. "I paid him for some *answers*. I'm not so optimistic that it will also keep him from talking."

Jack dropped himself into a particularly uncomfortable chair. "This is a disaster. They've been sold. And not just sold—they've been sold to two separate people! How are we supposed to rescue them now?"

Andrew tugged at the necklace, and Jack now saw that it held a small silver cross. "By faith, Jack. We'll rescue them by faith."

Andrew turned away from Jack and poured water from a pitcher into a bowl. He began to wash his face and neck. Jack dropped his chin onto his fist and, as he did, suddenly felt a strange tickling sensation go through his stomach. *Butterflies*, he thought. *I'm feeling nervous about Matt.*

But the butterflies flew on and Jack felt that weird surge through his body as if he were on a roller-coaster ride. He tried to stand up but couldn't. Alarmed, he called out to Reverend Andrew, who suddenly spun away from him—along with the room and the light—into darkness.

"What's going on here?" a deep, warm voice echoed in the darkness.

At that same moment, Matt was on the back of a wagon trying to comfort Eveline. She hadn't stopped crying since they had left the slave auction and drove away toward the colonel's plantation.

"They took my daddy, they took my daddy," she wept again and again.

His sides still hurting, Matt winced as he leaned close to her. "Don't worry. We'll find him."

"How?" Eveline sniffed.

"I don't know," Matt said. "But we will. I promise."

She put her head against his arm. "Promise?"

"Yeah," Matt replied and leaned his head against the coarse siding on the wagon. He closed his eyes wearily. His stomach lurched as if the wagon had suddenly slipped into a dip in the road. And that's when he heard the voice.

"What's going on here?" it asked.

It was so present that Matt thought someone had whispered in his ear. He opened his eyes while his stomach continued to do flips. Of course, he expected to see Eveline and the back of the wagon they'd been riding on. Instead, he found himself looking at a flashing red light.

CHAPTER NINETEEN

"WELL?" THE VOICE asked again.

"Who's there? Where are you?" Jack asked, still not able to see anyone. He was aware that his right arm felt prickly, as if it had fallen asleep. He pushed out with it and hit someone.

"Ouch. Cut it out."

Jack turned a little, and in the glow of a flashing red light he saw the outline of a face. "Matt?"

"Yeah, it's me," Matt answered. "I'm waiting for my stomach to settle down."

"Me, too. And I'm *really* confused," Jack said.

"So am I. How did we get here?"

"I don't know. I'm not sure where *here* is. Did you hear that voice?" Jack asked.

"Uh huh. Are we home?"

The voice bounced around them again. "Jack? Matt? Are you in there?"

"It's Mr. Whittaker," Jack said, elated. "We're here!"

With a *whoosh*, the door to the Imagination Station slid open. Light assaulted Jack and Matt so that they winced and had to lean back and cover their eyes.

Whit stood with his hands on his hips and a disapproving look on his normally friendly face. "Come out of there. I want to know what the two of you are doing in my machine without permission. Don't you realize how dangerous it is—messing around with something you don't understand? What if it locked you in and I didn't come back down as soon as I did?"

Jack sheepishly crawled out, explaining as he did, "We didn't know what it was. See, we were playing behind Whit's End and found the tunnel, and it led to here and we saw the machine and . . ." Jack's voice trailed off as he realized Whit was looking beyond him.

"Matt?" Whit called out.

Jack turned around to see that Matt was still inside the Imagination Station. "Come on, Matt," Jack insisted.

"No," Matt said in a small voice. "I can't."

Whit cocked one of his bushy white eyebrows. "You can't?"

"No, sir."

"Why not?"

"Because I promised," Matt said with a sniffle from the shadow of the machine.

Jack was surprised to realize that Matt had a choked crying sound in his voice.

"*What* did you promise?" Whit asked.

"I promised Eveline that I would help her find her father."

"Eveline?"

"The slave girl," Jack explained. "She and Clarence were captured by the slave hunters and taken to Alabama. They took Matt, too. Reverend Andrew and I followed them."

Matt continued from inside the machine, "They sold Clarence to another plantation, then they sold me and Eveline to some colonel. She was crying, Mr. Whittaker, and I promised. Please don't make me leave them there."

Whit stroked his mustache for a moment, then strolled over to his workbench. "That's not how the story went," he said as he picked up one of the books lying there.

"Story?" Jack asked.

"I've been programming the Imagination Station to play out different kinds of stories—from the Bible and from history." He flipped a few pages in the book, then turned to Jack. "I had set the Imagination Station in its program mode to input all kinds of information, including Clarence's and Eveline's story. They had been caught by the slave hunters here at Whit's End and taken south—"

"Just like we said!"

"Yes, but they weren't sold to separate slave owners in the original story. They were both sold to Colonel Alexander Ross. Later, Reverend Andrew showed up posing as an ornithologist—"

"Yeah! I was with Reverend Andrew!" Jack said excitedly. "I was his assistant!"

Whit shook his head. "It's very strange. You must have come in right after I went upstairs. I've only been gone for 15 minutes."

"Fifteen minutes!" Jack cried out. "We've been in there for almost two weeks!"

Whit scrubbed his chin. "The adventures work at an accelerated pace."

Jack couldn't believe it. "Wow," was all he could figure to say.

Whit continued, "But what doesn't make sense to me is why the story has changed." He fell silent for a moment, then suddenly snapped his fingers. "You two must have gotten into the Imagination Station while it was in the *middle* of inputting the program! Your interference changed the story."

Jack felt like Whit was blaming them for something, but he didn't understand enough of what he just said to know for sure.

"You mean we messed it up?" Matt asked.

Whit leaned against the door to the Imagination Station and peered in at Matt. "It looks that way."

That's what happens when you do things you're not supposed to do.

Though Whit didn't say those actual words, Jack and Matt both felt the sting as if he had.

Matt got that choked sound in his voice again. "But what's it mean? Are Clarence and Eveline in trouble because of us?"

Whit shrugged. "By getting into the machine when you did, you changed the program—and must have changed the story."

"Then we have to go back and fix it," Matt said urgently.

"It's only a story, Matt," Whit said.

"No, it isn't! It was real! *They* were real. You have to let me go back. I promised I'd help!" Matt's voice was high-pitched and panicked.

Whit gazed at Matt warmly, his eyes soft with understanding. "You're taking this pretty seriously."

"I promised," Matt said quietly.

Whit turned to Jack. "You, too?"

Jack nibbled on his lower lip, then nodded. "Yeah. Reverend Andrew was counting on me to help," he said with more confidence than he felt.

"Reverend Andrew's mission—and what happened to Clarence and Eveline—took a lot of courage. It won't be easy," Whit told them.

"It wasn't easy before," Matt said.

Whit glanced at his watch as if to confirm that they still had time enough to do it. He then waved his hand for Jack to get back into the machine. "Go on. But I'll be watching you closely this time. And when you're finished, we're going to have a talk about you sneaking in here in the first place."

Jack settled into the seat next to Matt again. Matt turned his face away, embarrassed that he had become so emotional.

"Just push the red button when you're ready," Whit said as the door closed.

"We have to be out of our minds to go back," Jack said in the darkness.

"Yeah. We probably are," Matt agreed.

Then Matt reached forward and pushed down on the flashing red button.

(To be continued)

FREEDOM RUN

INTRODUCTION

As part of the boys' "punishment" for getting into my workroom (and the Imagination Station) without permission, I made them write down the rest of their adventure. I polished it up a little, fixed the spelling, and edited it so readers can follow who is telling what part of the story where and . . . well, you'll see.

They wanted to call it *Jack's and Matt's Big Adventure*, but they got in a loud argument over whose name should go first. So I suggested we call it *Freedom Run* as a follow-up to *Dark Passage*. I'll stop taking up your time now and let the boys tell their own stories.

—John Avery Whittaker

CHAPTER ONE

Matt tells about the plantation.

I SCOOTED OVER IN the seat as Jack squeezed next to me in the Imagination Station. He didn't say anything. I was glad. Nothing a guy hates worse than to have his best friend make a fuss about the fact that he was crying. I turned away and rubbed my eyes. I hoped my nose wouldn't run. It always runs when I cry, and I didn't have a tissue.

It was kind of dumb to get so upset, I know. But I felt bad about promising to help Eveline find her father and then—*zing*—all of a sudden being yanked out of the slave wagon and brought back to my time. Don't get me wrong; I was happy to be home. I didn't think we'd *ever* get back. I hated being a black kid in a world where everyone thought blacks were good only for being slaves. I hated being treated worse than an animal. I wanted to get back to *my* Odyssey, where people treated me like . . . well, *me*.

But poor Eveline was stuck back there on that wagon without her father, and it was *my* fault in a way. If Jack and I hadn't gotten into the Imagination Station in the first place, things would've turned out the way they were supposed to. I mean, what could I do except go back and try to fix everything? What would *you* do?

"Just push the red button when you're ready," Mr. Whittaker said as the door to the Imagination Station *whooshed* shut. The lights on the panel blinked at us like a Christmas tree.

"We have to be out of our minds to go back," Jack said.

"Yeah, we probably are," I answered.

Jack reached over and pushed down on the flashing red button.

The machine hummed louder and louder until it felt like it had suddenly jumped forward. I had the same feeling in the pit of my stomach that I get on a roller-coaster ride. Or in the car when my dad hits a dip in the road too fast. It turned my stomach upside down and sucked the breath out of me. Everything went dark. For a minute, I wasn't sure where I was. Then I smelled old straw and heard the clip-clop of horses' hooves and the slow creaking of a wooden wagon. I guessed that somehow the Imagination Station had put me right back where I was before. Only now I was half-buried in a pile of straw. I sat up and my body ached all over. I forgot about being knocked around by Mr. Ramsay's overseer and kicked by the man at the slave auction.

"Are you all right?" Eveline asked. The tears were still in her eyes, but now they were wide like she'd just seen a ghost.

"I'm all right," I said. I had no idea what had happened—if I suddenly disappeared right in front of her when the Imagination Station took me back to my time, or if I just reappeared, or what. "Why?"

She watched me carefully. "You rolled under the hay all of a sudden. Were you afraid of something?"

"I . . . I . . ." I couldn't think of an answer that would make sense. "Never mind."

"You were crying, weren't you?" Eveline said softly.

Oh, brother, I thought.

"You two better shut your traps!" the wagon driver growled. He was a heavyset man named Master Kinsey. He was the overseer, the man in charge of the slaves, at Colonel Ross's plantation. "A few days in the field will take the spunk out of you," he threatened.

I believed him. But Colonel Ross was the owner of the plantation, and he had other ideas.

My mother once made me watch a movie called *Gone with the Wind.* I didn't like it much, because it was long and boring and all about a woman who didn't care who she hurt as long as she got what she wanted. There was a big fire in it, which I thought was okay, but other than that, the adults can have it. Anyway, Colonel Ross lived in a house like the one in the movie. It was real big, with large windows and giant pillars along the front. Master Kinsey pulled the wagon around the back where the sheds and barns were. Beyond them was a "compound" of shacks where the slaves lived. And beyond that was a field that went way out to the horizon.

The place was so pretty that I was beginning to think that it might not be so bad there after all. Then I remembered that I wasn't here as a visitor; I was a *slave.* How could I ever forget it?

A wiry man in a dark butler-type suit hustled down the stairs from the back door and raced to the wagon. He was out of breath with excitement. "Saints be blessed, they're here," he said.

I looked around to see who he was talking about and was surprised to realize that it was me and Eveline.

"You can just forget about it, Jonah," Master Kinsey said. "I'm putting them in the fields."

Jonah waved his arms around nervously. "No, sir, Master Kinsey. Colonel Ross said they're for the house. You can ask him yourself; they're for the house."

Master Kinsey punched the seat of the wagon. "You can be sure I will, you old liar." He leapt from the wagon and marched into the house.

"I'm Jonah," he said to me and Eveline. "Now, come down from the wagon, young'uns. Let me have a look at you." We jumped down and the jolt made my ribs hurt all over again. He circled us to get a good look. "I think little Nell's old clothes'll fit you," he said to Eveline. Then he eyed me up and down. "Nate's will do for you."

"Won't Nate mind me taking his clothes?" I asked.

"He might mind if he were here and still wanting to wear them," Jonah said.

"Where is he?" I asked.

"Got shot trying to run away."

The back door slammed and Master Kinsey stomped down the stairs, muttering the whole way. "He spoils these slaves, I tell you! You don't break them in and you have nothing but trouble from them." He climbed back onto the wagon, swearing and fuming, and slapped the reins for the horses to get moving.

Jonah smiled. "I reckon the Colonel told him. You're to work in the house with me."

Jonah led us into the back of the house to the kitchen. It was a massive room with a big, wooden table in the middle and a gigantic fireplace off to the side that someone had bricked up. Nearby sat an enormous cast-iron stove. A woman was fussing over the stove, trying to get a fire started in it. The walls were lined with shelves covered with plates and bowls. Pots and pans hung from the ceiling.

Jonah called out to the woman to say that the new house servants were here. "Looky here, Lizzie!" She waved at us without a lot of interest and returned to the stove.

A sturdy-looking beagle strolled into the kitchen to see what was going on. Jonah and Lizzie watched it nervously. "That's Scout," Jonah said. "Don't try to pet him; he'll take your hand off. He don't like slaves much."

"He doesn't? Why not?" I asked as I tucked my hands under my arms and froze in place while Scout sniffed at me.

"He's trained to catch runaways," Jonah replied.

Scout turned to Eveline.

"You're a pretty dog," she said and reached down to scratch him behind his ears. I braced myself for an attack. To everyone's surprise, Scout closed his eyes and panted happily.

"Well, look at that," Jonah said.

I breathed a sigh of relief.

Jonah waved at us to follow him up a narrow flight of stairs. At the top were a couple of rooms. He gestured to the one on the right. "That's my room. You're in this one." He pushed open a dried up, scarred, wooden door.

"We have our own room?" Eveline asked.

"You want us to *share* a room?" I asked. I couldn't believe it.

Jonah went on like he didn't hear me. "It's got its own window and two beds—"

Two *cots*, he meant.

Eveline raced over to one and dropped onto it. Dust flew everywhere. She bounced around like she'd just been given a bed at the White House or something. I didn't get it. They were two cots with ratty blankets on top. I kind of snorted to show I wasn't impressed.

"I'm not gonna sleep on *that*," I said.

Jonah suddenly grabbed my arm and leaned into my face. His eyes had a yellow color and his breath smelled of old cabbage. "Look, *boy*, you could be sleeping out in the compound with no bed and no blanket and working in the fields until you want to drop. You better thank the Lord you're in here. Got it?"

I nodded.

He let go, but kept a stern tone in his voice. "Let me tell you how things are around here. You're house servants and that means you have to behave. You do what I say, stay out of the master's way, and everything'll be good. Step the wrong way and you'll be licking Master Kinsey's boots."

"But we never liked the house slaves," Eveline said. She didn't mean anything by it, but said it as a matter of fact.

"You've been a field slave, haven't you?"

Eveline nodded.

Jonah hitched his thumbs in his pockets. "Well, I know field slaves don't trust us house slaves. That's how it is in some places. And I know some house slaves I wouldn't trust neither. But let me tell you that around here, we house slaves watch out for the ones working in the fields. So don't give me an attitude."

Eveline nodded again. For her, the case was closed.

It wasn't for Jonah. He continued, "I know the field slaves think we house slaves have it easy as pie. But we don't. You'll see that soon enough. You'll run errands, go to the market, work in the garden, milk the cows, serve meals, help take care of the horses, dust the house, sweep up, polish the silver, and set the table in the dining room. As a house slave you're always on duty—the master may call anytime day or night. You're the last one to bed and the first one to rise."

I got tired just listening to Jonah talk about all the work I'd do. The only thing that kept me hopeful was that I'd come back to help Eveline find her father—and then we'd all escape. The only problem was that I didn't know *how* we'd do it.

I wondered where Jack was—and if he and Reverend Andrew had come up with a plan.

CHAPTER TWO

Jack tells about the bird-watcher.

REVEREND ANDREW WASN'T Reverend Andrew anymore. He got rid of his clerical collar and all his antislavery stuff and became Andrew Jamison, a bird-watcher who was touring through the South to draw and collect all kinds of birds. I was his assistant. I called him "Uncle Andrew."

I guess I should explain that when Mr. Whittaker turned off the Imagination Station, I had been sitting in a chair in our hotel room in Huntsville, Alabama. Uncle Andrew was washing his face. He had just scolded me for not keeping my mouth shut when he was talking to the slave trader at the auction about where Eveline and Matt had been taken. I was moping and complaining when the butterflies suddenly went crazy in my stomach—and the next thing I knew, I was with Mr. Whittaker again. It was so weird because when I pushed the red button to go back to the adventure, the Imagination Station put me right where I left off in that hotel room. It was like hitting the pause button on a DVD player, then starting it again.

Uncle Andrew turned around to me from the washstand and asked, "What did you say?"

I felt embarrassed because I couldn't remember what I had said. I just shrugged.

"This evening we're going to the Mason plantation for dinner," Uncle Andrew explained.

I sat up in my chair. "The Mason plantation? But Matt and Eveline are at Colonel Ross's plantation!"

Uncle Andrew turned to face me. "How did you know that?"

His question made my brain seize up. *How did I know?* "You told me, didn't you?"

"The slave auctioneer told *me,* but I don't remember telling *you.*"

"You must have told me," I gulped. "How else could I know?"

The question must've stumped him because he didn't answer or ask me again.

"Anyway," Uncle Andrew went on, "we're going to the Masons'. I had already arranged it through my friend before we arrived. Mr. Mason is interested in ornithology."

"What's that mean again?" I asked.

"It's the study of birds."

"That's right," I said. "I keep thinking it's those dentists who put braces on teeth."

Uncle Andrew shot me a strange look but didn't say anything.

"So when are we going over to Colonel Ross's to rescue Matt and Eveline?" I asked.

"In due time," Uncle Andrew said firmly. "Our purpose here isn't just to rescue them. We have to help spread the word among the slaves about the Underground Railroad."

"Spread the word about it? Don't they know already?"

"No, many of them don't. Many of them are so isolated on the plantations that they have no way of knowing." Uncle Andrew dabbed a towel at his face. "And it'll be a lot easier to get to the slaves if I can build up a friendship with some of the plantation owners."

I knew that being impatient wouldn't help anything, so I agreed to do whatever Uncle Andrew wanted. I regretted it right away when he handed me a stiff suit with a collar like cardboard that cut into my neck.

"If we're going to a dinner party, then you have to *dress* for a dinner party," he said with a smile.

We hired a carriage to take us out to the Mason plantation just as the sun was going down. It must've taken us a half hour to get there and I was completely lost. I wondered out loud how the slaves ever knew which way to escape.

Uncle Andrew checked to make sure the driver couldn't hear us, then pointed out the carriage window to the sky. "The North Star," he said. "We tell them to follow the North Star."

We turned onto a dirt driveway where flickering lamps showed us the way to the Mason house. It was a mansion built in what Uncle Andrew said was the Greek Revival style of architecture, which was real popular then. I assumed he was talking about the large, white pillars along the front porch.

A servant ran down to meet our carriage and helped us out. I said "Thanks" but he didn't look at me or say anything. We strolled up to the front door, which was actually two *massive* doors, and another servant let us in. (Maybe I should mention that all the servants were black.)

We stepped through the front door and I have to tell you: this place was *huge*. It had a front hall you could've played basketball in. Off of that, the widest staircase I'd ever seen curved around up to the second floor. There were paintings of people all over the walls. The furniture was that rich, curlicue kind, with round backs on the chairs and legs that curve in and out. The house was full of fancy tables, gigantic mirrors, and sparkling chandeliers. Uncle Andrew pointed out that the chandeliers were "Waterford" and the furniture represented the Empire, Victorian, and Early American periods. All I know is I never saw anything like it at Sears.

I tugged at my collar and felt out of place. *It's going to be a long night*, I thought.

A tall man with a white beard and a woman with big curls in her hair came out to meet us. "Welcome to our home!" the man said as if he meant it. His hand was stuck out for Uncle Andrew to shake. He did. "I'm Richard Mason. This is my wife, Annabelle."

Annabelle curtsied.

"A pleasure to meet you," Uncle Andrew said, then bowed like a gentleman to Mrs. Mason. "I'd like you to meet my assistant, Jack."

Remembering Uncle Andrew's warning, I made sure to keep my mouth shut except to say "It's very nice to meet you."

Uncle Andrew said, "Thank you for opening your home to us so graciously."

Mr. Mason clapped Uncle Andrew on the back. "When John said you were coming to our fair town, I insisted you join us for a meal. Didn't I, Annabelle?"

"You certainly did," Annabelle said softly.

"Come into the living room," Mr. Mason said and led the way.

It was another gigantic room with a lot of fancy furniture and a huge, carved-wood fireplace. Uncle Andrew made a fuss over the "Chippendale mirror" above the "rosewood piano" and the authentic "French porcelain mantel clock." His compliments charmed the socks off of both Mr. and Mrs. Mason.

"I take it from your accent that you're from Britain," Mr. Mason said after we were all sitting down.

"England," Uncle Andrew clarified.

"A Johnny Bull! I have family in Runnymede," Mr. Mason exclaimed.

"Oh, please, Richard, they're hardly family," Mrs. Mason said. "Distant cousins, at best. Please, Mr. Jamison —"

"Andrew," he corrected her.

It looked to me as if she blushed. "*Andrew*. Tell us about your purpose here."

Uncle Andrew sat up proudly and told them all about the studies he wanted to do of the birds in the area and how he hoped to catch a few to take back north. I noticed that just saying the word "north" made Mr. and Mrs. Mason stiffen.

Mr. Mason said, "Tell me, sir, if all Northerners are opposed to slavery."

"Not all," Uncle Andrew replied honestly.

Mrs. Mason fanned herself as if she were too hot. "I shudder to think of the abolitionists who would wreak violence on us all."

"I take it, sir, that you are not of that mind," Mr. Mason said.

It felt like my collar shrunk around my neck while I waited for Uncle Andrew to answer.

He smiled politely, "Would I be here now if I were?"

The servant who let us in the front door suddenly appeared to say that dinner was served in the dining room. I was so relieved by the interruption that I nearly leaped to my feet.

Uncle Andrew frowned at me.

"Hungry, boy?" Mr. Mason said with a chuckle.

"Yes, sir." I smiled in my most angelic way.

"Then let's not dillydally!" Mr. Mason said.

During dinner—which was chicken, potatoes, and a green kind of vegetable I didn't recognize—Mr. Mason told us all about his grown-up sons who'd become successful lawyers and merchants in other parts of the South. Mrs. Mason beamed while he spoke. I watched them both while I ate and wondered how such nice people could *buy and sell* other human beings as slaves. It didn't make sense. Every time the servants came into the dining room to make sure we were okay, I had to remind myself that they weren't just waiters in some restaurant—they were *owned* and didn't have a choice about whether they wanted to be there.

Eventually Uncle Andrew steered the conversation back to birds and talked about his desire to spend time in the surrounding country-side, drawing and cataloging the native species. Mr. Mason took the hint and told Uncle Andrew he was more than welcome to bird-watch *their* property.

"In fact, I'm an amateur bird-watcher myself," Mr. Mason said. "I'm familiar with the works of Wilson. Wilson was from your country, wasn't he?"

I had a feeling that Mr. Mason was testing Uncle Andrew.

"If you mean Alexander Wilson, he was from Scotland," Uncle Andrew replied easily. "His nine-volume work *American Ornithology* was unsurpassed. That is, until Audubon published *his* definitive *Birds of America.*"

Mr. Mason knew his bluff had been called. "Yes, an excellent work. In any event, if it won't be intrusive, I might come along with you tomorrow!" Mr. Mason exclaimed.

I dropped my fork and it hit the plate with a deafening clang.

Uncle Andrew smiled. "That would be delightful!"

Mrs. Mason cleared her throat. "Richard, you're supposed to go into town tomorrow, remember?"

"Oh, blast it all!" Mr. Mason shouted. "That confounded meeting with the bankers. You're right, of course."

"Oh, too bad. Some other time perhaps," Uncle Andrew said.

A droplet of sweat tickled at the back of my neck.

"If you need anyone else to assist you, besides your young companion here, I'll be happy for one of my servants to accompany you," Mr. Mason offered.

Uncle Andrew said he was most kind. And as everyone was distracted by their plates of food again, he winked at me.

Jack tells about bird-watching.

"NOW, TELL ME HOW one identifies birds," Uncle Andrew asked the next day as we tramped across a field not far from Mason's house.

It was a pop quiz. Just that morning Uncle Andrew lectured me about how to be a bird-watcher. He said that if I was going to be his assistant, I had to at least sound like I knew what I was talking about.

I tried to think as I adjusted the sack hanging from my shoulder. In it were Uncle Andrew's pads of papers, pens, and watercolors so he could sketch some of the birds we hoped to find. "The marks around the eyes . . ." I said.

"And?"

I thought again. "The marks on their wings . . ."

"Very good. And what else?"

My mind was blank, so I guessed. "The color of their beaks?"

Uncle Andrew shook his head. "I suppose the *shape* of their beaks might be helpful, even the color. But you guessed the wrong end. The correct answer is: the marks on their outer tail feathers."

I frowned. "Oh, yeah."

We reached the edge of some woods and Uncle Andrew stopped. He pointed to a cavity in a nearby tree. "There."

I looked up but didn't see what he was pointing at.

"See? The Eastern Bluebird."

My eyes finally fixed on a bright-blue bird with an orangey chest sitting on a branch. Another bird just like it flew in from the field and landed on the branch. The high-pitched chirps from the tree said that it was a mom and dad watching over a nest.

"Do you want to draw them?" I asked.

"No, I've sketched some of them from a previous trip. But I wanted you to see them for yourself. That way, if anyone asks, you can say what kind of bird you saw and give a reasonable description."

"Eastern Bluebird," I repeated.

"Come along," he said and continued into the woods.

"Where are we going?"

Uncle Andrew spoke softly. "These woods circle Mason's plantation. I want to stroll around the perimeter, then 'accidentally' come upon the fields where the slaves will be working. Lord willing, I'll have a chance to talk to them."

We walked through the woods and every once in a while Uncle Andrew would stop to sketch on his pad, or he'd point out different birds to me. Eventually we got to the edge of a field. In the distance, we could see a group of slaves clearing the field. An overseer sat nearby and barked orders at them.

"Set up my easel here," Uncle Andrew said. "I'll go have a word with the overseer, so he won't chase us off."

I nodded and started to unpack the bag while he strode across the field in large steps. I had just set up the wooden legs of the easel when I heard the clanging of several bells. At first I thought it might be the cook signaling everyone that it was time for lunch and didn't pay attention. But the clanging came closer and closer, so I looked up. Three slaves were carrying a huge log away from the field and toward the woods. Two of the slaves looked the way the slaves normally looked, but the third had something on his head that looked like a large helmet. As they walked past with the log, I got a better look and noticed that the thing wasn't a helmet as much as a kind of cage. It had a circle of iron around the top of the slave's head, with several rods fixed to it that stretched down to another circle of iron that fit around the slave's neck. It was fastened shut by a large padlock at the throat. There were big bells hanging from the rods that knocked around to make the clanging I heard.

I know my mouth fell open. The cage-helmet looked incredibly heavy, and I couldn't imagine how the slave was able to walk at all, let alone carry a log. The slave turned to me as they walked by and I recognized him right away. It was Clarence, Eveline's father!

I wanted to shout, but Uncle Andrew's hand was on my shoulder. "I know," he said quietly. "Don't do anything that will draw attention to our knowledge."

I got busy with the easel again. "What was that thing on his head?"

"It's a way to punish slaves who've run away. They have to wear them day and night."

"It looks awful."

Uncle Andrew nodded. "It's worse than awful. With one of those contraptions on your head, you can barely stoop to work without straining all the muscles in your neck and shoulders. You can't put your head down to sleep; you have to crouch all night. But it serves its purpose. You can't run away without everyone hearing you." Uncle Andrew rubbed at his face, and I realized he was trying to get rid of the tears in his eyes.

"What are we going to do?"

"It's imperative we don't let on that we know Clarence."

"Okay."

Uncle Andrew rubbed his chin. "I think I have an idea."

Clarence and the two slaves threw the log into the woods, then came past us again. Uncle Andrew called out as he ran to them. The slaves looked stricken that this strange white man would approach like that. If Clarence recognized Uncle Andrew, he didn't let on.

"Pardon me," Uncle Andrew said, "but I'm doing some research on birds in this area."

The slaves shuffled their feet and looked anxiously toward the overseer, who now stood up and watched the scene from across the field.

"I believe one of you is named Clarence."

Clarence spoke reluctantly. "That's me, sir."

"I've been told that that you know a thing or two about birds. Is that true?"

"Well, sir . . ." Clarence spoke slowly as if he wasn't sure what the right answer was. "I know a thing or two about birds. Yes, sir."

"Hey!" the overseer shouted as he came closer.

"I may need some help with my research," Uncle Andrew said to Clarence.

The overseer was only a few yards away. "What's going on here? You three—get back to work!"

"Yes, sir," the slaves said and rushed away. Clarence staggered behind with the bells on his helmet ringing and clanging.

"You can look at birds all you want, but stay away from the slaves," the overseer said. "Distracts them from their work."

"I'm terribly sorry. It wasn't my intention to stir up trouble. But I'd like to talk to Mr. Mason about the one in the helmet."

"Why? What'd he do wrong?"

"Not a thing. I believe he may be of some assistance to us."

"Not that one. You can believe me."

"Jack, pack up our things. Let's go to the mansion and have a word with Mr. Mason."

The servant showed us in to the study, where Mr. Mason was seated at the desk. He rose to greet us. "How was the bird-watching today?" he asked.

"Slightly disappointing," Uncle Andrew answered. "We're having trouble tracking the little devils."

"I was certain that a man of your expertise would have no trouble finding the birds he wanted."

Uncle Andrew bowed modestly. "You esteem me too highly. I'm a rank amateur. However, there is someone in your service who may be of great help to me."

"Is there? Who?"

"One of your slaves."

"I'm astounded," Mr. Mason said. "I'm not aware that any of my slaves would have a special knowledge of birds."

"It's obviously a knowledge from experience, rather than books—of working the land and knowing the birds of the area as a result."

Mr. Mason shrugged. "Well, sir, if you want to borrow one of my slaves for a day's expedition, I don't mind. Which one is he?"

"The one with the unusual contraption on his head," Uncle Andrew said.

"Contraption?"

Uncle Andrew explained, "It looked like a cage with bells on it. Makes an infernal noise, I confess."

Mr. Mason thought for a moment, then realized whom Uncle Andrew meant. "You're talking about one of my new slaves. I'm sorry, sir, but I'm not sure it would be prudent to let him wander the country-side with you."

"I agree, sir," Uncle Andrew said carefully. "Particularly with that commotion on his head. I don't think the birds would stay still with him banging and clamoring like he does."

Mr. Mason frowned. "Do you know why that boy is wearing that hat with the bells? It's because he runs away. I bought him from Ramsay because Ramsay was tired of dealing with him. I apologize, but if I take off the helmet, there'll be no stopping him from running away again."

"What if I were to promise that he wouldn't? What if I took full responsibility for him while he's with me?" Uncle Andrew locked his gaze on Mason and waited patiently for an answer.

Mr. Mason thought about it for a few minutes, then shook his head. "I don't believe that would be a good idea. Not without the helmet."

"Perhaps we could take him with the helmet and the key to the padlock. If the bells scare off the birds, we can remove the helmet. If not, we'll leave it on."

It was a reasonable offer Mr. Mason couldn't refuse without looking like he didn't trust us. "If you'll take responsibility for him and use discretion in your choice, then how can I protest? When would you like to take him?"

"Tomorrow, if you don't mind."

Later, as we walked to the carriage, I had to ask Uncle Andrew: "Does Clarence really know about birds, or did you make it up?"

Uncle Andrew didn't smile, but there was laughter in his voice. "I haven't the foggiest idea. I suspect he knows as much about birds as you do."

"Uh-oh."

Jack tells about a plan.

"I DON'T LIKE IT. I don't like it one bit," the overseer—a man named Hickocks—complained as he gave us the key to Clarence's padlock.

"You worry too much," Mr. Mason said.

"You pay me to worry too much," Hickocks replied gruffly. "This buck'll run the first chance he gets."

"And I'll take responsibility for it if he does," Uncle Andrew said. "Unless you don't consider me a man of my word."

It was a challenge and Hickocks seemed to know it. With muttered curses he turned and walked off to a group of slaves who were waiting for him. "What are you standing around for, you good-for-nothings!" he shouted at them. He gestured for Clarence to join us.

"Hickocks is a little protective of our property," Mr. Mason said apologetically.

At the word *property* I looked hard at Mr. Mason. I wanted to say, "What do you mean by calling them property? They're not your property. They don't belong to *anybody*. And you have no right to think so." The words were right on the tip of my tongue, but I bit them back.

Clarence walked up to us with the bells on his hat banging away.

"Our guest seems to think you know a thing or two about birds," Mr. Mason told him.

Clarence wouldn't look Mr. Mason in the eye, but gave him a slight nod. "Yes, sir."

Mr. Mason held up a finger. "I'm entrusting you to Mr. Jamison. If you try to run away, not only will *I* be sorely put out, but so will Mr. Jamison. Between the two of us, I reckon we'll catch you and hang you in a most painful way. Do you understand?"

"Yes, sir."

"Good bird-hunting, then," Mr. Mason said.

We thanked him for his kindness and strolled with Clarence across the field and into the nearest patch of woods. Clarence did his best to keep his head still so the bells wouldn't clang, but it was no use. It sounded like a herd of cows with bells around their necks was on a stampede.

"We'll have to walk far enough away so they can't hear the bells," Uncle Andrew said.

Mr. Mason owned a lot of land, so we made it pretty far before Uncle Andrew stopped and faced Clarence directly. "We'll never find any birds like this," he said.

"Are we really looking for birds, sir?" Clarence asked.

"Only the kind to set free," Uncle Andrew replied, then produced the key to the helmet. "Is it safe?"

"We should be clear from the farm," Clarence said.

"I've been watching behind us to make sure no one was following," I said, proud of myself for thinking to do it.

"Good lad," Uncle Andrew said, then grabbed the padlock at the base of the helmet. "Let's get that thing off your head."

"Are you sure, sir? I mean, this whole thing seems risky to me," Clarence said, with a worried sound in his voice.

Uncle Andrew nodded. "I'm sure."

The lock was a little rusty, and it took a minute or two to get the key moving inside of it. I was afraid that Hickocks gave us the wrong key. (I wouldn't put it past him to do something like that.) Finally, something clicked and the lock came loose. We helped Clarence take the helmet off. Clarence immediately moved his head to the left, then to the right, then rolled it around and around on his shoulders. Each movement made him groan with pain.

With a victorious shout, Uncle Andrew and I threw the helmet into a pile of leaves.

"Cover it up, Jack," Uncle Andrew said.

I grabbed leaves and started to bury the ugly thing.

"What are you doing? I have to take it back!" Clarence said.

Uncle Andrew brushed his hands off. "I promised to bring *you* back, not that inhumane piece of iron."

Clarence reached out to Uncle Andrew. "Look, Reverend, forget about me. But I beg you to go to Colonel Ross's house and get my little girl. That's where she is. Your friend, too. It's only six miles away. Jake told me—he goes there on errands. He saw them with his own eyes."

"I won't forget about you, Clarence," Uncle Andrew said firmly. "If all goes according to plan, tomorrow night we'll *all* leave together."

"Tomorrow night? But how?"

"Yeah—goes according to *what* plan?" I asked.

Uncle Andrew smiled. "The plan I'm making up as we go along."

"Oh, Lord have mercy," Clarence said.

"I'm quite in earnest, Clarence. Without that helmet, do you think you can escape tomorrow night?"

Clarence gave the question some thought and then nodded his head. "If they don't put me in another helmet, I think I know a way out."

"Then we'll pray they won't have another helmet to put you in. One way or another, we'll know when we go back," Uncle Andrew said. "Now, let's go look at some birds."

We walked through the woods and fields of Mr. Mason's land, and I was surprised to find that Clarence really did know a lot about the birds we found. He even taught Uncle Andrew a couple of things. I tried to take notes about the birds so I could answer intelligently if anyone asked me. Eventually, I gave up. Once we got beyond blackbirds, sparrows, and mockingbirds, the names got too hard. They were called things like phoebe and nuthatch and waxwing and titmouse. Even now I'm not sure I'm getting them right.

When it was time to go back to the plantation, Uncle Andrew reminded Clarence about running away the next night, then said: "Whatever happens, let's decide now that our rendezvous point will be north—at the Hollow Tree by Griffith's Creek. A friend told me about it. It's about 20 miles. Do you know where that is?"

"I reckon if I head north along Griffith's Creek, I'll find it," Clarence answered.

"Good man. So, by the grace of God, we'll be on our way within the next 48 hours. Can you hold on until then?"

Clarence said, "I'll try. I've waited this long. I think I can wait another 48 hours. Just so you promise we won't go without my little girl. 'Cause I won't."

"I promise."

Clarence suddenly stopped and grabbed Uncle Andrew's hand. "Thank you, sir," he said with tears in his eyes.

Uncle Andrew gazed into his face, then simply said, "You're welcome."

Back at the plantation, Hickocks started sputtering and went red-faced with the news that we didn't have the helmet. "You said you *lost* it?"

"Yes," Uncle Andrew answered. "I'm so sorry. It was scaring the birds, so we took it off in the woods and moved on. For the life of me, I couldn't remember where we put it. Neither could Jack or your slave."

Hickocks took a deep breath as he looked at us warily. "I have no doubt that they couldn't! The Master'll be upset."

"I'll be happy to make full restitution for the item," Uncle Andrew said.

Hickocks glared at him. "Full restitution? You think you can just walk into a store and buy one of those things? I made it myself. It was the only one we have."

I was relieved to hear the news. That would make our escape plan a little easier.

"Please, just name the price and I'll pay it," Uncle Andrew said in a voice that was full of mock regret.

"It's not for me to say," Hickocks snapped. "Take it up with Mr. Mason."

"I will. Wait here, Jack." Uncle Andrew strolled off toward the house.

Hickocks eyed me, then Clarence. "I don't know what you're up to, but I don't like it. I don't like it one bit."

"Up to, sir?" I asked.

"I won't be made a fool," he said, then looked steely-eyed at Clarence. "Listen to me, boy. If you run away again, you better make sure you're never found—'cause I'll kill you if I catch you. You hear me? I'll kill you."

"Yes, sir," Clarence said.

It scared me to hear Hickocks talk like that and I was glad to hear Uncle Andrew and Mr. Mason return. Uncle Andrew must've charmed Mr. Mason again, because Mr. Mason didn't seem bothered about losing the helmet and insisted that his driver take us back to town.

At the carriage, Uncle Andrew told Mr. Mason that this was good-bye.

Mr. Mason was surprised. "I'm sorry to see you go so soon," he said sincerely.

"We won't be too far away," Uncle Andrew replied. "I want to go to Colonel Ross's plantation first thing in the morning. I was told that he has several species of woodpeckers on his property."

"Does he? How unusual. Several species? How marvelous for him. I never heard that."

"Perhaps I've got it wrong, but it will be worth investigating."

They shook hands, and then Mr. Mason signaled the driver to go. I glanced back and it looked as if Mr. Mason was still pondering how Colonel Ross was lucky enough to have so many woodpeckers to look at.

I quietly asked Uncle Andrew about the lies he kept telling.

He looked at me as if I'd shocked him. "Lies?" he replied.

"You said you heard that Colonel Ross has woodpeckers. You didn't really hear that, did you?"

"I *said* I might have heard wrong," he explained.

"You know what I mean," I persisted. "You also said we lost the helmet. Isn't it wrong to lie like that?"

Uncle Andrew looked at me with a serious expression, his eyebrows pushed together in a thoughtful frown. "Jack, I've asked myself that question time and time again. Is it wrong? Well, let me ask *you* a question. Was Rahab wrong?"

I thought about it, but I couldn't remember who Rahab was. I shrugged and said, "Rahab was in the Old Testament, right?"

He smiled sympathetically. "The story of Rahab is in Joshua, chapter 2. She hid a couple of Joshua's spies, then lied to her king's men to protect them. Was she wrong?"

"I don't know. Was she?"

"People have been debating that question for centuries," Uncle Andrew replied. "On one hand, she lied. On the other hand, she protected two of God's men. Do you remember what happened? God brought the walls of Jericho down for Joshua and the Israelites. Because of Rahab's faithfulness, she was saved by Joshua."

"So they rewarded her for lying?" I asked.

Uncle Andrew nodded. "It seems that way. And there's an even more interesting twist to the story."

"What?"

"Read Matthew, chapter 1. Rahab was an ancestor of King David, and in turn she was related to Jesus Himself. The apostle Paul even considered her a hero of the faith for what she'd done. What do you make of that?"

I didn't know what to make of it. "Are you saying that lying is okay?"

"Not necessarily," he replied. "God prohibits 'bearing false witness,' which means lying about your neighbor to bring unjust punishment against him. Rahab did not lie in that sense. Likewise, I am not breaking a commandment by what I do. I say what I say not to bring harm to anyone or to bring personal gain to myself, but to free men from their bondage."

We rode on silently while I thought about it. I kept thinking about it all the way through dinner, bedtime, and breakfast the next morning. As we got ready to go to Colonel Ross's plantation, I told Uncle Andrew what I thought about his explanation.

"I'm still not so sure about it," I said.

He smiled and clapped me on the back. "I thought that's what you'd say."

I waited to see if he had another answer.

His smiled faded and he looked deep into my face. "Jack, may God judge me if I'm wrong. But I am willing to risk His wrath to set these slaves free."

Matt tells about his confession.

OKAY, I NEED TO tell you right up front that it was hard working in Colonel Ross's house. Just in the couple of days I was there, I worked until every muscle in my body hurt. At night, when Jonah said I could go to bed, I barely had the energy to wash my face before I collapsed onto that straw mattress and snoozed away.

We—I mean, the house slaves—were the first ones up in the morning, even before sunrise, to milk the cows and get breakfast ready for the Colonel and his wife. There were logs to split and the house animals to be fed (except Scout; he only let Eveline feed him). Then we dug in the garden, swept the porches, set the dining room for the next meal, polished silver, and washed clothes—and I'm not talking about using a washing machine. We had to use a washboard and tub, scrubbing and scrubbing until our hands were all pruney. I was exhausted. Eveline, Jonah, Lizzie, and the other house slaves acted like there was nothing to it. If they were tired, they never let on, and they didn't complain.

Eveline amazed me. I don't know where she got all her energy. Only a couple of times did I see her standing still by the back door or a window, looking out with a sad look on her face. She was thinking about her dad, I knew.

The whole time I was working, I had to keep reminding myself that I was doing it so I could come up with a plan to help Eveline see her father again. That's why I came back. But I wasn't sure how to do it.

I also kept wondering where Jack was. Did the Imagination Station take him back to Reverend Andrew? If it did, why didn't he come to rescue us? Every time a wagon drove up or someone knocked on the door, I kept expecting it to be him and Reverend Andrew. But he didn't show up.

I imagined him hanging out with the white folks, eating a lot of good food and being able to do whatever he wanted. It didn't seem fair. It *wasn't* fair. Just because the color of our skin was different didn't make it right for him to be better off.

Jonah was friendly the whole time, teaching us what to do. And he told us over and over to thank God for having it so good. That was hard for me to do considering all the work we did, but he said it was a lot worse on the other plantations. "Colonel Ross is a good and kind man," Jonah insisted. "There's no better master in the area. He takes care of his slaves."

"But we're *still* slaves," I reminded him.

He simply wagged a finger at me and told me to watch my mouth. "It's going to get you in big trouble, you hear?"

I mumbled that what I said was still true.

"There's no other master who brings in a doctor for his slaves or puts them in such nice quarters and never uses the whip unless somebody really deserves it, and he even tries to keep the families together. No other master does that. But he does."

I didn't say a word, but that last part he said about keeping families together gave me an idea.

After breakfast on the third morning (I think it was the third morning, but I lost count), Jonah was upset because one of the field slaves had been disobedient about his work. I guess he pretended to be sick and then was found later behind one of the sheds, goofing off.

Kinsey, the overseer, brought the slave to the back door. "Jonah! I don't have time to deal with him. You know what to do."

"Yes, Master Kinsey," Jonah said in a shaky voice.

I found out later that one of the reasons the field slaves didn't like the house slaves was because the house slaves were sometimes told to whip the field slaves.

Jonah, who was carrying a tray of tea for the Colonel, pushed it into my hands. "Take this to the study," he ordered.

"Yes, sir."

As I turned to go, I heard Jonah stomp down the back stairs and say to the disobedient slave, "Why do you make me have to do this? You know I hate it. You know it makes me cry. Why can't you behave so I won't have to whip you, boy?"

I carried the heavy tray through the house and into Colonel Ross's study. He was leaning over some ledgers, concentrating hard, when I put the tea next to him.

"Your tea, sir," I said.

I guess he was expecting the voice to belong to Jonah and it surprised him to hear mine. He looked up and smiled, and his teeth glistened through his mustache and chin beard. "Thanks, son," he answered.

I didn't move away as I was supposed to. I had something I wanted to say. But I was scared and it took me a minute to get my nerves together. Outside, dark clouds rolled in and I heard some distant thunder.

"Is there something you want?" the Colonel asked.

I shuffled my feet a little. "Colonel—er, Master Ross? I was wondering if we could . . . uh, talk, just for a minute."

"Talk?"

"I mean, you seem like a nice guy and I thought maybe I could be honest with you about something."

Colonel leaned back from his desk and gave me his full attention. "Honest? Honest about what?"

I fiddled with the buttons on my jacket and worked up my courage. "The truth is . . . I'm not a slave."

"Aren't you?"

"No, sir. I'm free. I've always been free. The slave traders grabbed me and made me come here and then sold me, even though I told them I was free." There. It was out. I waited to see what he'd do.

The Colonel hit his palms against the top of his desk. "No! The scoundrels! How could they do that to you?"

I relaxed. "I don't know, but they did. You believe me, don't you?"

"Of course I do." The Colonel was on his feet in an instant and the size of him—he was *big*—made me a little nervous again. He rushed to the door and called out to whoever was in hearing distance. "I want Jonah in here right away!"

"Jonah?" I asked. "But he doesn't know anything about it."

The Colonel waved at me to stay put. "Listen, son, Jonah's going to help me get to the bottom of this. For one thing, I want him to call Kinsey in from the fields. Kinsey knows those slave traders. If there's something illegal going on, I want to get to hear about it. Now, tell me what happened."

I was so relieved that I told him just about everything—about Eveline, Clarence, Odyssey, and how the slave traders grabbed us and brought us south. I told him everything except the part about Jack and the Imagination Station, since I didn't want him to think I was completely crazy. By the time I finished, Jonah showed up at the study door.

"Yes, Master?" he asked, his body still shaking from the whipping he had just given that field slave.

"Jonah," the Colonel said, "step forward, please."

Jonah did, until he was standing next to my chair. He looked down at me, and I could tell he was confused. He knew something was going on but couldn't figure out what it was.

The Colonel sat down behind his desk again. "I want you to take this boy and teach him a thing or two about lying."

"Lying!" I cried out.

Jonah grabbed me by the shirt and said sadly, "I knew it. It was just a matter of time."

"But—" I tried to get out words of protest, but nothing came.

"And, boy," the Colonel said to me, "I suggest you keep your mouth shut in the future. Nobody here likes to think our fellow Southern gentlemen are cheats."

"Come on, son," Jonah said and yanked me out of the room and through the house.

"No! No!" I cried the whole way. I squirmed, but Jonah's grip was like a vise.

"I told you, boy. I told you to keep your mouth shut. Now look what you've gone and done. I get done with one, and now I have to deal with another."

Going through the kitchen, I saw Eveline rush forward to help me, but Jonah stopped her. "Nothing you can do, child. There's nothing you can do."

He dragged me down the back stairs to the same spot where he had whipped the field slave. Drops of sweat still spotted the dirt under our feet.

"No, Jonah, don't," I pleaded. "I'm sorry. I was trying to help!"

He tied my hands to the hitching post. He sounded as if he was going to cry. "I warned you, son. I warned you."

He picked up a long, slender switch. Thunder rolled above, and rain started to fall.

Jack tells about their arrival.

UNCLE ANDREW AND I got to Colonel Ross's plantation late in the morning. The carriage pulled up the drive as the rain stopped. We climbed out, and Uncle Andrew gave the driver instructions to take our belongings to an inn about a quarter of a mile up the road. As we walked to the stairs leading to the door, we passed a puddle of mud. I glanced down at it, trying to be careful not to step in, when Uncle Andrew gave me a slight nudge. It was just enough to knock me off balance and I fell on my knees—right in the mud.

"Hey!" I called out. "Why'd you do that?"

"You'll see," Uncle Andrew said.

The front door opened and a wiry, old servant with a worried look greeted us. We stepped into the front hallway as Uncle Andrew introduced himself. The servant's eye fell to the mud all over my pants, then back to Uncle Andrew. "I'll announce your arrival to the Colonel," he said before he shuffled off.

Colonel Ross came down the hall and I was surprised by how big he was. He wasn't heavy, just tall. And he had long curly hair, a mustache, and one of those little beards that stuck out from his chin. "The ornithologist!" he said. "I heard you were in the area. It's a pleasure to meet you. I'm Alexander Ross."

"This is my nephew Jack," Uncle Andrew said.

"An honor, Jack," the Colonel said, then looked down at the mud on my pants. "Did you have an accident?"

"Well, I—"

"Yes," Uncle Andrew cut in. "He tripped as we approached the porch. Would you mind if—"

"Jonah, take the young master here to the kitchen to see if you can wipe the mud off," Colonel Ross said.

"Yes, sir," Jonah replied and signaled me to follow him.

The Colonel invited Uncle Andrew into the family room, while we walked in the opposite direction down the hall.

In the kitchen, a black woman with a scarf on her head was busy getting lunch ready. She hardly looked at me. The servant named Jonah led me to a large tub of water, grabbed a rag, and knelt down to wipe at the mud on my pants and shoes.

"I'll do it," I said.

"No, sir. I'll do it."

It didn't take long for me to realize that Uncle Andrew knocked me in the mud so I could have a look at the servants' areas. If Matt and Eveline really were here, I'd probably see them in the back. I also remembered that the slave trader told Uncle Andrew that Matt and Eveline had been sold specifically as house slaves.

"Don't dillydally, girl," the woman in the scarf said.

I looked up to see who she was talking to. I was surprised and happy to see Eveline standing on the other end of the kitchen. She just stared at me, her mouth hanging open.

I wanted to say something to her—hello, and "Where's Matt?" and other things I was busting to ask—but she shook her head quickly.

"Go on, girl," the woman said. Eveline walked past me and out the back door.

"Unless you want me to wash your britches, that's the best I can do," the servant said.

I looked down and saw that Jonah had gotten rid of most of the mud. "I think that's good. Thanks."

Jonah took me back to the family room. I got the impression that Uncle Andrew and Colonel Ross had become fast friends. They talked like old buddies. The Colonel insisted that we have dinner with him, then apologized that his wife couldn't join us since she'd gone to visit her mother in Savannah.

"I don't know much about birds," the Colonel said, "but you're welcome to any resource I have that will assist your expedition."

"I'm obliged, sir," Uncle Andrew said, then hesitated as if he were about to ask the unaskable.

Colonel Ross picked up the hint. "You have a question, sir?"

"Mr. Mason was very kind to lend one of his slaves to me. Jack is capable, but he's—"

"Say no more," Colonel Ross said. "I can certainly provide you with a slave."

"I saw one in the kitchen that would be perfect," I jumped in.

Uncle Andrew shot a heedful look my way. "Did you?"

"It's a young girl. I think she's just the right size to climb trees and find the nests."

Colonel Ross tugged at his whiskers. "There are better and more experienced slaves to send with you. The girl is new, and I'm not entirely sure I can trust her in an open field."

"I would take full responsibility, of course."

"I have no doubt that you would," the Colonel replied. "But taking responsibility isn't the point. I believe it would be reckless to send her with you. I'll send Washington instead."

Washington was a field slave who was probably in his thirties, but looked as if he were my age. He talked more than any other slave I'd met—about his wife and children, the weather, the landscape, where we were from, birds—and I wondered if there was anything he *wouldn't* talk about.

I tuned out. My mind was on other things. I felt worried and discouraged that Washington went with us instead of Eveline or Matt. What were we going to do now? How would we contact them to say that we were all going to escape that night? Where *was* Matt anyway?

The dark clouds hung over us all afternoon. Uncle Andrew was real sneaky in how he asked Washington questions about his life as a slave and if he'd ever thought about escaping. Just then, Washington brought up the Underground Railroad.

"Yes, sir, I heard tell of a railroad for slaves. But I thought somebody made it up. Do you know anything about it, sir?" Washington asked.

I waited for Uncle Andrew to tell him the truth.

Instead, Uncle Andrew just shrugged. "Not very much. Perhaps less than you do."

Rain spat down at us in small sprinkles, and we decided to go back to the Colonel's. After we made sure that Washington was back in his slave quarters, I had a question for Uncle Andrew. "Why didn't you tell him about the Underground Railroad?"

"Didn't you notice how much he talked?"

"How could I *not* notice?" I snorted.

"If he talks that much about nothing in particular, how much more would he have to say about something really important—like us, or the Railroad?"

"You mean he might be like a spy or an informer?" I asked.

"Possibly," Uncle Andrew replied. "There was something about the way he asked me if I knew anything about the Railroad. He was too aggressive, particularly when you consider that I'm a complete stranger. How did he know I wouldn't turn the tables on him and report him to the overseer? So, if he isn't some sort of an informer, he's reckless, which can be just as bad."

We walked along quietly for a minute, then I asked, "What are we going to do, Uncle Andrew? I've seen Eveline, but I don't know where Matt is. How can we find them and talk to them without making everybody suspicious? Do you want to throw me in another mud puddle?"

Uncle Andrew chuckled, then looked down at our clothes. We were covered with mud and leaves. "I don't think that will be necessary. Let's simply walk to the back door of the main house and ask to be cleaned off. Chances are we'll see Eveline and Matt in the kitchen, preparing for the evening meal."

I didn't realize how cold it was outside until we stepped into the warmth of the kitchen. The woman in the scarf was there, wrestling with a large duck. Eveline was there, too, peeling potatoes.

She looked up at us but didn't react.

Uncle Andrew approached the woman with the scarf. "What's your name, my good woman?"

"I'm Lizzie," she answered.

"Lizzie, would you be so kind as to fetch us some fresh water so we can get the mud and leaves off our clothes?"

Lizzie looked down at her duck as if to say, "Can't you see I'm busy?" But Uncle Andrew kept his eyes on her, and she gave a quick curtsy and dashed out the door.

When we were sure it was safe, Uncle Andrew spoke softly to Eveline. "We're going to run away tonight, Eveline."

"Run away!" she gasped.

"Yes. We're going to run away and meet with your father."

Eveline's eyes went wide. "My daddy?"

Uncle Andrew nodded. "Now, how can we tell Matt?"

"Yeah," I asked, "where is he?"

Eveline's face fell. "Oh no . . . no . . . we can't run away tonight."

"Why not?" Uncle Andrew asked.

Eveline looked around nervously, then wiggled a finger at us. "Come here."

We followed her up a small staircase to a room on the second floor. Eveline opened the creaky wooden door. The room was dark. I could just barely make out the bed and the outline of someone in it.

"Matt?" Eveline whispered.

"Huh?" Matt answered weakly.

We moved closer to the bed. My heart pounded hard. I still couldn't see what was wrong with him, but I knew it wasn't good.

"Matt—it's me," I said.

"Hiya, Jack. Glad you could make it." Matt was lying on his stomach.

"What's wrong with you? Are you sick?" I asked.

"Yeah. Kinda."

Eveline whispered, "Jonah took a switch and whipped him. I don't know why."

"I talked too much," Matt groaned. "Colonel Ross made him do it."

Uncle Andrew lifted the blanket and winced as he looked at Matt's back. He gently put the blanket down before I could see.

"Are you all right?" I asked. I felt an angry burning in the pit of my stomach. How could Colonel Ross do this to Matt? What kind of man beats kids like that?

"It hurts, but Eveline keeps putting some kinda lotion on my back."

"Jonah gave it to me," Eveline explained.

I leaned close and whispered, "Matt, if you're hurt, I have to call for Mr. Whittaker. We have to get out of here."

"No," Matt said weakly. "I said I want to finish this and I will."

"Then you have to hurry up and get better," I said louder. "We're gonna run away tonight!"

Eveline pushed her knuckles against her mouth as if it would keep her from crying. "But don't you see? We can't! Matt can't go anywhere. Not like this."

Uncle Andrew lowered his head, and for a second I thought he was going to pray. "I'm afraid you're right, Eveline," he said. "We can't go anywhere tonight."

I looked at Uncle Andrew bug-eyed. "But Clarence is going to—"

"My daddy? You've seen my daddy?"

"Yes, Eveline. He's well. But we have a problem. Your father is going to try to run away tonight—and we won't be with him!"

Jack tells about the long night.

"WHY CAN'T I RUN back to Mr. Mason's to warn Clarence?" I asked after we left Matt to sleep in his room.

"It's too far to run and would draw suspicion," Uncle Andrew answered as we walked down the stairs. "We can only hope that if he does run tonight, he'll simply hide and wait for us at the hollow tree."

Lizzie was in the kitchen with our tub of water. She gave us an uneasy look as we came down the stairs from the servants' quarters, but didn't say anything except, "Your water is ready, sir. If you'll come over here, I'll clean off your trousers. Eveline, give us a hand."

I felt bad for Eveline. Watching her while she cleaned off our pants and shoes, I kept thinking about her daddy and what he was about to do. What would he think when he got to the hollow tree and we weren't there?

Uncle Andrew and I sat down at the dinner table with Colonel Ross, and all I could think about was that he ordered Matt to be beaten. I didn't know why. I didn't care. There was no excuse for it. I had to bite my tongue, because I wanted to say something nasty to him.

Uncle Andrew was friendly and nice to Colonel Ross. I figured he must be the world's greatest actor. He asked the Colonel about the local economy and the future of the South, and good investment practices.

Then dinner was served, and I felt bad all over again. Jonah brought in a large tray with the main course plates and, seconds later, Eveline and Matt came in to serve the dinner rolls and gravy. Matt looked terrible and walked as if every move he made hurt him a lot. He wouldn't look me in the eye.

I wanted to jump on the table and ask the Colonel just who in the world he thought he was to have my best friend whipped! I know it wasn't very Christian of me, but I imagined what it'd be like to have the Colonel himself whipped.

The storm that had been hanging around all day suddenly broke right after dinner. The lightning flashed through all the windows, and the thunder shook the house. The rain fell in buckets.

"Where are you staying tonight?" Colonel Ross asked after we settled by the fire in the family room.

"I had our luggage sent to the inn down the road," Uncle Andrew answered.

"I won't have it, " Colonel Ross said firmly. "You'll stay here tonight. I insist. I'll send Jonah to gather your things. I find you both good company and won't allow you to travel in such inclement weather. Jonah!"

I stood at the window and watched the rain fall against the glass. Uncle Andrew and Colonel Ross were playing chess at a small table on the other side of the room. The clock on the mantel chimed eight o'clock, and I wondered if Clarence had escaped yet. I had a tight feeling in my chest about it. It was awful, and the harder I tried not to think about Clarence running through the dark rain, the more I did.

"Sit down, Jack," Uncle Andrew said. "Read a book. You're making us both nervous standing there like that."

Colonel Ross agreed. "It's as if you're waiting for some bad news. You aren't, are you?"

"No, sir," I replied. "I'm just waiting for Jonah to come back with our suitcases."

Both of them looked at me as if I'd said a foreign word. It wasn't until later I learned that *suitcase* wasn't a normal word then. They used words like *trunks* or *baggage* or *luggage* instead.

A carriage raced up the driveway to the front porch and then stopped. I watched as Jonah leaped out and, along with the driver, started carrying our *trunks* up to the front door. The rain lashed at them as they did. The front door opened with a bang. Colonel Ross went to Jonah and barked instructions about where to put our belongings.

I think Jonah signaled the Colonel to come into the hall, because the Colonel said, "What? What is it?" and stepped out.

Uncle Andrew stood up at the table and we both found ourselves drifting toward the door so we could hear better.

The Colonel caught sight of us and waved for us to come out. "One of Mr. Mason's slaves ran away. Jonah heard about it at the inn."

My heart jumped into my throat.

"Truly? How did it happen?" Uncle Andrew asked coolly.

Jonah, still standing there dripping wet, explained, "It was one of Master Mason's new slaves. I guess he's run away before so they fixed an ornament of some bells to his head to keep him from running away again. Now, I don't know how, but the ornament came off in the woods behind Master Mason's land so Master Hickocks, the overseer, got his tracking dogs and found it hidden under some leaves."

I tried to keep from looking at Uncle Andrew. I suspected that we were thinking the same thing: We should have *buried* that helmet.

Jonah continued, "Master Hickocks took the ornament back to the slave and said he was going to fix it on his head good and tight. Then suddenly the slave acted like a mad man and attacked Master Hickocks until he was barely conscious and then ran away into the fields. They're looking for him now."

"Pity the poor creature. If they catch him, they'll kill him," Colonel Ross said, then clapped his hands together. "Shall we finish that game of chess, Andrew?"

I was in my room getting ready for bed when there was a knock at my door. I opened it and Matt pushed past me with an armload of wood. "This is for your fire," he said, then dumped the logs next to the stove in the corner.

"Matt!" I said and closed the door fast. "Are you all right?"

"My back still hurts, but I feel okay." He sat down where he was and slumped wearily. "Did you hear about Clarence?"

I nodded.

"It's all the slaves downstairs are talking about," he said.

"How's Eveline? Is she upset?" I asked.

"What do *you* think? How would you feel if *your* dad was being hunted like some kind of wild animal in the woods?"

"Okay, it was a stupid question."

We looked at each other for a minute. The rain had stopped and outside we could hear dogs barking somewhere far away. Were they chasing Clarence?

It was the unspoken question between us.

"What are we going to do?" Matt asked. "Does Reverend Andrew have a plan?"

"Sort of," I answered. "But we'll have to let you know what it is."

"Terrific," Matt said as if he didn't believe a word of it. He stood up to go. "I'm not going to fix your fire. You can figure out how to do that yourself."

"Do you want to stay in here tonight? You can sleep in my bed," I offered.

Matt looked at the big, cozy bed and, for a second, I could tell that it's what he wanted to do more than anything. But he shook his head no. "It'll get us in trouble."

When he reached the door, I said, "Matt, we can stop this story right now if you want to."

"Do *you* want to?" he asked.

"You're the one who's getting hurt," I said. "It's up to you."

He thought about it a moment. "I said I was going to finish this story and I am. If I go back now, I'll feel like a coward."

He slipped out the door and closed it quietly behind him.

I crawled into bed and wondered if I'd do the same thing in his place.

CHAPTER EIGHT

Jack tells about getting caught.

MORNING CAME AND the clouds went. The sun shone through my window bright and warm. My first thought was that it was a good day for an escape. My second thought was whether Clarence was caught or not. I prayed he wasn't.

I got dressed and went to Uncle Andrew's room just as he was coming out into the hall. "Good morning," he said without a lot of cheer. I guessed he was worried about Clarence, too. "Did you sleep well?"

"I slept okay," I said. "How about you?"

His voice went low. "Not well at all. I thought about Clarence mostly. Today we *must* work out an escape plan with Matt and Eveline."

Jonah appeared at the head of the stairs and said breakfast was being served in the dining room.

Colonel Ross was eating toast and sipping his coffee when we walked in. He stood up until we were seated, then called out for our food to be served. Matt and Eveline brought in plates of egg, ham, and bread. We exchanged cautious glances. The Colonel said that he had heard that the runaway slave from the night before hadn't been found yet.

"It's a nuisance," he said. "I can't imagine what goes through a slave's head. He has a place to live, steady work, food, and clothing. Why would he want to run away?"

I clenched my teeth to keep back what I wanted to say.

"Forgive me for saying so, Colonel," Uncle Andrew began, "but I believe that, for most of them, being a *slave* is cause enough to run away. I doubt that we as whites can appreciate what it is like to have one's freedom completely stripped away, but if we could imagine it, we wouldn't sit for it for very long. After all, what was your War of Independence for if not to be free from the rule of someone else?"

Colonel Ross gazed at Uncle Andrew. "By heavens, you almost sounded like one of those abolitionists."

Uncle Andrew chuckled as if the idea couldn't be more ridiculous. "I'm not a politician, sir, nor particularly active in your country's social issues. Would it be right for me, a foreigner, to intrude?"

"To be quite frank, I don't think it's right for *anyone* to intrude on the rights of a man and what he does with his possessions. You would no more want me to tell you what to do with the drawings you made of our birds, than I would want you to tell me what to do with my horses or cattle or slaves. Property is property, no matter how large or small."

I gripped my knife and fork until my knuckles turned white.

"To play the devil's advocate," Uncle Andrew replied, "we must remember that, in the case of slaves, we are talking about fellow human beings."

"Are we? I thought we were talking about *property*. And I will do with my property whatever I like, regardless of what those blasted abolitionists say."

I think it was probably the stress of the past couple of days, because Uncle Andrew went red in the face and looked as if he wanted to say a lot of things to set the Colonel straight. But he choked it all back. I mean, he *really* choked it all back—and started gasping.

The Colonel was on his feet right away and started pounding on Uncle Andrew's back. Finally, Uncle Andrew wheezed and got his breath back.

"Are you well, sir?" the Colonel asked.

Uncle Andrew nodded. "I'm so sorry. I simply found that hard to swallow."

"I suppose we've said enough about slavery," the Colonel said, then turned his head and raised his voice. "Have you heard enough?"

The doors to the dining room were thrown open and several men— including Mr. Mason—marched in and surrounded the table.

"I certainly have!" Mr. Mason said in a loud and excited voice.

"What is this?" Uncle Andrew asked.

Two of the men grabbed him, and one put a heavy hand on my shoulder. "Hey!" I cried out.

Mr. Mason pointed at Uncle Andrew. "There he is. Arrest him."

Another man with wild, white hair stepped forward with a pair of iron handcuffs to put on Uncle Andrew's wrists. "You, sir, are my prisoner."

"I demand to know the meaning of these actions!" Uncle Andrew shouted.

Mr. Mason leaned on clenched fists. "I charge you with being an abolitionist!"

"What?"

"You persuaded my slave to run away!" Mr. Mason said. "If I had any doubt before, your words just now proved it!"

The two men holding Uncle Andrew yanked him to his feet. The white-haired man—who I guessed was a sheriff—put the handcuffs on him. "Let's go," he ordered.

"Go where?" Uncle Andrew asked. "Am I supposed to believe you're taking me to jail somewhere? This is a well-dressed lynch mob."

"Close your mouth, slave lover," Mr. Mason said.

"Will you act the part of cowards by murdering me, or will you be brave and grant me a fair trial for these accusations?"

"Bring him!" Mr. Mason snarled.

Colonel Ross suddenly moved forward. "No. This man will not be taken from my house unless I have your word that he'll be given a fair trial. I won't be party to a lynching!"

Mr. Mason glared at the Colonel. "Are you taking the side of this man?"

"I'm taking the side of justice, sir," the Colonel answered. "If you have an accusation, then take it before our magistrate in Huntsville. Otherwise, leave now."

Mr. Mason snorted, then waved for the men to bring Uncle Andrew. "We will take him to the jail, on my word."

Colonel Ross stepped back.

"What about the boy?" the man with the heavy hand asked about me.

"Bring him along. He's probably an accomplice—or he'll make a good witness."

Mr. Mason and his men took us out to their wagon. As we pulled away, I saw Matt and Eveline watching us anxiously from the back of the house.

Jack tells about their day in court.

UNCLE ANDREW AND I were taken to the Huntsville jail and spent the rest of the day and that night in a cold and damp cell. The guards were polite, but didn't trust us. "You abolitionists are the curse of mankind," one of them said.

They asked us if we wanted to secure a defense lawyer.

Uncle Andrew chuckled. "Is there a lawyer in this town who would try to defend accused abolitionists? It's doubtful. I'll defend myself."

I spent most of the time worrying while Uncle Andrew read, prayed, and wrote in a diary.

"Aren't you afraid?" I asked at one point.

"Of course," he replied calmly. "But there's little sense in worrying about it. The outcome to this situation is entirely in God's hands."

I shivered most of the night, though I can't say whether it was because I was cold or scared.

The next morning we were taken to a crowded courtroom. "We must be quite a sensation," Uncle Andrew said as we sat down.

Judge Thadeus Stallcup sat behind a tall, wooden desk and wearily asked Mr. Mason what the charge was.

"This scoundrel is an abolitionist who enticed my poor, weak-minded slave to run away," Mr. Mason said. "The slave attacked my overseer, dashed into the cold, wet night, and has yet to be found. I have no doubt that this man will bear the brunt of the guilt if anything tragic happens to that unfortunate slave."

"Mr. Mason, you had better elaborate the circumstances of this accusation and why you believe this man to be an abolitionist," the judge said.

Mr. Mason paced around the court in a dramatic style. "I will make a statement and call witnesses who will support my claim."

"Proceed," the judge said.

Mr. Mason went on to say, "This man, who goes by the name of Andrew Jamison, called at my residence recently and requested permission to roam over my plantation to do a study of the birds there. In good faith, I granted it to him. He then claimed that one of my slaves—the one I had recently purchased called Clarence—knew something about local birds. He asked if Clarence might accompany him on his expedition, providing we removed the means we had secured to prevent him from running away again."

"Your slave has a history of running away?" the judge asked.

Mr. Mason nodded. "Yes, sir. When he was owned by Mr. Ramsay, he ran away to the North, and was captured and returned."

"And by what means did you secure him?"

"A head ornament with bells on it," Mr. Mason replied.

The judge turned to Uncle Andrew. "Why did you want the head gear removed?"

"The bells made an awful noise, which I was certain would scare away the birds I had hoped to study," Uncle Andrew replied.

The judge made a note of it, then waved at Mr. Mason to go on.

"He promised to take full responsibility if anything happened. They returned that afternoon without the head ornament. Mr. Jamison claimed that they had taken it off and forgotten where they left it. I realize now that it was merely a ploy to assist my slave's escape."

"Why do you believe it was a ploy?" the judge asked.

"Because my overseer later used his tracking dogs to find the head ornament. It had been clumsily stashed beneath a pile of leaves in the woods."

"Clumsily stashed?" the judge inquired.

"If they had simply forgotten it, then it would have been sitting next to a tree or on a log. But to be pushed under a pile of leaves makes me believe it had been intentionally hidden. Who but my slave, Mr. Jamison, or his young assistant would have done it?"

The judge conceded the point. "Any response, Mr. Jamison?"

Uncle Andrew shook his head. "Your Honor, I would have to be a clairvoyant to know how the helmet wound up under the leaves. We had misplaced it and, after searching and failing to find it, we returned to Mr. Mason's plantation. I offered to pay for the item, but he declined."

"Is that true?" the judge asked Mr. Mason.

Mr. Mason was momentarily flustered. "Yes, it's true. He cleverly offered. As a Southern gentleman, I refused his money out of courtesy. I have no doubt that as an abolitionist he has the financial backing of wealthy Northerners to pay for incidentals like that helmet. Unfortunately, it was the only one of its kind in this district. My overseer constructed it himself."

The judge scratched his temple. "Let me understand, then, that Mr. Jamison returned your slave to you, but without the helmet."

"Yes, sir," Mr. Mason answered.

"Then what happened?"

"As I said, the next day, my overseer took his tracking dogs into the woods and found the helmet. He returned to the plantation, whereupon he attempted to place it back on the head of my slave. But my slave refused, attacked my overseer, and ran away."

The judge thought for a moment, then said to Uncle Andrew, "Your response?"

Uncle Andrew stood up. "Your Honor, I'm a stranger in these parts and must submit myself to the mercy of the court. The evidence against me is circumstantial at best. I admit to borrowing Mr. Mason's slave and removing the helmet for the reason I had stated, but I see no proof that I enticed the slave to run away. That he did so was unfortunate for Mr. Mason and his overseer, but I cannot connect the event to anything I did. Surely you must be wondering the same thing, Your Honor."

The judge agreed. "Mr. Mason, if you are to make a case against Mr. Jamison, then you must have more evidence to prove that he was an abolitionist who enticed your slave."

I breathed a sigh of relief. I couldn't imagine that Mr. Mason could come up with anything else. I breathed too soon.

"I have other suspicious elements, Your Honor," Mr. Mason said.

"Speak, then."

"I recall that when Mr. Jamison first arrived at my residence, he said nothing about a slave of mine knowing much about birds. But after seeing Clarence in the field, he returned to say that he needed Clarence's assistance the following day. How did Mr. Jamison come by this knowledge that Clarence was experienced with birds?"

The judge tilted his head to Uncle Andrew. "Mr. Jamison?"

Uncle Andrew frowned. "I'm sorry, Your Honor, but my travels put me in contact with a large number of people, slaves included. I cannot recall where I was told that Clarence knew about birds."

There was a murmur through the crowd that told me that this wasn't a good answer.

"Perhaps you heard it from the slave auctioneer," Mr. Mason offered.

"I beg your pardon?"

Mr. Mason looked to the judge. "Your Honor, I have here a witness who will testify that Mr. Jamison had inquired about Clarence and two other slaves prior to setting foot on my property. Perhaps this gentleman told him about Clarence's knowledge of birds."

"Bring him forward," the judge said.

A large bearded man came up to the witness box, gave his oath to tell the truth, then sat down. I recognized him as the slave auctioneer that Uncle Andrew and I spoke to when we first got to Huntsville. He was named Peter Fields.

"Did Mr. Jamison approach you after the last slave auction?" Mr. Mason asked the man.

"He did indeed," Fields answered. "He wanted to know about the slave you keep calling Clarence—the one I sold to you, Mr. Mason. He also asked about Clarence's daughter and another boy that I sold to Colonel Ross."

"Were you aware that Clarence was an expert in birds?" Mr. Mason asked.

"No."

Mr. Mason directed his comments to the judge. "Is this mere coincidence, then, that Mr. Jamison came to my plantation and then went to the Colonel's? I believe he was trying to find Clarence with the intent of luring him away. Perhaps he had the same intent with Clarence's daughter and the other slave."

"That's merely conjecture, Your Honor," Uncle Andrew said. "I told Mr. Mason that I was going to Colonel Ross's—"

Mr. Mason cut in: "Because you had heard that the Colonel had several rare birds there. Again, I must ask, who told you that the Colonel had such birds? I've spoken with the Colonel, and he was not aware of having rare birds on his property."

Uncle Andrew stood up again. "I must say once more that I can't remember who told me about the Colonel's rare birds."

The crowd muttered to themselves, and I know I heard one or two voices say that the abolitionist should be punished. I felt frozen with fear about what would happen.

"How convenient," Mr. Mason snarled. "I'd like to ask Colonel Ross to please come into the courtroom, along with my other witness."

A bailiff called out the door for Colonel Ross. He entered and had Matt and Eveline with him, dressed smartly as attendants for the occasion, and the field slave named Washington.

On the stand, Colonel Ross admitted that he could not positively say that Mr. Jamison was an abolitionist—only that he was a man who was *not* sympathetic to slavery.

"Are there any rare birds on your property, Colonel?" Mr. Mason asked.

"None that I know of," he replied. "Come to think of it, I don't remember Mr. Jamison saying anything about rare birds either."

The crowd mumbled once more and I began to sweat. This wasn't looking good at all.

"You lent him one of your slaves, didn't you, Colonel?" the judge asked.

The Colonel said that he did. "I brought the slave with me to testify."

"So the slave is still here—he didn't run away?" Uncle Andrew asked. "I must be a poor abolitionist, then."

Laughter rippled through the crowd.

"Bring the slave to the witness stand," the judge said.

Washington took the stand and, after he'd been sworn in, was asked by Mr. Mason if he had talked to Mr. Jamison about anything in particular during their afternoon looking for birds.

"Yes, sir," Washington replied as he fixed his eyes on the hat in his lap.

"What did you talk about?" Mr. Mason asked.

"Me and Master Andrew talked about the Underground Railroad. I don't know why but he started telling me about it."

"That's a lie!" I shouted, then immediately regretted it when all eyes fell on me.

"Is there something you want to say, young man?" the judge asked me.

"No, sir," I said and sunk down in my seat.

Uncle Andrew patted my arm. "Your Honor, I believe this slave is confused. Our conversation was the other way around. *He* asked *me*

about the Underground Railroad and I told him as much as I knew—
which, in fact, was nothing."

Washington shook his head slowly.

The judge leveled a gaze at Mr. Mason. "Sir, I will not have a contest of the truth between a free white man and a slave. I believe I'll disregard this portion of your case."

Mr. Mason nodded and the crowd seemed to agree.

"Do you have anything else?" the judge asked.

Mr. Mason said, "No, Your Honor. I think what I've presented
speaks for itself. This gentleman has concocted a series of untruths for
some diabolical purpose—and since my slave has run away, I can only
conclude that he enticed him to do so. I demand that this court punish
him as a Negro thief, if not as a scheming abolitionist."

The crowd shouted their agreement.

After the judge quieted them down, he pointed at Uncle Andrew.
"Rise, sir, and give your defense before I render a judgment."

Uncle Andrew stood up again. I held my breath. Whatever he was
going to say had better be really good.

"Your Honor," he said respectfully, "the evidence is circumstantial
and, if one were to interpret it as diabolical, one could do so. However,
there was nothing diabolical in my activities. I can only submit myself
to the mercy of the court and hope that you will see that I am an innocent man."

The crowd called out for the liar to be hanged. Uncle Andrew sat
down and leaned over to me. "If he finds me guilty, run for your life."

The judge cleared his throat and spoke carefully. "I wish I could
believe in your innocence, Mr. Jamison. But the evidence speaks otherwise. If your intent was not to promote the abolitionist cause or give
assistance to the slave's escape, then please tell me your true purpose
here. Everything indicates that it was *not* to study birds."

A pause fell on the crowd as they strained to hear Uncle Andrew's
reply. But he didn't have a chance to give one. A commotion erupted in
the back of the courtroom. I turned around to see what was going on
and nearly fell out of my chair with surprise.

Clarence walked into the room.

Matt tells about the surprise witness.

AT THE BACK OF THE COURTROOM, I stood with my eyes wide open and my mouth hanging down. Clarence waited by the door for a moment, looking unsure about what to do. Then he saw Mr. Mason and rushed forward. The crowd parted for him and gaped in wonder as he fell at Mr. Mason's feet and said over and over, "I'm sorry, Master. I'm sorry I ran away."

The judge called for order in the court and insisted that Clarence take the stand and tell us what he was doing there. Looking tired and confused, Clarence agreed and sat down in the witness chair.

"All right, boy, tell us where you've been," the judge said.

"Well, sir, I'm sorry, I'm so sorry—"

The judge snapped impatiently, "You're sorry—that much we understand. Now tell us the rest."

Clarence swallowed hard, then began: "It's all my fault, sir. After Master Andrew here took off that terrible big head ornament with the bells—so we could look for birds like he wanted—I promised myself I never wanted that thing put back on my head. You don't know what it's like, sir, unless you had it on yourself. It must weigh almost 15 pounds, and my suffering was great. Not only did it make my head and neck ache something awful, but you can't even lie down to sleep. No, sir, I had to sleep crouching down like some kinda animal. And after it came off, I thought to myself that I was never gonna let it be put on again. Never again . . ." Clarence put his head down and started to cry.

Now, I have to say right here that I had talked to Clarence enough to know that he was a pretty smart man. But the Clarence who spoke in that courtroom wasn't anything at all like the person I knew. His voice was thick and shaky, and after a minute, it dawned on me that he was playing the part of the "dumb slave."

"Get control of yourself, boy!" Mr. Mason growled. "Tell us what happened!"

Clarence wiped his nose with the side of his sleeve. "I tried to hide that hideous helmet in the woods. But later on, when Master Hickocks showed up with it, I was afraid. I knew he was going to put it back on my head, and it was more than I could stand. As he came near me, I felt a horrible, horrible panic deep inside my soul and it was like I was taken over by a wild animal. That's what it was like, sir. I turned into a wild animal and knocked poor Master Hickocks down and ran for the woods. I didn't know what came over me, 'cept I couldn't bear the thought of carrying that contraption on my head again."

The crowd started mumbling to themselves. I couldn't figure out if they were sympathetic to Clarence's story or not.

"I hid in the woods until my senses came back to me," Clarence explained. "And I thought that I had to go back, 'cause I didn't wanna be a runaway anymore. Mr. Mason's is a good place to work—"

With that, Mr. Mason sat up in his chair and nodded.

"—so I thought that I would just turn around and go back. I'd beg for mercy and pray for forgiveness. That's what I was gonna do, too, but then I fell in a hole in the woods and hurt my ankle. The pain was so bad I couldn't move, so I just waited in the woods until I could walk again."

"Why did you come to this court?" the judge asked. "Why didn't you go back to the plantation?"

"I was going to, but on the road I heard it told that poor Master Andrew had been accused of helping me to run away. I felt awful, terrible. So I said to myself that I would come straight here so Master Andrew wouldn't be punished because of me. Here I am, Mr. Mason, and I'm sorry, sir. I'm sorry right down to my bones. I won't ever do anything like it again. You can even put the bells back on my head. That's how bad I feel."

Mr. Mason waved his hand at Clarence as if to say that all was forgiven and he wouldn't put the helmet back on.

"Mr. Jamison," the judge said, "considering this evidence, I order that you be released at once and please accept this court's apology for any inconvenience or slight of your character this case has caused."

Reverend Andrew stood up. "Thank you, Your Honor. I am grateful for your time and the fair manner in which you conducted this investigation."

"Case dismissed!" the judge shouted.

It's hard to describe the chaos of the courtroom then. The place erupted. Everyone crowded forward to shake Reverend Andrew's hand or commend Mr. Mason for getting his slave back. A lot of things happened at once. Everyone seemed amazed that it turned out the way it did. I glanced over at Jack, but I didn't dare yell or wave. Eveline and I had to stay still at Colonel Ross's side with serious expressions on our faces. I was pretty sure, though, that Eveline was bursting to see her dad.

Mr. Mason was all smiles again and shook Reverend Andrew's hand. "Mr. Jamison, I'm sorry for misjudging you. I should have respected my first impression that you were a true gentleman."

"Think nothing of it, Mr. Mason," Reverend Andrew said.

"There must be something I can do to make it up to you," Mr. Mason said. "Will you dine with me this evening? Allow me hours of contrition for what I've done."

"I will be happy to dine with you, sir, but I ask one other favor."

"Name it," Mr. Mason said.

"I beg you not to punish Clarence for what he's done. He admits he was a fool and behaved abominably against you and your overseer. But, for my sake, please do not punish him."

Mr. Mason looked as if he might not agree, then nodded yes. "I won't punish him."

Reverend Andrew shook Clarence's hand and they swapped an expression that made me realize how brave Clarence was to come back like he did. He risked his life for Reverend Andrew—and Jack. It'd be easy enough for Mr. Mason to go back on his word and punish Clarence hard for what he'd done. And I had no doubt that Mr. Hickocks, the overseer, would want a hand in that.

Somewhere in the confusion, Reverend Andrew leaned down and said something to Jack. Jack looked up at me as if he wanted to say something, but Colonel Ross signaled for us to follow him out of the courtroom. "Come on," he growled.

I reluctantly obeyed and slowly followed. I didn't want the Colonel to have the satisfaction of seeing I still hurt. When we got out to his carriage, another man shouted at the Colonel, and they walked off together to talk. Eveline and I waited. I knew what she was thinking: She wanted to run to her father. I figured it was all she could do to stand still and just wait the way she was supposed to.

Jack suddenly came rushing through the front door of the court building, then saw us and tried to act casual. I looked around to make sure we weren't being watched, then wiggled a finger for him to come over.

"That was a close call," he said.

"I was sweating bullets," I said. My eyes locked on Eveline's and for the first time I noticed she'd been crying.

"Are you okay?" I asked her.

"I wanted to be with my daddy," she said.

Jack double-checked to make sure no one was listening, then said quietly, "Maybe you can be with him *tonight*."

Her face lit up.

"What's the plan?" I asked.

Jack shrugged. "I don't know, but Uncle Andrew said to be ready tonight. Can you make it?"

I stood up straight as if to show him that my back wasn't bothering me. "I'll make it. I'm all better."

He looked at me as if he didn't believe me.

Jonah suddenly rounded the corner of the carriage and frowned when he saw Jack. "Scoot, boy," he said. "You're nothing but trouble around here. Go about your business."

"Yes, sir," Jack said and walked away.

He glanced back at me and Eveline one last time. I smiled and mouthed the word *Tonight*.

Jack tells about the plan to escape.

AT THE INN LATER that afternoon, Uncle Andrew and I packed up the last of our things. "I don't get it," I said. "Aren't we worse off than we were? How can we escape tonight?"

"Because after tonight, I don't believe Clarence will ever have a chance to escape again. Here's my idea: I will go to Mr. Mason's for dinner. After the meal, I will ask to see Clarence—to once again thank him for helping me today. I suspect that Mr. Mason won't put Clarence back in that atrocious head gear until he's certain I'm out of the area. After all, he promised he wouldn't punish the poor man."

I sat on the edge of the bed. "So you'll get Clarence and make a run for it after dinner?"

"Crudely put, but correct. I will make as if to leave right after I see Clarence, then circle around to his quarters and escape."

"What if Mr. Hickocks is there? What if they're keeping a close eye on him?" I asked.

Uncle Andrew looked at me impatiently. "I didn't say it was a *fool-proof* plan. Many things could go wrong. But we must pray that we'll overcome any and all obstacles."

I wished I had his confidence. "What about me?" I asked.

"I want you to run back to the Colonel's and help Matt and Eveline escape."

"Oh," I said. "Is that all? Just walk in and help them escape?"

Uncle Andrew chuckled. "I have a friend who will create a diversion to help you."

"You keep talking about a friend who's gotten you information and sets things up. Just who is this guy?" I asked.

"Jack, in times like these, you never know when or where a friend will turn up," he answered. "Just listen. Hide near the back door. When the diversion comes, take Matt and Eveline and run for the hollow tree."

I folded my arms skeptically. "I don't know where the hollow tree is."

Uncle Andrew grabbed a large sheet of paper from the dresser and spread it out on the bed. "Take a look at this map and you'll have all you need to know."

CHAPTER TWELVE

Matt tells about the escape.

I COULDN'T FIGURE OUT how in the world Reverend Andrew and Jack were going to get us all away. After the big courtroom drama, we went back to Colonel Ross's plantation and got to work as usual. Jonah told me to polish the silver in the dining room—which is what I was doing when the thunder roared and another storm dropped gallons of rain on us. The rain kept on going into the early evening.

The sun went down and Eveline and I kept looking at each other, wondering what was going to happen. It drove me crazy, waiting like that. To make matters worse, Jonah was in a bad mood and kept telling me to do things. I had a feeling that it was connected to the courtroom somehow. After all the excitement there, he seemed angry.

At one point, Scout, who was leashed to his doghouse just outside the back door, started barking at something. Jonah yelled at him to shut up.

I never heard Jonah yell like that.

"Go get some more wood for the fire," he said. I had just finished sweeping the kitchen floor while Lizzie had Eveline cutting up carrots for dinner.

I looked out the back door at the downpour and hesitated.

"I said to go get some more wood!" he said harshly.

"Yes, sir," I said and ran into the rain. Scout peeked his head out of the doghouse and snarled at me. I thought: *He's just waiting for the chance to bite me. I know it.* I ducked around the side of the shed to where we kept the split logs covered. Just as I reached down to grab an armload, someone grabbed me from behind.

I was afraid that it was Kinsey. He seemed to enjoy picking on the slaves—especially the house slaves, because he thought we were spoiled and pampered. I jerked away and spun around to face Jack.

"What took you so long?" I asked.

"I've been busy," Jack said.

"Busy with what?" I teased.

"Busy waiting out here in the rain for you to come out. I couldn't figure out how to get your attention without everybody seeing me," he said.

I smiled because he was soaked from head to toe, his dark hair matted against his face.

"What's so funny?" he asked.

I shook my head. "Nothing. What's the plan?"

"All I know is that a friend of Uncle Andrew's is going to create a diversion so you and Eveline can run out here. Then the three of us'll hightail it into the woods."

"*That's* the plan?" I couldn't believe it.

"What did you expect? A squadron of helicopters to fly in and get you?"

"But who's this friend?"

"I don't know. Hasn't anybody shown up?"

"No. It's just the usual people. Colonel Ross's wife is supposed to come home from her trip tonight, but that's it."

Jack rubbed his chin. "Do you think *she's* the friend?"

"Beats me."

"Well, I'll wait out here. Hopefully whatever's gonna happen will happen *soon*. I'm getting cold."

"You could always crawl in with Scout," I suggested.

"The dog? Are you kidding? I thought he was going to take my leg off when I first got here." Jack looked at the stupid grin on my face. "What? What's so funny?"

"You are," I said. I'd never admit it out loud, but it was really good to see him.

"Matthew!" Jonah shouted from the back door. "Where are you, boy?"

I started grabbing up some logs. "I better get back inside. Stay dry."

Jack nodded and retreated to wherever he had been hiding behind the shed.

Back in the kitchen, Jonah frowned at me. "What did you do, get lost?"

"No, sir." I threw some of the logs into the stove and leaned over to Eveline and whispered: "Be ready to run."

"What'd you say?" Jonah asked from the other side of the kitchen. "What's this whispering?"

"Nothing, sir," I said. Suddenly I was worried that Jonah would figure out what was going on and try to stop us from escaping.

Colonel Ross walked in the kitchen and pointed a finger at Eveline. "You—I want you to go up and prepare my wife's bedroom for her arrival tonight. I want it clean as a whistle."

"Yes, sir," she said and curtsied.

He looked at me. "Boy, I want you to give my boots a good polish. They're in my wardrobe."

"Yes, sir," I said. My mind went wild with the problems the Colonel's work would cause. If Eveline was in one room and I was in another, how would we talk? If we were upstairs, would we hear the diversion—whatever it was—when it happened?

I was surprised when Jonah spoke up. "Colonel, it might be better to wait until we have dinner all fixed and ready."

Colonel Ross looked at Jonah impatiently. "Are you telling me that you and Lizzie can't make dinner yourselves? You sure got the work done before we had this boy and girl. Are you getting lazy?"

"No, sir, Colonel," Jonah said.

"Then I expect the work to be done," the Colonel said, then turned on his heel and walked out.

Eveline and I looked worriedly at each other and slowly started to follow.

Just as we reached the door, Jonah put his hand on our shoulders and pulled us back. "Don't go," he said.

I looked at him, confused.

He gave a signal to Lizzie. She nodded and picked up a large bucket of fat.

"Ready?" he asked.

"I . . . I don't understand," I said.

"This is your way out," Jonah answered. "You two grab your coats and get ready to run."

"You mean, *you're* Reverend Andrew's friend?" I asked, shocked.

"*We* are," Lizzie said.

"I reckon you could call us the departure depot for the Underground Railroad," Jonah said. "Now get ready to run."

We grabbed our coats and bundled up as fast as we could.

"Jonah!" the Colonel shouted from down the hall. He was coming our way.

"Hurry!" Jonah whispered.

Eveline and I were as ready as we were going to be.

Jonah waved at Lizzie. "Go on, woman—watch yourself."

Lizzie tossed the fat on the fire. It spat, then roared at her in a burst of flame.

"Fire! Fire!" Jonah yelled as he pushed us out the back door. The rain was still falling. Scout leapt forward and ran at us until his rope yanked him back.

Jack rushed out from behind the shed. "Is that it?" he shouted.

"Let's go!" I yelled back. We ran straight for the field.

Kinsey rounded the corner of the house and ran right into us. "What's going on here?" he asked.

"There's a fire in the kitchen," I told him.

Kinsey looked at the flames rising in the kitchen window, but suddenly looked at Jack, then me and Eveline. "What are you doing out here? Where do you think you're going?"

The three of us were speechless.

"You three get over there by the door. You're going to help fight this fire," Kinsey said.

"Fight it yourself!" I said and threw myself into Kinsey to give him a push. He tumbled backward into a feeding trough that was filled with water. "Run!" I yelled.

We ran into the darkness of the field, our feet splashing through the puddles and mud.

I heard Kinsey shout and turned in time to see him scramble out of the trough. He grabbed Scout's collar and untied him. "Get 'em, Scout!"

Scout tore after us.

I shrieked, "Faster!" and we all picked up speed.

Just as we reached the edge of the woods, Scout caught up with us. I was sure he was going to dive at one of us, teeth first. But suddenly Eveline turned around and pointed a finger at him. "No, Scout! No!"

Scout stopped dead in his tracks and looked at her.

"Go home!" she said.

Scout looked like he couldn't make up his mind, barking and growling at us.

"Go home!" Eveline said more firmly.

Scout then turned and halfheartedly made his way back toward the house. I wanted to ask her how she made Scout obey like that. But there wasn't time.

"Come on," Eveline said and we followed her into the woods.

The rain fell hard as we ran and ran until we couldn't run anymore.

CHAPTER THIRTEEN

Matt tells about crossing the river.

SOMEHOW IN THE STORM we found an old barn where we hid under a moldy pile of hay. The next morning we woke up huddled together, cold and hungry. The rain had stopped.

"We have to go," Eveline said as she stood up.

As far as I could tell, the sun was just peeking over the horizon. Jack refused to budge.

I tried to stretch out my stiff arms and legs. They hurt.

Eveline stood in the middle of the barn with a stern expression on her face and firmness in her voice. "We have to go, y'hear?"

Somewhere in the silence of the morning, I heard dogs barking.

"Man, somebody owns a lot of dogs," Jack grumbled and rolled over.

"Those aren't dogs. They're hounds," Eveline said.

I sat up and looked at her to confirm what I thought she meant. "Hounds . . . that are hunting for us?"

She nodded.

"Jack!" I said and gave him a hard jab. "Those dogs want to have us for breakfast!"

Jack was on his feet before me and headed for the barn door. "We have to get out of here!"

"And go where?" I asked.

Jack jerked out a crudely drawn map from his pocket and pointed to it. "We've been following Griffith's Creek all the way up. We need to get across and find the hollow tree."

"How many miles do you think we ran last night?" I asked.

Jack shrugged. "I'm no good at figuring that kind of thing. It felt like a hundred."

"I reckon we ran about 10 miles," Eveline said.

"Which means we have to run another 10," Jack said wearily.

"We won't be running anywhere if we don't get out of here *now*," Eveline said. "Those dogs are getting closer."

She was right. I could hear them barking and yelping. We checked to make sure there wasn't anyone around the barn, then made a mad dash for Griffith's Creek.

Though the rain had stopped, Griffith's Creek was flooded. It poured over both banks in a torrent.

"What do we do now?" I asked as I tried to figure our chances of crossing over.

Jack, panicked, pulled out the map again, and looked for an alternate route.

"That won't help us," Eveline said. "We have to follow it north and hope to the Lord that we'll find a place to cross over."

Jack and I agreed with her and were just about to leave when a dog barked behind us. We nearly jumped out of our skins.

"Scout!" Eveline said.

I couldn't believe my own eyes. "Did he follow us?"

"Or maybe he's leading those hounds to us," Eveline said. "That's what he's trained to do."

Scout paced back and forth a few feet away from us.

"Go home, Scout!" Eveline shouted. He didn't obey her.

"Well?" Jack asked. "I'm all out of doggie biscuits."

"Should we throw rocks at him?" I asked.

"No," Eveline said. "It'll only make him mad—maybe attack us himself."

"He likes you. He wouldn't attack . . . would he?" I wondered.

Eveline watched Scout, then reached out and took my hand. "Hold hands," she ordered.

"What?"

"Hold hands real tight. We have to go into the creek," she said.

Jack hesitated. "But we don't know how deep it is."

"We can't stay here," Eveline said impatiently. "If we go in the creek, if we can make it across, the dogs'll lose our scent. Maybe even Scout won't follow us. He's not crazy enough to get in this water."

I protested, "If *he's* not that crazy, why should we be?"

"Because *he* won't get whipped and sold when they get him back to the plantation," Eveline answered.

The three of us grabbed hands and slowly waded into the cold, rushing water of Griffith's Creek. Scout whined at us from the creek's edge but didn't follow. In fact, he did something I never expected: He lay down and put his head between his two front paws.

"What's he doing?" I asked Eveline.

She glanced back. "I don't know. Funny, but if he's the lead dog of the pack, he should've run back to help guide the rest of the hounds to us."

The water was up to our waists, and we strained with all our might to hold on to each other. The current threatened to knock us over. One wrong step and I knew we'd be goners.

"This is no creek," Jack said, "it's a *river*."

The hounds were still in the distance, but getting closer all the time. Scout stayed where he was along the creek's edge. I didn't know much about dogs, but what he was doing didn't make any sense.

Suddenly Eveline let out a shriek. "It's the lead hound!" she cried.

I looked over my shoulder and saw a single mangy-looking dog follow our scent to the creek. He seemed excited by the scent. Oblivious to Scout who stayed put, the hound pranced back and forth, barking and howling. Even in that dim morning light, I saw his long, white teeth and the slobber that sprayed back and forth. I imagined a whole pack of them rushing into the water to make a meal out of us.

"What's that mean? There's only one," Jack said.

"The rest'll be here soon," Eveline said in a choked voice. "God have mercy!"

I didn't know which was worse, wading into that deep creek with the fear of falling and drowning, or facing the coming dogs.

It's hard to talk about what happened next because it was so horrible, but it saved our lives. Scout, who had been lying perfectly still, suddenly lunged out at the hound. I don't think it knew what hit him. In a flash, Scout had the hound's throat in his vicelike jaws. The hound yelped, but the sound was cut off instantly. It fought to get free, wrenching its head back and forth, but Scout wouldn't give up. Pretty soon the hound's struggle ended, and it went limp.

We stood mesmerized where we were in the water, too terrified to make a move. Scout shook the hound a couple of times and, sure that it was dead, dragged its carcass to the creek. The current caught the hound and sent it floating away downstream.

With tears streaming down her face, she cried out to Scout, "Thank you, Scout! Thank you! Oh, thank You, Lord."

"What happened?" I mumbled.

"The rest of the pack'll be lost without their lead hound," Eveline said. "Hurry! Move upstream!"

We got to shallower waters and waded against the current and away from Scout. He didn't follow but stood watching us.

"Come on, Scout!" Eveline called.

We joined in. He was our hero now. We didn't want to go on without him.

Scout just watched us for a moment, then suddenly turned and ran away into the woods. I wanted to believe that he was coming up with a scheme to lead the pack of hounds away from us. After what I had just seen, I could believe anything of that dog. The hounds' barking soon faded until we couldn't hear them anymore.

Staying in the creek, we waded about a quarter of a mile until we found a section with a fallen tree. It worked as a bridge for us to get across.

Safe and sound, Jack got a bright idea. "Let's try to knock the tree into the creek. Then it'll be even harder for anybody to follow us."

"What about my daddy and Reverend Andrew?" Eveline asked.

In our rush, I think I had it in my mind that they were already up ahead of us, waiting at the hollow tree. It hadn't occurred to me that they might still be somewhere behind us—*if* they were even able to escape at all.

Eveline's sad expression made me and Jack feel awful. We had forgotten, but she hadn't.

"How will they get across?" she asked on the verge of crying.

"What if we're *already* across?" Clarence asked as he stepped out from behind a tree. He stretched out his arms toward his daughter.

"Daddy!" she shouted and ran into one of the best hugs I've ever seen in my life.

"Hello, my baby," Clarence said.

"Well, boys? How did you do?" Reverend Andrew asked. He stepped out from behind another tree nearby. "I was getting worried about you."

"Uncle Andrew," Jack said, relieved to see him. "You were worried about *us*? Nothing to it. We were getting worried about *you*."

"It was a piece of cake for us—once I gave that overseer a good knock on the head," he replied.

"That makes two he's gotten in the last couple of days," Clarence said with a laugh.

"Why didn't you tell us that Jonah was the friend you kept getting your information from?" Jack asked.

"Because I didn't dare risk that you could expose him. He and Lizzie are two of the most valuable assets we have in the Underground Railroad. They feed us helpful information constantly—and the Colonel would never guess it. You see, Jack, you never know when or where your friends will turn up."

I thought about Scout and figured that truer words had never been spoken.

CHAPTER FOURTEEN

Matt tells about their "ride" on the Underground Railroad.

WITHIN A FEW HOURS AFTER we were all together again, Reverend Andrew led us to the first "stop" in the Underground Railroad to the North. It was a farmhouse in the middle of nowhere where an old man and woman fixed us a hot meal and let us sleep in some beds they'd set up in secret rooms near the back of the house. When night came, we headed out again. We walked for miles and miles along dirt roads, through damp woods, and across muddy fields. It was tiring, but just about the time we thought we couldn't walk anymore, we came to another "stop" and felt okay again. People all along the way greeted us like long-lost family. I knew then how it must have felt for blacks to go from the cruel treatment of the slave-owning whites to the kindness and generosity of those whites who wanted slavery abolished—and would sacrifice all they had to make it that way.

Jack and I talked about ending the adventure. Since Clarence and Eveline were back together again, we thought we could tell Whit to flip the switch that would stop the Imagination Station. But we both had a nagging feeling that the story couldn't really end until we were back where we started: in Odyssey.

There isn't much point to telling everything that happened on our journey. I guess it's enough to say that we made it back to Odyssey on a cold evening while the sun set over the town. We went straight to the church where Reverend Andrew—even Jack started calling him "Reverend" again—said he would start a fire in the big potbelly stove and would make us rest on the beds in the basement. But we had forgotten that the basement was torn up when the slave hunters broke in. *It was such a long, long time ago*, I thought.

"Then we'll go to my hotel," Reverend Andrew said.

We all reacted the same way, and basically it came down to: "Are you nuts? Don't you remember what happened before?"

Reverend Andrew shook his head. "I remember well enough—and after what we've been through, I defy *anyone* to bother us now."

Clarence spoke up first. "With respect, Reverend, I think we'd all feel better if you were *sure* we could get to the hotel safely. Otherwise, I'm happy to stay here—or move on to the next station—as long as I'm with Eveline."

Reverend Andrew looked at them both, then agreed. "Jack, do you want to come with me?"

"I guess so," Jack answered.

"We'll be back in an hour," Reverend Andrew announced.

But things weren't right in Odyssey, and it was a lot less than an hour before we saw them again.

Jack picks up the story.

Reverend Andrew and I walked to the hotel just as the shops were closing the day's business. I wish I could describe the looks on people's faces when they saw us (well, not *us* really—Reverend Andrew mostly). You could hear the "buzz" of everyone talking.

We got to the hotel and Reverend Andrew went straight up to the manager's office and knocked hard.

"Come in," a voice called from the other side.

Reverend Andrew opened it, and a well-dressed man with slicked-down, brown hair and a handlebar mustache stood behind a big, oak desk. He couldn't hide his surprise. "Reverend! You're back!"

"I am, indeed, Nathaniel," Reverend Andrew said. "I went south to reclaim those poor souls who were taken from me."

"Come in, come in, sit down," Nathaniel offered.

Reverend Andrew declined. "I'll get to the point, my good friend. I have the three Negroes with me, and I want to bring them back to my rooms for a bath and a rest. Do you have any grievances with that?"

Nathaniel's eyes bugged out. "Now, Reverend, you know that I, personally, do not have a grievance against it, but you've been away for a while and . . ." He signaled for us to come fully into his office, and after we did, he closed the door.

"This is a bad time, Reverend," he explained. "The town is torn apart by arguments between the abolitionists and the pro-slavery factions. Twice now we've had assemblies in the streets that I feared might lead to violence. If you brought your Negroes into the light of day—and to this hotel—I don't believe we'd survive it."

"Then so be it," Reverend Andrew said. "Perhaps it's time for Odyssey to make up its mind about what it believes."

Nathaniel's expression was calm, but his voice shook. "That may be true, but the law remains on the side of those who support slavery and the return of any runaway slaves. The slave hunters, those who caused all that trouble before, are here. You'll risk the lives of your friends by bringing them out into the open. The slave hunters will take them again."

"Perhaps it's time for Odyssey to force a change in the law. The slave owners are so adamant about states' rights, then what about *this* state's right to throw the slave hunters out on their ears?"

"I'm just a hotel manager," Nathaniel said as an appeal.

"And I'm just a pastor," Reverend Andrew said. "We all have a responsibility to our brothers in need."

Nathaniel frowned. "It's dangerous."

"Most of the great causes are. Will you send one of your trusted staff to Adam Green's place? Please tell him I've returned and that I'm expecting trouble."

"Then?"

"He'll know what to do."

We walked back into the lobby where the guests eyed us nervously. A short man with a twitchy face raced up to Reverend Andrew and whispered in his ear. Reverend Andrew nodded and thanked the man.

"I have a bad feeling about this," I said.

"So you should," Reverend Andrew said as he picked up his pace to a jog. "The slave hunters know we're here. We have to get back to the church immediately."

We got there in a few minutes, and we didn't like what we saw as we walked up to the door. Several men with torches sat on horseback. One climbed off and I remembered from before that he was the sheriff. He had black and white stubble all over his face and looked tired. Though it was a cool evening, there were dark rings of sweat around his armpits.

"Good evening, Sheriff," Reverend Andrew said cordially.

"Reverend, I'm glad to see you back in town."

"Thank you. I appreciate you coming here personally to say so."

The sheriff scratched at his stubble. "I'm here to make sure we don't have any trouble. Have you got runaways in your church?"

"I have a free man, his daughter, and a freeborn boy visiting my church," Reverend Andrew explained.

The sheriff winced. "Aw, now, Reverend . . . why? Do you have any idea of the problems I've been having around here?"

"You have my sympathy," Reverend Andrew said with a smile. "Let's go inside, Jack. We need to start that fire, make some tea, and fix up those beds."

He and I stepped toward the front door.

"Reverend—"

"Listen to me, Sheriff. I don't want any trouble, but I have a feeling it's going to come anyway. I suppose you and your men should decide now on which side of the trouble you wish to place yourselves." Reverend Andrew closed the door.

Just as Reverend Andrew said, we built a fire in the big potbelly stove, made some tea, and fixed the beds in the basement. No one felt much like sleeping.

"What do you reckon will happen?" Clarence asked.

Reverend Andrew shook his head. "Only God knows, Clarence. But my educated guess is that the slave hunters will come and try to take you back again."

"We won't go back," Clarence said firmly. "We'd rather die first."

Matt and I exchanged glances across the room. Was this part of the story? Were Clarence and Eveline really supposed to get hurt when they got back to Odyssey? Was our part in this whole thing just to bring them to their deaths?

A door slammed in the sanctuary upstairs, and Reverend Andrew excused himself to go investigate. I said I'd go with him, but he waved me back.

Eveline cupped her mug of tea in her hands and began to pray softly.

Clarence leaped to his feet. "No, sir, we haven't come all this way *again* just to get caught. No, sir. I won't let it happen."

I decided to creep upstairs to see what was going on.

"I'm coming with you," Matt said.

The front door of the church was open just a crack and we watched while Reverend Andrew talked to two of the slave hunters who'd captured Clarence, Eveline, and Matt before. One was tall and had a hooked nose and bushy mustache. "That's Hank," Matt whispered.

The other man had a round baby face and wore a vest stretched tight over his big belly. Matt said his name was Sonny.

The two slave hunters were arguing with the Reverend about handing over Clarence and Eveline. "We'll let you keep the one who says he's free," Hank said.

"Gentlemen," the Reverend said, "my church is a sanctuary and I warn you that if you enter it with the intention of capturing *anyone* inside, I will be forced to take action."

The sheriff stepped forward. "I believe there must be a peaceful solution to this conflict. I won't have violence in my town. I promise you, I won't."

"Then you better do something, Sheriff!" a man in the gathering crowd shouted. The light from a torch flickered on his face. I remembered him from before, too. He was a loudmouth who believed in slavery. "Some of us in town are getting sick of the way the Reverend here ignores the laws! These men have a *right* to take those runaway slaves back to their masters!" The crowd shouted their agreement.

"Now hold on, hold on," the sheriff said.

Another man pushed to the front of the crowd and shook a fist in the loudmouth's face. "No one has the *right* to take another man as a slave! And I'm telling all of you now, there are those of us in Odyssey who won't tolerate these slave hunters anymore!"

"There are those of us who won't tolerate you slave lovers anymore!"

The two men started pushing each other. The sheriff stepped in. "Stop it, boys!" he ordered.

They pushed him away. Then the crowd moved forward with shouts from both sides. Fists started flying. We stepped aside so that Reverend Andrew could back into the church and close the door. Then he locked it.

"Is that a riot?" I asked, wondering why I wasn't more afraid.

"I always knew it would come to this," he said sadly. "Citizen against citizen, brother fighting against brother. That's what the cruelty of slavery does to men's hearts." Bodies banged against the door as the shouts continued. I thought I heard a gun go off.

Matt said, "One of them's missing, Reverend Andrew. I didn't see Boss."

"Boss?"

"He's the leader. Remember? There were *three* slave hunters. Why wasn't he out there?"

Just then we all got the same idea: "He's sneaking in through the tunnel!"

We ran back through the church and started down the wooden steps to the basement. Eveline was sitting on the edge of her bed. Clarence was using a poker to jab at the fire. Boss, a squinty-eyed man with thick eyebrows and permanent frown on his hard face, was sneaking in through the tunnel door. He had a gun drawn.

First, Reverend Andrew shouted from the stairs. "Boss!"

Boss looked up and Clarence, thinking fast, spun around with the poker and threw it at the slave hunter. Boss raised his arm and deflected the poker away onto one of the mattresses. In that split second, Clarence leapt like a tiger onto Boss. They slammed against the wall, the gun waving around wildly in Boss's hand, and then they fell onto the mattress where the poker was. Clarence was on the bottom, and his back pressed against the hot spike. He screamed and threw Boss off. The gun slipped from Boss's hand and landed at Reverend Andrew's feet as he was rushing toward the two men. Reverend Andrew snatched up the gun just as Boss grabbed the poker. Boss was just about to hit Clarence with the poker when Reverend Andrew fired the gun. Boss grabbed his side as he spun around, then collapsed with a groan on the ground.

We stared at Reverend Andrew. I think he was as shocked as we were at what he'd done.

"Through the tunnel," he shouted. "We have to get out of here!"

"What about me?" Boss cried out, still clutching his side.

"I'll come back for you, son," Reverend Andrew said as he picked up an oil lamp. "You deserve to be left here, but I'm a servant of God and I'll come back. I promise."

We followed Reverend Andrew through the door into the dark tunnel. He lit the lamp. "This way," he said.

Somewhere, farther up the tunnel, we heard shouts. Boss must've heard the shouts, too, because he started calling for whoever it was to come help. "They're in here! Don't let them get away!"

"Where do we go now?" Clarence asked.

Reverend Andrew suddenly stopped midway up the tunnel and turned to the wall. "Push this," he told us. He pushed at the wall. The rocks gave way and spilled inward. We helped until we'd cleared the entrance to *another* tunnel. "It's my emergency escape," he said.

We ran down the tunnel, skipping over fallen rocks and coughing at the thick air.

"Are you sure this leads somewhere?" Clarence asked.

"To the old rectory," Reverend Andrew explained. "It's the ruined house not far away."

I remembered seeing it the first time we tried to escape from the church.

We reached the end of the tunnel and saw a wooden ladder. "Hold this, please," Reverend Andrew said and passed the lamp to Clarence. He climbed up the ladder and pushed at something above. It sounded like a latch. With a rusty groan, it opened, and a burst of fresh air poured in. Scrambling up the ladder, he called for us to follow.

I nearly had a heart attack when we got to the top. We were in the middle of what looked like the remains of a house. A band of men with torches and horses surrounded us, and I thought for sure that we were caught.

"Thank you for coming, Adam," Reverend Andrew said to a man at the front of the group.

"Glad you're back, Reverend," Adam said. "What would you like me to do?"

Reverend Andrew gestured to us. "Take these friends of mine to the next station on the Railroad. They're not safe here."

"Yes, sir," Adam said. "Can you ride horses?"

Clarence nodded. "I can. My daughter can ride with me."

"Then get on. I don't think it'll be long before that riot makes its way here."

We looked in the direction of the church. The shouts and chaos were unmistakable. It was a full-scale riot.

"Oh no," Reverend Andrew said. Flames reflected off the glass on the inside of the church. "They're burning my church down!"

Clarence climbed on the horse and then pulled Eveline up to his lap.

"What about your two boys?" Adam asked.

"We're staying," Matt said.

Reverend Andrew turned to face us. "You can't. They'll try to take you as a slave again."

"They won't be able to," Matt said.

Reverend Andrew persisted, "I don't know that I can stop them."

"You won't have to stop them," I said with a strange confidence. "We have another way out."

"How?"

I smiled at him. "You never know when or where your friends will turn up."

Reverend Andrew waved at Adam. "Go, then. Hurry."

"Right," Adam said and gave his horse a nudge.

"No, wait," Clarence said. "Reverend . . . Matt . . . Jack . . . I don't know how to thank you." He reached down and shook our hands.

"Thank you," Eveline said. She had tears in her eyes. Suddenly, with Clarence holding on, she threw herself halfway off the horse and grabbed Matt to kiss him. She pulled me close, too, and kissed me on the cheek. Then Reverend Andrew.

"Lord love you," she whispered.

Clarence pulled her back up, tugged at the reins on his horse, and steered it away. Adam and his men followed. With a "Hyah," they raced off into the night.

The mob around the front of the church drifted to the side and someone saw us. With shouts and angry gestures, the crowd moved our way.

Reverend Andrew gestured to us. "Well, boys? Care to run for the woods?"

I looked at Matt, and we both knew it was time to go home.

"Good-bye, Reverend Andrew," I said. "Thank you for everything."

He shook my hand. "You're welcome, Jack. You made a nice nephew for a while."

"See ya, Reverend Andrew," Matt said and held out his hand.

Reverend Andrew took it but pulled him close for a hug. He then wrapped his other arm around me.

My face was buried in his side so that all was dark. I felt that roller-coaster feeling again and thought my legs might slip out from under me.

I heard Matt say, "Hey, what's going on?"

And then the Imagination Station wound down.

CHAPTER FIFTEEN

Matt wraps it up.

THE IMAGINATION STATION door *whooshed* open. Mr. Whittaker stood just outside with his hands on his hips. "Well?"

Jack crawled out. "What an adventure!" he said.

I got out behind him and realized right away that I didn't feel stiff or sore. I reached up and touched my back where I'd been whipped. It felt fine. "That's weird. I wasn't hurt."

"I hope not," Mr. Whittaker said with concern. "Whatever you experienced in the Imagination Station should never come out with you—except what you learned, of course."

"So . . . was it *all* just in our imaginations?" Jack asked.

"Yes . . . and no," Mr. Whittaker smiled. "The stories you went through are based on the truth, on history. It was your imaginations that let you take part in them."

"What happened after we left?" I asked. "What became of Reverend Andrew and Clarence and Eveline and—"

Mr. Whittaker held up his hand. "One thing at a time. Let's talk about Odyssey."

"Yeah, we left in the middle of a riot. I didn't know we had riots in Odyssey," Jack said.

Mr. Whittaker pointed to the old newspaper on the workbench. "The Odyssey Riots of November 1858 are well known to anyone who's studied our local history. They caused several things to happen . . . some good, some not so good. The town finally made up its mind about how it felt toward the slavery issue—and became the first in the state to refuse to cooperate with slave hunters."

"That's good," I said. "What's not so good?"

"The church burned down."

"No!" Jack cried out.

"Everything except for the church tower. It was the only thing left standing. You can still see it."

"Where?" I asked.

"Right upstairs," Mr. Whittaker answered. "It's the tower you see on the side of Whit's End."

"*What?*" Jack and I said together.

His white mustache spread out in a broad smile. "Uh-huh. This building was built on the site of the church. The tunnel leading into this very workroom was used by Reverend Andrew and the Underground Railroad."

"What happened to Reverend Andrew?" Jack asked.

"Reverend Andrew Jamison later became a leading light in the fight against slavery. He later lost his life while ministering to Union soldiers during the Civil War."

This made Jack and me go quiet for a moment. Somehow I think we had hoped that he lived on for years and years.

"It shouldn't surprise you that he would sacrifice himself that way," Mr. Whittaker observed. "He said he was God's servant and believed it through to death."

"How about Clarence and Eveline?" I asked.

Mr. Whittaker smiled again. "You'll like this part. Clarence and Eveline took the Underground Railroad all the way to Canada, where they were reunited with Lucy—Clarence's wife and Eveline's mother. They lived there until Clarence died, then Lucy and Eveline moved to Chicago. Eveline got married to a fine gentleman named William Teller, and they had children of their own."

I thought about it quietly for a minute and had a strange feeling. "Maybe one day we'll bump into someone who was related to them. Maybe they don't know all that their ancestors went through to be free."

"Maybe so," Mr. Whittaker said. "But now *you* know, right? You've seen what it's like to be in a time when you couldn't take freedom for granted."

We nodded.

He said, "I hope that makes you appreciate your freedom even more now—that it's something to be treasured."

As a kid who never thought much of being black, I realized I had a lot to be thankful for.

◎ ◎ ◎

When I got home, I asked my mom and dad if we had any books or papers about the history of our family. They were surprised that I would ask, but then said they did. Dad took me into our little family library and pulled out a book with "Our Family Record" stamped in gold on the front.

"Because our ancestors were slaves, the records don't go back very far," my dad explained.

"How far back does it go?" I asked.

He pointed to the top of a page where a tree had names filled in on various branches. "Right there."

Clarence and *Lucille*, it said on one side.

He traced his finger down to the next line. *William & Eveline Teller* it said.

I followed the lines down the page until the names came to my grandfather, then my father and his family. "No way," I said in complete and absolute disbelief. "You mean, I'm related to Clarence and Eveline?"

Dad looked at me, puzzled. "Sure. Why? Do you know something about them?"

"Oh, Dad," I said with a laugh, "have I got a story for you!"

BOOK FOUR

THE STRANGER'S MESSAGE

Note: In 1897, Charles Sheldon wondered what would happen if an entire town decided to "do as Jesus would do" throughout their homes and workplaces. The answer was the classic novel *In His Steps*. It is this author's hope that our *Odysseyized*-adaptation of the same concept will inspire readers to go back to the original book and take to heart its simple yet powerful message.

CHAPTER ONE

"LORD, HELP ME," John Avery Whittaker said under his breath as he sat down once again at the oak desk in his study. His plea for help had an uncharacteristic edge to it. He had been trying to assemble the questions for a Bible contest he was hosting at his shop, Whit's End, later that evening, but one interruption after another conspired to keep him from his work. Three phone calls, a door-to-door salesman, the postman, and a pesky fly that kept dive-bombing for his nose pushed the normally affable man to the limits of his patience.

He glanced around his study suspiciously, wondering what would interrupt him next. Maybe one of the many bookshelves would suddenly collapse, or the window shade would violently flap upward, or a leg on the desk chair would break. It felt to him as if the very silence of the room might scream, if only to ruin his concentration. He stroked his bushy white mustache and waited. Nothing happened.

Satisfied that he could resume his work, Whit (as he was best known) opened his Bible to find a verse in the book of James. He accidentally opened a couple of pages past it and found himself looking at a verse in the first letter of Peter, chapter two, verse 21. It said simply:

> To this you were called, because Christ suffered for you, leaving
> you an example, that you should follow in his steps.

He stared at the verse with an unexplainable feeling that the words there were significant. After a moment he dismissed the feeling then turned to the book of James.

The doorbell rang.

"I knew it," Whit groaned. He sat still as if afraid that if he moved, the bell might ring again. He secretly hoped whoever it was would go away. The doorbell rang again. Whit sighed, stood up, and gently moved the curtain aside on a window that gave him a clear view of the front porch. A man stood on the steps, dressed in worn, dirty clothing. He had greasy, matted hair that looked as if it hadn't been washed or combed in a long time. Frowning at the work yet to be done on his desk, Whit went down the stairs to the door. It was the last straw—the last interruption he would tolerate—and he yanked the door open as if to warn whoever it was that he wasn't in a mood to be trifled with.

The stranger looked at Whit with a startled expression, as if he didn't expect anyone to answer the door. Whit gazed at him, not sure what to make of someone who looked so bad, then asked, "Can I help you?"

The stranger coughed nervously. "I'm out of work, sir, and thought you might know of someone who's hiring. Maybe to do some odd jobs . . ."

"I'm really sorry," Whit replied, "but I don't know of anything off-hand. Try the shops downtown." He slowly began to close the door.

"Anything at all," the man said as he struggled to smile. "Just point me in the right direction." His teeth appeared yellow behind the gray stubble on his face. The lines around his eyes seemed to point like arrows at their redness.

Whit tried to imagine who he'd send a man in this condition to, but he couldn't think of anyone. "I wish I could help you," he said. "I really don't know of anyone who's hiring. And I don't have anything around here that needs done. I'm sorry. I hope you find something."

"Thanks anyway," the man said as he turned to leave. Whit closed the door and went back up to his study. He was about to start working again but first yielded to the temptation to look out the window. The man had walked down the sidewalk to the street and now stood as if he couldn't decide which way to turn.

Whit let the curtain fall back into place. He felt a pang of guilt. He could have offered the man something temporary at Whit's End, he knew. There were floors to be swept, windows to be washed, dishes to be cleaned. Even around the house, Whit could have paid the man a few dollars to rake the leaves. A list formed in Whit's mind of all the things he could have done for the stranger but didn't think about at the time because he *had to* get the questions for the Bible contest finished.

It's not too late, Whit thought and leapt to his feet. He tossed aside the curtains and reached for the window, preparing to throw it open and call for the man to come back. His fingers were clasped around the latch when he saw the sidewalk and street were empty. The man was gone.

With a heavy heart, Whit sat down at his desk and slowly returned to the Bible contest questions. There were no other interruptions that afternoon.

Tom Riley, Whit's best friend, arrived as planned at 5:30 to pick Whit up for the evening's activities at Whit's End.

"Ready?" Tom asked in his gentle, folksy accent as Whit climbed into the passenger side of the car.

"I think so," Whit answered. "How did it go at the shop this afternoon?"

Tom pulled the car out of the driveway and into the street. "No particular problems," he said. "Except you might want to take a look at the train set. The Baltimore and Ohio keeps coming off the tracks. It won't be too long before they all come apart."

"I'll look at it later tonight," Whit said, knowing his friend was trying to make a point. *You need help*, is what Tom Riley was really saying behind his comment about the train set. Whit knew it was true. Apart from sporting the county's largest running train set, Whit's End also had an ice-cream parlor, a library, a theater, and dozens of rooms filled with interactive displays. It was little wonder that Whit's End had become one of the most popular places for the children in Odyssey to play. But the success of the shop made it hard for Whit to keep up with all the things needing taken care of, and harder still for him to find the right kind of people to work there.

Employees came and went quickly. Whit was never satisfied with any of their work. He figured he could do it all better himself. Tom had said just the other day that Whit was being "too picky." *Maybe he was right*, Whit thought. In all of Odyssey, Tom was the only one Whit trusted in the shop. Earlier in the afternoon Tom had kept an eye on things while Whit worked on the Bible contest questions.

"You can't do it all," Tom said. "And I can't keep helping you. I have a farm to run."

"I know, Tom, and I'm grateful." Whit watched the evening light explode blues, yellows, and oranges behind the houses and, in the distance, the larger buildings of downtown Odyssey. They were approaching the edge of McAlister Park, where the autumn leaves spread like a carpet over the playing fields and under large collections of trees. Tom would have to drive around the edge of the park for another mile before reaching the Victorian-style building housing Whit's End.

Tom adjusted the shoulder strap on his overalls. "There was one peculiar thing that happened today," Tom said.

"Oh?" Whit's thick white eyebrows lifted and nearly blended with the wild, white hair on the top of his head.

Tom nodded. "A man I'd never seen before came in to Whit's End. He was a little shabby-looking, like he hadn't had a bath or changed his clothes in a long time."

Whit thought of the man who had come to his door that afternoon. "Did he say anything?"

"That's what was so odd. I thought he was going to ask for a handout, but he didn't. He just sat in one of the booths for a while and drank some water. He showed an interest in the posters for the Bible contest tonight, but didn't say anything else. After a while, he left."

Whit scrubbed his chin thoughtfully and felt the pang of guilt again. He should have done something for the man. "Sounds like the same man who came to my door this afternoon. I'm ashamed to say I was so preoccupied with the Bible contest, I didn't offer to help him. I feel bad about it now."

Tom shook his head. "Funny you should mention it," he said. "I kept thinking to myself that I should give the man some food, but I got so busy with the kids that I never did it. He was gone before I realized."

"So much for good intentions," Whit said.

They reached the front of Whit's End where kids were already lined up to take part in the Bible contest. Whit grabbed his Bible and stack of questions from the front seat and didn't think again about the stranger—until later that evening when the stranger would be *all* he'd think about.

"WHAT DID JAMES SAY was like the small rudder of a ship?" Whit asked from his podium on the Little Theatre stage in Whit's End.

The remaining group of contestants, sitting in a semicircle, wiggled in their chairs and scratched their heads. Only five players remained. The rest had been eliminated throughout the evening by not knowing the answers to where specific Bible verses were found, or who wrote what books, or which person did what and where it was done.

The Bible contest was one of the many ways Whit used to help bring the Bible to life for kids. He believed the more fun they had with Scripture, the more they'd get out of it. This evening's contest proved the point: The kids cheered for the various contestants, calling out answers and groaning when an obvious answer escaped them. They didn't do it for the prize (which, in this case, was a week's worth of ice cream at Whit's End). They did it for the fun.

"The tongue!" Karen Crosby exclaimed in a burst of excitement and nearly fell out of her chair.

"You're right," Whit said. The crowd applauded as Whit turned over his question card. He picked up another. "Which three disciples went with Jesus to a high mountain where they saw Him speak with Elijah and Moses?"

Oscar's hand shot up. "Peter, John, and Matthew!" he shouted.

Whit smiled at the round-faced boy. "Sorry, Oscar. It wasn't," he said.

"Oh, man." Oscar frowned and gave up his seat on the stage. Whit was sorry to see the boy leave, since he was often teased for not being very bright. He had surprised everyone by making it so far into the contest.

"It was Peter, John, and *James*!" Lucy Cunningham-Schultz cried out in her mousy voice.

"You're correct!" Whit announced.

Lucy giggled and Karen said graciously, "Good going, Lucy."

"All right, Lucy!" Jack Davis cheered from the audience. Then he and Matt Booker began to chant, "Looo-seee! Looo-seee! Looo-seee!" until Whit waved his arms to quiet them down.

It was down to Lucy, Karen, Mike Henderson (a pastor's son), and Jamie Peck, a boy of 10 who was extremely smart for his age. Whit couldn't imagine who the winner would be since they were all so evenly matched.

He continued, "In the Gospel of Mark, chapter 10, a young man asks Jesus what he must do to inherit eternal life. In verse 21, Jesus gave the young man specific instructions. What did He say to do?"

The contestants squirmed awkwardly as they each tried to think of the answer.

"Sell what you own and give the money to the poor and follow Me," an adult voice said from the back of the auditorium.

It was such a surprise that Whit almost said "Right!" before he realized the wrong person spoke. Heads turned and necks craned to see who had spoken. Whit shielded his eyes from the stage lights. He barely made out the form as it moved forward to the center of the audience.

"I'm sorry, but we don't allow answers from the audience," Whit said, still unable to see who had spoken.

"But that's the right answer," the man said. "Sell what you own and give the money to the poor and follow Me."

The auditorium was completely silent as the kids and some of the few attending parents watched the stranger with wide, worried eyes. Tom, who'd been standing in the wings, now took a few steps onto the stage just to show that another adult was present—just in case the man meant to cause trouble.

The man walked closer to the stage and Whit finally recognized him. It was the same one who had come to his door earlier in the afternoon. He was in the same drab, dirty clothes with matted hair and scratchy stubble. Whit found nothing dangerous in the man's tone or in how he moved. In fact, Whit thought he looked like a man who might be walking and talking in his sleep. There was an unreal calm, even sadness, in his demeanor.

He rubbed a hand over his greasy hair and said, "I'm sorry to interrupt. I really am. But I was watching this contest—watching how good these kids are with their Bibles—and I thought I oughtta say something. You see, I've been out of work for about 10 months. I was a printer in

Connellsville, and the new computers took away my job. I don't have anything against computers or the folks who use them, but they put me out of work. What could I do? Printing is all I know—"

Whit held up a hand. "Look, sir, maybe we should talk about this somewhere else."

The stranger shook his head. "Please," he said. "I won't take much of your time. I just thought you Bible-believing people might be interested in what I have to say. I'm not complaining. I was just sitting in the back thinking that *knowing* about the Bible is one thing, while *doing* what the Bible says is another.

"You folks seem to have it all worked out about what Jesus said in the Bible, and that's a good thing. Even the young man in the chapter you read seemed to have it all worked out. He kept the Ten Commandments. But Jesus said to *follow* Him and, well, the young man went away sad. I just wonder if we understand what it means when Jesus says to follow Him. Do we?"

Here the man slowly turned to look at his audience. The kids clung to every word. "What do we Christians mean by following in the steps of Jesus?

"I've been wandering around your town for two days trying to find a job. I don't mean printing, I mean *any kind* of job. And in all that time I haven't had a word of sympathy or comfort from anyone, except your Mr. Whittaker here who said he was sorry for me. Everyone else turned away—or turned me away.

"Now I know you can't all go out of your way to find jobs for people like me. I'm not asking you to. I'm just trying to figure out how those words in the Bible connect to our lives, to what we should say or do when someone in need comes up to us. When Jesus said to follow Him, *what did He mean*? Did He mean to just get on with our lives, or was He talking about something more—something that would make a difference in our world?"

He scanned the audience, then slowly continued, "I know what you're thinking. You're thinking I should be able to get a job somewhere if I really wanted one. That's what all the people who have jobs and homes and money say. They don't understand how hard it is. My wife died a few months ago and I thank God she's out of this trouble. My daughter is . . . well, she's taken care of. I never wanted to be a burden to her or anybody else. But nobody in Connellsville could help me, so I made my way toward Odyssey. I thought, *Here's a place where folks are living well. There's got to be something there for me.*"

The man stopped for a moment and pressed his hand against his mouth as if trying to stifle a scream. He swayed slightly. Whit and Tom took a step toward him, but stopped when he spoke again. "I'm puzzled, that's all. Everyone's doing so well in this town, and Jesus said things like 'Sell what you own, give money to the poor, and follow Me' and I'm trying to figure it out in my mind. My wife died in a tenement building in Connellsville. It was owned by a Christian landlord and, even though she died, he told me I had to pay my rent or leave right away. He was a Christian man and said he felt bad for making me leave. I guess he felt bad the same way the young man in the story felt bad.

"Jesus said to follow Him, and we always feel bad when we don't. Maybe we just don't understand what He means. Or maybe we do and we just feel bad because we don't think we can do what He wants. I don't know. Maybe we don't even ask ourselves what it really means to follow Him. Do we ever ask, 'What would Jesus do if He were in my situation?' What would Jesus do if He had a nice house and a good job and decent family but knew there were folks outside who didn't have any of those things? What would Jesus do to help folks like me who have to walk the streets or who die in tenements or who—?"

The man suddenly jerked toward the stage as if someone had punched him from the side. He reached his hands out wildly, then fell to his knees. Spinning out of control, he grabbed the edge of the stage with a grimy hand for only a second before collapsing to the floor.

CHAPTER THREE

WHIT RODE WITH THE unconscious stranger in the back of the ambulance to the hospital. A team of doctors and nurses met the gurney as it was brought into the ward. Whit started to follow as they wheeled it past a curtained area, but a doctor stopped him.

"Please wait out here," he said, pulling the curtains together.

Dazed by everything that had happened, Whit slowly paced back and forth in the lounge of the emergency area.

"I need some information about the patient," a nurse with a clipboard told him. "Name?"

"I don't know," Whit said.

"Do you know *anything* about him?"

Whit shook his head. "Not really. He's a stranger. He collapsed in my shop."

"Then he isn't insured, is he?" the nurse asked.

"If you're worried about who'll pay," Whit replied, "I'll take care of everything. Just help him, all right?"

The nurse handed Whit the clipboard. "Then I'll need you to fill this out and sign at the bottom."

Whit mechanically obeyed. Even as his fingers moved the pen through the little boxes asking for his name, address, and financial information, his mind raced with everything the stranger had said earlier. *Do I know what Jesus meant?* he asked himself again and again. *What does it really mean to follow Him? What does it mean to walk in His steps?*

The hands of the clock above the nurses' station moved indifferently past the hour—then past another hour. Whit sat staring at the torn black leather on the waiting lounge sofa. The television was on but the sound was off. Whit didn't pay attention to the fast-cutting images that flickered and flashed on the screen. *Does following Jesus mean just trying to be good, or does it mean something more? What does it mean to walk in His steps?*

"Well, Whit?"

Before he looked up, Whit knew the voice. It was Captain Wilkins from the Odyssey police.

"Hi, Joe," Whit said.

Captain Wilkins sat down on a small chair nearby. He was dressed in casual clothes, as if he'd been called from an evening at home. His jacket was partially zipped up over a flannel shirt.

"Is it cold outside?" Whit asked. He had forgotten to bring his own coat.

"A typical fall night. Crisp," the captain replied. "Tom told me what happened at Whit's End. I guess some of the kids and parents are still shook up. What can you tell me about the stranger?"

Whit sighed. "Not much. He said he was an unemployed printer from Connellsville. His wife died a few months ago in a tenement owned by a Christian. He has a daughter, but didn't say where she was. That's all."

"It's a start," Wilkins said. "He didn't have a wallet or any identification. I can check with the printers' union, though. And the Connellsville police may be able to help me with tracking down information about the dead wife."

Whit glanced at the captain. His words sounded so cold and clinical, as if the stranger was an abandoned car instead of a human being.

The captain leaned toward Whit. "They told me you're going to take care of his bills. Why? You've never seen him before today, right?"

"He came to my door this afternoon and the shop tonight."

"You don't have to feel obligated, Whit," Captain Wilkins said. "He's not your responsibility."

"Isn't he?" Whit asked.

Dr. Morton appeared in the doorway to the waiting lounge. Her white coat was rumpled and her hands were shoved deep in its pockets. She looked tired. "Whit?"

Whit looked up at her.

"Your friend has a damaged heart," she said. "There isn't much we can do. Right now he's in a coma."

The doctors moved the stranger to the intensive care ward. Since no one had been able to find any information about the next of kin, Dr. Morton gave permission for Whit to sit with him. Apart from a patient across the floor, all the other beds were empty. The stranger was attached to all kinds of tubes and equipment. A heart monitor blipped a green line on a black screen. Its effect on Whit was hypnotic. Up and down, up and down the line went.

It was close to ten o'clock when one of the nurses signaled Whit to come out in the hall. Tom Riley was waiting for him, clutching a coat in his hands.

"How's our mystery man?" Tom asked.

"In a coma," Whit answered, then moved to the vending machine to get a cup of coffee. He slid the coins into the slot and watched as the cup dropped and slowly filled with the dark brown liquid. "He has a bad heart."

Tom shook his head. "That's too bad. Are you planning to spend the night here?"

"I think I should. Don't you?"

Tom shrugged. "I can stay with him for a while if you get tired."

"Thanks."

The two men looked at each other with a deep understanding. They were both affected by the stranger and all he had said. His words hadn't been idle or the ramblings of a lunatic. He had spoken calmly and asked them a simple question that cut to the very heart of their Christianity. The Bible spoke of entertaining angels unaware. Whit and Tom took the notion seriously. And even if the stranger wasn't an angel, his words seemed to come from heavenly places.

"We canceled the contest," Tom said. "I used the rest of the time talking to the kids and their parents. Some of them were pretty upset. I guess we were all just trying to figure out what to make of what he said."

"Did any of you come to a conclusion?" Whit picked up the cup of coffee and blew the steam across the top.

"No. There wasn't much to say—everyone felt bad—we all wished we had done more to help him." Tom shuffled uneasily. "I think most of us got to wondering about his question. You know, what does it mean to follow Jesus?"

"Me, too."

They stood in silence again. The hospital hallway was empty.

"Let's pray, Tom."

Tom agreed and the two men bowed their heads then and there. They didn't say much out loud, except to ask God to heal the stranger and to help them understand the meaning behind the evening's events.

When they finished, Tom held up the coat in his hand. It was plain brown, torn, and grease-smeared. "I found this in the back of the auditorium. I think it's his."

Whit took it. "Thanks for everything, Tom."

"Oh, and I brought your car. Third row back from the front entrance." Tom handed him the extra set of keys Whit kept at the shop for emergencies. "I'll get a lift back from Donnie Armstrong. He's an orderly downstairs. His shift is about to end. Good kid. Used to be in my Sunday school class."

Whit nodded. He remembered Donnie.

"You call me if you want me to come back. I mean it. I'll stay."

"I will." Whit watched his friend walk down the hallway with a renewed feeling of gratitude.

Back in the intensive care unit, the stranger remained unconscious. Whit sat down with his coffee and realized that the stranger's coat might have some identification in the pockets. He checked the outside ones first, discovering only a fragment of an old sandwich and some plastic-wrapped saltine crackers. His fingers felt the inside breast pocket and made contact with a small paper bag that had been carefully folded down to a rectangle. Whit opened the bag: It held three letters. Each one was addressed to Raymond Clark. In the upper left-hand corner, above an address in Columbus, Ohio, was the name of Christine Holt.

Whit slipped out of the room to phone Captain Wilkins.

"Raymond Clark of Connellsville," Captain Wilkins confirmed an hour later over the phone. "His wife's name was Mary. Christine Holt is his daughter. Holt is her married name. We've been trying to reach her in Columbus, but haven't had much success. I think the Columbus police are going to send someone around to the address you gave me. I'll let you know if we learn any more."

"Joe," Whit said slowly, his speech a little slurred from his weariness, "if it's a matter of money . . . I mean, if his daughter needs help to get here . . . leave it to me."

"If you say so," Captain Wilkins said. They hung up. Whit was aware of a surge of activity down the hall—in the intensive care unit—and felt a sick feeling go through his stomach. He walked quickly and then found himself running back to Raymond Clark's bed. Two nurses were at its side, adjusting equipment and checking his vital signs.

"Promise me . . ." Raymond Clark was saying when Whit arrived.

"He's talking?" Whit asked, surprised.

"Stay back, Mr. Whittaker," one of the nurses said.

"Promise me," Raymond Clark said again. His voice was a harsh whisper.

Whit got as close to the bed as he could without getting in the nurses' way.

"Promise you what?" Whit asked gently. "Mr. Clark?"

Raymond Clark turned his head slightly. His eyes were red and wet, but he fixed them on Whit. "You're a kind man. My daughter. Promise me you'll tell her where I am."

"I promise," Whit said. "In fact, we found her letters in your coat pocket. We're going to bring her to see you as fast as we can."

"She won't . . ." his voice trailed off to a mumble, then returned with, ". . . in time. I know. I'm not afraid. Do you see Him? Jesus is . . ." his voice trailed off again.

Raymond Clark slowly closed his eyes. The green line on the heart monitor machine stopped bouncing and went flat across the screen. The room was filled with the sound of a solitary, unending beep.

The nurses and doctors were powerless to save his life.

"Go home and get some sleep," Dr. Morton advised Whit later in the waiting lounge. "There's nothing you can do."

Whit rubbed his eyes. They burned from lack of sleep and the tears that wouldn't fall. *Nothing you can do*, Whit thought again and again as he drove home. In a few hours another Sunday morning would arrive in

Odyssey. People would get up and go to church like they always did, unaware—or uncaring—about the Raymond Clarks in the world who had slept hungry the night before . . . or died.

Nothing you can do, Dr. Morton had said.

Whit brought his car to a halt in his driveway and leaned against the steering wheel.

Well, he thought, *we'll just see about that. . . .*

Lucy walked into the sanctuary of Odyssey Community Church and scanned the half-filled pews. It was still early. Most of the congregation hadn't wandered in from their various Sunday school classes. Lucy clutched her Bible and noticed smudges of white powder on the cover. She smiled to herself. It was baby powder from changing David Kemper's diapers in the nursery.

Karen Crosby waved from her normal spot on the pew on the side of the church. She was sitting with Jack, Matt, and Oscar—*The Three Musketeers*, Lucy called them, because they'd been together so much lately. Lucy strolled over and slid in next to the gang.

"Where've you been?" Karen asked. "You weren't in Sunday school."

Lucy held out her white fingers. "Nursery."

"Something's going on," Matt said.

"What do you mean?"

Jack leaned forward. "Mr. Whittaker wasn't in Sunday school. Mrs. Winger covered for him."

Oscar piped in, "When we asked if he was sick, she said no and not to ask any questions because we'd find out in church. Isn't that weird? Mr. Whittaker *never* misses teaching his class."

"I think it has something to do with the man," Karen said.

"The one who barged in on the contest last night," Jack clarified, as if Lucy had already forgotten the incident.

Oscar looked around nervously, then said: "I heard he was a lunatic and they took him away to the asylum."

"I heard he was once the pastor of *this* church and came back because they fired him," Jack said.

"Cut it out," Lucy said. "You guys don't know what you're talking about."

"But something happened," Karen affirmed.

Mr. Shelton started playing a hymn on the organ as a signal for all talking to stop. The sanctuary slowly filled up with the regular church attendees and a few people Lucy didn't recognize. During the first hymn, Pastor Henderson walked up to his chair behind the pulpit. Whit followed and sat down in the guest chair next to it.

"See? I told you," Jack said, gesturing to Whit.

Whit looked tired, as if he'd been sick or up all night. Lucy tried to take in the eyes beneath the wild white hair. They were puffy. And his normal smiling expression seemed undone by a sad droop in his mustache.

The church service proceeded as usual, with hymns, Scripture readings, announcements, and the offering. After the collection plates had been passed, another hymn was sung as a lead-in to the pastor's sermon. The hymn was "Take My Life and Let It Be." As the last note of the hymn echoed through the church, Pastor Henderson stepped up to the pulpit. He spoke in a tone so serious that Lucy instinctively drew her arms around herself. "Good morning, ladies and gentlemen. Thank you for joining us. I'm sure by now most of you have heard about what happened at Whit's End last night. But just in case you haven't, allow me a minute to explain."

He went on to tell the congregation about the Bible contest at Whit's End, how it had been interrupted by the stranger, what he said before he collapsed, and how he was taken to the hospital where he later died.

Lucy put her hand over her mouth as she gasped along with others in the congregation. She didn't know what she expected to have happened to the stranger, but she never expected for him to die.

The pastor continued, "John Whittaker, who was with the stranger until the end, has asked to talk to the church this morning. After hearing what he wants to say, I believe it's the best thing for all of us. Please give him your full attention. Whit?"

"Thank you, Pastor Henderson," Whit said when he reached the pulpit. He spoke so softly that Lucy had to strain her ears to hear him. "I'm grateful to those of you who were at Whit's End last night—and to those of you who prayed for Raymond Clark. That was his name. We still don't have all the details about him, but I understand he has a daughter who is being notified."

Whit clutched the pulpit as if it was the only thing stopping him from falling over. Lucy felt an unfamiliar tightness in her chest.

Surveying the audience, Whit continued, "The appearance of Mr.

Clark at Whit's End last night startled us all. It's not very often we have a complete stranger come in, looking like he did and talking the way he talked. But I have to tell you honestly: His words hit me right here—" Whit put his hand over his heart. "And when I think that those were nearly the last words he spoke before he died, they hit me even harder.

"Do you know what he asked us? He wanted to know what it means when we say we're followers of Jesus. What difference does it make to our lives? Ask anyone who heard him. He wasn't harsh or judgmental. He simply asked the question, then pointed out how different following Jesus is from how we normally live our lives. I wish I could ignore Mr. Clark and his words—it'd be easier that way—but I can't. What he said was true. What he asked was something we should all be asking ourselves every day of our lives. What does it mean to follow Jesus? What would change in my life if I truly walked in His steps?"

Whit paused again. The congregation shuffled uncomfortably. Someone coughed. Lucy braced herself—for what, she didn't know. But all her best instincts said that this was serious—*very* serious.

"I have a plan in mind," Whit said. "Call it a challenge, if you want. But I've been thinking about Mr. Clark's question and how to answer him. What I propose now is something that shouldn't be peculiar to any of us, but will probably sound ridiculous, even impossible. Basically, I'm looking for volunteers to pledge themselves—for just a couple of weeks—to do only what Jesus would do."

The congregation came alive with buzzing and whispers.

Whit held up his hand. "The idea is for us not to do anything without first asking the question, *What would Jesus do?* And afterward, we ought to act as we believe Jesus Himself would act if He were in our place. I'm pledging myself to that challenge right here and now. I'm asking for others to join me—men and women, boys and girls. Make no mistake. It's a simple challenge, but it won't be easy. But I'm willing to try. If you are, too, meet me at Whit's End this afternoon at 3:00. That's all I have to say."

Whit stepped away from the pulpit and Pastor Henderson returned to close the service in prayer. After the final hymn, the entire auditorium exploded in conversation.

Lucy wondered if she should take Whit up on his challenge.

What would Jesus do? she asked herself.

"HE DIDN'T GET VERY many people to show up," Jack observed from the booth in the far corner of Whit's End soda shop. He was there with Lucy, Karen, Matt, and Oscar. They had all agreed after church to go to the meeting. Lucy and Karen were serious about taking Whit up on his challenge. Jack, Matt, and Oscar just wanted to see what would happen next.

"I count 16 adults," Oscar said. "So, counting us that would be—"

"Twenty-one," Matt finished for him with a bored tone in his voice.

Lucy adjusted her glasses and scanned the room to see who had shown up. Most of them were leaders from the church, including Pastor Henderson and Tom Riley, who was a deacon. The others were parents (including Lucy's and Karen's parents and Oscar's mom).

"They're the ones I figured would come," Jack said.

Matt nodded. "They *had* to show up—or they'd look like they weren't spiritual."

"Maybe they thought it was a good idea," Karen said, annoyed at Jack and Matt's sarcastic attitude. She slumped down on the table and weaved a finger through her chestnut hair. That's what she did when she was bothered about something.

Whit stood up in front of the small gathering. "Thank you for coming," he said. He looked pale and even more tired than he had just a couple of hours before. Lucy thought he was on the verge of tears. "Let's pray."

Everyone bowed their heads. From Whit's very first words—"Dear Father"—something about the room seemed to change. Lucy felt it so precisely that she glanced up as if someone had tapped her on the shoulder. She caught eyes with Karen, who was also now looking around with a confused expression on her face. Oscar furrowed his brow while Jack and Matt, eyes still closed, wiggled in their seats. Out of the corner of her eye, Lucy saw the adults in the room also reacting to whatever it was that seemed to be happening because of Whit's prayer. The hair stood up on the back of her neck—but not from fear, from *excitement*. It was as if the room was suddenly charged with electricity.

"The Holy Spirit," Karen whispered.

Lucy bowed her head and knew He was there. She felt it as surely as she felt the presence of the rest of the kids at her table. And somehow she knew this wasn't just an experiment or a game. Whit's challenge was *real*—and not to be taken lightly. But she knew she *would* take the challenge. She *would* try to follow in the steps of Jesus in what she did over the next couple of weeks. The presence of the Spirit—if that's what it really was—confirmed in her heart that she *had to*.

When Whit finished his prayer, everyone sat silently, their heads still bowed, as if they were hesitant to interrupt whatever they were feeling.

Whit's face was wet with tears. He pulled a handkerchief from his pocket and wiped his eyes. "I hope we understand what we're here to do. Basically, we're here to pledge to ask what Jesus would do with *everything* in our lives. Then we will act on the answer we get, regardless of the consequences. Do we all agree?"

Karen suddenly raised her hand. "Excuse me, Mr. Whittaker. I have a question."

"Go ahead, Karen."

She cleared her throat shyly, then said: "Well, I want to do what Jesus would do. But I'm not really sure I *know* what He would do. I don't remember any stories in the Bible about Jesus taking a math class or learning to play volleyball in gym class."

A few scattered chuckles echoed around the room. Whit smiled. "That's a very good question, Karen. My guess is that all of us will have to consider carefully how Jesus would act in our homes or schools or offices. It's a different world now than the one He lived in, yet His truth is timeless. The only thing we can do is study Jesus in Scripture and rely on the Holy Spirit to guide us. There are no easy rules for how to do it. We just have to read our Bibles, pray, and talk to people who are wiser than we are."

"But what if someone disagrees and says Jesus wouldn't do what we think He'd do?" Pastor Henderson asked.

Whit shrugged. "That'll probably happen. I don't expect everyone to agree with what we're trying to do or how we do it. There'll be some struggles to get it right. We just have to be completely honest and open with ourselves about our decisions. If someone says we're wrong, then we'll have to prayerfully consider their opinion and test it to see if the Spirit is speaking through them. But, in the long run, I think there'll be consistency in our decision making. If we're in tune with the Holy Spirit, then there shouldn't be any confusion in how we decide. But we have to be committed once we've made our decision. Right?"

The adults nodded their agreement. Then someone else asked another question which led to a long grown-up conversation that didn't interest the kids in the corner booth very much.

Lucy turned to Jack and Matt. "Are you going to do it?"

"Are you?" Matt asked.

Lucy said yes.

"If it's good enough for you, it's good enough for us," Jack said, then nudged Oscar. "Right?"

"Right," Oscar said.

"It's not a competition," said Lucy.

Jack rolled his eyes. "I know," he said as if stating the obvious.

But Lucy suspected deep inside that he *didn't* know.

"Look, it's not like it's going to be so hard," Matt said. "I mean, it's not as if we have anything really serious to deal with. For me it'll be trying to figure out what Jesus would do with my next English assignment."

"I think there's more to it than that," Karen said. "It's going to affect *everything* in our lives. I'm the president of the student council. What would Jesus do with our student council?"

"Tell them all to resign," Jack laughed.

Lucy frowned. "Oh boy. I'm the editor of the *Odyssey Owl*. How would Jesus edit a school newspaper?"

Lucy and Karen exchanged uneasy glances.

"We don't have anything to worry about," Matt said. "Do we?"

Oscar didn't look convinced. He was chewing the inside of his mouth like he did when he was trying to think.

"What's wrong, Oscar?" Jack asked him.

"Well," Oscar said carefully, "I was just trying to figure out what Jesus would do when Joe Devlin and his gang try to beat me up after school."

"Turn the other cheek?" Karen asked.

"That's what I *always* do," Oscar said. "It doesn't help."

Whit was suddenly standing next to the booth and Lucy realized the meeting had broken up and the adults were leaving. "I don't know if doing what Jesus would do will always *help* things," Whit said. "At least, not in the ways we expect. It's not like a magic formula to take our problems away or make us successful. Following Jesus is just . . . well, walking where He leads us. The question is, are we all committed to following Him wherever He goes?"

Whit's gaze fell from one face to another.

"Yes," Lucy said.

"Uh-huh," Matt said.

Jack nodded. "Yep."

"Yes, sir," Oscar piped in.

"Me, too," Karen said. Then she sighed with a string of hair curled around her finger. "I hope we know what we're getting ourselves into."

THE NEXT MORNING, Lucy slipped into the room that served as the main office for the *Odyssey Owl*. The bell wouldn't ring for school to start for another 15 minutes. She sat down next to a large, rectangular table covered with finished articles, assignment sheets, and clip-art catalogs. The silence of the room filled her with peace. She had determined to start the day the way Jesus often started His: with prayer. *I'm going to need it,* she thought.

She folded her hands and bowed her head, but it didn't feel right. She scooted the chair back, slid off, and knelt with her elbows on the edge of the seat. Her heart pounded a little harder as she whispered, "Dear God . . ."

She'd only been praying for a minute when Mike Colman, one of the *Owl*'s reporters, walked in. Embarrassed, Lucy leapt to her feet.

"What's wrong?" Mike asked as he tossed his books on the table.

"Nothing," Lucy answered. "You startled me."

Mike cocked an eyebrow at her, then peered at the base of the table. "What were you doing down there? Did you drop something?"

"Never mind," Lucy said. "What are you doing here?"

Mike looked at her suspiciously. "It's Monday, right? Assignments for this week's issue?"

Lucy blushed. "Oh yeah." She fumbled for the assignment sheet that she'd worked out last Friday. "Let's see . . ."

"I was thinking I'd like to do something different this week," Mike said.

Lucy looked up at him.

"I want to do a movie review. I saw Sylvester Kostenagger's latest over the weekend. *Blood Runs Deep*. It was amazing."

"But that's an adult movie," Lucy said. "I heard it's nothing but violence and killing from the beginning to end."

Mike put his hands on his hips. "You heard wrong. They stop blowing people away long enough to do a love scene in the middle."

"You're kidding."

"Nope." Mike smiled at her. His perfect white teeth, dimples, and curly black hair reminded Lucy she once had a crush on him. "All the kids are talking about this movie. We have to review it. Besides, I got to interview Sylvester Kostenagger on the phone."

"*What?*"

Mike said proudly, "My dad's lawyer's brother-in-law is an agent in Sylvester's talent agency and he set it up for me to interview him. We talked for a whole five minutes. I even recorded it. I could do a review of the movie *and* print the interview!"

Lucy was instantly excited for Mike. What a scoop! And it was true that all the kids in the school had been looking forward to this new action thriller. Most of the kids' parents would take them to see it—or they'd sneak in like Mike probably had. The theater owners didn't seem to care as long as they got their money. But to have an interview with the actor himself—that's the kind of thing that could get the *Owl* mentioned in the *Odyssey Times*!

Lucy very nearly said "Okay" but stopped herself just before the word came out. What happened to the pledge she made? "I'm going to have to think about it," she finally said.

"Think about it?" Mike was aghast. "What's to think about?"

She didn't dare tell him that she first had to decide what Jesus would do. Would Jesus, if He were editor of the *Owl*, allow a review to be printed about a movie that blatantly glorified violence?

Of course He wouldn't, Lucy knew. She then asked herself *how* she knew it. And in an instant, her mind worked through her reasons. For one thing, Jesus said to love each other—our neighbors, even our enemies. There was no room for that kind of love in movies where people got shot and buildings were blown up just for the fun of it. Lucy also remembered her parents complaining how violent movies made people less than humans—they were just nameless and faceless characters who died—and Jesus certainly wouldn't approve of that. There was never a point to those violent movies, except to show more and more violence. They never taught the kinds of things that Jesus taught about: mercy, compassion, self-sacrifice. There were more reasons, but Lucy figured she had enough.

"No," she said to Mike. "No review."

Mike was clearly disappointed, but rallied. "We'll just do the interview then."

"Huh-uh," she said and braced herself for the explosion.

"Are you nuts?" Mike shouted. "I talked to *Sylvester* on the phone! He answered my questions! He even said he'd send me an autographed picture!"

"No, Mike."

"Why not?" he demanded.

"Because movies like *Blood Runs Dark—*"

"Deep," he corrected her. "*Blood Runs Deep.*"

"Movies like that aren't healthy for kids like us. They're probably not even healthy for adults either. And actors like Sylvester what's-his-name don't even care what kind of effect his movies have on us. He's just out to make money."

"So what?"

"So, there's nothing that says I have to promote his movie by printing a review or promote *him* by printing an interview."

Mike stared at her with his mouth hanging down. He looked like he might rush into the hall and call for the school nurse to help poor Lucy who'd finally flipped her wig. "This is a joke, right? You're pulling my leg."

"No, I'm not."

"Then you've gone out of your mind!" he cried out. "How could you *not* print a review, *especially* when I have an interview with the country's *biggest selling star* to go with it!? What kind of editor are you, anyway?"

Lucy weighed her options carefully. There was a time when Mike and his family went to her church. They stopped going a couple of years ago and, for all she knew, had started going somewhere else. She didn't know. But one thing was certain: She had to tell him the real reason she couldn't print his review and interview.

"Close the door," she said softly.

He looked at her puzzled, then obeyed.

Once the door was closed and he returned to face her, she explained, "Mike, the truth is, I can't print your stuff because . . . well, it isn't something that Jesus would do."

He stared at her for a moment, then blinked a couple of times as if he hadn't heard right. "Jesus? You mean, like, Jesus in the Bible?"

Lucy nodded. "I made a pledge yesterday to do everything the way I think Jesus would do things. That includes how to edit the *Owl*. I don't think Jesus would print your review or interview. Do you?"

"No, He probably wouldn't." Then Mike shook his head quickly. "But . . . but this is crazy. You can't edit a paper like Jesus would. He never even edited a paper, did He? If He did, do you think any of the kids in this school would read it? I wouldn't."

"That's not the point. I made a pledge—no matter what," Lucy said.

"It's nuts," Mike said. "You'll get yourself in big trouble."

Lucy shrugged. "It's a risk I'll have to take."

At lunch, Lucy found Karen in the cafeteria praying over her meal. Lucy had never seen Karen—or anyone, for that matter—pray over a school lunch. Lucy followed her lead, and when she sat down with her own sack lunch, she bowed her head and offered a quick prayer.

"Well?" Lucy asked after she said amen.

"Well what?" Karen chomped down on a fish stick.

"How's it going on the first day of your pledge?"

"Okay, I guess," Karen replied. "I nearly got in an argument with Donna Barclay about borrowing my brush, but realized it wasn't something Jesus would argue about. Didn't He say something about giving away your coat if someone asked?"

Lucy nodded. "And to walk an extra mile."

"Yeah. So I gave Donna my brush." Karen pushed a lock of her hair away from her plate. "I have to meet this afternoon with Mr. Laker to talk about the stationery for the student council. Big deal."

"The student council is getting its own stationery? Why?"

"To write down all the high-powered decisions we're going to make," Karen said. "I voted against the idea. I thought we could use the money to do more important things. But I was in the minority, and it's my job to pick what it'll look like. How about you? How's the pledge going?"

"I'm not sure." Lucy bit into her ham sandwich. "I think everything's all right."

Karen looked at her skeptically. "That's not what I heard. Mike's been telling everyone you dumped his review and interview because you're on some wacko religious kick."

"Oh, no!" Lucy groaned.

"I couldn't believe you did it," Karen said proudly. "That must've been hard for you."

Lucy shook her head. "It wasn't as hard as I thought it would be. Once I figured out *why* Jesus would have said no to the movie and inter- view, I knew I had a good case against it. But maybe that's the trick here: *Doing* the right thing might start off easy, but living with the out- come may be the tough part."

"Mike says he's going to complain to Mrs. Stegner," Karen said. Mrs. Stegner was an English teacher and the faculty sponsor of the *Odyssey Owl*. Ultimately, she was responsible for everything to do with the newspaper. "Do you think she'll back you up?"

"I guess I'll find out when she calls me in."

"What if she doesn't?"

"Then I'll have to decide what Jesus would do next."

Mr. Art Laker was the school administrator, which meant he was in charge of the school's money. It was his responsibility to make sure the textbooks were ordered and teachers had enough whiteboard pens and erasers and the secretary had all the paper clips she needed. He was a tall, heavyset man with a shiny, bald head, small eyes, and a face that went beet red whenever he got agitated. Karen always felt uncomfort- able around him for no other reason than the feeling that he didn't really like his job. She had heard the other day that he was going to retire at the end of the school year. *He probably can't wait*, Karen thought as she walked into the school office.

Mrs. Stewart smiled as Karen stepped up to the office counter. "Hi, Karen."

"Hi. I'm here to see Mr. Laker," Karen said.

Mrs. Stewart looked puzzled. "Oh? Well, I'm sorry, but he had an unexpected meeting at the district office. What were you meeting him about? Maybe I can help."

"I have to pick out the stationery design for the student council," Karen explained.

Mrs. Stewart chuckled. "Ah, the president is making big executive decisions, huh?"

"Yeah," Karen grinned. "Our lives will never be the same once we have this stationery."

Gesturing to the small door leading behind the counter, Mrs. Stewart said, "Come on back to his office. He was looking at designs this morning, probably to get ready for your meeting together."

They walked back to Mr. Laker's closet-sized office down the corridor from the other, more important offices. Karen suspected that Mr. Laker probably resented being stuck down the hall in a tiny office when Principal Felegy and Vice Principal Santini had offices that were so much bigger and nicer looking. Even the school nurse had a larger work area.

"There it is," Mrs. Stewart said, pointing to the stationery book spread across Mr. Laker's plain metal desk. "Have a seat and pick out what you want."

Karen sat down at the desk to look through the various designs. The catalog had all types and sizes. Some of the lettering was boxy-looking, some had curlycues, some looked too boyish, and others were too girlie. Choosing one wasn't going to be easy. Ten minutes later, after her eyes started to hurt, Karen found one that she liked best: an austere "Times New Roman" type set at 14 points. She scribbled down what she thought the letterhead should say. "From Your Student Council." She figured that phrase would encompass everything they needed to communicate with both the faculty and students.

"It looks like it has strength and authority," Mrs. Stewart said when she saw Karen's choice.

"Yeah, I guess," Karen said with a shrug. It was hard for her to take the job very seriously. "Now we have to get bids."

"Bids?"

"You know—I have to ask some printing companies how much it'll cost to make the stationery, then go with the cheapest."

"I know what bids are," Mrs. Stewart replied, "but you don't have to go to all that trouble. We have a company who'll do all the printing for you."

Karen frowned. "But Mr. Felegy told me at the beginning of the year that we always had to get bids on *everything* we do. He said it was county education policy or something like that."

"Mr. Laker has one company that he always works with," Mrs. Stewart explained patiently.

Karen felt confused about the contradiction between what Mr. Felegy had said and what Mr. Laker did, but she honestly didn't care enough to argue. "What's their phone number?" she asked.

Mrs. Stewart pulled open a drawer on a tall, gray filing cabinet. She thumbed through some of the manila-colored folders. "It *should* be here," she said. She looked around the office, then spied something in an open briefcase. After a quick look she grabbed it. "Here it is. Ballistic Printing."

"Funny name."

Laura Szypulski, a student-assistant in the office, appeared in the doorway and breathlessly said, "Mrs. Stewart! Mr. Felegy wants you in the gym right away! Somebody fell off the balance beam and got knocked out!"

"Oh!" Mrs. Stewart cried out. She tossed the file in Karen's lap. "Take it," she said, then waved wildly for her to get out. "Students aren't allowed in here unsupervised. I have to lock everything up."

"But the file—"

"Just bring it back later."

Karen obeyed, clutching the file while Mrs. Stewart and Laura ushered her out, locked the main door to the office, and scurried down the hall toward the gym.

"What's this all about, Lucy?" Mrs. Stegner asked. They were sitting in the *Owl*'s so-called office. Lucy had been asked to stop in before going on to her last class of the day. "Mike makes it sound like you've joined some kind of cult. I half-expected you to walk in with your head shaved."

Lucy giggled. "No, ma'am."

"Then what's going on? Why did you refuse to print Mike's review and interview?"

Lucy took a deep breath, then tried to explain her reasons without mentioning her pledge to do what Jesus would do. Mrs. Stegner nodded quietly as Lucy spoke.

"I understand," she said when Lucy finished her list of reasons.

Lucy was relieved. "Do you?"

"Yes, your reasons are sound," Mrs. Stegner said. "But what confuses me is why you're taking this position *now*. We've printed reviews of movies that were far more questionable than this one by Sylvester who-ever-he-is. Why are you making an issue of it now?"

Lucy looked Mrs. Stegner in the eyes. "Because I made a pledge to do what Jesus would do, and I don't think He'd support that movie."

"Ah, I see," Mrs. Stegner said as she leaned back in her chair. "You're trying to act as Jesus would act. That certainly explains the rumors."

"I don't know why everyone has to make a fuss about it," Lucy said.

Mrs. Stegner smiled. "They're making a fuss because it's a rather . . . *different* idea. By deciding not to print Mike's material, you're taking a moral stand that you haven't taken before. That's going to stir some people up. Not everyone thinks that it's the editor's job to bring his or her personal morality into the newsroom. Some might say that you're shoving your beliefs down other people's throats."

"Am I?" Lucy asked sincerely. She didn't want to argue, but felt it was worth defending her position. "I mean, if I went ahead and printed Mike's stuff, then I'd be making a moral decision, right? I'd be saying that Sylvester Kostenwhatsit's movies are okay and that kids should go see them. Why does it only seem 'moral' when you hold something back?"

"Good question," Mrs. Stegner said.

Lucy felt flushed now, but continued: "And since when does a person have to split up what they believe personally from what they do at school, or an office, or at a newspaper? Didn't you just teach last week that most of our newspapers were started by people who *always* brought their personal perspectives to what they printed? They still do, except they never admit it now. Didn't you say so?"

"As a matter of fact, I *did* say that, but—"

"Then why can't I do that with the *Owl*?"

Mrs. Stegner laughed. "You're a sharp girl, Lucy. I respect what you think—you're sensible and show good judgment—that's why I asked you to be this year's editor. I'm not saying I disapprove of what you're trying to do. In fact, I'm very curious about it, as a sort of experiment."

"Really?"

Mrs. Stegner sat up in her chair and leaned forward on the table. "I assume you have other ideas for the newspaper. Surely we're doing a lot of things that Jesus wouldn't approve of."

"We sure are!" Lucy said excitedly. "I was thinking that we should get rid of that sarcastic tone we always seem to write in. Why can't we be more positive about our news?"

"Give me an example."

"Bruce Goff's column is one. He's always writing about how bad it is here at school and what a pain in the neck homework is and how bad the cafeteria food is."

Mrs. Stegner picked up a pen and tapped it against her notepad. "Bruce probably speaks for most of the students."

"He doesn't speak for anybody *I* know," Lucy said. "If things were as bad as Bruce says, we'd all be homeschooled."

"That's just his particular perspective."

"Not just his perspective, but everybody who writes for the *Owl*. I know because I write that way myself. We're always talking about what's wrong. Why do we have to be so negative?" Lucy shook her head. "I'm not afraid to report things that are really important, but I think it should be balanced by articles that show what's going *right* around here, too. I'd like to try it."

"It won't sell newspapers. It never does," Mrs. Stegner said.

"But if I'm going to keep my pledge, I have to try." Lucy paused for a moment, weighing carefully what she had to say next. "Mrs. Stegner, if this pledge doesn't work . . . I mean, if my decisions wreck the paper for some reason, I'll resign. I won't be editor anymore. Is that a deal?"

Mrs. Stegner gazed at Lucy soberly, then said, "Deal."

Lucy stood up to leave. "Thanks for being so understanding."

"Like I said, this is an interesting experiment," Mrs. Stegner said. "I sincerely hope that it works."

Mr. Laker walked into the school office with his coat draped over his arm. Though it was overcast and crisply cool outside, he perspired. He waved at Mrs. Stewart as he walked past her desk.

"How was your meeting?" she asked.

He grunted. "The usual nonsense. Did I miss anything here?"

"Kevin Cassidy fell off of the balance beam and hit his head. Three stitches."

"That's too bad," Mr. Laker said. He walked into his office. Mrs. Stewart followed. "We weren't at fault, were we?" he suddenly asked.

"Not that I know of. He was playing around."

"Oh." He stood behind his desk and looked down at the stationery catalog.

"Karen Crosby came in for her meeting with you."

"Meeting?"

She gestured to the catalog. "To choose the student council stationery. Remember?"

"Oh, that's right." He tossed his coat over the top of the filing cabinet.

"She picked a nice design, I think," Mrs. Stewart said.

"Good."

"She wanted to get bids for the job, but I told her we have a company we regularly work with." She put a finger to her chin as she remembered something. "Oh, I have to get that file back from her."

"File?" Mr. Laker asked as he sat down.

"For Ballistic Printing. In the panic that Kevin Cassidy caused, I gave her your file so she could call them."

Mr. Laker ran a hand over his bald scalp. "Why would *she* call them? That's for our office to do."

"Because she's the president of the student council and she's supposed to take responsibility for it. Practical experience, you see."

"I get it." He sat down as if to start working, then suddenly looked up at Mrs. Stewart. "Did you say you *gave* her my file? Which file? I took it with me to my meeting."

"No, you didn't. It was right there in your briefcase."

His face turned a slight pink. "You should never give my files to the students. Particularly files from my briefcase!"

"I'm sorry, I was—"

"What if she loses it? What if there's something confidential in it?" His face went to a darker shade of red.

Mrs. Stewart was surprised by his reaction. "In a printer's file? What kind of confidential material would—"

"It doesn't matter," he snapped. "Just get that file back immediately!"

Mrs. Stewart wasn't used to being spoken to so sharply and glared at her boss.

"Never mind. *I'll* do it!" Mr. Laker said and stormed out to find Karen.

CHAPTER SEVEN

THE BELL HAD JUST RUNG for the end of the school day. In no time at all, the kids poured out of the classroom leaving Karen alone with Mrs. Biedermann.

"Is everything all right, Karen?" Mrs. Biedermann asked as she erased the whiteboard. "Karen?"

Karen, who was staring at the open file from Mr. Laker's office, jumped. "What?"

"I know my classes are incredibly interesting, but school's out. You can go home now."

Fumbling to close the file and gather her books, Karen mumbled an apology and made her way out of the classroom. Once she was in the hallway, she stopped and opened the file again. *Something is wrong,* she thought.

"Hi, Karen," Lucy said.

Again, Karen jumped. "Don't do that!" she whispered.

"Didn't you see me come up? I was right in front of you."

"No, I didn't," Karen replied, her gaze falling back to the file.

Lucy peered over her shoulder. "Ballistic Printing? What's this?"

"A file from Mr. Laker's office. It's for the printer they use for all the school's forms and stuff," Karen explained. "Mrs. Stewart gave it to me so I could call them about our stationery. I'm supposed to take it back to her."

"Oh. Well, hurry up so we can go home," Lucy said.

Karen didn't move. She continued to flip through the pages in the file. "I nearly forgot I had it," Karen said as if Lucy had asked her another question. "Then I opened it up to get the phone number and I saw all these invoices and bids and receipts."

"So?"

Karen looked at Lucy with panic in her eyes. "I wasn't trying to snoop. I just couldn't find the phone number."

"What are you talking about?" Lucy asked. "Who said you were snooping?"

"Nobody—*yet*. But they will if I don't get this file back." Karen started to walk away, but Lucy caught her arm.

"What's wrong, Karen? Why are you acting so weird?" Lucy asked.

"It's probably nothing," Karen said in a tone that meant it was probably something. "It just doesn't make sense, that's all."

Lucy said impatiently, "*What* doesn't make sense?"

Karen looked around to make sure no one was watching, then held up a small stack of forms. "These are bids from last year to print new report-card forms for the school."

"Bids?"

"Yeah. Like when you bid at an auction. Except, in this case, printers bid for business."

"I don't get it."

Karen explained, "It's like my stationery. Normally, I would ask two or three companies to give me their best prices on what they'd charge to print everything. When they give me the prices, it's called a *bid*."

Lucy nodded. "Okay, I get it. Then you'd go with whoever cost less, right?"

"Right. But that's what's weird about this file. There are three bids for the report-card forms but Mr. Laker obviously went with Ballistic Printing, even though they're the most expensive."

"Maybe he has high-class tastes," Lucy suggested.

"But Mr. Felegy made it absolutely clear to me that it was the school district's policy to always go with the lowest price." Again, Karen checked the hallway to make sure they were alone.

Lucy shrugged. "I'm sure Mr. Laker had his reasons."

"I'm sure he did, too," Karen said suspiciously. "Look at this note."

Lucy leaned over and read the typed letter on Ballistic Printing's letterhead. It thanked Mr. Laker for his business, then detailed a lot of form numbers and charges. "What am I supposed to see here?" Lucy asked.

Karen pointed to the P.S. at the bottom of the letter. "See this?"

Lucy adjusted her glasses and read a handwritten scrawl: "P.S.— Art, your 'gift' is enclosed as usual for services rendered." The letter was signed Jim Forrester, President of Ballistic Printing, with a "J.F." scribbled after the P.S.

"Gift?"

Karen held up a photocopy of a check for $2,000 payable to Art Laker from Ballistic Printing. Lucy gasped.

"Why would Ballistic Printing pay Mr. Laker $2,000?" Karen closed the file.

Lucy's best instincts as a reporter kicked into gear. "Wait a minute. So what we have here is a company that does *all* of the school's printing—even though it's *more* expensive—because Mr. Laker is given money by the owner." Now it was Lucy's turn to check the hallway. She whispered, "But that's wrong!"

"It sure is," Karen answered.

Now Lucy understood why Karen looked so worried. She had accidentally stumbled onto a small case of corruption in the upper ranks of their school.

"What am I going to do?" Karen asked, then paused thoughtfully. "What would *Jesus* do?"

Lucy put her hand on Karen's shoulder. "I'm not so sure what Jesus would do, but a good reporter would take this file back to the *Owl*'s office and make copies of those bids, that letter, and the check!"

Lucy and Karen made their way through the *Owl*'s office and into the adjoining closet. It was a cramped little room with metal shelving piled high with reams of paper, envelopes, textbooks about journalism, old issues of the *Owl*, and a small photocopier that had been donated to the *Owl* by Mr. Whittaker two years ago. Karen watched nervously while Lucy made copies of the incriminating documents.

"So, what would Jesus do about this?" Lucy asked.

Karen chewed on a fingernail. "I don't know. Would Jesus have sneaked a peek in the file in the first place?"

"You didn't *sneak* a peek," Lucy rebuked her. "You were looking for a phone number and saw the rest of it by accident. *If* it was an accident."

"What do you mean, *if*? I didn't do this on purpose!"

"I know *you* didn't. But maybe somebody else did."

"Like who?"

"God." Lucy made the last copy and handed the original pages back to Karen. "Mr. Whittaker is always telling us how God answers our prayers in unexpected ways. You said you want to follow in Jesus' steps. Maybe this is His way of testing your pledge."

Karen groaned. "But I thought God was going to show me how to do better on my homework or get along with people I didn't like. I didn't think He'd drop me in the middle of a school scandal!"

"What would Jesus do?" Lucy asked simply.

"I don't know," Karen admitted.

Lucy giggled and said, "Jesus said to go into our closets to pray . . . and this is a closet. So let's pray about it and see what happens."

Karen said it was a good idea and they stood next to the humming copier and prayed for God to help Karen understand what Jesus would do.

"Lucy? Karen? Is anyone in here?" a voice called from the office.

Karen barely stifled a shriek. It was Mr. Laker!

"We're in here," Lucy called back and quickly shoved the copies she'd just made under a package of paper.

"What do I do? What do I say?" Karen asked quickly.

"Just get out of here. We can't let him see us next to the copier!" Lucy whispered and pushed Karen toward the closet door.

Karen stumbled into the *Owl*'s office. Mr. Laker was crossing the room and looked at her suspiciously. "Hi. I've been looking all over for you. Mrs. Biedermann said she saw you together and had a wild hunch that you'd be here. It looks like her hunch was right."

Lucy came out of the closet and closed the door behind her. "Hi, Mr. Laker," she said pleasantly.

Karen stared at her wordlessly.

"I came to get the Ballistic Printing file," Mr. Laker said. "Do you still have it?"

"Oh, yeah," Karen said and snatched it from her notebook. She handed it over.

"Did you get what you wanted?" asked Mr. Laker.

Karen swallowed hard as her mouth went dry. "Yes, sir. The phone number."

"Good. Y'know, I wasn't very happy with Mrs. Stewart. She shouldn't have let that file out of the office." He patted the file. "Oh, well. No harm done, I guess."

"No, sir," Karen said.

"See you tomorrow, then," Mr. Laker said and walked out.

"No harm done," Karen repeated softly.

"*Yet*," Lucy added.

Back in his office, Mr. Laker opened the Ballistic Printing file. He hadn't actually looked at its contents for a long time. Invoices, receipts, and letters had been randomly shoved inside without his thinking that anyone else would ever see them. It was one of several files that he kept at home. He had a "modified" version of the Ballistic Printing file in the school office. It was a safer version.

He chastised himself for bringing the file from home. He'd had a meeting with Jim Forrester a few days ago and wanted it on hand. It should have gone back into the filing cabinet at home right away. Obviously, he was getting careless in his old age. Leaving it in his briefcase was a stupid thing to do. He sighed. He should have cleaned the file out ages ago anyway.

He flipped through the pages, checking each one to see if there was anything unusual—anything that might draw the wrong kind of attention.

The report card bids caught his eye. What were they doing in there? He thought he'd thrown them away. He swore to himself and laid the bids on the desk. He'd use the office shredder to take care of them.

His gaze drifted back down to the file in his lap. He saw the letter from Jim Forrester, the P.S., and the copy of the check—and slammed his fist against the desk.

WHIT STOOD ON THE LONG stretch of land behind Whit's End and absentmindedly raked wayward autumn leaves into small piles. His mind was on Raymond Clark. Raking leaves was one of the jobs Whit knew he could have offered to the man. He sighed heavily and looked at his watch. It was a little after 3:00 P.M. He knew he needed to hurry up: The after-school rush of kids would keep him busy inside until dinnertime. He gazed down at the street in front of his shop, just as a young woman—probably in her early twenties—rounded the corner. She stopped when she saw him.

"Hello," she called out.

Whit walked toward her, skirting the shop to lean the rake against the wall. "Hi," he said. "Can I help you?"

As he got closer to the woman, he was struck by her square face and kind eyes—a clear resemblance to Raymond Clark. No doubt it was his daughter.

"Are you John Whittaker?" she asked.

"Yes, I am."

She held out her hand. "I'm Christine Holt—er, *Clark*. You helped my father, I was told. I came to say thank you."

Whit shook her hand. "No thanks are necessary."

"I disagree. You've been extremely kind and generous and—" She stopped as tears came to her abruptly. "I'm sorry," she whispered.

Whit put his arm around her and led her to the back entrance of the shop. "Come in and sit down. I'll make us some coffee."

He sat her down at the large wooden table in the kitchen and, once the coffee had been made and poured, eased into a chair across from her. She got her tears under control and sat quietly for a moment. Then she explained, "I went to the hospital to identify him and fill out a dozen different forms. When I asked about settling our bill with the doctors, they said you had taken care of everything. So I'm here to settle accounts with you."

Whit sipped his coffee. "There's nothing to settle, Mrs. Holt."

"Christine."

"Christine, then." Whit looked at her earnestly. "I'd be insulted if you insisted on paying me back. I did what I did as a matter of conscience. I only wish I could have done more—and sooner."

"That makes two of us," Christine said, wrapping her fingers around the coffee cup as if to keep them warm. A silent moment passed. "You're wondering how he wound up like he did."

"You don't have to explain anything."

"No, I owe you that much. Though I'm not sure about all the details myself." An ironic smile crossed her face. "That must sound terrible coming from his only daughter. But there's so much I didn't know. I'm not even sure where to begin."

"Where are you from?"

"I grew up in Chicago. That's where we lived most of my life. Dad was a press operator for various printers. It was never a great money-making job, but it was all he knew. His father was a printer, too." She lifted the cup to her lips and blew gently across the top to cool the coffee down. "All I remember growing up was how little we had. We weren't poverty-stricken, but we were pretty poor. Mom and I did what we could to help out. Dad didn't want us to work, though. He insisted on being the breadwinner of the family. No matter how bad it got, he wouldn't let us find jobs. In fact, he did everything he could to hide how bad things were financially."

"That's how it was with men from the older generation," Whit said.

Christine continued, "I left home to go to college. I worked nights to do it. Dad felt terrible. He kept saying that he should pay my tuition. I didn't mind doing it myself. Let's see. That was four years ago. I met Robert on campus—he's my husband—and we moved to Columbus because that's where his work was. He's a legal assistant right now. He's studying to be a lawyer."

"How did your father wind up in Connellsville?" Whit asked.

Christine replied, "The new computer technology kept putting Dad out of work, so he and Mom moved there. Staying in touch got harder and harder from so far away. I wrote and called, but he wouldn't tell me what was happening. He didn't tell me how sick Mom was with cancer. I barely found out just before she died. He also didn't mention that he'd lost his job. I kept meaning to come visit him, but we couldn't find the time."

Whit frowned. *Couldn't find the time.* How well he knew that reason. Or was it an excuse? "Why did your father keep so much to himself?"

"He knew I would have insisted that he come live with us in Columbus," Christine said.

"He didn't like Columbus?"

Christine smiled and, for a moment, Whit saw a fresh-faced young girl, instead of a grieving daughter. "He didn't want to be a burden to me or Robert."

"If you can't turn to your own family, who can you turn to?" Whit asked softly.

"That's right," Christine said, then lowered her head. "I had no idea he was walking the streets, begging for work. The doctors said he had a very weak heart. If he had only told me—if I'd only known . . ." She pressed a hand to her mouth to stifle a sob.

Whit reached across the table and gently placed his hand over hers.

"I don't know whether I feel sad or extremely angry at him for hiding so much from me." She wiped her nose with a balled-up tissue.

"Tell me about your father's faith. He said a lot of things to us that made me think he was a Christian. Was he?"

Christine nodded. "Oh, yes. He was an elder in our church for years. That's one thing he didn't hide: his faith. I think he struggled with it sometimes. I know he questioned God when he couldn't keep a job— and when Mom got sick and died. He never said anything outright, just little things that made me believe he was wrestling with what it all meant. The last time I saw him, at Mom's funeral, he asked me if I understood what it really meant to be a Christian. It's as if he was trying to figure out what makes a Christian different from other people. He never said anything judgmental. It was like he was sorting it out for himself."

"He asked us those same questions before he collapsed. It's caused quite a stir. Some of us are doing a lot of soul-searching because of him."

"I hope none of you blame yourselves," Christine said. "He was a stranger to you."

Whit looked her directly in the eyes. "He was a stranger, but none of us took him in."

Christine shook her head. "It's not realistic to expect any to . . ."

"Put ourselves on the line like Christians have for the past thousand years?"

"You're being too hard on yourself," she replied.

"Not at all. I'm merely asking the same question your father asked: What does it mean to follow in the footsteps of Jesus? It's an important question to answer."

"*Can* it be answered?" Christine asked.

"Not without great sacrifice, I suspect."

They sat quietly for another moment. The bell above the front door jingled as kids made their way in.

"I think I have some customers," Whit said.

Christine stood up. "My husband is coming tomorrow to help make arrangements for my father. We're going to bury him in Connellsville next to my mother. Will you come to the funeral?"

"Of course," Whit said warmly. "And if you need any help—with *anything*—money or— well, just ask."

Christine took Whit's hand and smiled gratefully. "You've done enough already. Just come to the funeral."

When Tom Riley stopped by to visit later in the evening, Whit told him about his visit with Christine.

"She seemed like a very sweet girl," Whit said in conclusion.

"I'm sure she is," Tom said. "I'd like to join you for that funeral, if you don't mind."

"I'd appreciate the company."

Tom climbed onto a stool at the soda counter and eyed his friend. "Well?"

Whit wiped off a table with a damp cloth and picked up someone's sticky, empty ice-cream bowl. "Well what?"

"You've got that pinched look in the corner of your eyes. There's something on your mind," Tom said.

Whit took the dirty dishes back to the counter and lingered there while his mind worked out what he wanted to say. "Tom, this whole thing has done something to me."

"I can see that."

"It's created an ache in my heart that I can't get rid of. And I don't mean feelings of guilt. It's more than that." Whit wiped the counter with the cloth. "Raymond Clark could be any one of us. He was a good man, a *Christian* man, and yet there he was at the end of his life still wondering what it meant to be a Christian."

"I wonder about it all the time. Don't you?"

Whit shrugged. "I guess I thought I'd have some of it figured out by now. Isn't that one of the benefits of growing old?"

"Says who?" Tom chuckled. "I don't remember anybody giving us guarantees about what we should or shouldn't know. All I remember is that the Bible tells us to be obedient, whether we can figure things out or not."

"I know, I know," Whit said. "But it seems strange to be a Christian as long as I've been and find myself right back at the start. *What would Jesus do?* It's such a basic question and I've never practiced finding an answer to it."

Tom laughed. "When have you ever had the time, Whit? Look at the hours you put into this shop—not to mention all the other things you do with the church and various city committees. You're constantly on the run. Not even Jesus tried to do *everything*."

The Starduster careened downward toward the village of Mythopoeic, its hyper-blast guns trained on the group of unsuspecting citizens going about their business on the main avenue. The Evil Overlord Latas gently squeezed the firing stick. The Starduster jerked as laser-balls burst forward. Each one hit the village below, disintegrating the people into clouds of dust and leaving behind craters of black soot. Leisha, daughter of the once-powerful Madrigal, turned and cried for help from the gods of Avaline. Latas trained his sites on her—because she was his only reason for attacking the village in the first place . . .

Matt suddenly paused the DVD player. "Was that a car door? I thought I heard a car door slam."

"I didn't hear anything. Now turn the movie back on; this is the best part," Jack said, then turned to Oscar, who was hiding his eyes behind a pillow. "You can come out now, Oscar."

Oscar peeked at Jack. "This stuff gives me nightmares. That Overlord Latas and his army reminds me of Joe Devlin and his bullies."

Matt listened for a moment to make sure his parents hadn't come home early from their meeting. "I could've sworn I heard them."

"Come on, Matt. This is where Leisha calls down the lightning from Natrom." Jack grabbed for the remote control.

"Wait a minute," Matt said, holding the remote out of Jack's reach.

"What's the matter? Your parents aren't home yet."

"I know, but . . ." he hesitated. "It just suddenly occurred to me that this is wrong."

Jack scrunched his eyebrows down. "*What's* wrong?"

"Watching a movie that I *know* my parents wouldn't want me to watch," answered Matt.

"They didn't say you *couldn't* watch it," Jack reminded him.

"But they didn't say I *could*, either. You brought it over. They don't know anything about it." Matt turned the movie off.

Jack groaned. "It's only a movie."

"When Leisha prayed to those gods like she did . . . well, it seemed wrong. There's only one God," Matt said.

"I was thinking the same thing myself," Oscar piped in.

Jack folded his arms impatiently. "It's a story that takes place in a different dimension. What's with you guys?"

"We promised that we'd ask what Jesus would do about *everything*," Matt said. "Would Jesus watch this movie—especially when He didn't have His parents' permission?"

"I don't know," Jack shrugged. "They didn't have movies when Jesus was a kid."

Matt persisted: "They probably had a lot of things like movies, though. Storytellers or books or whatever. The question is, would Jesus watch a movie where the bad guys kill everyone and the good guys pray to gods who aren't God?"

"Beats me. How do we find out?"

"Mr. Whittaker said we'd have to study Jesus in the Bible," Oscar offered. "Do you have one around here? I'd like to see what it says about Joe Devlin."

Matt thought about it. "I have a Bible in my room. And there's one that my Dad uses in his den."

They turned off the television and Jack grabbed the DVD to put back into his backpack. He looked at the cover one last time: where starships fired at innocent villagers and a dazzling blonde woman shot lightning from her fingertips at a gruesome monster. For a fleeting second, Jack thought he saw the picture as Jesus would've seen it—and he felt sad. It was only a story, all right, but was it a story that Jesus would like? As he slipped the movie into his backpack, Jack knew he would never watch the film again.

Bibles in hand, the three boys sat down in the living room to see if they could find out what Jesus would do about movies and bullies and anything else they could think of. No one was more surprised by the scene than Matt's parents when they got home.

CHAPTER NINE

"LUCY!" KAREN CALLED down the hallway the next morning at school.

"Hi, Karen."

Karen was breathless as she spoke. "He wants to see me."

"Who does?" Lucy asked.

"Mr. Laker! He wants to see me in his office," Karen gasped, looking left and right as if the man himself might be standing nearby.

Lucy looked at Karen wide-eyed, then fought to keep control of her own fear. It wouldn't help for both of them to be panicked. "Really?" she said calmly.

"'Really?' Is that all you can say? What am I going to do?" Karen asked in a harsh whisper.

"What would Jesus do?"

Karen held her books close to her chest while she rubbed her eyes wearily with her free hand. "I read my Bible last night—I prayed—I'm still not sure. Oh, I wish I never looked at that stupid file! I didn't get any sleep last night."

"I wonder if Jesus had any sleepless nights from worry?" Lucy asked, more as an accusation than a question.

Karen frowned at her friend. "Cut it out. I'm not Jesus. I'm just trying to follow Him. And right now it's scaring me to death."

"Did you tell your parents about the file?"

"No," Karen said quickly. "Telling them would be the same as telling everyone else. I'm not ready to do that yet. This is so serious. They'd make me confront Mr. Laker. I don't know if I can do that."

Lucy turned to face Karen. "Jesus exposed the darkness in the world. He got after the religious leaders for leaving God out of all their rules. Isn't it the same here?"

"Maybe it is," Karen said. "But they crucified Jesus in the end, remember?"

"And God raised Him from the dead," Lucy pointed out.

Karen groaned. "But will He raise *me* after Mr. Laker gets done with me? I wish I could pretend I didn't see anything. I'm a nervous wreck!"

Lucy ached for her friend, but could only say, "I'm sorry, Karen, I want to help you. But I'm not the Holy Spirit. Is there time to go somewhere and pray?"

"No! I have to go meet him *now.*"

Lucy scratched her chin thoughtfully. "Maybe Mr. Laker won't even bring it up. You know, he might want to meet with you about something else."

Karen looked at her friend hopefully. "Do you really think so?"

"That could be your test. Why don't you wait and see if Mr. Laker brings it up? If he does, then you'll probably have to tell him what you know. You can't lie. Jesus wouldn't. But if he *doesn't* mention it, then you'll have time to think about what to do. You'll have to tell your parents, you know."

"I know. And I will." Karen backed away from Lucy to go to the office. "Pray for me," she said.

Lucy watched Karen disappear around the corner, then slumped against the wall. She was trying to be strong for her friend. She wanted to encourage her to do the right thing. Yet, in her heart, Lucy was deeply afraid of what Mr. Laker might do to Karen. If he was truly guilty of breaking the school's policy—a policy that was put there for very good reasons—then he might try to protect himself. How, though? How far would Mr. Laker go to keep himself out of trouble? The possible answers worried Lucy.

Mr. Laker waved to the metal chair just opposite to his desk. "Sit down, Karen."

"Yes, sir," Karen said and sat down. She still held her books close, pressing them against her lap.

"I'll come right to the point. You're an impressive young girl, Karen. Talented, too. You play the oboe, I know."

Karen wasn't sure what to say. Discussing her oboe-playing wasn't what she thought they were going to do. "The oboe? Yes, I do," she stammered.

"I heard you at the last school concert. You're quite remarkable."

Karen blushed and said, "Thank you."

"Are you familiar with the Campbell County Youth Orchestra?" he asked, peering at his nails indifferently.

Karen brightened. "Are you kidding? Sure I've heard of it. It's the best there is."

Mr. Laker chuckled and said, "There're probably one or two that's better. But you're right: They're the best in this state for their age group. They take only the brightest students and the most talented players."

"Yes, sir. I hope to play with them one day. Maybe next year."

"How about *this* year?"

Karen tilted her head, unsure of how to take the question. "I beg your pardon?"

Mr. Laker sat forward in the chair again. "Karen, I'm pleased to tell you that you've been selected to play the oboe for the Campbell County Youth Orchestra."

"What?" Karen sat up so quickly that she spilled her books. As she retrieved them from the floor, she asked, "Me? Did you say me? Play in the Campbell County Youth Orchestra?"

Mr. Laker nodded his head happily. "It's a paid position, with money going to your future education. You, of course, know the orchestra's sterling reputation—not to mention the many opportunities it presents."

Karen was genuinely speechless. "I don't know what to say, Mr. Laker! How did it happen? I mean, why did they suddenly choose me?"

"They had an unexpected opening and . . ." He paused and looked away as if he was suddenly embarrassed. "I shouldn't say."

"Shouldn't say what?"

"Well, I'm a member of the orchestra's selection committee. I put your name forward as a candidate. Just last night, as a matter of fact. The rest of the committee agreed unanimously."

"I can't believe this!" Karen squealed and nearly dropped her books again.

He raised a finger. "Oh—there's only one tiny drawback."

"Drawback?" she asked anxiously.

"Yes," he said. "You'll have to resign as president of the student council. The orchestra puts in an awful lot of practice hours, you know. That's why they're so good. You wouldn't have time for both."

Karen was awash with relief. "Is that all? Who cares about being on the student council when I can perform with the orchestra!"

"I thought as much," Mr. Laker said with a smile.

In her excitement, Karen suddenly wondered why she had always been so afraid of Mr. Laker. *He's a nice man*, she thought. She'd misjudged him. Maybe even the file had an easy explanation; it was a mistake; she had misunderstood what she saw. Who cared about it now? *She was going to play for the Campbell County Youth Orchestra!*

Unexpectedly, a small voice whispered in the back of her mind: *What would Jesus do?*

The answer this time seemed obvious to her. Jesus would use His God-given talents to play for the orchestra. It wasn't as if being president of the student council had anything to do with her future anyway. Jesus would say yes.

Would He? The question made her terribly uncomfortable.

Mr. Laker's smile faded. "Karen?"

"I need to talk to my parents," she suddenly heard herself saying. Even as the words came out, she wanted to stop them. She was afraid he'd take the offer back just because she didn't say yes right away.

"I'd never let you do it without talking to your parents first."

"Thank you, Mr. Laker." She stood up to leave and said again awkwardly, "Thank you."

"You're welcome." He thrust his hand out to her and she shook it.

It was cold and clammy. A chill went up and down her spine.

JACK FINISHED THE LAST of his French fries and pushed the plate and the cafeteria tray aside. Matt was still eating his hamburger.

"Where's Oscar?" asked Jack, scanning the large room and all the students who were eating their lunches.

Matt glanced around. "Is today when he meets Mrs. McKenzie in the library? She's been helping him with his reading lately."

"I don't think so."

Joe Devlin, a large kid with greasy dark hair, walked up to the table with a lunch tray. He was followed by a couple of the members of his gang, whose sole purpose in life was to laugh at Joe's jokes and win his fights. "It's Tweedle-Dee and Tweedle-Dum," Joe said to Jack and Matt.

Joe's pals snickered obediently.

"And you must be the Three Stooges," Matt said.

"Do we want to make these two clowns move so we can sit here, boys?" Joe asked his cohorts.

"You'll have to wait until I'm finished eating," Matt said.

Joe reached over and shoved his forefinger through the top of Matt's hamburger. "Feels cold," he said with a smirk. "You don't want to eat the rest of that anyway. Get lost."

Matt leapt to his feet. "That's not funny, Joe!"

"You gonna do something about it?" Joe challenged him.

"Yeah . . ." Matt sneered, then quickly grabbed the hamburger off of Joe's tray and took a bite out of it.

"Hey!" Joe shouted and slammed his tray down on the table.

Matt laughed at him until Jack suddenly said, "What would Jesus do, Matt?"

This was enough to stop Matt—and Joe, turning to Jack, asked, "What did you say?"

"Is everything all right here?" a deep baritone voice asked. It was their principal, Mr. Felegy. He stood well over six feet tall, with a barrelchest, thin sandy-brown hair, and piercing eyes that defied anyone to rebel against his authority.

"No, sir," each of them mumbled.

"Then I suggest you find a table and eat your lunch before the bell rings," he said and was gone as quickly as he'd arrived.

Joe forced a chuckle. "It's okay. Keep the hamburger. I have plenty of money for another lunch today. Compliments of the First Bank of Oscar." He laughed viciously and his two friends cackled along with him as they walked off.

Jack and Matt exchanged looks as the meaning of Joe's words sunk in. They raced out of the cafeteria.

Jack and Matt found Oscar at the end of the hallway beyond the gym. He sat with his arms wrapped around his bent knees and rocking slightly.

"Oscar," Matt called out as they got closer.

"Are you all right?" asked Jack.

He looked up at them with pain in his eyes.

Matt knelt next to him. "Did they hurt you?"

He shook his head no.

"Then what happened? They got your lunch money, right?" Jack asked.

He nodded.

Matt looked him over. "But they didn't beat you up. You just *gave* it to them?"

He nodded again, then buried his face in his arms and cried softly.

"Aw, don't do that," Jack said as he sat down next to him.

Oscar sniffled. "You don't know what it's like. They pick on me all the time, no matter where I am. They don't even have to beat me up anymore. I just give them what they want so they'll go away."

Matt clenched and unclenched his fists. "I'm getting pretty tired of Joe. I think it's time he got taught a lesson."

"No," Oscar said, then lifted his head and spoke louder. "No. You can't do anything."

"Who says we can't?" Jack growled.

Oscar looked at Matt, then Jack, and said, "Would Jesus get revenge?"

Jack groaned. Matt hit his fist against the floor and complained, "I *knew* you were going to say that!"

"We made a promise," Oscar reminded them. "What would Jesus do about this?"

"I wish we never went to that meeting," Jack said under his breath.

Matt stood up and paced angrily. "I won't ever make a promise— ever again."

"I thought you guys were Christians," Oscar said.

"Don't start preaching to us, Oscar," Jack said. "It's bad enough that I didn't see the rest of my movie last night."

Oscar shook his head. "I'm not preaching. I'm just saying that we promised to try to follow Jesus. Why did we spend two hours reading through the Bible last night? What did we say? We said that Jesus knew what He was talking about and we should listen to Him."

Matt looked at Jack and spread his hands. "He's preaching to us anyway."

Oscar slowly got to his feet. "Getting revenge isn't what Jesus would do. He said to turn the other cheek. He said to pray for guys who persecute us. He said that people who live by the sword die by the sword."

"My dad has a Civil War sword in his den," Matt said thoughtfully, as if he meant to use it on Joe.

"So what do you suggest, Reverend Oscar?" Jack asked irritably. "How are we going to stop Joe Devlin? You'll never eat another lunch as long as he's around. Unless you want to tell on him."

"No," Oscar said. "I don't want to be teased for being a tattletale. Besides, he'll just pick on me when the teachers aren't around."

"So what should we do?" Matt asked. "This isn't right!"

Oscar looked at Matt and Joe and spoke sincerely. "Don't do anything. Don't even say anything."

"I don't get it," Jack said.

Oscar picked up his schoolbooks. "Remember? Jesus didn't say anything to those guys who crucified Him. He didn't fight back. He didn't argue. That's what I'm going to try with Joe and his gang. I won't fight back and I won't fuss. He may get what he wants from me, but it won't be any fun for him."

Though it was a cool autumn day, Lucy and Karen ate their lunches on the patio behind the cafeteria. The air had a hint of winter around its edges, as if it was snowing somewhere far away. Lucy pulled her jacket around her.

"So, they don't like any of your ideas?" Karen asked Lucy. They had been talking about Lucy's meeting that morning with the staff of the *Owl*.

"They think I'm crazy."

Karen shook her head. "You want to do positive articles. You want to have a more healthy attitude about the news. Why is it crazy to want to do *good* things?"

"Because they don't understand," Lucy said. She put her sandwich down on the plastic wrap that served as a plate. "I've been thinking about it a lot this morning. Y'know, I don't *really* know any of the kids I work with. I don't know if any of them are Christians—"

"Mike is, isn't he?"

Lucy shrugged. "I don't know for sure. Funny, he's probably the loudest about me being out of my mind. He said I should resign before I ruin everything and lose all our readers."

"Don't listen to him."

"But I know why he's so mad," Lucy said. "I understand how they feel. I'd feel the same way if Mrs. Stegner suddenly walked in and said, 'I'm a Buddhist and I want the *Owl* to write about Buddhist ideas.'"

"That's not what you're doing," said Karen.

"I'm sure it seems like it to them. Out of the blue, I come marching in with a whole different way of doing things and it's like I'm forcing everyone to follow what I believe." Lucy nibbled at her sandwich, lost in her thoughts, then said, "You see, when Jesus went into various towns and villages, they didn't know who He was. But when they heard the kinds of things He said, and saw the love He had and the way He healed people, they figured He was someone to listen to. What am I showing the staff of the *Owl*? It's not like I took time to get to know them, or do anything except throw my beliefs at them."

"What were you supposed to do, walk on water? Heal their acne?"

"Somehow I should've shown that I *care* about them—the way Jesus cared. Then maybe they'd be more open to my ideas."

A somber silence followed for a minute. Both of the girls seemed to realize the significance of what Lucy was trying to do. The stakes were high. It was entirely possible that it would end with Lucy having to resign.

"Forget about the *Owl*," Lucy abruptly said. "I want to hear *your* news. You've been bursting to tell me ever since we sat down, and I haven't given you the chance."

Karen looked at her coolly. "Oh, it's nothing special."

Lucy raised her eyebrow like a question mark.

With growing excitement, Karen said, "It's only that Mr. Laker has asked me to play oboe with the Campbell County Youth Orchestra!"

Lucy dropped her sandwich. "What?" she squeaked. "Is that why he wanted to see you?"

Karen nodded quickly. "Yeah! Isn't that great?"

"Congratulations!" Lucy said as she half-hugged Karen across the table.

"The only problem is that I'd have to resign as president of the student council. But I don't care. Though . . ."

"Though what?"

"I remembered to stop and ask myself what Jesus would do," Karen said proudly. "So I didn't tell Mr. Laker yes or no."

"Good for you. What do you think Jesus would do?"

As with so many situations they'd already encountered, Karen gave the standard answer: "I don't know. Would Jesus play for an orchestra? Would He use His talents like that? Y'know, we keep running into this same brick wall. 'What would Jesus do?' 'I don't know.' It's enough to drive me crazy. I didn't realize how ignorant I was about Jesus until now."

Lucy took her glasses off and cleaned them with a napkin. "There's something else to consider. What if Mr. Laker is doing this to cover himself."

Karen said she didn't understand.

"What if he's afraid you looked through the file? What if he's doing this to sort of bribe you to keep your mouth shut?" Lucy asked.

Karen's face fell. "I hadn't thought of that."

Lucy said, "Just because he got you a place on the orchestra doesn't mean you should forget what you saw."

Karen blushed. Whether she meant to or not, she *had* put the file out of her mind. She was ready to drop it. "Oh, Lucy," she said in despair, "what *are* we going to do? If I blow the whistle now, I'll never get to play with the orchestra."

"If you blow the whistle, some people will call you a tattletale," Lucy added. "You could lose your position as president of the student council, too."

Karen put her face in her hands. "What am I going to do?"

Lucy gently touched her arm. "Maybe it's time we went back to Mr. Whittaker and asked him about some of this stuff. He's the one who started this situation in the first place. He might have some answers."

Karen agreed. "Let's go after school."

Heather Carr caught Karen just as she was headed out the door after school.

"I've been looking for you," Heather said. They were best friends, though Karen hadn't seen her since the "pledge."

"Hi, Heather. Sorry, but I have to go. I'm late." Karen was in a rush to get to Whit's End. She was meeting Lucy there. She had also bumped into Jack, Oscar, and Matt earlier in the hall and they agreed they'd go to Whit's End for a few answers of their own.

"A bunch of us are going to the mall," Heather said. She sounded annoyed. "Do you want to come with us?"

Karen replied, "I can't. I have a meeting."

"With who? *Lucy?*" The accusation was unmistakable.

"Yeah, with Lucy. Why?"

"It just seems like you've been hanging out with her a lot. You don't have time left for your *old* friends—like me," Heather said testily.

"Cut it out, Heather." Karen didn't have the patience for this encounter, but she wanted to explain anyway. "Weren't you in church last Sunday?"

"No. I was out of town, remember? I told you we were going to my grandmother's."

"I forgot. Sorry. Anyway, some of us made a commitment to do everything the way Jesus would do it and it's . . . complicated things."

"I heard all about your complications," Heather countered. "And I heard that you were offered to play oboe for the orchestra. Thanks for telling me yourself. Do you know how embarrassing it is to learn that your *best friend* had something exciting happen and didn't tell you? But now that you're part of this holier-than-thou club, I guess it's too much to expect."

Karen grimaced. "I'm sorry, Heather. I was going to tell you myself, but I haven't seen you. Besides, I don't know that I'm going to do it."

"Too good for the orchestra now?" Heather asked sharply.

"Give me a break. That's not it. Look, why don't you come with me to Whit's End? Then you can see what we're talking about."

"No, thanks. I already told the rest of the girls I'd meet them at the mall. Jesus would want me to keep my commitments, wouldn't He?" She grinned sarcastically, turned away, and walked off.

"Heather, wait!" Karen called out. "You don't understand."

Heather didn't look back or respond.

Karen grumbled under her breath, then remembered the many friends and family members that Jesus had lost due to misunderstanding. She made her way toward Whit's End.

"SO, WHAT WOULD YOU LIKE to talk about?" Whit asked as he turned the sign on the front door of Whit's End so the "Closed—Be Back In Thirty Minutes" faced outside. He didn't want this meeting to be disturbed. "Well? Things aren't going the way you thought?"

The five of them—Lucy, Karen, Jack, Matt, and Oscar—looked at each other across the table where they had gathered. No one knew who should speak first.

Lucy cleared her throat, then said, "One of the biggest problems is that we don't know Jesus well enough to figure out what He'd do."

Whit sat down at the table with them. "We said from the start that that might be a problem. We have to know Him to follow Him. But He didn't leave us high and dry. We have the Bible and the Holy Spirit."

"It's not helping," Matt complained. "We spent hours looking through the Bible last night and Oscar still got robbed by Joe Devlin."

Whit turned to Oscar. "Do you want me to talk to Joe's parents?" he asked.

"No," Oscar said. "It won't help. Unless you give me police protection 24 hours a day, Joe will get to me somehow."

"Mr. Whittaker," Karen said. "It might sound a little weird, but we don't want you to do *anything* about what we have to say. We just need you to listen and . . . give us some advice."

He looked into the faces of the five kids, then nodded. "Okay. But I reserve the right to *advise* you to talk to your parents. Now, let's take this one at a time. Joe Devlin keeps picking on Oscar. What would Jesus do about that?"

"Hit Joe with lightning bolts from heaven," Matt suggested.

"Hardly."

Jack chimed in: "Jesus said to turn the other cheek and now Oscar's got some whacko idea to—" He hooked his thumb at Oscar. "You tell him, Oscar, and see what he thinks."

Oscar explained to Whit that he should act like Jesus did before they crucified Him. "He didn't argue, He didn't fight back, so that's what I'm going to do with Joe. I'll keep my mouth shut and won't do anything."

Whit stroked his mustache as if he was considering the idea. "For two thousand years people have tried to decide what Jesus meant by 'turn the other cheek.' And for that same amount of time, kids have been dealing with bullies and wondering if what Jesus said applied to their situation. I've talked to some parents who say that the only way to lick a bully is to knock him flat."

"Yeah!" Matt said.

"Other people think that fighting only begets more fighting until someone gets *really* hurt." Whit gazed at Oscar. "Chances are, you couldn't knock Joe flat, right?"

"Nope," Oscar replied.

"Then you should try your plan to see if it works. What have you got to lose?" Whit concluded.

"Is that it?" Jack asked. "*That's* how you figure out what Jesus would do?"

"Following Jesus doesn't mean you throw away your good sense, Jack," said Whit. "You've studied your Bibles, you've explored what Jesus said, and now you're putting it into action. This is what Oscar believes he should do. It's *his* decision—not yours, or Matt's. God will honor what's in his heart."

Both Jack and Matt slid down in their chairs and folded their arms. They didn't agree, but they kept their mouths shut.

Whit looked at Lucy. "How are you doing, Lucy?"

Lucy shrugged. "Okay, I guess. I didn't realize that this little experiment would make me feel so . . . so *alone*. I've got everybody on the *Owl's* staff against me."

"But you've got *God* for you," Whit said. "And we're with you in this, too. To listen, to pray . . ."

"Yeah, I know. And I appreciate it." Lucy hesitated, then asked, "Do you think Jesus ever felt alone?"

The kindness in Whit's eyes seemed to sparkle as he looked at Lucy. "I'm sure He did sometimes. In the Garden of Gethsemane, Jesus was probably the loneliest person in all of history. But He still said, 'Thy will be done.'"

Somewhere a clock ticked and one of the ice-cream freezers rattled and hummed.

"Karen?" Whit asked.

"It's lonely," she said. "And people don't understand why we're doing this. They think we're trying to be better than everyone else."

"Misunderstanding is part of it," Whit said. "They misunderstood Jesus and they've misunderstood His followers for two thousand years. More often than not, we're perfectly understood and they *still* don't like what we stand for."

"Isn't there something else you want to say, Karen?" asked Lucy.

"No. I don't have anything else right now," she said.

Lucy looked surprised. "You don't?"

"No," Karen said simply, then glanced away.

Whit observed the unspoken argument going on between the girls, then said as if to change the subject, "Would it help if we met like this more often? I get together with some of the adults who made the pledge every couple of days. Mostly we pray. Would you like to do that?"

Each of them mumbled their assent.

Whit chuckled to himself. *Their enthusiasm is breathtaking*, he thought.

"Let's spend a little bit of time in prayer, and then I need to open the shop again."

They bowed their heads.

"What happened?" Lucy asked as they walked down the sidewalk away from Whit's End. "Why didn't you tell Mr. Whittaker about Mr. Laker?"

"I didn't need to. I know what I have to do," Karen said.

"What?"

"The thing I was supposed to do all along."

Lucy navigated a step in front of Karen and stood directly in her way. "*What* are you going to do?"

Karen spoke on the verge of tears. "Did you hear what he said about Jesus? He was all alone in the Garden of Gethsemane. He gave up everything He had—even His life—to do God's will. Why am I worried about playing for an orchestra? Why should I care if I'm president of the student council? 'Thy will be done,' He said. Those words burned inside me." Karen fought to hold back a sob. "I've known all along what I was supposed to do, but I was being a coward. I won't be one anymore."

The dam of tears broke. Karen pushed past Lucy and ran down the sidewalk.

FIRST THING THE NEXT MORNING, Karen found herself pacing back and forth in front of Mr. Laker's office door. He walked in through the main door, dressed in a heavy coat and furry hat. He stopped suddenly when he saw her. "Hi, Karen. What are you doing here?"

"I need to talk to you, Mr. Laker."

"About the orchestra," he said as he shoved his key into the door lock. He pushed the door open. "Come in."

She followed him in, her stomach churning nervously. Did Jesus feel this way when He confronted the Pharisees? Did He want to throw up when He stood before Pilate?

Mr. Laker hung his coat and hat on the coatrack. "Did you talk to your parents?"

"No, sir. Not yet," she said and swallowed hard. Oh *why* didn't she talk to her parents first? She was afraid to, that's why. She thought her dad would make a federal case out of it. She imagined him calling the police and making her go to court and sit on the witness stand. This way, she could talk to Mr. Laker alone and maybe he'd confess and promise to make amends and then she could forget about the whole thing.

Mr. Laker watched Karen for a moment. "Why not?"

"Because I wanted to talk to you again first," she said.

"Oh?"

"Yes, sir." She paused, wishing she had a glass of water. "I'm sorry but I have to say no about the orchestra."

Mr. Laker looked genuinely disappointed. "That's too bad. You'd be a wonderful asset, I'm sure. Why won't you do it?"

"Because . . . I'm afraid there's a price tag attached to it that I can't afford."

"A price tag? What kind of price tag?"

She'd practiced the speech a hundred times that morning. None of the words came to mind. "Let's see . . . does the phrase *bribery* mean anything to you?"

He blinked a couple of times, but kept his face solidly straight. "You thought I bribed someone to get you on the orchestra?"

Karen tugged at her collar. It seemed awfully hot all of a sudden. "Mr. Laker, I don't know how to start. But I saw some things in the Ballistic Printing file that you probably didn't want me to see."

"Like what?"

"Well . . ."

"Shall I get the file for you? Maybe that'll help." He opened the large filing cabinet drawer and pulled out a manila folder. "You have me worried, Karen. You're acting like something is seriously wrong."

He handed the file to her. She was stunned by his behavior and didn't know what to make of it. Was it some kind of trick? Did he *want* to get in trouble? She opened the file and worked through the various documents. The papers looked similar, but not identical to the ones she'd seen before. In less than a minute she'd reached the bottom. The bids, the letter, and the copy of the check were gone.

"You took them out," she said.

"Took what out?"

"Those bids—and the letter—and the check."

"Bids? Letter? Check?"

Karen turned red. "There were bids in here to print our report cards. Two printers were cheaper than Ballistic Printing, but you went with Ballistic anyway. It's against school policy to go with a more expensive printer when you have *two* who are less expensive."

Mr. Laker chuckled. "I think you must be feverish, Karen. Do you want me to call the school nurse?"

"No, sir." She took a deep breath to control her quavering voice. "You took a bribe, Mr. Laker. I saw the P.S. on the letter about your so-called gift. And I saw the check. Why would they pay you $2,000 unless it was to keep your business?"

Mr. Laker's cheeks turned pink, then he forced a smile. "You don't know what you're getting into, Karen."

"I . . . I want you to admit to what you did and talk to Mr. Felegy. Maybe they won't fire you," she said, trying to stick to her plan.

"Maybe they'll send me to bed without my supper," Mr. Laker said laughing. "I don't know what you're talking about. And you can see for yourself that there's no letter or check in the file."

"They were there and you know it!"

"Don't get hysterical," he urged.

"You got rid of the evidence! I saw them with my own two eyes!"

"Then you better get your eyes checked."

Karen's mouth moved, but nothing came out. She could insist over and over, but it wouldn't make any difference without proof.

"Now, can we stop this nonsense, please?" In the main office area, a door slammed. Someone had arrived. "Good morning!" Mrs. Stewart called from the other room. Karen could hear her drop her purse on the desk.

Mr. Laker spoke louder, as if having a new witness was important. "I don't know what your problem is, Karen. I tried to do something nice for you by getting you on the orchestra and this is how you say thanks. I feel sorry for you. You need to see a counselor. Get some help."

"But . . . but . . ."

"There's nothing left to say. You're going to be late for class."

Karen turned to leave. All the feeling in her mind and body seemed to disappear.

"Karen," Mr. Laker added in a low voice, "you're in over your head with things you know very little about. I'd keep my lips sealed if I were you. Wild accusations will only come back to hurt *you*. Do you understand?"

Lucy discovered Karen crying in a stall in the bathroom. Recognizing her shoes under the short gray door, she knocked softly. "Karen," she whispered.

The sniffling from the other side of the door suddenly stopped. "Lucy?"

"Yeah, it's me."

The door jerked open and Karen threw herself into Lucy's arms. "It was awful!" she said. "Awful!"

"What was?" Lucy held her tight for a moment, then held her away at arm's length. "You have to hurry and tell me—the bell's about to ring."

Karen dabbed at her eyes with some toilet tissue. "I talked to Mr. Laker."

"This *morning*? Why didn't you tell me?"

"I wanted to handle it myself—like Jesus did." Karen walked over to the sink and despaired of her looks. Her eyes were puffy and her nose rubbed raw from the cheap toilet paper.

"What happened?" Lucy asked as she watched Karen get herself cleaned up.

"He cleaned the file out," Karen said. "In fact, I'm not even sure it was the *same* file we saw. I looked like an idiot."

Lucy leaned against the sink and folded her arms. "What did you think he'd do, break under the truth and confess everything?"

"Yeah, I guess maybe I did," Karen said, half-smiling. "But he denied everything and said I was ungrateful and needed to see a counselor and . . . and it's all true! I must've been crazy. What could I do without any proof?"

"Did you tell him about the copies?"

"Copies?"

"The copies we made," Lucy said. "Remember?"

Karen pressed her hand to her mouth from shock and embarrassment. "My brains have been so tied up that I forgot all about them! I kept thinking about what Jesus would do. And I didn't think that Jesus would ever need *proof*."

"Oh, Karen . . ." Lucy put her head in her hands and shook her head.

"Where are they?" Karen asked, grabbing for this shred of hope.

"I gave them to you," Lucy said.

"You did?" She thought about it a moment. "No, you didn't. You kept them."

"Honest, Karen, I don't have them. Check your desk, your notebooks, *everywhere*. You must have hidden them."

Karen looked panicked again. "But I *didn't*. You made the copies and kept them with you! I'd remember!"

Lucy eyed her skeptically. "How could you remember *that* when you didn't even remember there were copies at all?"

"Don't yell at me," Karen said. "I'm feeling fragile right now."

Lucy groaned. "Okay. Maybe I'm wrong. Let's *both* check. One of us hid them somewhere!"

"Hey, look! It's our old buddy Oscar!"

Oscar stopped on the playground and turned to face Joe Devlin and his gang. Out of the corner of his eye, Oscar saw Jack and Matt step through the door into the school building with the rest of the class. Joe and his pals surrounded Oscar like they always did.

"How's it going, Osc?" Joe asked as he poked a finger into Oscar's shoulder. "Did you have fun playing soccer in P.E.?"

Oscar took a deep breath, then merely gazed at him.

"What's the matter, cat got your tongue?" Joe laughed. The gang chortled with him.

Oscar didn't reply. He simply looked at Joe and waited.

Joe eyed him carefully. "What's the matter with you? You got laryngitis? Say something."

Oscar didn't move, didn't twitch a face muscle, didn't react at all.

Joe pushed him. "I said *say something*."

Oscar stared at Joe like a little lamb.

"You heard him," one of the other gang members suddenly said, and shoved him in another direction. "Speak!"

Still no sound from Oscar.

The gang began to taunt him, pushing and jabbing from all sides until he bounced between them like a pinball in a machine. Still, he didn't say a word. When they tired of that little game, Joe grabbed Oscar by the front of his shirt and pulled him close.

"Say something," he hissed.

Oscar looked into his eyes, but wouldn't obey.

Joe thrust him away. "This is getting on my nerves. I'm tempted to give you a good pounding for being so rude."

Oscar reached into his pocket and silently held out his lunch money.

Joe slapped the money away. "I don't want your stupid money. I want you to *talk to me*!"

Oscar continued to look at him without a sound.

Clenching his fists, Joe stepped forward as if he might slug Oscar. "That's it!"

Oscar closed his eyes and waited for the blow.

It never came. Joe snarled, then turned and marched away. With a few extra shoves for good measure, Joe's pals brushed past Oscar and followed their leader across the playground toward the school.

Oscar slowly slumped to the ground, tense from fear but happy at the same time. He slowly picked up his lunch money.

At lunch, Jack and Matt weren't as pleased as Oscar about the encounter with Joe.

"He still pushed you around," Jack complained.

Matt agreed. "The point is his bullying has got to *stop!*"

Oscar swallowed a bite of bologna sandwich. "But I think it *will* stop. Even if it doesn't, I'm still doing what I think Jesus would do and that makes me feel *great*! I got to keep my lunch money, too!"

"I don't care," Jack said. He and Matt looked at one another.

Matt nodded with understanding. "Okay, this afternoon."

Oscar peered at Jack, then Matt, then asked, "This afternoon? What about this afternoon?"

"None of your business," Matt said.

"What are you guys up to?" Oscar asked, instantly worried. "Remember: What would Jesus do?"

Jack leaned toward Oscar and told him, "You just leave it to us."

Matt also leaned forward and smiled. "Don't forget that Jesus made whips and drove the money changers out of the temple."

"Did you find the copies?" Karen asked Lucy anxiously when they sat down at lunch.

"No. I guess you didn't either, huh?"

Karen shook her head. "No sign of them. What did we do with them, Lucy?"

"You didn't take them home, did you?"

"I don't remember ever having them! How could I know if I took them home?" Karen asked.

"Well, I know *I* didn't," Lucy said.

"Maybe Mr. Laker will forget I ever brought it up," Karen wished. "Without those copies, I'm just an insane kid who makes stupid accusations."

"Uh-oh," Lucy said, looking over Karen's shoulder.

Karen turned and saw Mrs. Stewart crossing the cafeteria toward her. A sinking feeling worked through her stomach.

Mrs. Stewart arrived. Her face looked pinched and worried. "Mr. Felegy wants to see you right away," she said.

Karen shot a parting glance to Lucy and followed Mrs. Stewart out of the cafeteria.

"Thank you for coming so fast," Mr. Felegy said when Karen arrived at his office and had taken a seat.

Karen nodded. "You're welcome." She wondered if Mr. Laker had said something to Mr. Felegy about their conversation that morning and tightly clung to the arms of the chair.

"This is a little awkward, Karen. You're a student whom I trust and hold with great respect. For those reasons, I thought I'd talk to you before I called your parents."

"Call my parents? But—why?"

Mr. Felegy handed her a computer printout. At the top, it said: Student Council Finance Statement. Underneath were columns of figures related to how the student council had been spending its small budget. Karen recognized the form. As president she had to be familiar with it, but she couldn't imagine why Mr. Felegy was showing it to her. "You know this."

"Yes, sir."

"Then perhaps you can explain that bottom line. The one that says 'Miscellaneous Expenses.'"

She looked down the page until she came to the phrase. Next to it was the figure "$347.00," and in parenthesis it said, "(Karen Crosby)."

"I don't know what that means," Karen said.

"Don't you?" Mr. Felegy asked. "It means that you personally spent $347 on something, but we can't find out what it was. There are no records in the student council files, except a receipt showing that you'd taken the money out of the account. Think, Karen. Why did you need the money?"

Karen worked through her memory of any time or reason she may have used money from the student council funds. "I had posters made for the charity car wash . . . the walk-a-thon . . . the fund-raiser for the trip to Chicago . . ."

"All of those expenses are accounted for elsewhere," Mr. Felegy said.

Karen was at a loss. She couldn't remember spending as much as $347 on anything. Even if she had, she would have filed the receipts so that a strict accounting could be made. "I don't know, Mr. Felegy. Why did this come up?"

"The school is being audited by the district office and Mr. Laker pointed out that—"

"Mr. Laker?"

Mr. Felegy explained, "As school administrator, he's in charge of all the finances. You know that."

"I know, but . . . did *he* bring this to you?" she asked.

"Yes. He said he didn't consider it a major problem, except that it seemed irregular. But *I* consider it a problem when $347 disappears from the student council funds and we don't know where it went." He kept his gaze fixed on her.

"Mr. Laker keeps all this stuff on his computer?" she asked.

"Yes."

Suddenly it clicked into place. Karen bit her nail and thought it through: Mr. Laker must have somehow juggled the figures on his computer. But did she dare say so to Mr. Felegy? Perhaps this was the moment of truth. What choice did she have?

"Karen, it's an awful lot of money and I certainly don't consider you irresponsible. But I need you to think very hard and tell me where you spent it."

"I didn't," Karen said, working up to her confession.

"Then who did?"

"I don't know, but it wasn't me," she said. "Maybe nobody spent it. Maybe it was never there."

Mr. Felegy looked at her quizzically. "Explain, please."

"Well," Karen began slowly. "I work on our computer at home with my dad. I've seen him do our finances. Last April, he pulled a joke on my mom by putting in the computer that she had spent $1,000 on groceries in one day."

Mr. Felegy frowned and said, "Why are you telling me this story?"

"Because I think Mr. Laker put in a bogus figure to get me in trouble," said Karen. There. It was out in the open.

Mr. Felegy pushed back from his desk and looked at her with a strained calmness. "Why would Mr. Laker want to get you in trouble?"

"Because I was going to get *him* in trouble."

"Oh boy," Mr. Felegy groaned. "I don't like the sound of *that*. You better tell me everything."

So Karen did: from when Mrs. Stewart gave her the file until her conversation with Mr. Laker that morning. It sounded almost ridiculous even to Karen's ears, but it was the truth and it had to be said.

"These are serious accusations, Karen," Mr. Felegy said after a long pause.

"I know."

"Do you have any proof?" he asked.

Karen cringed. "I knew you were going to ask me that."

"Well?"

"I *do* have proof," Karen said. "Somewhere. I just can't find it."

Mr. Felegy sighed. "Karen, you're putting me in a very difficult position. I've got a computer printout that shows you spent $347 that wasn't yours to spend, and you're telling me that Mr. Laker is on the 'take' with our best printing company, but you don't have proof. Do you realize how this looks?"

"Yes, sir."

"How do you suggest I proceed?" he asked.

Karen closed her eyes and prayed for a miracle. "Let's get Lucy. Maybe she found the copies we made of the documents in his file."

LUCY WAS HAVING PROBLEMS of her own. After lunch, she went to the *Odyssey Owl* office to make sure their next issue was coming together the way she'd hoped. Three of the *Owl*'s reporters—Mike, Sean Campbell, and Debbie Calhoun—were gathered around the table, talking in low, conspiratorial voices with Mrs. Stegner.

"What's going on?" Lucy asked.

Startled, they spun around.

Lucy approached them. "Come on, guys. What're you talking about?"

"A friend of yours," Mrs. Stegner said.

"*Which* friend?" Lucy asked.

"Karen," Mike replied, and handed her two sheets of notepaper.

Lucy looked down at the pages. The first was an accounting of the student council's funds. Highlighted in yellow was a column that said "Miscellaneous Expenses: $347.00 (Karen Crosby)." She didn't know what to make of it. "So?"

"Keep reading," Mike said. He had a smile on his face, but it wasn't friendly. He seemed to be taking pleasure from Lucy's ignorance.

Lucy held up the other page. It was a plain sheet of paper with a note typed to Mike:

Mike,
You're the "hot" investigative reporter for the *Owl*, so this information will be interesting to you. There's a deficit in the student council funds. (See highlight on the next page.) It's obvious who took the money. Maybe your editor knows her, too. Worth a story?
          —An Anonymous Friend.

That's why Karen got called to the office, Lucy thought. She was dumbfounded. This was the kind of thing that happened to big-city newspapers, not little school papers. "A news leak? A news leak in our school?"

"Interesting, isn't it?" Mrs. Stegner said.

"Well, Miss Crusading Truth-Finding Editor, can I do an article about it?" Mike asked.

"No!" Lucy snapped.

Mike gestured to Mrs. Stegner, Sean, and Debbie. "What did I say? She's going to cover for her friend."

Lucy turned on Mike. "I'm not covering for anybody! For one thing, Karen wouldn't steal the council's money. For another thing, we don't have any of the facts besides this anonymous note and the treasury report!"

"Those are two pretty good pieces of evidence," Debbie said. "What more do we need?"

"These aren't *facts,* they're circumstantial evidence." Lucy appealed to Mrs. Stegner. "I'm right, aren't I? We can't write an article *speculating* about missing money and then suggest that Karen took it. Since when do we write about *any* of our fellow students like that? We're a school newspaper, not muckrakers!"

"What do we do then?" Mrs. Stegner asked.

"Nothing—until we get more information," Lucy said.

"A cover-up!" Mike cried out. "If it wasn't Karen and you weren't in your do-as-Jesus-would-do phase, you'd jump all over this story. You'd have us running ourselves ragged digging out the facts!"

Mrs. Stegner nodded. "He's right, Lucy. I'm not sure you're being objective about this. Are you sure you're not protecting Karen?"

"I don't have to protect Karen. She wouldn't steal, it's as simple as that. But I'm not afraid of searching for the *truth.*"

"Newspapers aren't interested in only the truth, Lucy," said Mrs. Stegner. "They're interested in reporting the *facts*—as they emerge. If a bank gets robbed, you don't wait until you have the whole *truth* of what happened, you report what happened *when* it happened."

"But we don't even have all the facts, Mrs. Stegner," Lucy said.

"Then *what do you do next?*" she prodded.

Lucy hesitantly answered, "We investigate the story and assemble more facts."

"Right."

"But we won't print anything until we have them all," Lucy added as a qualifier.

"I'll go talk to Mr. Laker," Mike said enthusiastically.

Lucy looked surprised. "Mr. Laker?"

"Sure, he's in charge of the school finances. He has to know about it."

Lucy smiled knowingly. *Mr. Laker is the anonymous note-writer*, she realized. He's setting her up! She looked at the faces of her coworkers and knew she couldn't tell them. But suddenly it changed everything for her. "You're in over your head," Mr. Laker had said to Karen.

The reporters took off with various ideas about tracking the story, leaving Lucy and Mrs. Stegner alone.

"It's hard for you," Mrs. Stegner said sympathetically. "But this is what being an editor's all about."

Lucy nodded sadly. "I won't betray my friend."

There was a knock at the door. Mr. Felegy opened it and peeked in. "Sorry to interrupt," he said as he stepped fully into the room. Karen followed him, looking lost and helpless.

"What can I do for you?" Mrs. Stegner asked.

"It's what *Lucy* can do, actually," Mr. Felegy said. "We were wondering if she found the mysterious copies that Karen needs right now."

"Copies?" Mrs. Stegner asked.

"I haven't found them," Lucy admitted quietly. She spread her arms to Karen, as if to say, *What can I do?*

Karen turned to Mr. Felegy. "I don't blame you if you won't believe me, but . . . I didn't take the money, Mr. Felegy."

Mr. Felegy shook his head. "Karen—"

Karen interrupted him: "At the council meeting tomorrow, I'll . . . I'll resign as president."

CHAPTER
FOURTEEN

JOE DEVLIN GAVE HIS friends a few parting punches on their arms—just to remind them who was boss—and ducked into the woods. He followed the path through the bare trees like he always did at this time of day. He had to get home in time for dinner. His mom got very angry when Joe was late. And Joe knew it was dangerous to make his mom mad.

The fallen leaves crunched under his leather boots. He liked the sound. It made him feel powerful, as if he were destroying entire cities under his feet like Godzilla in those Japanese movies. He marched on through the woods, oblivious that he was being watched.

The trees suddenly gave way to a clearing and, a few yards beyond, Joe heard the creek pouring over the time-worn stones. The wind kicked up, so he tugged the zipper up on his leather jacket. He made his way to the large tree that had conveniently fallen to bridge one side of the creek to the other. He had crossed it so often that he didn't think twice about whether or not it was safe. He jumped on and strolled ahead.

When he reached the halfway point—identified by a rotted branch that stuck out of the side of the log—he heard a noise. It wasn't any of the familiar sounds he took for granted—the snapping of old bark from the tree, the creek gurgling below, birds singing somewhere in the forest—that made him stop and listen. This one was different. Joe waited and it came again: It was the unmistakable sound of someone clearing his throat.

Joe turned around quickly and saw Matt standing on the bank behind him. Something rustled in front and he looked to see Jack positioned on the bank ahead.

"Oh, it's you," he said.

"Yeah, it's us," Jack answered.

Joe took a step forward but halted when Jack raised his hand. In it was a whip. Jack flicked his arm and, in turn, snapped the whip. It cracked loudly, scattering the birds in a nearby tree. Jack smiled, impressed with himself.

Joe squinted his eyes in a way he thought looked vicious. "Nice whip. Are you boys playing *Indiana Jones* this week?"

Matt cracked his whip, too, and Joe nearly lost his balance on the log from the fright. "My dad is a collector."

"I'm happy for him," Joe said sarcastically.

"We've been thinking about it, Joe," Matt said. "We decided that we're sick and tired of you bullying Oscar."

"Am I supposed to care about what you think?" Joe said.

"You oughtta care right now. Because you're not coming off that bridge until you promise to leave Oscar alone," Jack said.

"Oh, yeah? What're you going to do if I refuse?"

Both boys cracked their whips.

Joe sneered at them. "You're pretty tough when it's two against one."

"And *you're* pretty tough when it's you and seven other guys against Oscar," Matt said. "Funny, but you're not so tough now."

"What're you going to do, whip me?" Joe challenged them.

"Worse than that," Matt said. "We're going to give you a bath."

"What?"

Jack continued, "If you don't promise to stay away from Oscar, you're going into the creek."

Joe nearly laughed at them. A dunk in the creek was nothing to him. "You think a little bit of water scares me?"

Jack cracked the whip at Joe. Joe flinched and took a step backwards. "Watch it with that thing!"

"You probably don't care about the water yourself," Matt informed him. "But that leather jacket and those leather boots won't enjoy it very much. Water ruins leather, doesn't it?"

"It does if you're drenched in it," Jack said.

Joe realized what they were up to and looked stricken. "You clowns better not try it. You ruin my jacket and boots and you'll pay for them."

"Why should we?" Matt asked. "You won't have any proof that we got them wet. You fell off the log on your way home."

"Besides, you probably bought them with the money you keep stealing from Oscar," Jack said.

"You force me into that water and you won't live to regret it!" Joe shouted.

Jack laughed. "What'll you do? Get your gang together and beat us up?"

"Count on it," Joe said.

"Yeah, but you can't always be with your gang, Joe," Matt countered. "Just like now. Whatever you do to us, we'll catch you alone and do back."

Jack cracked the whip again. "Y'see? You guys aren't the only ones who can play rough."

"On the other hand," Matt said, "all you have to do is promise that you'll quit bullying Oscar."

Joe spat at them. "I'm not making any deals with you sissies."

"I guess that's his answer," Matt said, and cracked the whip at Joe.

"Sounds like it," Jack agreed and flicked his whip at Joe, too. They were careful not to hit him, but he didn't know that. He moved first in one direction, then the other, struggling to keep balance on the log.

"Promise?" Matt called out again as they slowly worked their whip ends closer to him.

"No!" Joe yelled back.

The two boys inched their whips closer and closer. Jack got a little too close and hit Joe on the hand.

"Ouch!" Joe cried out. "That hurt!"

Jack was surprised, but didn't show it. Having Joe in a state of fear encouraged him. "Now you know how it feels when you hurt other people."

Joe paced like a lion between two tamers. His mind raced, trying to think of a way out—besides going into the water.

"Just promise, Joe!" Matt said.

Joe considered promising—and then going back on his word—but couldn't get the words out. It was galling to him to make any kind of promise to Matt and Jack. His pride wouldn't let him.

"That's it," Jack announced. "You're going in!"

Matt and Jack increased the flicks of their whips toward Joe. They had him dead center between them now. Joe looked down at the water and cursed loudly at the two boys. The whips cracked harder and got closer until it seemed like Joe had no choice: He had to jump into the water.

"Stop it! Stop it!" came a voice from the clearing behind Matt.

Matt didn't turn to look, for fear that Joe might go for him. "Who is it?" he shouted at Jack.

Jack and Joe both looked beyond Matt. Oscar rushed toward them, waving his arms and yelling.

"Stop! Stop!" he cried out. He reached the end of the log on Matt's side and breathlessly said, "This is wrong. Don't do it."

Matt lowered his whip. "Oscar, listen—"

Joe started for Matt, but Matt was too quick. He flicked the whip at Joe to force him back.

"You just stay where you are," Matt said to Joe.

Jack shouted at Oscar. "Get out of here. We're trying to help you."

"No!" shouted Oscar, red-faced. "This is wrong! What happened to your pledge? What happened to doing what Jesus would do?"

"Oh, brother," Joe mumbled. "I should've figured it was one of those religious things."

Matt said, "Jesus took action against the money changers and so *we're* taking action."

"It's the wrong kind of action," Oscar maintained.

"This is for *you*, you moron!" Jack shouted, clearly annoyed.

"If it's for me, then put your whips down!"

"Yeah, listen to him," Joe said.

"Be quiet," Jack growled and snapped the whip at him.

"It's *wrong*!" Oscar pleaded. "This *isn't* what Jesus would do. There are other ways to stop kids like Joe."

"Yeah, like what? Not speak to him?" Jack said sarcastically.

"Maybe. And maybe we're supposed to just put up with him, too. Maybe we're supposed to put up with him and even forgive him, just like God puts up with us and forgives us!" Oscar said firmly, "Now put your whips down and let him go!"

Matt wasn't ready to give in. "But he has to promise first!"

"I don't want his promise!" Oscar cried out. "I don't want anything from him. I want you to let him go."

"No can do," Jack said. "I'm tired of his bullying everyone around. If we can't do this for you, we can do this for someone else."

"Yeah, and then what? As soon as he gets away from here, he'll get his gang and hunt you down," Oscar said.

"Big deal," Jack replied. "Then we'll hunt *him* down. If he wants a war, he can have one. We have friends. We have kids who'll help."

Oscar waved a finger at him in accusation. "Then you'll be just like him—*bullies*. Is that what you want? You want to ignore your pledge to be like Jesus in order to turn into another bunch of bullies like Joe and his gang? Is that what you're telling me? Because if you do, then you'll have to give up friends like me and Lucy and Karen and the people at church! Don't you get it? This isn't the way to do it! Jesus had the better way! Now, are you going to put your whips down or not?"

Matt and Jack looked at each other, trying to make a silent decision. They both knew Oscar was right. Their hearts told them so.

"'Vengeance is mine,' says the Lord," Oscar reminded them. It was a verse they had seen the other night when they read their Bibles together.

Jack rolled his eyes, muttered under his breath, and stepped away from Joe. Leaping down from the log onto the bank, he slowly coiled up the whip.

"Ha!" Joe snorted and crossed the log. "I won't forget this," he said to Jack as he walked past. He sauntered away without looking back.

Jack and Matt glared at Oscar.

"It's what Jesus would do," Oscar said.

THE FUNERAL FOR Raymond Clark was a small affair held at the Chapel of Rest on the outskirts of Connellsville. Apart from Christine, her husband, Robert, and Whit and Tom, there were three former coworkers from the printing company where Raymond had once worked and been fired. It was hard for Whit to believe that only a few days had passed since Raymond Clark had entered his life. Now he was gone.

"Jesus said, 'I am the resurrection, and the life: he that believeth in me, though he were dead, yet shall he live; and whosoever liveth and believeth in me shall never die,'" the presiding minister read over the plain brown casket. "The eternal God is thy refuge and underneath are the everlasting arms."

He prayed a simple prayer about being comforted by God and to look beyond this life to the next one. "Help us to see the light of eternity," he concluded, "so we may find the grace and strength for this and every time of need. Through Jesus Christ our Lord. Amen."

Christine read a collection of psalms reminding them all of God's everlasting love. Robert, a tall young man with dark, curly hair and wire-rimmed glasses, read passages from the New Testament about the peace of Christ and the never-failing love of God.

The minister then prayed, "Eternal God, who committest to us the swift and solemn trust of life, since we know not what a day may bring forth but only that the hour for serving Thee is always present, may we wake to the instant claims of Thy holy will, not waiting for tomorrow, but yielding today."

That's what it's all about, Whit thought. *The days are so short, our time to serve God is so brief. Why do we spend so much time on things that don't really matter?* Whit echoed the words in his heart: "May we wake to the instant claims of Thy holy will, not waiting for tomorrow, but yielding today."

The late afternoon sky was alive with colorful contrasts: the brown carpet of fallen leaves on the cemetery lawn, a cloudless sky, pale marble tombstones that glimmered orange in the fading sunlight. "Not a bad day to go home," Tom whispered to Whit at the grave site.

"Lord, have mercy," the minister said.

"Christ have mercy," the small gathering replied. They said the Lord's Prayer together, and the minister said a few concluding remarks about God's compassion, then ended with, "The grace of the Lord Jesus Christ, and the love of God, and the communion of the Holy Spirit be with you all. Amen."

Whit and Tom were formally introduced to Robert, then given heartfelt hugs from Christine. "Thank you for coming," she said tearfully. "My father had few friends here."

"I only wish we could have been better friends when it really mattered," Whit said.

Christine pulled Whit close and whispered in his ear, "You can let go of that now. It's finished. If you were really in the wrong, then consider it closed. My father forgives you. I forgive you. God has always forgiven you. What more do you want?"

"To follow Jesus," Whit whispered back, emotion rising in his throat. "But thank you for saying so, Christine. Bless you."

"Bless *you*, John Whittaker," she said.

Tom and Whit walked silently back to the car. After they climbed in and they began the drive back to Odyssey, Tom asked, "So what now?"

"What do you mean?" Whit asked.

Tom stole a glance at his friend. "This whole experience is percolating inside of you. I can tell. Where do you think it's leading?"

Whit shrugged. "That's what I keep thinking about. It'd be easy for me to feel guilty and start giving my time to every charity in town."

"You're doing that already," Tom pointed out. "Where in the world will you find *more* time to give?"

Whit shook his head. "I don't have any more time. So I have to prioritize the time I have. That's it, isn't it?"

Tom chuckled softly. That's what he'd been trying to tell his friend for weeks.

"You've been absolutely right, Tom," Whit said.

Tom looked surprised. "Really? About what?"

"About my time." Whit casually rubbed the top of the dashboard.

"Jesus did His Father's work. That's why He said yes to certain things, and no to others. Jesus knew how to prioritize. That's what you've been trying to tell me. I realize it now."

"Terrific," Tom said, impressed. "So where do you start?"

"The same place Jesus started."

Tom looked at his friend quizzically.

"Jesus often went off alone to pray," Whit said. "And that's exactly what I'm going to do."

Two hours later, Whit returned to Whit's End where Oscar, Jack, and Matt were waiting on the porch.

"Is it time for another meeting?" he asked as he opened the front door.

"We think so," Matt said. "If you have the time."

"I'll make the time," Whit said. It was dinnertime—a slow period for Whit's End's business. He let the three boys in, then closed the door behind them and locked it. He gestured to a table. "Sit down. Aren't Lucy and Karen coming?"

"We don't know where they are," Oscar said. "*Two of us* left school as soon as the bell rang in order to—" He stopped, then turned to Jack and Matt. "Maybe you should tell him."

Jack and Matt squirmed in their seats. Whit watched them curiously.

"Yeah, I guess we should," Matt said. "Go ahead, Jack."

"Me! Why do I have to confess?"

"Confess?" Whit asked.

"Oh, *I'll* do it," Matt said, and told Whit what had happened with Joe at the creek. All in all, Whit was impressed with how well Matt told the story: He admitted fairly what he and Jack had done wrong, and included what Oscar did right.

When he finished, Whit patted Matt's arm. "Well done, Matt."

Matt shrugged awkwardly.

"Oscar, I want to commend you for the way you handled Joe," Whit said. "I think you're on the right track with him. Who knows? Maybe you'll lead him to Jesus eventually."

Oscar blushed.

"You two, on the other hand," Whit said to Jack and Matt, "should be ashamed of your behavior."

Matt slouched in his chair. Jack fiddled with a plastic spoon to keep from looking anyone in the eye.

"How did you *ever* think that threatening Joe with whips and trying to ruin his clothes in the creek was a good idea?" Whit asked.

Matt shook his head. Jack looked as if he might say something, then changed his mind. Instead he muttered, "Jesus did it."

"What Jesus did when He drove the money changers out of the temple was vastly different from what you did to Joe," Whit said. "Jesus was purifying God's holy place of worship. What were you two doing?"

"Trying to get Joe to leave Oscar alone," Jack said.

"Is that all?"

"Getting revenge," Matt admitted. He looked to Jack. "Come on, you know it's true. We wanted to get back at Joe for causing us so much trouble."

Jack nodded. "Yeah, I guess."

"Do you see what happened? You willfully distorted Scripture so you could vent your anger and get revenge." He sighed deeply, then smiled. "Welcome to the human race."

Matt and Jack perked up as if they hadn't heard him correctly.

Whit continued, with deep understanding in his voice, "Boys, you did what some Christians have been doing for two thousand years. You twisted the Bible around to suit your desires. It's sad, but true. So let's learn from this mistake, all right? It's the Spirit within us that helps us to understand God's Word and lead us into the *right* action. We have to be very, very careful not to confuse our ideas of what Jesus would do with what we want to do. Do you remember what the apostle Paul wrote about the fruit of the flesh versus the fruit of the Spirit?"

They shook their heads no.

"Let's see if I can paraphrase what he said. It's in Galatians, chapter 5. The fruit of the flesh is immorality, impurity, idolatry, *hatred*, *quarreling*, jealousy, *anger*, dissensions, envy . . . well, I think you get the idea. But the fruit of the Spirit is love, joy, peace, patience, kindness, goodness, faithfulness, gentleness, and self-control. See the difference? It's a good checklist when you're trying to decide whether or not you're behaving the way Jesus wants you to. Got it?"

"Yes, sir," Jack said.

"Would it be okay if we started over?" Matt asked.

"Start what over?" Whit asked in return.

"Our pledge," he replied, then nudged Jack. "From now on, we'll honestly try to do what Jesus wants us to do. Right?"

"Right," Jack said.

"Most of us have to 'start over' as Christians *every day*," Whit smiled. They fell silent for a moment. Whit looked at the two empty chairs and said, "I wonder what happened to Karen and Lucy?"

"Why didn't you tell us about this before?" Karen's father asked her.

"I thought I could deal with it myself," she replied. Karen, her father and mother, and Lucy were in the Crosbys' living room. Somewhere a radio played soft guitar music. Karen and Lucy sat on the couch, facing Mr. and Mrs. Crosby who nestled into two easy chairs. "I'm really, really sorry," she added.

Lucy felt awkward being there for this family meeting, but Karen wanted her nearby, if only for moral support. They had eaten dinner together, then moved to the living room to talk about Karen's troubles.

"Don't ever let things go so far before you talk to us," Mr. Crosby said as a final reprimand.

"Is there anything we can do?" Mrs. Crosby asked her husband as she reached over and gently took his hand. Mrs. Crosby was a beautiful woman with blonde hair and large blue eyes who once was a model but left the business to get married and raise a family.

Mr. Crosby was a handsome, easygoing man with friendly eyes, a ready smile, and plenty of jokes for Lucy whenever she came around. But he was deadly earnest now. "Without any proof, there isn't anything we can do about Mr. Laker."

"What about the missing money?" Karen asked.

"Unfortunately, they have all the proof they need for that." He tilted his head and looked thoughtfully at the fireplace. The flames crackled and popped there. "I suppose we can refuse to pay the money, especially since Karen didn't steal it. But the school district won't sit still for that."

Mrs. Crosby rested her chin on her fist. "What if we refuse to pay and demand some kind of inquiry? Maybe that'll shake a few apples out of Mr. Laker's tree. If the money really is missing, then he must've put it somewhere."

"It won't be an inquiry, darling. It'll be a *battle*," Mr. Crosby said. "Are we ready for that?"

"What would Jesus do?" Lucy asked them.

Mr. Crosby released his wife's hand to tend to the fire. He picked up a poker and jabbed at the logs a couple of times. "I get the impression from Scripture that it's better to be wronged than to fight or go to court. Jesus said it when He talked about turning the other cheek and Paul wrote about it in First Corinthians."

"The truth is, Karen's reputation is solid," Mrs. Crosby said. "People who know her will also know that she didn't steal the money. We can't worry about the rest."

"Then I'm right?" Karen asked. "I should resign from the student council?"

Reluctantly, Mr. Crosby nodded. "Yes, sweetheart. You probably should. Otherwise you'll spend the rest of the year battling this incident—trying to stay credible with those who are against you. Life's too short and you're too young for that."

"Do you mind?" Mrs. Crosby asked.

Karen considered the question. "Being president hasn't been so special, but I hate to quit like this. It's like admitting I'm guilty."

"I know, I know," Mr. Crosby said. "But unless you find those copies, there's nothing else you can do."

Lucy stood up. "I'm going home and ransacking my house one more time."

"I'll look around here again," Karen said.

"Meanwhile, girls, I suggest we all do a lot of praying," Mr. Crosby said. He gave the fire one last poke and it spat sparks back at him.

When Lucy got home, her mother informed her that Mrs. Stegner had called. Lucy slipped into the study and dialed the number her mother had scribbled on the pad. Somehow it felt very serious calling a teacher at home.

"Thanks for calling back," Mrs. Stegner said after they said their hellos.

"I was over at Karen's, talking to her parents," Lucy explained.

"No doubt they have a lot to talk about," Mrs. Stegner said. "I phoned to tell you that Mike's been working on an article about Karen's resignation. I assume she's still going to resign tomorrow?"

"Yes, ma'am."

The line hissed for a moment, then Mrs. Stegner said, "You're so close to this situation, Lucy, that I'm pulling rank on you. I'm making the decision to print an article about Karen's resignation and the allegations about the missing money."

"I figured you would," Lucy said.

"However, I want *you* to write an editorial. Make it a rebuttal, if you want. But I want to print your response to what's happened. Will you do that for me?"

Lucy thought about the opportunity to set the record straight—or, at least try to. "Yes, ma'am. Thanks for giving me the chance."

"I need it by tomorrow morning," Mrs. Stegner said.

"Okay," Lucy said. "I'll do my best."

"Thank you. And, again, I'm sorry your friend is having such a hard time."

"So am I, Mrs. Stegner."

They said good-bye and Lucy hung up the phone.

She glanced over at the cursor on her parents' computer as it sat indifferently on the desk. It winked at her over and over again. *I'm going to have to write the best editorial of my life*, she thought.

CHAPTER SIXTEEN

IT WAS JUDGMENT DAY—or so Jack took to calling it later.

The day began with Lucy and Karen meeting to pray together before school. They huddled outside next to a side door and asked God in hushed tones to be with them both, to give them courage to do what was right, and to allow the truth to come to light. It didn't seem like much to ask. But they both remembered Jesus' night in the Garden of Gethsemane, His betrayal at the hands of Judas, and the long road to that cross on top of the hill.

"Thy will be done," Karen whispered, and meant it. At some point in the night, as she wrote her speech, she felt her heart release the future. Whatever happened was God's business. It always was, she knew, but now she felt it deep in her heart.

Lucy had spent the night writing and rewriting her editorial for the paper. It was harder than she expected. In one version, she told the whole story about the file and Mr. Laker's misdeeds. She threw it away, though. Without proof, it was like bad gossip and would demean the good she'd hoped to do Karen. She wrote six versions before she settled on the one she liked the most. She was desperate to get it right for reasons even Karen didn't know.

"Are you coming to the meeting?" Karen asked.

"Only one reporter from the *Owl* is allowed to go to the student council," Lucy reminded her.

"That's silly. Whose idea was that?"

"Yours," Lucy chuckled. "It was the first rule you got passed when you became president."

"Oh," Karen giggled. "Well, I'm *still* the president and I say you can come in."

They both thought how nice it was to see the other smile. It felt like a long time since they had.

"I'll be there after I turn in my editorial to Mrs. Stegner," Lucy promised.

With a last hug for encouragement, the two girls went their separate ways: Karen to the library for the student council meeting and Lucy to the *Odyssey Owl*'s office. Only God knew where they would go from there.

Mrs. Stegner hadn't arrived at the *Owl* yet, so Lucy took out her editorial and set it on the table. She then took out another sheet of paper, looked it over one last time, then placed it next to the editorial.

It was her resignation.

As Lucy had asked herself again and again what Jesus would do with the *Owl*, she decided that He wouldn't go along with the hairsplitting between "truth" and "facts," between sarcastic reporting and honest news. Mrs. Stegner was a good teacher and had been more than fair to her, but Lucy felt it was wrong to teach kids that reporting was merely presenting facts without truth. Where was hope? Where was the belief that journalism could help lift people up, rather than constantly drag them into the mud? The questions made Lucy feel tired, mostly because the answers weren't easy to figure out.

Maybe one day Lucy could start her own newspaper—one in which she would try to make telling the truth fairly and positively her highest priority.

She was about to leave, when she suddenly decided that Mr. Felegy should see her editorial and resignation. Snatching them back up, Lucy went over to the storage closet to make copies. She turned the copier on and had to wait for a couple of minutes while it warmed up. *It was only a couple of days ago*, she thought, *that we were here making copies of Mr. Laker's file*.

"What did we do with those copies?" she asked herself, pressing the side of her head as if it might jog her memory.

Lucy placed the first page of her editorial on the glass, lowered the lid, and pushed the copy button. It hummed at her as the light flashed under the lid. A copy of page one slid out of the side and settled into the rack. She was about to put page two down when suddenly the machine stopped and a red symbol flashed.

"Out of paper," she muttered. Turning to the metal shelves behind her, she looked for packages of the right kind of paper for the copier. She knew from experience that to put the wrong kind in would jam it up. "There it is," she said and reached up for the half-opened ream. She caught the flap on the end and pulled the package toward her. It slid off the shelf and into her hands. A few pages dropped to the floor. She hated it when the kids were too lazy to close the half-opened wrappers holding the paper. They *always* lost a few sheets to the floor or under the cabinet.

Not this time, she thought and bent down to retrieve the fallen pages.

Lucy's hand was poised in midair, her fingers just about to touch one of the sheets, when she suddenly cried out.

"The meeting will now come to order," Sarah Hogan announced, ful- filling one of her duties as the "clerk" to the student council after she'd called roll. Everyone was present and accounted for.

Karen sat in her usual chair at the front desk in the library. To her left was Brad O'Connor, the vice president. To her right was Olivia Bennett, the treasurer. Karen couldn't help but notice that neither one of them would look her in the eye.

Along the wall next to the main library door sat Mr. Felegy and Mr. Laker. Mr. Felegy watched her with a sad expression on his face. Mr. Laker's expression was cold and stony.

Not far from Mr. Laker, Mike sat with his notepad in hand. He didn't want to miss a word for the *Owl*.

No one in the room betrayed that they knew what Karen was about to do, but they all knew. Karen was sure of it. There was something about the stillness—the lack of the usual jokes from the usual kids— that told her they were waiting.

Karen decided to surprise them by going through their usual proce- dure. She stood up and asked, "Any old business?"

No one spoke.

"No old business? How about new business?"

Heather raised her hand. "Yeah. I want to hear you explain what happened to $347 of our money."

Karen felt wounded. She expected someone to attack, but not Heather, not someone who was supposed to be a good friend.

Is this how Jesus felt when Judas kissed him? she wondered.

"We're checking into it," Karen said calmly. Why did she feel such a profound peace in the midst of this emotional hurricane?

"Who's checking into it?" Heather challenged her.

"I'll be working with Mr. Felegy to—"

"But aren't *you* responsible for the missing money?" Don Kramer asked from the other side of the room. "You're the president. You were the one who took the money out, right? Isn't that what the sheet says?" He held up the financial statement.

Karen felt flustered. Did everyone get a copy of the statement?

Olivia Bennett waved at Don Kramer. "As treasurer, let me say—"

"We don't care what you have to say, Olivia," Heather snapped. "We want to hear what Karen has to say. We want an explanation. Rumors are flying all over the school that she stole the money."

Some of the rest of the council joined in, calling out for Karen to explain what was going on.

Karen held up her arms to quiet them down. "Look, it's confusing right now. The statement *looks* like there's money missing, but we're not sure there is."

"It says what it says," Heather pointed out. "How could the statement be wrong?"

Karen was stuck. She didn't want to mention Mr. Laker. It was pointless without any proof.

"What are you going to do about this?" Carol Cofield asked. "It looks pretty bad when the president of our council is accused of swiping—"

"I didn't swipe anything!" Karen shouted. "Who's spreading these rumors? Who passed out those statements? Why am I being accused without the benefit of the doubt? Something looks fishy, but it's not what you think."

"Then what is it?" Don called out.

Karen shook her head. "I can't say."

Someone booed her. She didn't look to see who. She didn't care. Someone else yelled "cover-up" then booed as well. Then it seemed she was in front of a chorus of "boos" and "cover-up!"

Do it now, she thought. *Resign before you start crying.*

"All right, calm down. Listen to me." The council calmed down. Karen stared at the top of the table, her eyes and face burning. Her well-rehearsed words stumbled forward. "Since I can't offer a good reason for the confusion about—"

"Confusion!" someone called out indignantly.

Brad O'Connor hit the table with his hand. "Let her talk, for crying out loud!"

The room fell silent.

Karen looked at Brad out of the corner of her eye. "Thank you," she whispered.

"Go ahead," he said back to her.

"Since I can't offer a good reason for the confusion about that mysterious statement, and you guys obviously want to believe the worst about me—even though I've never done anything to betray your trust—I want to offer my res—" That was as far as she got. The tears filled her eyes and got caught in her throat. She struggled to continue. "I want to offer my resignation, effective immediately."

She glanced up at the council through misty eyes, only to realize that they weren't listening to her. They were all facing the door. Karen hadn't heard the door open, nor did she see Lucy enter with a handful of papers.

Everyone else saw it, though. It was like watching a silent movie. Lucy ran in, saw Mr. Felegy sitting next to the door, and frantically pushed the pages into his face. Most of them didn't know what it meant. They had no idea why Mr. Laker suddenly went pale and nearly fell out of his chair.

The only thing any of them knew for sure—and could agree about when they gossiped for the rest of the day—was that Mr. Felegy stood up and dismissed them.

"This meeting has to be postponed," he announced. "Lucy, Karen, I'd like to see you in my office right away. You, too, Mr. Laker."

"THEY'RE FRAUDS," Mr. Laker said with a red face. He paced around Mr. Felegy's office impatiently, pausing only to scowl at Karen and Lucy.

Mr. Felegy looked over the bids for the report cards, the letter with its incriminating "P.S.," and, of greater interest to him, the copy of the check for $2,000. "They look pretty genuine to me, Art. Where would these girls get the technology to put together forgeries?"

Mr. Laker grunted. "Kids can do everything with computers these days."

Karen and Lucy watched the proceedings silently. They both knew there was little for them to say. The evidence had to speak for itself.

"Are you telling me you've *never* received any money from Ballistic Printing?" Mr. Felegy asked.

"Well," Mr. Laker stammered, "what do you mean by 'received'?"

"Good grief, Art!" Mr. Felegy cried out. "Do you realize what this means? What about your retirement? Your pension!"

Mr. Laker abruptly turned to Karen and Lucy. "Get out!"

The girls looked to Mr. Felegy.

"Thank you both for . . . er, all your help. I'll call you when I need you again," he said.

The girls stepped out of the office and into the main office area. Mr. Laker slammed the door behind them. Maybe they imagined it, but the muffled shouts on the other side of the door had the sound of justice being done.

Mrs. Stewart looked at them warily.

Suddenly the door opened again and Mr. Felegy said, "Mrs. Stewart, will you please get the district office on the phone?"

Mrs. Stewart's eyes bulged. "Anyone in particular?"

"Superintendent Murphy," said Mr. Felegy as he closed the door. Then he opened it again and added, "You'd better get someone from the legal department, too." He closed the door.

"This must be serious," Mrs. Stewart said excitedly as she picked up the phone.

Karen and Lucy looked soberly at each other.

"It's serious, all right," Lucy said.

WHIT DROPPED THE NEWSPAPER onto the counter. "Well, what do you know about that?" he said.

It wasn't the *Odyssey Owl*, but the *Odyssey Times* he'd been reading. It chronicled the forced resignation of Mr. Art Laker and the school district's investigation of his business practices as a school administrator over the past few years. The article also hinted at further investigations by the district attorney's office into Ballistic Printing and the many questionable "gifts" they had paid out to influential decision-makers in Connellsville's and Odyssey's governments.

"You two really were in the middle of it, weren't you?" Matt said to Lucy and Karen.

"Yeah! You turned out to be the opener of a big can of worms," Jack said with a laugh.

"Please, Jack, I'm eating," Karen said as she scooped in a mouthful of ice cream.

Lucy smiled. "You should've seen Mr. Laker's face when I walked in with those copies."

"I'll bet he nearly had a heart attack," Oscar said. He jammed a straw in his mouth and slurped his milk shake.

"Now I understand why you were so hesitant to talk to me about it," Whit said to Karen. "But where does that leave you?"

Karen swallowed her ice cream, then explained, "I'm still president of the student council. Mr. Felegy said that he believes Mr. Laker juggled the numbers in our account to make it look like I'd taken the money."

"Mr. Laker was in a panic," Lucy said. "He was ready to do anything to keep Karen from being believed."

Whit nodded sympathetically. "He was so close to retirement. To be caught now jeopardizes his pension, his future, *everything*. It's sad, really."

"I'll feel bad for him later," Karen said. "Right now I'm too relieved to think about how he feels."

"What would Jesus do?" Whit asked.

"Forgive him, pray for him," Karen replied while she scraped the last of the ice cream out of the bowl.

"Will you?"

Karen replied while she licked the spoon. "Yeah. Probably. I made a promise, remember?"

"What about you, Lucy?"

"I resigned as the editor of the *Owl*," Lucy said. "But Mrs. Stegner wouldn't accept it. She said she needs me there."

"That's not *all* she said," Karen interjected. "She said that the school needed someone with Lucy's 'personal integrity' in charge of the newspaper. She's even going to let Lucy keep experimenting to make it more positive."

"To try to do what Jesus would do," Lucy said cheerfully.

"What about you boys? Do you have any new insights after all you've been through?"

The three of them looked at each other and shrugged.

"Typical," Lucy laughed.

"I'm gonna be honest," Jack said. "Following Jesus is tough. It's the hardest thing I've ever done, in fact. I don't know if I can do it. But I'll try."

"Me, too," Oscar said.

"All for one and one for all," Matt joined in. "I don't remember what verse that is."

Whit smiled and said, "*Three Musketeers*, I think."

"What are you going to do when Joe catches up with you?" Lucy asked them.

Jack grinned and said, "Turn the other cheek."

Matt began to laugh. "Joe's going to think we're crazy. First, Oscar won't talk to him, then he saves him from getting dunked in the creek. And if he tries to get revenge on us, we won't fight back! It'll drive him up the wall!"

The three boys laughed, as only boys can about fighting. Karen and Lucy thought they were terribly immature.

"So it's a happy ending all the way around," Matt concluded.

Whit shook a finger at him. "Not a happy ending. This is just the beginning. We have a lot more challenges ahead of us."

"See ya, Oscar!" Matt called out.

Oscar turned to wave at Matt and Jack, then walked on up the street to his house.

"Shortcut?" Jack asked, hooking a thumb to the woods.

Matt nodded. "Yeah."

They strolled down the path into the late afternoon shadows of the trees.

"It feels like snow," Jack said.

Matt agreed. "It sure does. I'm going to have to dig my sled out of the garage. I think my dad's been using it to store paint cans on."

"I hate it when they do that," Jack said.

The sudden rustling of leaves and crackling of branches all around didn't give Matt or Jack time to react. Before they knew it, they were surrounded by Joe Devlin and his gang.

"It's payback time," Joe said.

"What would Jesus do?" Matt asked Jack.

As if to say, "Come and get it," Jack spread his arms. "Turn the other cheek," Jack said.

Joe and his gang closed in on the two boys. But any enjoyment they might have had with their revenge was robbed by the maddening way Jack and Matt kept laughing.

Whit and Tom sat quietly at the counter of Whit's End later that night. Whit was about to lock the front door, but he enjoyed the silence of the building so much that he didn't want to move.

"It's nice when it's quiet like this," Whit said as he sipped his coffee.

"Yep," was Tom's only reply.

Whit glanced down at the newspaper again, then casually flipped the pages over. It didn't appear as if he was looking for anything special, but it turned out that he was. "Here it is," Whit said and spun the paper on the counter so Tom could see.

It was an obituary for Raymond Clark. Christine had provided the newspaper with an older photograph of the man. He looked healthy and robust in the posed family portrait. Whit figured it was taken several years before, in happier times.

"Well, that's something," Tom said as he pointed to a line in the obituary.

"What?" Whit asked and peered over to look.

"It says here that he was an employee of Ballistic Printing until they laid him off a few months ago." Tom clicked his tongue. "Amazing."

Whit thought about it for a few minutes. "What are we supposed to think about that?" he wondered aloud. "Ballistic Printing fired Raymond Clark, so he came to Odyssey where he died. Because of him, we made promises to do what Jesus would do, which is why Karen decided to expose Mr. Laker rather than hide the truth—the truth about the very company that had fired Raymond Clark in the first place."

"It boggles the mind," Tom said. "Coincidence, you reckon?"

"I don't believe in coincidences. Just God," Whit said with a smile.

PASSAGES™

What if history repeated itself — with you in it? "Passages" takes familiar stories and retells them from a kid's perspective. Loosely based on the popular "Adventures in Odyssey" series, "Passages" books begin in Odyssey and take you to a fantasyland, where true belief becomes the adventure of a lifetime! Look for all the exciting "Passages" adventures, including *Darien's Rise*, *Arin's Judgment*, *Annison's Risk*, *Glennall's Betrayal*, *Draven's Defiance*, and *Fendar's Legacy*.

Request the entire set or each book individually at www.whitsend.org/passages.

Their town is Ambrosia . . . their headquarters is a vintage B-17 bomber . . . and they are The Last Chance Detectives . . . four ordinary kids who team up to solve mysteries no one else can be bothered with. Now, for the first time, the three best-selling episodes in the series are available in one DVD gift set.

Request this collector's edition set by calling the number below. And see if you can crack the cases of *Mystery Lights of Navajo Mesa*, *Legend of the Desert Bigfoot*, and *Escape from Fire Lake*.

And for the latest audio exploits of The Last Chance Detectives, call that same number. Request your copy of *The Day Ambrosia Stood Still*, *Mystery of the Lost Voices*, and *Last Flight of the Dragon Lady*.

Phone toll free: (800) A-FAMILY (232-6459)